Washington Irving.
Hearthside Tales

Signature Series
Frank Gado, General Editor

WASHINGTON IRVING

# HEARTHSIDE TALES

Selections from
The Sketch Book
Bracebridge Hall
and
Tales of a Traveller

*Selection and Introduction by*
PATRICK F. ALLEN

SIGNATURE SERIES

Union College Press
Schenectady, New York

## Also in the Signature Series

Sherwood Anderson
*The Teller's Tales*

Henry James
*Tales of Art and Life*

Nathaniel Hawthorne
*The Violated Heart*

Stephen Crane
*Drawn from Life*

William Gilmore Simms
*Tales of the South*

Second Printing of *Hearthside Tales*

Copyright 1983 by Union College Press
ISBN 0-912756-10-1
Library of Congress Catalog Card Number 83-81804

Hearthside Tales

# Contents

# Introduction

No American man of letters, not even Emerson, surpassed Washington Irving in the nation's esteem during the half century before the Civil War; the very features that once raised him to such eminence, however, have also operated to diminish his stature in our time. To a generation unschooled to appreciate style, Irving's finesse seems a vapid substitute for thought, satirical bite, and originality. Another modern prejudice takes his popularity as proof that he was a lesser artist, essentially an author for children—or, at least, for the unsophisticated. Even judgment from an historical perspective has not worked in his favor. His comparison, first with Addison and then with Scott— in turn, the greatest accolades his contemporaries could bestow—signaled a pivotal shift to the Romantic course that would dominate our literary tradition; but to a twentieth-century critical establishment preoccupied with evidence of a new nativism among the first generation of post-Revolution writers, these same affinities have made him vulnerable to discounting as a pale imitator of European models who led toward the sentimentality of Bryant, Kennedy, and Longfellow. Finally, although a few of his pieces are known by almost every literate American, that very fame, by calling attention to the abundance of second-and third-rate work in which they are imbedded, has also paved the way for reproach.

One must concede, of course, that the same stimuli responsible for his memorable performances also lie behind the melodramatic excess that flaws too much of the rest, and certainly, to claim as high a place for Irving, even at his best, as his more celebrated successors in the "renaissance" period would be folly. Nevertheless, if that recognition were permitted to excuse the critical neglect of Irving in our century, it would mean the loss of a valuable insight into the evolution of one of our major writers—and thereby, of a central branch in our literary genealogy. Just as surely as a new Russian fiction emerged from Nikolai Gogol's "The Overcoat," the new American fiction of the century sprang from Irving's tales. It was he who designed many of the elemental patterns and subjects and who took the first tentative steps toward the formulation of a different concept of story. Moreover, the record of his groping for an innovative mode of fiction, followed by his lapse into flaccid imitation when confronted with critical hostility, forms one of the more intriguing chapters in our literary history.

During his first seven years of literary activity, a period that began with his imitation of *The Spectator* in *Salmagundi* (1807–08) and culminated with the brilliant *A History of New York* (1811), Irving aspired to be one of the "laughing philosophers" who understood that "true wisdom is a plump, jolly dame who sits in her arm chair and laughs right merrily at the face of life—and takes the world as it goes." Such "philosophizing," cast in the form of amiable satire, suited his pose of the cultured gentleman who only dallied with the muse while he tested careers in the law, journalism, and commerce. But when *The Analectic Magazine,* for which he had assumed editorial responsibility, collapsed under him in 1814, the game he had been playing came to an abrupt halt. Startled by the realization that he had reached the age of thirty-one without having established himself in a stable profession, he decided to abandon his pen and move to England to join the family business.

Ironically, this choice for a comfortable life of stolid burgher respectability plunged him into a financial crisis: the Irving firm, he discovered upon arriving in England, was sliding irreversibly toward bankruptcy. As his private papers reveal, he quickly began longing for the literary occupations he had so recently, and so resolutely, put behind him, but the struggle with the "mere pounds, shillings, and pence business" depleted his energy. "I have little leisure for writing—and when leisure does come," he complained ruefully, "I find every gay thought or genteel fancy has left my unhappy brain, and nothing remains but the dry rubbish of accounts."

Alarmed by his despair, friends sought to rally his spirits by urging him to return to his writing desk. In a letter posted in May of 1817, the Scottish poet James Oglivie predicted he would win acclaim within a year: "Yet in the flower of youth, in possession of higher literary reputation than any of your countrymen have hitherto claimed—you want nothing but a stimulus strong enough to overcome that indolence which, in a greater or lesser degree, besets every human being." Another encouragment came from an honored countryman, the painter Washington Allston, who appended his praises to a packet of his illustrations for a new edition of *A History.* The drawings pricked Irving's imagination, leading him to consider a rewriting of the book to complement Allston's artwork. Perhaps, he reflected, he had been too hasty in dismissing the prospects of a literary life. After taking up residence in London, he set himself to writing sketches in a new manner which, he confided to his closest friend, Henry Brevoort, he dared believe might provide him "a scanty but sufficient means of support."

The most powerful inducement, however, was the now legendary visit to Sir Walter Scott's Abbotsford in 1817. For one week, Irving spent all of his waking hours in Scott's company discussing literature, languages, folklore, and local customs. Their mutual passion for the picturesque, the supernatural, and the remnants of a medieval past sealed a psychic kinship. The older Scott became a father-figure who, unlike Irving's own father (a curt, dour Philistine in cultural matters), luxuriated in the imagination and was proud to display it. When Scott added his voice to the chorus urging Irving to return to writing, the American resolved to redeem his mentor's confidence. Romantic mould, Irving now saw clearly, was the proper nourishment for his talent. Before meeting Scott, Irving had already completed an essay or two for the first number of what was to become *The Sketch Book*, but he still had not formulated a comprehensive plan for his book or any clear-cut strategy for his career. At Abbottsford—itself a monument of the Romantic imagination—he conceived a guiding vision.

Vowing not to sail for home "until I have sent some writings before me that shall, if they have any merit, make me return to the smiles, rather than sulk back to the pity of my friends," Irving labored over *The Sketch Book* through most of 1818. Six years later, he would be enjoying the smiles not only of his friends but of the rest of the world as well. The career reborn in those months of lonely effort proved that an American writer could win Europe's respect. Also, perhaps fraught with greater consequence because of the emulation it inspired, Irving's example demonstrated that literature could lead an American to affluence—indeed, to an aristocratic way of life beyond the dreams of the writers who had struggled for subsistence only a decade before. These effects on the status of the American writer may not have been altogether a product of chance. Among Irving's closest associates were a colony of American painters (consisting, in addition to Allston, of Charles Leslie, Stuart Newton, Peter Powell, and William Welles) who met regularly at the York Chop House to discuss the imperatives for a distinctively American art; Irving's title for his new book—a far cry from *salmagundi*, the commoner's hash denoted by the title he had chosen a decade before—suggests he was consciously enlisting in his friends' cause.

A sketch book, in the early nineteenth century, was a painter's repository for drawings meant as a *preliminary* to a finished, important work; in this sense, the title serves most appropriately to describe the book's place both in the Irving canon and in American literary history. Already by the time the first number appeared (the book was serially published in packets of five or six interrelated pieces), Irving was confident of his purpose: "I have preferred addressing myself to the feelings and fancy of the reader, more than to his judgment," he wrote to his friend Brevoort in 1818. "My writings, therefore, may appear light and trifling but if they possess the merit in the class of literature to which they belong, it is all to which I aspire in the work"—even if this were "only to blow a flute accompaniment in the national concert."

One of the major contributions to this "concert" was his invention of an "instrument," Geoffrey Crayon, the supposititious author who transparently represents Irving himself. The use of a narrative frame to house a gathering of tales harks back to *The Thousand and One Nights*, *The Decameron*, and *The Canterbury Tales* (to which Irving may have been nodding by borrowing

Chaucer's Christian name), but Crayon plays a rather different role as the source of the narratives in that the miscellany of painterly descriptions mixed with anecdotes and legends directly reflects his (and thus, Irving's) interests and personality. Irving, of course, had employed a persona to good effect before—most notably, Diedrich Knickerbocker. Unlike the voice that narrated *A History*, an eighteenth-century rasp satirically describing human foibles, Crayon's utterance bespeaks Irving's newly-acquired Romantic disposition toward the world. It was obviously a comfortable accent: Crayon would continue to reappear in later books. (Knickerbocker, of course, does enter *The Sketch Book* twice, but the reason is patently a matter of convenience: Irving could not easily transport Crayon back to America. This Knickerbocker, however, bears little resemblance to his former self.) Crayon's shadow, however, would lengthen over more than Irving's subsequent works. The most widely read authors of the next generation, Nathaniel Parker Willis and Bayard Taylor, directly imitated the convention in their elevation of the travel narrative into the dominant genre of the nineteenth century. He also influenced American travel literature of a different sort. Sophisticated, erudite, polished in manner, and the possessor of an understated ironic wit, Crayon became the model for the numerous judges, journalists, and small-town aristocrats who, from Longstreet through Hooper, chronicled life among the lowly on the Old Southwestern frontier. Indeed, even the complex psyche of Samuel Clemens/Mark Twain traces back, in some measure, to Crayon.

Beyond the figure of Crayon was the cluster of aesthetic attitudes enunciated through him that forecast our American literary character. Anticipating, in remarkably similar language, the plaints of Hawthorne, James, Henry Adams, and even some of the twentieth-century expatriates, Crayon confesses his longing "to tread in the footsteps of antiquity—to loiter about the ruined castle—to meditate on the falling tower—to escape, in short, from the commonplace realities of the present, and lose myself among the shadowy grandeurs of the past." One rather obvious solution was to skirt the American deficiencies by relying instead on European materials; the other—to which he resorted less frequently but with greater effect—was to recreate an American past by reverting to materials provided by the Dutch settlement that he had earlier exploited in *A History*.

Neither course, however, led toward a simple realism. If scenic description figured as a key ingredient in the Romantic mix, it must nevertheless be treated in a manner designed to enhance qualities from which the picturesque could arise. Moreover, as several essays in *The Sketch Book* reveal, Irving insisted that the writer's choice of natural surroundings must harmonize with the mental associations they inspire. The principle stated here portends no incipient transcendentalism, nor does it suggest the abstract metaphysical concerns soon to flower in American literature in the next decades; rather, while assigning a primary function to actual experience, it stresses the secondary effect that actuality has in stimulating the imagination. What he intended was the cultivation of a penumbral realm—that border between reality and dream Hawthorne would later call "an intermediate space" in "The Haunted Mind" and "the genial atmosphere which a literary man requires in order to ripen the best harvest of his mind" in "The Custom-House" preface to *The Scarlet Letter*.

Nowhere does Irving illustrate the point—and its attendant danger—more forcefully than in "The Mutability of Literature." Wandering in Westminster Abbey, Crayon descends deeper into its dark interior, and consequently further from the noise and commerce of humanity. On arriving in the library at the building's heart, Crayon encounters hundreds of entombed volumes. When one of the books laments its unconscionable neglect for generations, Crayon somewhat pompously objects that only those writers who portray nature faithfully, render the choicest thoughts in the choicest language, and live by the rule of self-abnegation deserve to survive. For the true artist alone is "the intercourse between the author and his fellowman ... ever new, active, and immediate. He has lived for them more than for himself; he has sacrificed surrounding enjoyments, and shut himself up from the delights of social life." But his dedication, as Hawthorne also was to recognize, exacts both an artistic and a personal price. In creating the illusion of life, the isolated artist risks severing the most vibrant ties to life itself, thus robbing his art of its vitality and denying himself the pleasures of society.

Another major theme, which would pervade his writings for the rest of his career, surfaces in "Roscoe" and "The Wife," the third and fourth sketches in the volume's first number. Albeit in a didactic and treacly manner, they argue the artist's obligation to continue his struggle in the face of crippling financial reverses—an unmistakable reflection of the psychological wound Irving had recently sustained (and that was still throbbing.) In "The Wife," the theme is somewhat disguised: the husband in the tale, having failed in his financial speculation, fears the ruin of his marriage, but after he shares his secret with his bride, the couple finds happiness in a humble rural retreat. Although this man who is so fortunate in having wed a self-sacrificing woman is not identified as an artist, the description of their haven as suitable "for the most pastoral poet" indicates the drift of Irving's thoughts. Curiously, "Roscoe," in addressing the problem of the artist more directly, advocates an opposite course from the seclusion so endearingly extolled in "The Wife." Its central figure, an historian (at a time when history was within the realm of the muses), loses everything as a result of "having been unfortunate in business"; nevertheless, Irving pleads, he deserves admiration. Instead of indulging "in the selfishness of lettered ease," Roscoe has "gone forth into the highways and thoroughfares of life," using his literary gifts to effect a "union of commerce and the intellectual pursuits."

If one regards the various parts of the first number as exploring the implications in pursuing a life in art, "Rip Van Winkle," the number's last section, assumes an aspect rather different from that which readers have usually seen. Rip is an autobiographical projection of Irving himself. At the outset, the protagonist lacks commitment: a mere entertainer content to spin stories for children, he neglects his farm and family—and is consequently held in low esteem by his fellow citizens. In escaping to the woods and then meeting the legendary crew of Hendrick Hudson, however, Rip, like Irving after discovering the possibilities of Romance at Abbotsford, has stumbled onto the subject matter that will give him an honored place in the community. Furthermore, the true Americans who gather to hear Rip's tales at the story's conclusion are no longer the colonists who disparaged him before he made his trek—just as Rip himself is now not quite the same man he had been. In a sense, this ending reaches beyond itself: it enacts Irving's own return to his native land through the initial number of *The Sketch Book* and expresses the author's faith that his countrymen were at last ready to welcome a storyteller working in indigenous materials.

The wish that drove "Rip Van Winkle" was, of course, doubly fulfilled: not only did the story's success pave the way for Irving's triumphant career but Rip himself has become an American archetype. As numerous critics have noted, this "man-boy" stands first in a long line of "outsiders" in American fiction—those good bad "boys," such as Huck Finn and Randall Patrick McMurphy, who live by their dreams to escape the "civilizing" influences of a hard-driving, pragmatic society.

The only rival to the fame of "Rip Van Winkle," "The Legend of Sleepy Hollow" is better known for the images it has contributed to American popular iconography than for its literary qualities. But in contrast to the mythic proportions Rip has assumed, Ichabod, Brom Bones, and the pumpkin-head carried by the Headless Horseman are cartoon figures in a delightful national joke not deemed worth critical attention; indeed, more than any of his other writing, "The Legend of Sleepy Hollow" is responsible for its author's relegation to the shelves of children's literature. Yet, on closer examination, this final tale in *The Sketch Book* reveals that Irving was now fully in command of both his craft and his genius.

Cast as "sportive gothic" (a sub-genre which simultaneously exploits gothic conventions and parodies them), "The Legend" begins with an evocation of mystery appropriate to a Romantic tale—"the place still continues under the sway of some witching power," we are told, "that holds a spell over the minds of good people." Once Katrina Van Tassel, ostensibly the lady fair of the legend, enters the narrative, however, the tone changes. The only child of a wealthy farmer—and "plump as a partridge [in a day when that was an unambiguous merit]; ripe and melting and rosy cheeked as one of her father's peaches, and ... withal a little of a coquette" to boot—she is a prize meant by fate for a doughty young man with a future in the region's society rather than for a dessicated schoolmaster who is tolerated but scarcely admired by the citizenry. The powers of Romance will be laughably inadequate in the cause of wooing her.

Ichabod Crane, the lank scholar who does not realize his suit is doomed, is a more erudite edition of Rip. Like Rip, he helps with his neighbors' chores and, outside the confines of his schoolhouse, is beloved by children (the association may also extend to the fact that, when he ventures forth from his little corner of authority—*i.e.*, his *winkle*—to court Katrina, he borrows a horse—whose name, Gunpowder, recalls Rip's expedition into the mountains—from a farmer named Van Ripper). But the key to the resemblance rests in Ichabod's belief in the supernatural (Cotton Mather is his favorite author) and his inclination toward the world of imagination (indicated, among other things, by his outpourings of conventionally Romantic poetry to Katrina); in short, he represents the artist.

His rival, Brom Bones, embodies quite different values. (There is an evident parallel between "The Legend of Sleepy Hollow" and Hawthorne's "The Artist of the Beautiful": Ichabod is a comic version of Owen Warland; Brom has the role of Robert Danforth.) A "burly, roaring, roystering blade," a man's man who also sets the hearts of comely women aflutter, Brom has no reason to doubt that he will win Katrina and eventually, in keeping with the mission implied by his given name (Abraham), become the patriarch of an honored tribe. But Brom is not content merely to allow his advantages to determine the contest; as though responding to a deep fear (as well as disdain) of what Ichabod represents, he successfully contrives to rid his future of the schoolmaster by "becoming" the ghost that strikes terror in Ichabod's soul. In a sense, Ichabod and Brom, the dreamy poet and the solid burgher, are two manifestations of one mind—Irving's own. Significantly, after the persistent chase of the gothic specter has caused Ichabod to flee the precincts of Sleepy Hollow, he is reported to have taken up the study of law, entered politics, electioneered, and written for the newspaper—a profile of the very career for which, earlier in the decade, the young Washington Irving had been laying a foundation.

The reception of *The Sketch Book* on both sides of the Atlantic gratified the burgher in Irving as much as it did the artist. The reaction of the British, who had previously been unable to muster more than patronizing approbation for an American author, must have been especially pleasing: not only did the first edition sell out rapidly but, in addition, the rumor spread that the author was actually Walter Scott! Irving had realized his ambition to demonstrate it was possible for *"an American to write decent English"*; in fact, enthusiasm for the transplanted New Yorker reached such a pitch that his friend Peter Powell could comment, without much exaggeration, "there seems to be a *conspiracy* to hoist you over the heads of your contemporaries." The next step was clear: a second book, built on the plan of the first, to secure his reputation. But if the strategy seemed obvious, the execution proved difficult: almost two years would pass, during which he made several false starts, before *Bracebridge Hall* arrived in the bookstalls.

The book itself provides several clues as to the reason for the delay. Instead of ranging hither and yon for his subject matter as he had in *The Sketch Book*, the new work concentrates on life in and about the Bracebridge family estate in rural England. Perhaps, as has often been suggested, this focus on the squirearchy betrays Irving's aristocratic predilections, but a more convincing explanation has to do with his desire for English approval. Having won recognition as an American, he was now more eager to gain acceptance as a writer of English within the British tradition. If, today, *The Sketch Book* is chiefly remembered as the depository for "Rip Van Winkle" and "The Legend of Sleepy Hollow," these glories were not nearly so prominent at the time. Indeed, the former had been composed in one night—scarcely representing the kind of studied effort that Irving had preached literary immortality required—and the latter, he had depreciated as only "a random thing, suggested by the recollection of scenes and stories about Tarrytown." To a writer convinced (with good reason for thinking so) that fame must rest on an English base, tales of the Hudson Valley may have held the danger of stigmatizing their author with a Colonial tar brush; using a thinly-drawn plot line about the complications surrounding the nuptials of Guy Bracebridge to support descriptions of local customs and legends ran no such risk.

The second clue may be found in the volume's subtitle—*The Humorists*—which evidently pointed toward the theory of personality outlined in Galen's medicine rather than toward the laugh-provoking characters Irving had created in *A History* and in the two Sleepy Hollow tales. In 1817, he had confided to Allston that, in his earlier works, he may have been guilty of "the *grosserie* into which the writer of a work of humor is apt to run." For the most part, the gentleman writer who emerges in *Bracebridge Hall* eschews such a course. As a result, the volume consists mainly of mildly entertaining caricatures guided by the humor theory of behavior, sentimental essays and sketches, and conventionally Romantic accounts of country lore and superstition. In this respect as in his veering from the source of his best writing in *The Sketch Book*, Irving was denying himself the proper exercise of his genius. At best, the Bracebridge material imitates the more pallid sections of the previous book.

*Bracebridge Hall* does, however, contain two exceptions to the rest of its fare which, significantly, Irving was unable to integrate structurally or thematically into the whole. The first of these, "The Stout Gentleman," seems on the surface a mere bagatelle, a ruse played on those listening to the story (and, of course, on the readers as well) who are infected by the storyteller's mounting curiosity as to the elusive stout gentleman's identity only to be utterly disappointed at the end. But more is to be gained here than a thumping heartbeat generated by the chase after the shaggy dog. For one, it offers the delight of observing a writer's superb performance with language. Nothing Irving ever wrote manifests surer control or greater deftness. In its opening, for example, the author not only provides a lesson in the use of words as though they were a steel tip applied to an engraver's plate but also anticipates Stein and Hemingway in orchestrating variations of an image to intensify the reader's sensory experience of the scene.

The second reason "The Stout Gentleman" deserves closer attention may help to explain the first. The story's narrator, "a thin, pale, weazened gentleman who is shrunk up in the corner of the room like a turtle in a shell," claims he will amaze his audience with "A Stagecoach Romance" (the story's subtitle), the most exciting adventure tale since *The Man in the Iron Mask*. In strictly mechanical terms, this is, of course, the "set up" which makes possible the crash of expectations at the end. Also, as some commentators have noted, it serves to satirize the bad taste of audiences gourmandizing on a diet of such romances as Dumas cooked. Perhaps the most important function of this frame, however, is what it reveals about Irving. In traveling down Scott's path, he was by no means happily disposed to clutch all the baggage of Romantic fiction. (Indeed, even amid the baldly Romantic material that surrounds this tale, Crayon laments the unrealistic plots of popular novels and plays that end with marriage—and then, as though bowing to the readers' Romantic wishes, he concludes his own "plot" in the very same way!) If, in writing *Bracebridge Hall* to assure himself of a comfortable future, he was willing to satisfy what he perceived to be his public's appetites, he also felt the need, somewhere, to satisfy his own. "The Stout Gentleman" marks one such moment of self-indulgence. It mocks the conventions of the Romance plot and, in the process, makes a hero of the imagination.

In a different way, the role of the imagination is also central to the longest of the volume's tales, "Dolph Heyliger." The idea for the story may have come from adjoining tales in *The Thousand and One Nights*, which, Irving read avidly while at work on *Bracebridge Hall*. Scheherazade's account begins with Sinbad, a humble porter, gazing in wonder at a splendid mansion and lamenting the burden of poverty he must bear while others live in comfort. Then, unexpectedly, the owner appears, invites the bedraggled man of the street into the magnificent house, and proceeds to entertain him for seven days with the adventures at sea that swelled his treasure. That this wealthy seaman should also be named Sinbad is, of course, the key to the tale's significance: the second Sinbad is a figment of the first, a fantasy-self freed from the constraints of hard work, responsibility to others, and morality. Beneath the complexities of "Dolph Heyliger" lies this same, simple tension between the snare of reality and the unfettered flights of the pleasure-principle.

Irving's study of *The Thousand and One Nights* may also have influenced him to devise an elaborate construction of frames within frames; certainly, no previous Irving story is so intricate in its design. In the frame sketch, "The Haunted House," the revamped Diedrich Knickerbocker creates a Romantic backdrop for the action to follow by recounting the rumors, folklore, and history connected with the Heyliger house. Later, Knickerbocker yields to another narrator, John Vandermoere, an old Dutchman who is his mirror image. This replication of narrators has a corollary in the multiplication of narratives—what begins as sportive gothic becomes a ghost story, then metamorphoses into an adventure romance that braces a second ghost story— which reflect each other in curious ways. The experiment ultimately fails, for in wending his way through the maze of his invention, the author sometimes loses hold of his narrative thread, yet the reach of the effort makes "Dolph Heyliger" one of the most intriguing pieces in all of early American fiction.

Wild, pleasure-loving young Dolph shares none of his widowed mother's desire to see him with "an M.D. at the end of his name—one of the established dignitaries of the town"; even so, he is apprenticed to a quack physician, Doctor Knipperhausen, and submits to the discipline of endless chores and pestle-wielding. (The Knipperhausen mansion corresponds to the palace of Sinbad the Sailor, and Dolph, like Sinbad the Porter, is learning to shoulder his responsibilities in life.) But if one route to wealth would be to follow the path of the hard-working Dr. Knipperhausen, a more exciting possibility of attaining riches is that offered by another presence in the house, the ghost of an ancestor named Vanderspiegel. After noticing that Vanderspiegel resembles him (the ghost's name means "from the mirror" in German), Dolph obeys his regenerated instincts and sails into the wilderness of the Hudson River valley.

The real import of this adventure, obviously, is that it liberates his true self. Emancipated from society's strictures, the young man's senses expand to take in every natural detail, and, in keeping with this symbolic rebirth, he acquires a new "father": Anthony Vander Heyden, who, though an Albany burgher, shares Dolph's penchant for pleasure. Vander Heyden not only instructs his adopted son in the arts of the woods but also, by telling him two vastly improbable ghost stories, furnishes an example in giving full license to the imagination. The confident, initiated Dolph who emerges from the woods seals his arrival at maturity by marrying Vander Heyden's daughter and undertaking the support of his destitute mother. (Thus, the twin identities, Sinbad the Porter and Sinbad the Sailor, fuse into one.) More important than the suggestion Irving may have drawn from the Arabian source, however, is the parallel between Dolph's adventure and his own personal story: the escape from drudgery into the woods and the resurrection effected through the acquisition of a new father clearly reflect Irving's escape from the rigors of his ill-chosen career in business that he achieved after discovering a psychic father in Scott and accepting his Romantic creed.

To his public and the book's reviewers, *Bracebridge Hall* confirmed the testimony of *The Sketch Book* that Irving was the paramount American author. Their praise, however, focused on the sentimental sketches that later generations would ignore, not on the inventiveness evident in the construction of the volume's more intricate fiction. Whether because Irving was too pleased by the book's brisk sale or too intent on exploring further possibilities in tale telling, he failed to see a warning that he was moving beyond what his audience expected of him. Apparently having lost interest in the sketch, he spent most of the next two years working on full-blown stories, without a plan, as he was to note in his journal, of "how to arrange the Mss. on hand." During this period, he also entertained the thought of producing a new English version of *The Thousand and One Nights;* the project was abandoned after just a few weeks, but it seems to have inspired him to find an answer to his problem in the practice of Scheherazade, of Boccaccio, and, most elaborately, of Chaucer. Instead of relying principally on the personality of a single narrator or on a single locale to unify the volume, he would organize what he had written into four tale cycles. Except for the last—which has supposedly been "found among the papers of the late Diedrich Knickerbocker—these would be loosely bound as reports of encounters with sets of storytellers by that extraordinary sojourner, Geoffrey Crayon. Each cycle would be framed by circumstances (a literary dinner, a hunting party, a gathering of travelers, and a discussion about pirate gold) promoting an exchange of stories. To avoid boring the reader through a mere accretion of tales, the cycle would consist of a variety of "movements." Some tales would be unabashed fantasy; others, purportedly, true-life accounts. Furthermore, the style of the tales would vary from lampoons to serious treatments of popular genres. Irving, delighted by the solution he had devised, drew confidence from the reaction of friends: "those who have seen various parts," he reported in a letter, "think the work will be the best thing I have written."

The initial section of *Tales of a Traveller*, entitled "Strange Stories by a Nervous Gentleman," is ostensibly composed by the same anxiety-ridden man who narrated "The Stout Gentleman"—here introduced as ten times more nervous than when he related that tale. The three sportive gothic tales that follow—"The Adventure of My Uncle," "The Adventure of My Aunt," and "The Bold Dragoon"—in making fun of the narrator's ingenuous belief in the paraphernalia of gothic fiction, reveal more about him than about the tales' characters. But after mocking the gothic genre and its audience, Irving then offers a few stories embodying his ideas of how gothic characteristics can be employed for more sophisticated purposes. "The Adventure of the German Student," the pivot for this change in orientation, has been reprinted more often than any other tale in the volume; unfortunately, lifted from its context, its essential ambiguity has evaded most of its readers.

On the most superficial level, young Wolfgang's sudden love for the beautiful French girl he finds on a Paris street, his discovery the morning after consummation of their "marriage" that she had been guillotined before they had met, his shock when her head separates from her body and rolls to the floor, and his subsequent commitment to a madhouse can be read as a simple horror story, similar to the garish tales Poe set out to imitate. The careful reader, however, will notice Irving's exaggeration of grotesque details (such as, in the frame, the narrator's dangling "haunted eye"), the underlying humor in much of the narration, and the subversion of veracity in the disclosure, at the end, that the authenticity of the events depends upon the word of a certified madman; from this perspective, the tale obviously aims at parody. But neither interpretation is wholly satisfactory. If the reader is too naive in surrendering to the emotional effect intended by the conventional claptrap of the ghost story, he is also too condescending in regarding the account as a joke. Despite the narrator's undercutting remarks, the fact remains that the shy recluse who pursues the French Revolution is a model idealist. The student's fantasy of unwitting necrophilia may represent the implications of an idealism that refuses to respect a common-sense view of life. Read in this way, the story assumes the aspect of a metaphysical parable as a journey through a mental labyrinth that ends with a fall into a pit of insanity when the lofty ambitions of philosophy prove incapable of altering the ugly reality of history.

Although "The Money-Diggers," the concluding cycle in *Tales of a Traveller,* lies too far removed from "The Adventure of the German Student" to be considered its complement, the aggregation traces a similar moral—*viz.,* that the imagination must be tempered by recognition of reality. "Hell-Gate," the frame that establishes the perspective from which the subsequent stories are to be judged, focuses on the unearthing of a Negro farmer's skull. While its discoverers speculate in elaborate rumors of murder, kidnapping, and betrayal that incorporate several variations of pirate atrocities, the narrator (presumably Knickerbocker) keeps his knowledge that the old Negro died of natural causes to himself. By thus introducing the results of his "diligent research" into the "fable and romance" of his Hudson River neighborhood that is "like the straits of Pelorus of yore," the narrator acknowledges the tendency of fantasy to displace fact. Although he is too charmed by the power of story to wish it were otherwise, he also issues a warning against emulating the characters in these tales who stake their lives on romance.

Following "Kidd the Pirate"—which, in installing the subject of the buried pirate treasure, plants the seed-corn of romance from which the cycle's tales spring—Irving produces a whaler who narrates the events of "The Devil and Tom Walker" as a sermon against the blasphemy of ill-gotten gain. The story itself anticipates Hawthorne's "Young Goodman Brown," not only in its use of the forest as a metaphor for the evil region within the soul but also in its ascription of all success to pacts with Satan. In the hands of the worldly Irving, however, the principal intention seems to be to demonstrate the danger of the imagination's effect on the whaler's misanthropic religiosity. The whaler is fascinated by the most gruesome details he can conjure up, and his speculations always assume the very worst about his fellow man. Ironically, of course, his Calvinist diatribe against blasphemy is itself blasphemous in supposing the devil to be the author of all good fortune.

Irving reserves his most intriguing variation on the cycle's central theme for the last story, "Wolfert Webber, or Golden Dreams"—a comic extravagance that also serves as coda to the entire volume. The Webber family's wealth has been generated through the cultivation of cabbages; now, however, the spread of the city to the family's fields threatens Wolfert with financial ruin. Instead of grappling with this reality, Wolfert, seduced by rumors of buried pirate loot exchanged at the local tavern, lays waste to his cabbage patch in searching for treasure. The stakes in the opening phase of this folly are relatively small, but after the arrival of a mysterious seaman at the tavern inspires one of the topers to spin a yarn about Kidd's cache along the Hudson, Wolfert—"like the greedy inhabitant of Bagdad, when his eyes had been greased with the magic ointment of the dervise, that gave him to see all the treasures of the earth"—risks his life in pursuit of the gold mentioned in the tale that his "infected fancy" takes for fact. Mere chance saves him from being killed by smugglers, just as, subsequently, good luck enables him to convert the cabbage patch into a fortune in real estate, but the fatuous Wolfert accredits the happy outcome to his superior intelligence. At the story's end, the unlikely new aristocrat adopts a family crest consisting of a cabbage and the motto, "*Alles Kopf,* that is to say, all head."

The key to the story is Irving's extensive punning on "cabbage"—used both as a noun and as a verb meaning "to come or to grow to a head." The first connection between cabbages and heads occurs when the narrator speaks of the Webber ancestry's having devoted "its entire intellect to growing cabbages," with the result that the portraits of all its males resemble that vegetable. After noting that changing times have made the old "head" work obsolete, the author shifts the connotation: responding to the heady fantasies of the tavern's habitues, Wolfert yields to his imagination and begins to "overturn the old 'heads'" by digging up the cabbage patch in a quest for treasure. Finally, the triumph of the imagination is both complete and of dubious value: if Wolfert's riches insure the protection of his self-delusion, he remains, for all his aristocratic posturing, the same cabbage-headed dolt he was at the start.

The comedy of "Wolfert Webber" thus envelops a central ambiguity: while the story laughs at the stupid parvenu, it ridicules those gulled by their "Golden Dreams." The pretentious oaf, of course, has always been a tempting target for comic thrusts, and that the artistocratically-inclined Irving should have set his barbs in such a figure at a time when so many ignorant men were using newly-acquired fortunes to boost themselves above their class is not especially remarkable; that the author of "Dolph Heyliger" should also deride the lure of illusion, however, *is* noteworthy and provides a clue toward understanding the imminent change in his literary career. Apparently, despite Irving's disdain for the dullness of business and his encomium for the humble pastoral poet in "The Wife," the attraction of the hard-headed pragmatist remained a strong force within him. Through *The Sketch Book* and *Bracebridge Hall*, Irving had performed the trick, previously impossible for an American, of riding his pen to wealth; the experiment with fiction in *Tales of a Traveller*, he had expected, would extend that phenomenal success. But when the critics and the public, discovering nothing original nor interesting in his manner, attacked it viciously (indeed denounced it as sacrilegious), his artistic courage failed.

Two years after the stunning setback, Irving went to Spain to translate documents pertaining to the voyage of Columbus; the result of the initial impulse, four years later, was a monumental biography of the Discoverer of America that enjoyed enormous respect and popularity. Another search into history, *A Chronicle of the Conquest of Granada*, was published the next year. It was not until 1832 that his public once again would read an Irving book similar to those of the early 1820's—and significantly, *The Alhambra* was only an uninspired imitation of the least vibrant aspects of his first sallies into fiction. During the rest of his life, he concentrated his literary efforts on accounts of the American frontier *(Astoria* and *The Crayon Miscellany)*, and on biographies of Oliver Goldsmith, Mahomet, and George Washington.

Although Irving neglected the ground he had prepared, his successors would sow it with the seeds of American literary greatness. Explicit acknowledgements of his importance as a pioneer by the giants of the American Renaissance are few in number—Poe's accolade, that *Tales of a Traveller* contained the only "American tales of real merit" prior to the appearance of Hawthorne's *Twice-Told Tales*, and Melville's little-known homage in "Rip Van Winkle's Lilac" stand out—but the implicit signs of his influence pervade our nineteenth-century fiction. Far from being the author of charming trivialities assumed by modern critics who have not traversed beyond a casual reading of the Sleepy Hollow tales, Irving was a forebear of singular importance.

Patrick F. Allen
Clifton Park, New York

# THE MUTABILITY OF LITERATURE

## A Colloquy in Westminster Abbey

> I know that all beneath the moon decays,
> And what by mortals in this world is brought,
> In time's great period shall return to nought.
> I know that all the muse's heavenly lays,
> With toil of sprite which are so dearly bought,
> As idle sounds, of few or none are sought,
> That there is nothing lighter than mere praise.

DRUMMOND OF HAWTHORNDEN

There are certain half-dreaming moods of mind, in which we naturally steal away from noise and glare, and seek some quiet haunt, where we may indulge our reveries and build our air castles undisturbed. In such a mood I was loitering about the old gray cloisters of Westminster Abbey, enjoying that luxury of wandering thought which one is apt to dignify with the name of reflection; when suddenly an interruption of madcap boys from Westminster School, playing at football, broke in upon the monastic stillness of the place, making the vaulted passages and mouldering tombs echo with their merriment. I sought to take refuge from their noise by penetrating still deeper into the solitudes of the pile, and applied to one of the vergers for admission to the library. He conducted me through a portal rich with the crumbling sculpture of former ages, which opened upon a gloomy passage leading to the chapter-house and the chamber in which doomsday book

is deposited. Just within the passage is a small door on the left. To
this the verger applied a key; it was double locked, and opened with
some difficulty, as if seldom used. We now ascended a dark narrow
staircase, and, passing through a second door, entered the library.

I found myself in a lofty antique hall, the roof supported by massive
joists of old English oak. It was soberly lighted by a row of Gothic
windows at a considerable height from the floor, and which apparently
opened upon the roofs of the cloisters. An ancient picture of some
reverend dignitary of the church in his robes hung over the fireplace.
Around the hall and in a small gallery were the books, arranged in
carved oaken cases. They consisted principally of old polemical writers,
and were much more worn by time than use. In the centre of the
library was a solitary table with two or three books on it, an inkstand
without ink, and a few pens parched by long disuse. The place seemed
fitted for quiet study and profound meditation. It was buried deep
among the massive walls of the abbey, and shut up from the tumult
of the world. I could only hear now and then the shouts of the school-
boys faintly swelling from the cloisters, and the sound of a bell tolling
for prayers, echoing soberly along the roofs of the abbey. By degrees
the shouts of merriment grew fainter and fainter, and at length died
away; the bell ceased to toll, and a profound silence reigned through
the dusky hall.

I had taken down a little thick quarto, curiously bound in parchment, with brass clasps, and seated myself at the table in a venerable
elbow-chair. Instead of reading, however, I was beguiled by the solemn
monastic air, and lifeless quiet of the place, into a train of musing.
As I looked around upon the old volumes in their mouldering covers,
thus ranged on the shelves, and apparently never disturbed in their
repose, I could not but consider the library a kind of literary catacomb,
where authors, like mummies, are piously entombed, and left to blacken
and moulder in dusty oblivion.

How much, thought I, has each of these volumes, now thrust aside
with such indifference, cost some aching head! how many weary days!
how many sleepless nights! How have their authors buried themselves
in the solitude of cells and cloisters; shut themselves up from the face
of man, and the still more blessed face of nature; and devoted themselves to painful research and intense reflection! And all for what? to
occupy an inch of dusty shelf—to have the title of their works read

now and then in a future age, by some drowsy churchman or casual straggler like myself; and in another age to be lost, even to remembrance. Such is the amount of this boasted immortality. A mere temporary rumor, a local sound; like the tone of that bell which has just tolled among these towers, filling the ear for a moment—lingering transiently in echo—and then passing away like a thing that was not!

While I sat half murmuring, half meditating these unprofitable speculations with my head resting on my hand, I was thrumming with the other hand upon the quarto, until I accidentally loosened the clasps; when, to my utter astonishment, the little book gave two or three yawns, like one awaking from a deep sleep; then a husky hem; and at length began to talk. At first its voice was very hoarse and broken, being much troubled by a cobweb which some studious spider had woven across it; and having probably contracted a cold from long exposure to the chills and damps of the abbey. In a short time, however, it became more distinct, and I soon found it an exceedingly fluent conversable little tome. Its language, to be sure, was rather quaint and obsolete, and its pronunciation, what, in the present day, would be deemed barbarous; but I shall endeavor, as far as I am able, to render it in modern parlance.

It began with railings about the neglect of the world—about merit being suffered to languish in obscurity, and other such commonplace topics of literary repining, and complained bitterly that it had not been opened for more than two centuries. That the dean only looked now and then into the library, sometimes took down a volume or two, trifled with them for a few moments, and then returned them to their shelves. "What a plague do they mean," said the little quarto, which I began to perceive was somewhat choleric, "what a plague do they mean by keeping several thousand volumes of us shut up here, and watched by a set of old vergers, like so many beauties in a harem, merely to be looked at now and then by the dean? Books were written to give pleasure and to be enjoyed; and I would have a rule passed that the dean should pay each of us a visit at least once a year; or if he is not equal to the task, let them once in a while turn loose the whole school of Westminster among us, that at any rate we may now and then have an airing."

"Softly, my worthy friend," replied I, "you are not aware how much better you are off than most books of your generation. By being stored away in this ancient library, you are like the treasured remains

of those saints and monarchs, which lie enshrined in the adjoining chapels; while the remains of your contemporary mortals, left to the ordinary course of nature, have long since returned to dust."

"Sir," said the little tome, ruffling his leaves and looking big, "I was written for all the world, not for the bookworms of an abbey. I was intended to circulate from hand to hand, like other great contemporary works; but here have I been clasped up for more than two centuries, and might have silently fallen a prey to these worms that are playing the very vengeance with my intestines, if you had not by chance given me an opportunity of uttering a few last words before I go to pieces."

"My good friend," rejoined I, "had you been left to the circulation of which you speak, you would long ere this have been no more. To judge from your physiognomy, you are now well stricken in years: very few of your contemporaries can be at present in existence; and those few owe their longevity to being immured like yourself in old libraries; which, suffer me to add, instead of likening to harems, you might more properly and gratefully have compared to those infirmaries attached to religious establishments, for the benefit of the old and decrepit, and where, by quiet fostering and no employment, they often endure to an amazingly good-for-nothing old age. You talk of your contemporaries as if in circulation—where do we meet with their works? what do we hear of Robert Groteste, of Lincoln? No one could have toiled harder than he for immortality. He is said to have written nearly two hundred volumes. He built, as it were, a pyramid of books to perpetuate his name: but, alas! the pyramid has long since fallen, and only a few fragments are scattered in various libraries, where they are scarcely disturbed even by the antiquarian. What do we hear of Giraldus Cambrensis, the historian, antiquary, philosopher, theologian, and poet? He declined two bishoprics, that he might shut himself up and write for posterity; but posterity never inquires after his labors. What of Henry of Huntingdon, who, besides a learned history of England, wrote a treatise on the contempt of the world, which the world has revenged by forgetting him? What is quoted of Joseph of Exeter, styled the miracle of his age in classical composition? Of his three great heroic poems one is lost forever, excepting a mere fragment; the others are known only to a few of the curious in literature; and as to his love verses and epigrams, they have entirely disappeared. What is in current use of John Wallis, the Franciscan, who acquired the name of the tree of life? Of William of Malmsbury;—of Simeon of Durham;—of Benedict of Peterborough;—of John Hanvill of St. Albans;—of—"

"Prithee, friend," cried the quarto, in a testy tone, "how old do you think me? You are talking of authors that lived long before my time, and wrote either in Latin or French, so that they in a manner expatriated themselves, and deserved to be forgotten,* but I, sir, was ushered into the world from the press of the renowned Wynkyn de Worde. I was written in my own native tongue, at a time when the language had become fixed; and indeed I was considered a model of pure and elegant English."

(I should observe that these remarks were couched in such intolerably antiquated terms, that I have had infinite difficulty in rendering them into modern phraseology.)

"I cry your mercy," said I, "for mistaking your age; but it matters little: almost all the writers of your time have likewise passed into forgetfulness; and De Worde's publications are mere literary rarities among book-collectors. The purity and stability of language, too, on which you found your claims to perpetuity, have been the fallacious dependence of authors of every age, even back to the times of the worthy Robert of Gloucester, who wrote his history in rhymes of mongrel Saxon.† Even now many talk of Spenser's 'well of pure English undefiled,' as if the language ever sprang from a well or

---

*In Latin and French hath many soueraine wittes had great delyte to endite, and have many noble things fulfilde, but certes there ben some that speaken their poisye in French of which speche the Frenchmen have as good a fantasye as we have in hearying of Frenchmen's Englishe.—*Chaucer's Testament of Love.*

†Holinshed, in his Chronicle, observes, "afterwards, also, by deligent travell of Geffry Chaucer and of John Gowre, in the time of Richard the Second, and after them of John Scogan and John Lydgate, monke of Berrie, our said toong was brought to an excellent passe, notwithstanding that it never came unto the type of perfection until the time of Queen Elizabeth, wherein John Jewell, Bishop of Sarum, John Fox, and sundrie learned and excellent writers, have fully accomplished the ornature of the same, to their great praise and immortal commendation."

*mutability* (handwritten annotation)

fountain-head, and was not rather a mere confluence of various tongues, perpetually subject to changes and intermixtures. It is this which has made English literature so extremely mutable, and the reputation built upon it so fleeting. Unless thought can be committed to something more permanent and unchangeable than such a medium, even thought must share the fate of every thing else, and fall into decay. This should serve as a check upon the vanity and exultation of the most popular writer. He finds the language in which he has embarked his fame gradually altering, and subject to the dilapidations of time and caprice of fashion. He looks back and beholds the early authors of his country, once the favorites of their day, supplanted by modern writers. A few short ages have covered them with obscurity, and their merits can only be relished by the quaint taste of the bookworm. And such, he anticipates, will be the fate of his own work, which, however it may be admired in its day, and held up as a model of purity, will in the course of years grow antiquated and obsolete; until it shall become almost as unintelligible in its native land as an Egyptian obelisk, or one of those Runic inscriptions said to exist in the deserts of Tartary. "I declare," added I, with some emotion, "when I contemplate a modern library, filled with new works, in all the bravery of rich gilding and binding, I feel disposed to sit down and weep; like the good Xerxes, when he surveyed his army, pranked out in all the splendor of military array, and reflected that in one hundred years not one of them would be in existence!"

"Ah," said the little quarto, with a heavy sigh, "I see how it is; these modern scribblers have superseded all the good old authors. I suppose nothing is read now-a-days but Sir Philip Sydney's Arcadia, Sackville's stately plays, and Mirror for Magistrates, or the fine-spun euphuisms of the 'unparalleled John Lyly.'"

"There you are again mistaken," said I; "the writers whom you suppose in vogue, because they happened to be so when you were last in circulation, have long since had their day. Sir Philip Sydney's Arcadia, the immortality of which was so fondly predicted by his admirers,* and which, in truth, is full of noble thoughts, delicate

---

*Live ever sweete booke; the simple image of his gentle witt, and the golden-pillar of his noble courage; and ever notify unto the world that thy writer was the secretary of eloquence, the breath of the muses, the honey-bee of the

images, and graceful turns of language, is now scarcely ever mentioned. Sackville has strutted into obscurity; and even Lyly, though his writings were once the delight of a court, and apparently perpetuated by a proverb, is now scarcely known even by name. A whole crowd of authors who wrote and wrangled at the time, have likewise gone down, with all their writings and their controversies. Wave after wave of succeeding literature has rolled over them, until they are buried so deep, that it is only now and then that some industrious diver after fragments of antiquity brings up a specimen for the gratification of the curious.

"For my part," I continued, "I consider this mutability of language a wise precaution of Providence for the benefit of the world at large, and of authors in particular. To reason from analogy, we daily behold the varied and beautiful tribes of vegetables springing up, flourishing, adorning the fields for a short time, and then fading into dust, to make way for their successors. Were not this the case, the fecundity of nature would be a grievance instead of a blessing. The earth would groan with rank and excessive vegetation, and its surface become a tangled wilderness. In like manner the works of genius and learning decline, and make way for subsequent productions. Language gradually varies, and with it fade away the writings of authors who have flourished their allotted time; otherwise, the creative powers of genius would overstock the world, and the mind would be completely bewildered in the endless mazes of literature. Formerly there were some restraints on this excessive multiplication. Works had to be transcribed by hand, which was slow and laborious operation; they were written either on parchment, which was expensive, so that one work was often erased to make way for another, or on papyrus, which was fragile and extremely perishable. Authorship was a limited and unprofitable craft, pursued chiefly by monks in the leisure and solitude of their cloisters. The accumulation of manuscripts was slow and costly, and confined almost entirely to monasteries. To these circumstances it may, in some meas-

---

daintyest flowers of witt and arte, the pith of morale and intellectual virtues, the arme of Bellona in the field, the tonge of Suada in the chamber, the sprite of Practise in esse, and the paragon of excellency in print.—*Harvey Pierce's Supererogation.*

ure, be owing that we have not been inundated by the intellect of antiquity; that the fountains of thought have not been broken up, and modern genius drowned in the deluge. But the inventions of paper and the press have put an end to all these restraints. They have made every one a writer, and enabled every mind to pour itself into print, and diffuse itself over the whole intellectual world. The consequences are alarming. The stream of literature has swollen into a torrent— augmented into a river—expanded into a sea. A few centuries since, five or six hundred thousand volumes; legions of authors at the same time busy; and the press going on with fearfully increasing activity, to double and quadruple the number? Unless some unforeseen mortality should break out among the progeny of the muse, now that she has become so prolific, I tremble for posterity. I fear the mere fluctuation of language will not be sufficient. Criticism may do much. It increases with the increase of literature, and resembles one of those salutary checks on population spoken of by economists. All possible encouragement, therefore, should be given to the growth of critics, good or bad. But I fear all will be in vain; let criticism do what it may, writers will write, printers will print, and the world will inevitably be overstocked with good books. It will soon be the employment of a lifetime merely to learn their names. Many a man of passable information, at the present day, reads scarcely any thing but reviews; and before long a man of erudition will be little better than a mere walking catalogue."

"My very good sir," said the little quarto, yawning most drearily in my face, "excuse my interrupting you, but I perceive you are rather given to prose. I would ask the fate of an author who was making some noise just as I left the world. His reputation, however, was considered quite temporary. The learned shook their heads at him, for he was a Greek, and had been obliged to run the country for deerstealing. I think his name was Shakspeare. I presume he soon sunk into oblivion."

"On the contrary," said I, "it is owing to that very man that the literature of his period has experienced a duration beyond the ordinary term of English literature. There rise authors now and then, who seem proof against the mutability of language, because they have rooted themselves in the unchanging principles of human nature. They are like gigantic trees that we sometimes see on the banks of a stream; which, by their vast and deep roots, penetrating through the mere surface, and laying hold on the very foundations of the earth, preserve the soil around them from being swept away by the ever-flowing current, and hold up many a neighboring plant, and, perhaps, worthless weed, to perpetuity. Such is the case with Shakspeare, whom we behold defying the encroachments of time, retaining in modern use the language and literature of his day, and giving duration to many an indifferent author, merely from having flourished in his vicinity. But even he, I grieve to say, is gradually assuming the tint of age, and his whole form is overrun by a profusion of commentators, who, like clambering vines and creepers, almost bury the noble plant that upholds them."

Here the little quarto began to heave his sides and chuckle, until at length he broke out in a plethoric fit of laughter that had well nigh choked him, by reason of his excessive corpulency. "Mighty well!" cried he, as soon as he could recover breath, "mighty well! and so you would persuade me that the literature of an age is to be perpetuated by a vagabond deer-stealer! by a man without learning; by a poet, forsooth—a poet!" And here he wheezed forth another fit of laughter.

I confess that I felt somewhat nettled at this rudeness, which, however, I pardoned on account of his having flourished in a less polished age. I determined, nevertheless, not to give up my point.

"Yes," resumed I, positively, "a poet; for of all writers he has the best chance for immortality. Others may write from the head, but he writes from the heart, and the heart will always understand him. He is the faithful portrayer of nature, whose features are always the same, and always interesting. Prose writers are voluminous and unwieldy; their pages are crowded with commonplaces, and their thoughts expanded into tediousness. But with the true poet every thing is terse, touching, or brilliant. He gives the choicest thoughts in the choicest language. He illustrates them by every thing that he sees most striking in nature and art. He enriches them by pictures of human life, such as it is passing before him. His writings, therefore, contain the spirit, the aroma, if I may use the phrase, of the age in which he lives. They are caskets which inclose within a small compass the wealth of the language—its family jewels, which are thus transmitted in a portable form to posterity. The setting may occasionally be antiquated, and require now and then to be renewed, as in the case of Chaucer; but the brilliancy and intrinsic value of the gems continue unaltered. Cast a look back over the long reach of literary history. What vast valleys of dulness, filled with monkish legends and academical controversises! what bogs of theological speculations! what dreary wastes of metaphysics! Here and there only do we behold the heaven-illuminated bards, elevated like beacons on their widely-separate heights, to transmit the pure light of poetical intelligence from age to age."*

I was just about to launch forth into eulogiums upon the poets of the day, when the sudden opening of the door caused me to turn my head. It was the verger, who came to inform me that it was time to close the library. I sought to have a parting word with the quarto, but the worthy little tome was silent; the clasps were closed: and it looked perfectly unconscious of all that had passed. I have been to the library two or three times since, and have endeavored to draw it into further conversation, but in vain; and whether all this rambling colloquy actually took place or whether it was another of those odd day-dreams to which I am subject, I have never to this moment been able to discover.

> \*Thorow earth and waters deepe,
>   The pen by skill doth passe:
> And featly nyps the worldes abuse,
>   And shoes us in a glasse,
> The vertu and the vice
>   Of every wight alyve;
> The honey combe that bee doth make
>   Is not so sweet in hyve,
> As are the golden leves
>   That drop form poet's head!
> Which doth surmount our common talke
>   As farre as dross doth lead.
>                                   *Churchyard*

# RIP VAN WINKLE

## A Posthumous Writing of Diedrich Knickerbocker

By Woden, God of Saxons,
From whence comes Wensday, that is Wodensday,
Truth is a thing that ever I will keep
Unto thylke day in which I creep into
My sepulchre—

CARTWRIGHT

[The following Tale was found among the papers of the late Diedrich Knickerbocker, an old gentleman of New York, who was very curious in the Dutch
history of the province, and the manners of the descendants from its primitive
settlers. His historical researches, however, did not lie so much among books
as among men; for the former are lamentably scanty on his favorite topics;
wheras he found the old burghers, and still more their wives, rich in that
legendary lore, so invaluable to true history. Whenever, therefore, he happened upon a genuine Dutch family, snugly shut up in its low-roofed farmhouse, under a spreading sycamore, he looked upon it as a little clasped
volume of black-letter, and studied it with the zeal of a book-worm.

The result of all these researches was a history of the province during
the reign of the Dutch governors, which he published some years since. There
have been various opinions as to the literary character of his work, and, to
tell the truth, it is not a whit better than it should be. Its chief merit is its
scrupulous accuracy, which indeed was a little questioned on its first appearance, but has since been completely established; and it is now admitted into
all historical collections, as a book of unquestionable authority.

The old gentleman died shortly after the publication of his work, and
now that he is dead and gone, it cannot do much harm to his memory to say
that his time might have been much better employed in weightier labors. He,
however, was apt to ride his hobby his own way; and though it did now and
then kick up the dust a little in the eyes of his neighbors, and grieve the

spirit of some friends, for whom he felt the truest deference and affection; yet his errors and follies are remembered "more in sorrow than in anger," and it begins to be suspected, that he never intended to injure or offend. But however his memory may be appreciated by critics, it is still held dear by many folks, whose good opinion is well worth having; particularly by certain biscuit-bakers, who have gone so far as to imprint his likeness on their new-year cakes; and have thus given him a chance for immortality, almost equal to the being stamped on a Waterloo Medal, or a Queen Anne's Farthing.]

WHOEVER has made a voyage up the Hudson must remember the Kaatskill mountains. They are a dismembered branch of the great Appalachian family, and are seen away to the west of the river, swelling up to a noble height, and lording it over the surrounding country. Every change of season, every change of weather, indeed, every hour of the day, produces some change in the magical hues and shapes of these mountains, and they are regarded by all the good wives, far and near, as perfect barometers. When the weather is fair and settled, they are clothed in blue and purple, and print their bold outlines on the clear evening sky; but, sometimes, when the rest of the landscape is cloudless, they will gather a hood of gray vapors about their summits, which, in the last rays of setting sun, will glow and light up like a crown of glory.

At the foot of these fairy mountains, the voyager may have described the light smoke curling up from a village, whose shingle-roofs gleam among the trees, just where the blue tints of the upland melt away into the fresh green of the nearer landscape. It is a little village of great antiquity, having been founded by some of the Dutch colonists, in the early times of the province, just about the beginning of the government of the good Peter Stuyvesant, (may he rest in peace!), and there were some of the houses of the original settlers standing within a few years, built of small yellow bricks brought from Holland, having latticed windows and gable fronts, surmounted with weather-cocks.

In that same village, and in one of these very houses (which, to tell the precise truth, was sadly time-worn and weather-beaten), there lived many years since, while the country was yet a province of Great Britain, a simple good-natured fellow, of the name of Rip Van Winkle. He was a descendant of the Van Winkles who figured so gallantly in the chivalrous days of Peter Stuyvesant, and accompanied him to the siege of Fort Christina. He inherited, however, but little of the martial character of his ancestors. I have observed that he was a simple good-natured man; he was, moreover, a kind neighbor, and an obedient hen-pecked husband. Indeed, to the latter circumstance might be owing that meekness of spirit which gained him such universal popularity; for those men are most apt to be obsequious and conciliating abroad, who are under the discipline of shrews at home. Their tempers, doubtless, are rendered pliant and malleable in the fiery furnace of domestic tribulation; and a curtain lecture is worth all the sermons in the world for teaching the virtues of patience and long-suffering. A termagant wife may, therefore, in some respects, be considered a tolerable blessing; and if so, Rip Van Winkle was thrice blessed.

Certain it is that he was a great favorite among all the good wives of the village, who, as usual, with the amiable sex, took his part in all family squabbles; and never failed, whenever they talked those matters over in their evening gossipings, to lay all the blame on Dame Van Winkle. The children of the village, too, would shout with joy whenever he approached. He assisted at their sports, made their playthings, taught them to fly kites and shoot marbles, and told them long stories of ghosts, witches, and Indians. Whenever he went dodging about the village, he was surrounded by a troop of them, hanging on his skirts, clambering on his back, and playing a thousand tricks on him with impunity; and not a dog would bark at him throughout the neighborhood. *exemption from punishment*

The great error in Rip's composition was an insuperable aversion to all kinds of profitable labor. It could not be from the want of assiduity *constant effort* or perseverance; for he would sit on a wet rock, with a rod as long and heavy as a Tartar's lance, and fish all day without a murmur, even though he should not be encouraged by a single nibble. He would carry a fowling-piece on his shoulder for hours together, trudging through woods and swamps, and up hill and down dale, to shoot a few squirrels or wild pigeons. He would never refuse to assist a neighbor even in the roughest toil, and was a foremost man at all country frolics for husking Indian corn, or building stone-fences; the women of the village, too, used to employ him to run their errands, and to do such little odd jobs as their less obliging husbands would not do for them. In a word Rip was ready to attend to anybody's business but his own; but as to doing family duty, and keeping his farm in order, he found it impossible.

*(margin annotations: agreeable; adaptable; violent)*

In fact, he declared it was of no use to work on his farm; it was
the most pestilent little piece of ground in the whole country; every
thing about it went wrong, and would go wrong, in spite of him. His
fences were continually falling to pieces; his cow would either go astray,
or get among the cabbages; weeds were sure to grow quicker in his
fields than anywhere else; the rain always made a point of setting in
just as he had some out-door work to do; so that though his patrimonial
estate had dwindled away under his management, acre by acre, until
there was little more left than a mere patch of Indian corn and potatoes,
yet it was the worst conditioned farm in the neighborhood.

His children, too, were as ragged and wild as if they belonged to
nobody. His son Rip, an urchin begotten in his own likeness, promised
to inherit the habits, with the old clothes of his father. He was generally
seen trooping like a colt at his mother's heels, equipped in a pair of
his father's cast-off galligaskins, which he had much ado to hold up
with one hand, as fine a lady does her train in bad weather.

Rip Van Winkle, however, was one of those happy mortals, of
foolish, well-oiled dispositions, who take the world easy, eat white
bread or brown, whichever can be got with least thought or trouble,
and would rather starve on a penny than work for a pound. If left to
himself, he would have whistled life away in perfect contentment; but
his wife kept continually dinning in his ears about his idleness, his
carelessness, and the ruin he was bringing on his family. Morning,
noon, and night, her tongue was incessantly going, and every thing
he said or did was sure to produce a torrent of household eloquence.
Rip had but one way of replying to all lectures of the kind, and that,
by frequent use, had grown into a habit. He shrugged his shoulders,
shook his head, cast up his eyes, but said nothing. This, however,
always provoked a fresh volley from his wife; so that he was fain to
draw off his forces, and take the outside of the house—the only side
which, in truth, belongs to a hen-pecked husband.

Rip's sole domestic adherent was his dog Wolf, who was as much
hen-pecked as his master; for Dame Van Winkle regarded them as
companions in idleness, and even looked upon Wolf with an evil eye,
as the cause of his master's going so often astray. True it is, in all
points of spirit befitting an honorable dog, he was as courageous an
animal as ever scoured the woods—but what courage can withstand
the ever-during and all-besetting terrors of a woman's tongue? The

moment Wolf entered the house his crest fell, his tail drooped to the ground, or curled between his legs, he sneaked about with a gallows air, casting many a sidelong glance at Dame Van Winkle, and at the least flourish of a broomstick or ladle, he would fly to the door with yelping precipitation.

Times grew worse and worse with Rip Van Winkle as years of matrimony rolled on; a tart temper never mellows with age, and a sharp tongue is the only edged tool that grows keener with constant use. For a long while he used to console himself, when driven from home, by frequenting a kind of perpetual club of the sages, philosophers, and other idle personages of the village; which held its sessions on a bench before a small inn, designated by a rubicund portrait of His Majesty George the Third. Here they used to sit in the shade through a long lazy summer's day, talking listlessly over village gossip, or telling endless sleepy stories about nothing. But it would have been worth any statesman's money to have heard the profound discussions that sometimes took place, when by chance an old newspaper fell into their hands from some passing traveller. How solemnly they would listen to the contents, as drawled out by Derrick Van Bummel, the schoolmaster, a dapper learned little man, who was not to be daunted by the most gigantic word in the dictionary; and how sagely they would deliberate upon public events some months after they had taken place.

The opinions of this junto were completely controlled by Nicholas Vedder, a patriarch of the village, and landlord of the inn, at the door of which he took his seat from morning till night, just moving sufficiently to avoid the sun and keep in the shade of a large tree; so that the neighbors could tell the hour by his movements as accurately as by a sun-dial. It is true he was rarely heard to speak, but smoked his pipe incessantly. His adherents, however (for every great man has his adherents), perfectly understood him, and knew how to gather his opinions. When any thing that was read or related displeased him, he was observed to smoke his pipe vehemently, and to send forth short, frequent and angry puffs; but when pleased, he would inhale the smoke sometimes, taking the pipe from his mouth, and letting the fragrant vapor curl about his nose, would gravely nod his head in token of perfect approbation.

From even this stronghold the unlucky Rip was at length routed by his termagant wife, who would suddenly break in upon the tran-

quillity of the assemblage and call the members all to naught; nor was
that august personage, Nicholas Vedder himself, sacred from the daring
tongue of this terrible virago,* who charged him outright with en-
couraging her husband in habits of idleness.

Poor Rip was at last reduced almost to despair; and his only alternative, to escape from the labor of the farm and clamor of his wife,
was to take gun in hand and stroll away into the woods. Here he would
sometimes seat himself at the foot of a tree, and share the contents of
his wallet with Wolf, with whom he sympathized as a fellow-sufferer
in persecution. "Poor Wolf," he would say, "thy mistress leads thee a
dog's life of it; but never mind, my lad, whilst I live thou shalt never
want a friend to stand by thee!" Wolf would wag his tail, look wistfully
in his master's face, and if dogs can feel pity I verily believe he
reciprocated the sentiment with all his heart.

*what a dirge* In a long ramble of the kind on a fine autumnal day, Rip had
unconsciously scrambled to one of the highest parts of the Kaatskill
mountains. He was after his favorite sport of squirrel shooting, and
the still solitudes had echoed and re-echoed with the reports of his gun.
Panting and fatigued, he threw himself, late in the afternoon, on a
green knoll, covered with mountain herbage, that crowned the brow
of a precipice. From an opening between the trees he could overlook
all the lower country for many a mile of rich woodland. He saw at a
distance the lordly Hudson, far, far below him, moving on its silent
but majestic course, with the reflection of a purple cloud, or the sail
of a lagging bark, here and there sleeping on its glassy bosom, and at
last losing itself in the blue highlands.

On the other side he looked down into a deep mountain glen, wild,
lonely, and shagged, the bottom filled with fragments from the impending cliffs, and scarcely lighted by the reflected rays of the setting
sun. For some time Rip lay musing on this scene; evening was gradually
advancing; the mountains began to throw their long blue shadows over
the village, and he heaved a heavy sigh when he thought of encoun-
tering the terrors of Dame Van Winkle.

As he was about to descend, he heard a voice from a distance,
hallooing, "Rip Van Winkle! Rip Van Winkle!" He looked round,
but could see nothing but a crow winging its solitary flight across the
mountain. He thought his fancy must have deceived him, and turned
again to descend, when he heard the same cry ring through the still

evening air; "Rip Van Winkle! Rin Van Winkle!"—at the same time Wolf bristled up his back, and giving a low growl, skulked to his master's side, looking fearfully down into the glen. Rip now felt a vague apprehension stealing over him; he looked anxiously in the same direction, and perceived a strange figure slowly toiling up the rocks, and bending under the weight of something he carried on his back. He was surprised to see any human being in this lonely and unfrequented place, but supposing it to be some one of the neighborhood in need of his assistance, he hastened down to yield it.

On nearer approach he was still more surprised at the singularity of the stranger's appearance. He was a short square-built old fellow, with thick bushy hair, and a grizzled beard. His dress was of the antique Dutch fashion—a cloth jerkin strapped round the waist— several pair of breeches, the outer one of ample volume, decorated with rows of buttons down the sides, and bunches at the knees. He bore on his shoulder a stout keg, that seemed full of liquor, and made signs for Rip to approach and assist him with the load. Though rather shy and distrustful of this new acquaintance, Rip complied with his usual alacrity; and mutually relieving one another, they clambered up a narrow gully apparently the dry bed of a mountain torrent. As they ascended, Rip every now and then heard long rolling peals,* like distant thunder, that seemed to issue out of a deep ravine, or rather cleft, between lofty rocks, toward which their rugged path conducted. He paused for an instant, but supposing it to be the muttering of one of those transient thunder-showers which often take place in mountain heights, he proceeded. Passing through the ravine, they came to a hollow, like a small amphitheatre, surrounded by perpendicular precipices, over the brinks of which impending trees shot their branches, so that you only caught glimpses of the azure sky and the bright evening cloud. During the whole time Rip and his companion had labored on in silence; for though the former marvelled greatly what could be the object of carrying a keg of liquor up this wild mountain, yet there was something strange and incomprehensible about the unknown, that inspired awe and checked familiarity.

On entering the amphitheatre, new objects of wonder presented themselves.

On a level spot in the centre was a company of odd-looking personages playing at nine-pins. They were dressed in a quaint outlandish

*loud, prolonged ringing of bells

fashion; some wore short doublets, others jerkins, with long knives in their belts, and most of them had enormous breeches, of similar style with that of the guide's. Their visages, too, were peculiar: one had a large beard, broad face, and small piggish eyes: the face of another seemed to consist entirely of nose, and was surmounted by a white sugar-loaf hat, set off with a little cock's tail. They all had beards, of various shapes and colors. There was one who seemed to be the commander. He was a stout old gentleman, with a weather-beaten countenance; he wore a laced doublet, broad belt and hanger, high-crowned hat and feather, red stockings, and high-heeled shoes with roses in them. The whole group reminded Rip of the figures in an old Flemish painting, in the parlor of Dominie Van Shaick, the village parson, and which had been brought over from Holland at the time of the settlement.

What seemed particularly odd to Rip was, that though these folks were evidently amusing themselves, yet they maintained the gravest faces, the most mysterious silence, and were, withal, the most melancholy party of pleasure he had ever witnessed. Nothing interrupted the stillness of the scene but the noise of the balls, which, whenever they were rolled, echoed along the mountains like rumbling peals of thunder.

As Rip and his companion approached them, they suddenly desisted from their play, and stared at him with such fixed statue-like gaze, and such strange, uncouth, lack-lustre countenances, that his heart turned within him, and his knees smote together. His companion now emptied the contents of the keg into large flagons, and made signs to him to wait upon the company. He obeyed with fear and trembling; they quaffed the liquor in profound silence, and then returned to their game.

By degrees Rip's awe and apprehension subsided. He even ventured, when no eye was fixed upon him, to taste the beverage, which he found had much of the flavor of excellent Hollands. He was naturally a thirsty soul, and was soon tempted to repeat the draught. One taste provoked another; and he reiterated his visits to the flagon so often that at length his senses were overpowered, his eyes swam in his head, his head gradually declined, and he fell into a deep sleep.

On waking, he found himself on the green knoll whence he had first seen the old man of the glen. He rubbed his eyes—it was a bright sunny morning. The birds were hopping and twittering among the bushes, and the eagle was wheeling aloft, and breasting the pure mountain breeze. "Surely," thought Rip, "I have not slept here all night." He recalled the occurrences before he fell asleep. The strange man with a keg of liquor—the mountain ravine—the wild retreat among the rocks—the wobegone party at nine-pins—the flagon—"Oh! that flagon! that wicked flagon!" thought Rip—"what excuse shall I make to Dame Van Winkle!"

He looked round for his gun, but in place of the clean well-oiled fowling-piece, he found an old firelock lying by him, the barrel incrusted with rust, the lock falling off, and the stock worm-eaten. He now suspected that the grave roysterers of the mountain had put a trick upon him, and, having dosed him with liquor, had robbed him of his gun. Wolf, too, had disappeared, but he might have strayed away after a squirrel or partridge. He whistled after him and shouted his name, but all in vain; the echoes repeated his whistle and shout, but no dog was to be seen.

He determined to revisit the scene of the last evening's gambol, and if he met with any of the party, to demand his dog and gun. As he rose to walk, he found himself stiff in the joints, and wanting in his usual activity. "These mountain beds do not agree with me," thought Rip, "and if this frolic should lay me up with a fit of the rheumatism, I shall have a blessed time with Dame Van Winkle." With some difficulty he got down into the glen: he found the gully up which he and his companion had ascended the preceding evening; but to his astonishment a mountain stream was now foaming down it, leaping from rock to rock, and filling the glen with babbling murmurs. He, however, made shift to scramble up its sides, working his toilsome way through thickets of birch, sassafras, and witch-hazel, and sometimes tripped up or entangled by the wild grapevines that twisted their coils or tendrils from tree to tree, and spread a kind of network in his path.

At length he reached to where the ravine had opened through the cliffs to the amphitheatre; but no traces of such opening remained. The rocks presented a high impenetrable wall over which the torrent came tumbling in a sheet of feathery foam, and fell into a broad deep basin, black from the shadows of the surrounding forest. Here, then, poor Rip was brought to a stand. He again called and whistled after his dog; he was only answered by the cawing of a flock of idle crows, sporting high in air about a dry tree that overhung a sunny precipice; and who, secure in their elevation, seemed to look down and scoff at the poor man's perplexities. What was to be done? the morning was passing away, and Rip felt famished for want of his breakfast. He grieved to give up his dog and gun; he dreaded to meet his wife; but it would not do to starve among the mountains. He shook his head, shouldered the rusty firelock, and, with a heart full of trouble and anxiety, turned his steps homeward.

As he approached the village he met a number of people, but none whom he knew, which somewhat surprised him, for he had thought himself acquainted with every one in the country round. Their dress, too, was of a different fashion from that to which he was accustomed. They all stared at him with equal marks of surprise, and whenever they cast their eyes upon him, invariably stroked their chins. The constant recurrence of this gesture induced Rip, involuntarily, to do the same, when, to his astonishment, he found his beard had grown a foot long!

He had now entered the skirts of the village. A troop of strange children ran at his heels, hooting after him, and pointing at his gray beard. The dogs, too, not one of which he recognized for an old acquaintance, barked at him as he passed. The very village was altered; it was larger and more populous. There were rows of houses which he had never seen before, and those which had been his familiar haunts had disappeared. Strange names were over the doors—strange faces at the windows—every thing was strange. His mind now misgave him; he began to doubt whether both he and the world around him were not bewitched. Surely this was his native village, which he had left but the day before. There stood the Kaatskill mountains—there ran the silver Hudson at a distance—there was every hill and dale precisely as it had always been—Rip was sorely perplexed—"That flagon last night," thought he, "has addled my poor head sadly!"

It was with some difficulty that he found the way to his own house, which he approached with silent awe, expecting every moment to hear the shrill voice of Dame Van Winkle. He found the house gone to decay—the roof fallen in, the windows shattered, and the doors off the hinges. A half-starved dog that looked like Wolf was skulking about it. Rip called him by name, but the cur snarled, showed his

teeth, and passed on. This was an unkind cut indeed—"My very dog,"
sighed poor Rip, "has forgotten me!"

He entered the house, which to tell the truth, Dame Van Winkle
had always kept in neat order. It was empty, forlorn, and apparently
abandoned. This desolateness overcame all his connubial fears—he
called loudly for his wife and children—the lonely chambers rang for
a moment with his voice, and then all again was silence.

He now hurried forth, and hastened to his old resort, the village
inn—but it too was gone. A large rickety wooden building stood in
its place, with great gaping windows, some of them broken and mended
with old hats and petticoats, and over the door was painted, "The
Union Hotel, by Jonathan Doolittle." Instead of the great tree that
used to shelter the quiet little Dutch inn of yore, there now was reared
a tall naked pole, with something on the top that looked like a red
night-cap, and from it was fluttering a flag, on which was a singular
assemblage of stars and stripes—all this was strange and incomprehensible. He recognized on the sign, however, the ruby face of King
George, under which he had smoked so many a peaceful pipe; but
even this was singularly metamorphosed. The red coat was changed
for one of blue and buff, a sword was held in the hand instead of a
sceptre, the head was decorated with a cocked hat, and underneath was
painted in large characters, GENERAL WASHINGTON.

There was, as usual, a crowd of folk about the door, but none that
Rip recollected. The very character of the people seemed changed.
There was a busy, bustling, disputatious tone about it, instead of the
accustomed phlegm and drowsy tranquility. He looked in vain for the
sage Nicholas Vedder, with his broad face, double chin, and fair long
pipe, uttering clouds of tobacco-smoke instead of idle speeches; or Van
Bummel, the schoolmaster, doling forth the contents of an ancient
newspaper. In place of these, a lean, bilious-looking fellow, with his
pockets full of handbills, was haranguing vehemently about rights of
citizens—elections—members of congress—liberty—Bunker's Hill—
heroes of seventy-six—and other words, which were a perfect Baby-
lonish jargon to the bewildered Van Winkle.

The appearance of Rip, with his long grizzled beard, his rusty
fowling-piece, his uncouth dress, and an army of women and children
at his heels, soon attracted the attention of the tavern politicians. They
crowded round him, eyeing him from head to foot with great curiosity.

The orator bustled up to him, and, drawing him partly aside, inquired "on which side he voted?" Rip stared in vacant stupidity. Another short but busy little fellow pulled him by the arm, and, rising on tiptoe, inquired in his ear, "Whether he was Federal or Democrat?" Rip was equally at a loss to comprehend the question; when a knowing, self-important old gentleman, in a sharp cocked hat, made his way through the crowd, putting them to the right and left with his elbows as he passed, and planting himself before Van Winkle, with one arm akimbo, the other resting on his cane, his keen eyes and sharp hat penetrating, as it were, into his very soul, demanded in an austere tone, "what brought him to the election with a gun on his shoulder, and a mob at his heels, and whether he meant to breed a riot in the village?"—"Alas! gentlemen," cried Rip, somewhat dismayed, "I am a poor quiet man, a native of the place, and a loyal subject of the king, God bless him!"

Here a general shout burst from the by-standers—"A tory! a tory! a spy! a refugee! hustle him! away with him!" It was with great difficulty that the self-important man in the cocked hat restored order; and, having assumed a tenfold austerity of brow, demanded again of the unknown culprit, what he came there for, and whom he was seeking? The poor man humbly assured him that he meant no harm, but merely came there in search of some of his neighbors, who used to keep about the tavern.

"Well—who are they?—name them."

Rip bethought himself a moment, and inquired, "Where's Nicholas Vedder?"

There was a silence for a little while, when an old man replied, in a thin piping voice, "Nicholas Vedder! why, he is dead and gone these eighteen years! There was a wooden tombstone in the church-yard that used to tell all about him, but that's rotten and gone too."

"Where's Brom Dutcher?"

"Oh, he went off to the army in the beginning of the war; some say he was killed at the storming of Stony Point—others say he was drowned in a squall at the foot of Antony's Nose. I don't know—he never came back again."

"Where's Van Bummel, the schoolmaster?"

"He went off to the wars too, was a great militia general, and is now in congress."

Rip's heart died away at hearing of these sad changes in his home and friends, and finding himself thus alone in the world. Every answer puzzled him too, by treating of such enormous lapses of time, and of matters which he could not understand: war—congress—Stony Point—he had no courage to ask after any more friends, but cried out in despair, "Does nobody here know Rip Van Winkle?"

"Oh, Rip Van Winkle!" exclaimed two or three, "Oh to be sure! that's Rip Van Winkle yonder, leaning against the tree."

Rip looked, and beheld a precise counterpart of himself, as he went up the mountain: apparently as lazy, and certainly as ragged. The poor fellow was now completely confounded. He doubted his own identity, and whether he was himself or another man. In the midst of his bewilderment, the man in the cocked hat demanded who he was, and what was his name?

"God knows," exclaimed he, at his wit's end; "I'm not myself—I'm somebody else—that's me yonder—no—that's somebody else got into my shoes—I was myself last night, but I fell asleep on the mountain, and they've changed my gun, and every thing's changed, and I'm changed, and I can't tell what's my name, or who I am!"

The by-standers began now to look at each other, nod, wink significantly, and tap their fingers against their foreheads. There was a whisper, also, about securing the gun, and keeping the old fellow from doing mischief, at the very suggestion of which the self-important man in the cocked hat retired with some precipitation. At this critical moment a fresh comely woman pressed through the throng to get a peep at the gray-bearded man. She had a chubby child in her arms, which, frightened at his looks, began to cry. "Hush, Rip," cried she, "hush, you little fool; the old man won't hurt you." The name of the child, the air of the mother, the tone of her voice, all awakened a train of recollections in his mind. "What is your name, my good woman?" asked he.

"Judith Gardenier."

"And your father's name?"

"Ah, poor man, Rip Van Winkle was his name, but it's twenty years since he went away from home with his gun, and never has been heard of since—his dog came home without him; but whether he shot himself, or was carried away by the Indians, nobody can tell. I was then but a little girl."

Rip had but one question more to ask; but he put it with a faltering voice:

"Where's your mother?"

"Oh, she too had died but a short time since; she broke a blood-vessel in a fit of passion at a New-England peddler."

There was a drop of comfort, at least, in this intelligence. The honest man could contain himself no longer. He caught his daughter and her child in his arms. "I am your father!" cried he—"Young Rip Van Winkle once—old Rip Van Winkle now!—Does nobody know poor Rip Van Winkle?"

All stood amazed, until an old woman, tottering out from among the crowd, put her hand to her brow, and peering under it in his face for a moment, exclaimed, "Sure enough! it is Rip Van Winkle—it is himself! Welcome home again, old neighbor—Why, where have you been these twenty long years?"

Rip's story was soon told, for the whole twenty years had been to him but one night. The neighbors stared when they heard it; some were seen to wink at each other, and put their tongues in their cheeks: and the self-important man in the cocked hat, who, when the alarm was over, had returned to the field, screwed down the corners of his mouth, and shook his head—upon which there was a general shaking of the head throughout the assemblage.

It was determined, however, to take the opinion of old Peter Vanderdonk, who was seen slowly advancing up the road. He was descendant of the historian of that name, who wrote one of the earliest accounts of the province. Peter was the most ancient inhabitant of the village, and well versed in all the wonderful events and traditions of the neighborhood. He recollected Rip at once, and corroborated his story in the most satisfactory manner. He assured the company that it was a fact, handed down from his ancestor the historian, that the Kaatskill mountains had always been haunted by strange beings. That it was affirmed that the great Hendrick Hudson, the first discoverer of the river and country, kept a kind of vigil there every twenty years, with his crew of the Half-moon; being permitted in this way to revisit the scenes of his enterprise, and keep a guardian eye upon the river, and the great city called by his name. That his father had once seen them in their old Dutch dresses playing at nine-pins in a hollow of

the mountain; and that he himself had heard, one summer afternoon, the sound of their balls, like distant peals of thunder.

To make a long story short, the company broke up, and returned to the more important concerns of the election. Rip's daughter took him home to live with her; she had a snug, well-furnished house, and a stout cheery farmer for a husband, whom Rip recollected for one of the urchins that used to climb upon his back. As to Rip's son and heir, who was the ditto of himself, seen leaning against the tree, he was employed to work on the farm; but evinced an hereditary disposition to attend to any thing else but his business.

Rip now resumed his old walks and habits; he soon found many of his former cronies, though all rather the worse for the wear and tear of time; and preferred making friends among the rising generation, with whom he soon grew into great favor.

Having nothing to do at home, and being arrived at that happy age when a man can be idle with impunity, he took his place once more on the bench at the inn door, and was reverenced as one of the patriarchs of the village, and a chronicle of the old times "before the war." It was some time before he could get into the regular track of gossip, or could be made to comprehend the strange events that had taken place during his torpor. How that there had been a revolutionary war—that the country had thrown off the yoke of old England—and that, instead of being a subject of his Majesty George the Third, he was now a free citizen of the United States. Rip, in fact, was no politician; the changes of states and empires made but little impression on him; but there was one species of despotism under which he had long groaned, and that was—petticoat government. Happily that was at an end; he had got his neck out of the yoke of matrimony, and could go in and out whenever he pleased, without dreading the tyranny of Dame Van Winkle. Whenever her name was mentioned, however, he shook his head, shrugged his shoulders, and cast up his eyes; which might pass either for an expression of resignation to his fate, or joy at his deliverance.

He used to tell his story to every stranger that arrived at Mr. Doolittle's hotel. He was observed, at first, to vary on some points every time he told it, which was, doubtless, owing to his having so recently awaked. It at last settled down precisely to the tale I have related, and not a man, woman, or child in the neighborhood, but knew it by heart. Some always pretended to doubt the reality of it, and insisted that Rip had been out of his head, and that this was one point on which he always remained flighty. The old Dutch inhabitants, however, almost universally gave it full credit. Even to this day they never hear a thunderstorm of a summer afternoon about the Kaatskill, but they say Hendrick Hudson and his crew are at their game of nine-pins; and it is a common wish of all hen-pecked husbands in the neighborhood, when life hangs heavy on their hands, that they might have a quieting draught out of Rip Van Winkle's flagon.

## NOTE

The foregoing Tale, one would suspect, had been suggested to Mr. Knickerbocker by a little German superstition about the Emperor Frederick *der Rothbart*, and the Kypphaüser mountain: the subjoined note, however, which he had appended to the tale, shows that it is absolute fact, narrated with his usual fidelity:

"The story of Rip Van Winkle may seem incredible to many, but never-theless I give it my full belief, for I know the vicinity of our old Dutch settlements to have been very subject to marvellous events and appearances. Indeed, I have heard many stranger stories than this, in the villages along the Hudson; all of which were too well authenticated to admit of a doubt. I have even talked with Rip Van Winkle myself, who, when last I saw him, was a very venerable old man, and so perfectly rational and consistent on every other point, that I think no conscientious person could refuse to take this into the bargain; may, I have seen a certificate on the subject taken before a country justice and signed with a cross, in the justice's own handwriting. The story, therefore, is beyond the possibility of doubt. D.K."

## POSTSCRIPT

The following are travelling notes from a memorandum-book of Mr. Knickerbocker:

The Kaatsberg, or Catskill Mountains, have always been a region full of fable. The Indians considered them the abode of spirits, who influenced the weather, spreading sunshine or clouds over the landscape, and sending good or bad hunting seasons. They were ruled by an old squaw spirit, said to be their mother. She dwelt on the highest peak of the Catskills, and had charge of the doors of day and night to open and shut them at the proper hour. She hung up the new moons in the skies, and cut up the old ones into stars. In times of drought, if properly propitiated, she would spin light summer clouds out of cobwebs and morning dew, and send them off from the crest of the mountain, flake after flake, like flakes of carded cotton, to float in the air; until, dissolved by the heat of the sun, they would fall in gentle showers, causing the grass to spring, the fruits to ripen, and the corn to grow an inch an hour. If displeased, however, she would brew up clouds black as ink, sitting in the midst of them like a bottle-bellied spider in the midst of its web; and when these clouds broke, woe betide the valleys!

In old times, say the Indian traditions, there was a kind of Manitou or Spirit, who kept about the wildest recesses of The Catskill Mountains, and took a mischievous pleasure in wreaking all kinds of evils and vexations upon the red men. Sometimes he would assume the form of a bear, a panther, or a deer, lead the bewildered hunter a weary chase through tangled forests and among ragged rocks; and then spring off with a loud ho! ho! leaving him aghast on the brink of a beetling precipice or raging torrent.

The favorite abode of this Manitou is still shown. It is a great rock or cliff on the loneliest part of the mountains, and, from the flowering vines which clamber about it, and the wild flowers which abound in its neighborhood, is known by the name of Garden Rock. Near the foot of it is a small lake, the haunt of the solitary bittern, with water-snakes basking in the sun on the leaves of the pond-lilies which lie on the surface. This place was held in great awe by the Indians, insomuch that the boldest hunter would not pursue his game within its precincts. Once upon a time, however, a hunter who had lost his way, penetrated to the garden rock, where he beheld a number of gourds placed in the crotches of trees. One of these he seized and made off with it, but in the hurry of his retreat he let it fall among the rocks, when a great stream gushed forth, which washed him away and swept him down precipices, where he was dashed to pieces, and the stream made its way to the Hudson, and continues to flow to the present day; being the identical stream known by the name of the Kaaters-kill.

# THE LEGEND OF
# SLEEPY HOLLOW

## Found Among the Papers of
## the Late Diedrich Knickerbocker

A pleasing land of drowsy head it was,
Of dreams that wave before the half-shut eye;
And of gay castles in the clouds that pass,
For ever flushing round a summer sky.

CASTLE OF INDOLENCE

In the bosom of one of those spacious coves which indent the eastern shore of the Hudson, at that broad expansion of the river denominated by the ancient Dutch navigators the Tappan Zee, and where they always prudently shortened sail, and implored the protection of St. Nicholas when they crossed, there lies a small market-town or rural port, which by some is called Greensburgh, but which is more generally and properly known by the name of Tarry Town. This name was given, we are told, in former days, by the good housewives of the adjacent country, from the inveterate propensity of their husbands to linger about the village tavern on market days. Be that as it may, I do not vouch for the fact, but merely advert to it, for the sake of being precise and authentic. Not far from this village, perhaps about two miles, there is a little valley, or rather lap of land, among high hills, which is one of the quietest places in the whole world. A small brook glides through it, with just murmur enough to lull one to repose; and the occasional whistle of a quail, or tapping of a woodpecker, is almost the only sound that ever breaks in upon the uniform tranquillity.

I recollect that, when a stripling, my first exploit in squirrel-shooting was in a grove of tall walnut-trees that shades one side of the valley. I had wandered into it at noon time, when all nature is peculiarly quiet, and was startled by the roar of my own gun, as it broke the Sabbath stillness around, and was prolonged and reverberated by the angry echoes. If ever I should wish for a retreat, whither I might steal from the world and its distractions, and dream quietly away the remnant of a troubled life, I know of none more promising than this little valley.

From the listless repose of the place, and the peculiar character of its inhabitants, who are descendants from the original Dutch settlers, this sequestered glen has long been known by the name of SLEEPY HOLLOW, and its rustic lads are called the Sleepy Hollow Boys throughout all the neighboring country. A drowsy, dreamy influence seems to hang over the land, and to pervade the very atmosphere. Some say that the place was bewitched by a high German doctor, during the early days of the settlement; others, that an old Indian chief, the prophet or wizard of his tribe, held his pow-wows there before the country was discovered by Master Hendrick Hudson. Certain it is, the place still continues under the sway of some witching power, that holds a spell over the minds of the good people, causing them to walk in a continual reverie. They are given to all kinds of marvellous beliefs; are subject to trances and visions; and frequently see strange sights, and hear music and voices in the air. The whole neighborhood abounds with local tales, haunted spots, and twilight superstitions; stars shoot and meteors glare oftener across the valley than in any other part of the country, and the nightmare, with her whole nine fold, seems to make it the favorite scene of her gambols.

The dominant spirit, however, that haunts this enchanted region, and seems to be commander-in-chief of all the powers of the air, is the apparition of a figure on horseback without a head. It is said by some to be the ghost of a Hessian trooper, whose head had been carried away by a cannon-ball, in some nameless battle during the revolutionary war; and who is ever and anon seen by the country folk, hurrying along in the gloom of night, as if on the wings of the wind. His haunts are not confined to the valley, but extend at times to the adjacent roads, and especially to the vicinity of a church at no great distance. Indeed, certain of the most authentic historians of those parts, who have been

careful in collecting and collating the floating facts concerning this
spectre, allege that the body of the trooper, having been buried in the
church-yard, the ghost rides forth to the scene of the battle in nightly
quest of his head; and that the rushing speed with which he sometimes
passes along the Hollow, like a midnight blast, is owing to his being
belated, and in a hurry to get back to the church-yard before daybreak.

Such is the general purport of this legendary superstition, which
has furnished materials for many a wild story in that region of shadows;
and the spectre is known, at all the country firesides, by the name of
the Headless Horseman of Sleepy Hollow.

It is remarkable that the visionary propensity I have mentioned is
not confined to the native inhabitants of the valley, but is unconsciously
imbibed by every one who resides there for a time. However wide
awake they may have been before they entered that sleepy region, they
are sure, in a little time, to inhale the witching influence of the air,
and begin to grow imaginative—to dream dreams, and see apparitions.

I mention this peaceful spot with all possible laud; for it is in such
little retired Dutch valleys, found here and there embosomed in the
great State of New-York, that population, manners, and customs,
remain fixed; while the great torrent of migration and improvement,
which is making such incessant changes in other parts of this restless
country, sweeps by them unobserved. They are like those little nooks
of still water which border a rapid stream; where we may see the straw
and bubble riding quietly at anchor, or slowly revolving in their mimic
harbor, undisturbed by the rush of the passing current. Though many
years have elapsed since I trod the drowsy shades of Sleepy Hollow,
yet I question whether I should not still find the same trees and the
same families vegetating in its sheltered bosom.

In this by-place of nature, there abode, in a remote period of
American history, that is to say, some thirty years since, a worthy
wight of the name of Ichabod Crane; who sojourned, or, as he expressed
it, "tarried," in Sleepy Hollow, for the purpose of instructing the
children of the vicinity. He was a native of Connecticut; a State which
supplies the Union with pioneers for the mind as well as for the forest,
and sends forth yearly its legions of frontier woodsmen and country
schoolmasters. The cognomen of Crane was not inapplicable to his
person. He was tall, but exceedingly lank, with narrow shoulders,
long arms and legs, hands that dangled a mile out of his sleeves, feet

that might have served for shovels, and his whole frame most loosely
hung together. His head was small, and flat at top, with huge ears,
large green glassy eyes, and a long snipe nose, so that it looked like
a weather-cock, perched upon his spindle neck, to tell which way the
wind blew. To see him striding along the profile of a hill on a windy
day, with his clothes bagging and fluttering about him, one might
have mistaken him for the genius of famine descending upon the earth,
or some scarecrow eloped from a cornfield.

His school-house was a low building of one large room, rudely
constructed of logs; the windows partly glazed, and partly patched
with leaves of old copy-books. It was most ingeniously secured, at
vacant hours, by a withe twisted in the handle of the door, and stakes
set against the window shutters; so that, though a thief might get in
with perfect ease, he would find some embarrassment in getting out;
an idea most probably borrowed by the architect, Yost Van Houten,
from the mystery of an eel-pot. The school-house stood in a rather
lonely but pleasant situation, just at the foot of a woody hill, with a
brook running close by, and a formidable birch tree growing at one
end of it. From hence the low murmur of his pupils' voices, conning
over their lessons, might be heard in a drowsy summer's day, like the
hum of a beehive; interrupted now and then by the authoritative voice
of the master, in the tone of menace or command; or, peradventure,
by the appalling sound of the birch, as he urged some tardy loiterer
along the flowery path of knowledge. Truth to say, he was a conscientious man, and ever bore in mind the golden maxim, "Spare the
rod and spoil the child."—Ichabod Crane's scholars certainly were not
spoiled.

I would not have it imagined, however, that he was one of those
cruel potentates of the school, who joy in the smart of their subjects;
on the contrary, he administered justice with discrimination rather than
severity; taking the burthen off the backs of the weak, and laying it
on those of the strong. Your mere puny stripling, that winced at the
least flourish of the rod, was passed by with indulgence; but the claims
of justice were satisfied by inflicting a double portion on some little,
tough, wrong-headed, broad-skirted Dutch urchin, who sulked and
swelled and grew dogged and sullen beneath the birch. All this he
called "doing his duty by their parents;" and he never inflicted a
chastisement without following it by the assurance, so consolatory to

*A person who lives in the labor of others*

the smarting urchin, that "he would remember it, and thank him for it the longest day he had to live."

When school hours were over, he was even the companion and playmate of the larger boys; and on holiday afternoons would convoy some of the smaller ones home, who happened to have pretty sisters, or good housewives for mothers, noted for the comforts of the cupboard. Indeed it behooved him to keep on good terms with his pupils. The revenue arising from his school was small, and would have been scarcely sufficient to furnish him with daily bread, for he was a huge feeder, and though lank, had the dilating powers of an anaconda; but to help out his maintenance, he was, according to country custom in those parts, boarded and lodged at the houses of the farmers, whose children he instructed. With these he lived successively a week at a time; thus going the rounds of the neighborhood, with all his worldly effects tied up in a cotton handkerchief.

That all this might not be too onerous on the purses of his rustic patrons, who are apt to consider the costs of schooling a grievous burden, and schoolmasters as mere drones, he had various ways of rendering himself both useful and agreeable. He assisted the farmers occasionally in the lighter labors of their farms; helped to make hay; mended the fences; took the horses to water; drove the cows from pasture; and cut wood for the winter fire. He laid aside, too, all the dominant dignity and absolute sway with which he lorded it in his little empire, the school, and became wonderfully gentle and ingratiating. He found favor in the eyes of the mothers, by petting the children, particularly the youngest; and like the lion bold, which whilom so magnanimously the lamb did hold, he would sit with a child on one knee, and rock a cradle with his foot for whole hours together.

In addition to his other vocations, he was the singing-master of the neighborhood, and picked up many bright shillings by instructing the young in psalmody. It was a matter of no little vanity to him, on Sundays, to take his station in front of the church gallery, with a band of chosen singers; where, in his own mind, he completely carried away the palm from the parson. Certain it is, his voice resounded far above all the rest of the congregation; and there are peculiar quavers still to be heard in that church, and which may even be heard half a mile off, quite to the opposite side of the mill-pond, on a still Sunday morning,

which are said to be legitimately descended from the nose of Ichabod
Crane. Thus, by divers little make-shifts in that ingenious way which
is commonly denominated "by hook and by crook," the worthy pedagogue got on tolerably enough, and was thought, by all who understood nothing of the labor of headwork, to have a wonderfully easy
life of it.

The schoolmaster is generally a man of some importance in the
female circle of a rural neighborhood; being considered a kind of idle
gentlemanlike personage, of vastly superior taste and accomplishments
to the rough country swains, and, indeed, inferior in learning only to
the parson. His appearance, therefore, is apt to occasion some little
stir at the tea-table of a farmhouse, and the addition of a supernumerary
dish of cakes or sweetmeats, or, peradventure, the parade of a silver
tea-pot. Our man of letters, therefore, was peculiarly happy in the
smiles of all the country damsels. How he would figure among them
in the churchyard, between services on Sundays! gathering grapes for
them from the wild vines that overrun the surrounding trees; reciting
for their amusement all the epitaphs on the tombstones; or sauntering,
with a whole bevy of them, along the banks of the adjacent mill-pond;
while the more bashful country bumpkins hung sheepishly back, envy-
ing his superior elegance and address.

From his half itinerant life, also, he was a kind of travelling gazette,
carrying the whole budget of local gossip from house to house; so that
his appearance was always greeted with satisfaction. He was, moreover,
esteemed by the women as a man of great erudition, for he had read
several books quite through, and was a perfect master of Cotton Mather's history of New England Witchcraft, in which, by the way, he
most firmly and potently believed.

He was, in fact, an odd mixture of small shrewdness and simple
credulity. His appetite for the marvellous, and his powers of digesting
it, were equally extraordinary; and both had been increased by his
residence in this spellbound region. No tale was too gross or monstrous
for his capacious swallow. It was often his delight, after his school was
dismissed in the afternoon, to stretch himself on the rich bed of clover,
bordering the brook that whimpered by his school-house, and there
con over old Mather's direful tales, until the gathering dusk of the
evening made the printed page a mere mist before his eyes. Then, as
he wended his way, by swamp and stream and awful woodland, to the

farmhouse where he happened to be quartered, every sound of nature, at that witching hour, fluttered his excited imagination: the moan of the whip-poor-will* from the hill-side; the boding cry of the tree-toad, that harbinger of storm; the dreary hooting of the screech-owl, or the sudden rustling in the thicket of birds frightened from their roost. The fire-flies, too, which sparkled most vividly in the darkest places, now and then startled him, as one of uncommon brightness would stream across his path; and if, by chance, an huge blockhead of a beetle came winging his blundering flight against him, the poor varlet was ready to give up the ghost, with the idea that he was struck with a witch's token. His only resource on such occasions, either to drown thought, or drive away evil spirits, was to sing psalm tunes;—and the good people of Sleepy Hollow, as they sat by their doors of an evening, were often filled with awe, at hearing his nasal melody, "in linked sweetness long drawn out," floating from the distant hill, or along the dusky road.

Another of his sources of fearful pleasure was to pass long winter evenings with the old Dutch wives, as they sat spinning by the fire, with a row of apples roasting and spluttering along the hearth, and listen to their marvellous tales of ghosts and goblins, and haunted fields, and haunted brooks, and haunted bridges, and haunted houses, and particularly of the headless horseman, or galloping Hessian of the Hollow, as they sometimes called him. He would delight them equally by his anecdotes of witchcraft, and of the direful omens and portentous sights and sounds in the air, which prevailed in the earlier times of Connecticut; and would frighten them wofully with speculations upon comets and shooting stars; and with the alarming fact that the world did absolutely turn round, and that they were half the time topsy-turvy!

But if there was a pleasure in all this, while snugly cuddling in the chimney corner of a chamber that was all of a ruddy glow from the crackling wood fire, and where, of course, no spectre dared to show his face, it was dearly purchased by the terrors of his subsequent walk homewards. What fearful shapes and shadows beset his path

---

*The whip-poor-will is a bird which is only heard at night. It receives its name from its note, which is thought to resemble those words.

amidst the dim and ghastly glare of a snowy night!—With what wistful
look did he eye every trembling ray of light streaming across the waste
fields from some distant window!—How often was he appalled by some
shrub covered with snow, which, like a sheeted spectre, beset his very
path!—How often did he shrink with curdling awe at the sound of
his own steps on the frosty crust beneath his feet; and dread to look
over his shoulder, lest he should behold some uncouth being tramping
close behind him!—and how often was he thrown into complete dismay
by some rushing blast, howling among the trees, in the idea that it
was the Galloping Hessian on one of his nightly scourings!

All these, however, were mere terrors of the night, phantoms of
the mind that walk in darkness; and though he had seen many spectres
in his time, and been more than once beset by Satan in divers shapes,
in his lonely perambulations, yet daylight put an end to all these evils;
and he would have passed a pleasant life of it, in despite of the devil
and all his works, if his path had not been crossed by a being that
causes more perplexity to mortal man than ghosts, goblins, and the
whole race of witches put together, and that was—a woman.

Among the musical disciples who assembled, one evening in each
week, to receive his instructions in psalmody, was Katrina Van Tassel,
the daughter and only child of a substantial Dutch farmer. She was a
blooming lass of fresh eighteen; plump as a partridge; ripe and melting
and rosy cheeked as one of her father's peaches, and universally famed,
not merely for her beauty, but her vast expectations. She was withal
a little of a coquette, as might be perceived even in her dress, which
was a mixture of ancient and modern fashions, as most suited to set
off her charms. She wore the ornaments of pure yellow gold, which
her great-great-grandmother had brought over from Saardam; the
tempting stomacher of the olden time; and withal a provokingly short
petticoat, to display the prettiest foot and ankle in the country round.

Ichabod Crane had a soft and foolish heart towards the sex; and it
is not to be wondered at, that so tempting a morsel soon found favor
in his eyes; more especially after he had visited her in her paternal
mansion. Old Baltus Van Tassel was a perfect picture of a thriving,
contented, liberal-hearted farmer. He seldom, it is true, sent either
his eyes or his thoughts beyond the boundaries of his own farm; but
within those every thing was snug, happy, and well-conditioned. He
was satisfied with his wealth, but not proud of it; and piqued himself

upon the hearty abundance, rather than the style in which he lived. His stronghold was situated on the banks of the Hudson, in one of those green, sheltered, fertile nooks, in which the Dutch farmers are so fond of nestling. A great elm-tree spread its broad branches over it; at the foot of which bubbled up a spring of the softest and sweetest water, in a little well, formed of a barrel; and then stole sparkling away through the grass, to a neighboring brook, that bubbled along among alders and dwarf willows. Hard by the farmhouse was a vast barn, that might have served for a church; every window and crevice of which seemed bursting forth with the treasures of the farm; the flail was busily resounding within it from morning to night; swallows and martins skimmed twittering about the eaves; and rows of pigeons, some with one eye turned up, as if watching the weather, some with their heads under their wings, or buried in their bosoms, and others swelling, and cooing, and bowing about their dames, were enjoying the sunshine on the roof. Sleek unwieldly porkers were grunting in the repose and abundance of their pens; whence sallied forth, now and then, troops of sucking pigs, as if to snuff the air. A stately squadron of snowy geese were riding in an adjoining pond, convoying whole fleets of ducks; regiments of turkeys were gobbling through the farmyard, and guinea fowls fretting about it, like ill-tempered housewives, with their peevish discontented cry. Before the barn door strutted the gallant cock, that pattern of a husband, a warrior, and a fine gentleman, clapping his burnished wings, and crowing with his feet, and then generously calling his ever-hungry family of wives and children to enjoy the rich morsel which he had discovered.

The pedagogue's mouth watered, as he looked upon this sumptuous promise of luxurious winter fare. In his devouring mind's eye, he pictured to himself every roasting-pig running about with a pudding in his belly, and an apple in his mouth; the pigeons were snugly put to bed in a comfortable pie, and tucked in with a coverlet of crust; the geese were swimming in their own gravy; and the ducks pairing cosily in dishes, like snug married couples, with a decent competency of onion sauce. In the porkers he saw carved out the future sleek side of bacon, and juicy relishing ham; not a turkey but he beheld daintily trussed up, with its gizzard under its wing, and, peradventure, a necklace of savory sausages; and even bright chanticleer himself lay sprawling on his back, in a side-dish, with uplifted claws, as if craving that quarter which his chivalrous spirit disdained to ask while living.

As the enraptured Ichabod fancied all this, and as he rolled his great green eyes over the fat meadow-lands, the rich fields of wheat, of ruddy fruit, which surrounded the warm tenement of Van Tassel, his heart yearned after the damsel who was to inherit these domains, and his imagination expanded with the idea, how they might be readily turned into cash, and the money invested in immense tracts of wild land, and shingle palaces in the wilderness. Nay, his busy fancy already realized his hopes, and presented to him the blooming Katrina, with a whole family of children, mounted on the top of a wagon loaded with household trumpery, with pots and kettles dangling beneath; and he beheld himself bestriding a pacing mare, with a colt at her heels, setting out for Kentucky, Tennessee, or the Lord knows where.

When he entered the house the conquest of his heart was complete. It was one of those spacious farmhouses, with high-ridged, but lowly-sloping roofs, built in the style handed down from the first Dutch settlers; the low projecting eaves forming a piazza along the front, capable of being closed up in bad weather. Under this were hung flails, harness, various utensils of husbandry, and nets for fishing in the neighboring river. Benches were built along the sides for summer use; and a great spinning-wheel at one end, and a churn at the other, showed the various uses to which this important porch might be devoted. From this piazza the wondering Ichabod entered the hall, which formed the centre of the mansion and the place of usual residence. Here, rows of resplendent pewter, ranged on a long dresser, dazzled his eyes. In one corner stood a huge bag of wool ready to be spun; in another a quantity of linsey-woolsey just from the loom; ears of Indian corn, and strings of dried apples and peaches, hung in gay festoons along the walls, mingled with the gaud of red peppers; and a door left ajar gave him a peep into the best parlor, where the claw-footed chairs, and dark mahogany tables, shone like mirrors; and irons, with their accompanying shovel and tongs, glistened from their covert of asparagus tops; mock-oranges and conch-shells decorated the mantle-piece; strings of various colored birds' eggs were suspended above it: a great ostrich egg was hung from the centre of the room, and a corner cupboard, knowingly left open, displayed immense treasures of old silver and well-mended china.

From the moment Ichabod laid his eyes upon these regions of delight, the peace of his mind was at an end, and his only study was how to gain the affections of the peerless daughter of Van Tassel. In this enterprise, however, he had more real difficulties than generally fell to the lot of a knight-errant of yore, who seldom had any thing but giants, enchanters, fiery dragons, and such like easily-conquered adversaries, to contend with; and had to make his way merely through gates of iron and brass, and walls of adamant, to the castle keep, where the lady of his heart was confined; all which he achieved as easily as a man would carve his way to the centre of a Christmas pie; and then the lady gave him her hand as a matter of course. Ichabod, on the contrary, had to win his way to the heart of a country coquette, beset with a labyrinth of whims and caprices, which were for ever presenting new difficulties and impediments; and he had to encounter a host of fearful adversaries of real flesh and blood, the numerous rustic admirers, who beset every portal to her heart; keeping a watchful and angry eye upon each other, but ready to fly out in the common cause against any new competitor.

Among these the most formidable was a burly, roaring, roystering blade, of the name of Abraham or, according to the Dutch abbreviation, Brom Van Brunt, the hero of the country round, which rang with his feats of strength and hardihood. He was broad-shouldered and double-jointed, with short curly black hair, and a bluff, but not unpleasant countenance, having a mingled air of fun and arrogance. From his Herculean frame and great powers of limb, he had received the nickname BROM BONES, by which he was universally known. He was famed for great knowledge and skill in horsemanship, being as dexterous on horseback as a Tartar. He was foremost at all races and cock-fights; and, with the ascendency which bodily strength acquires in rustic life, was the umpire in all disputes, setting his hat on one side, and giving his decisions with an air and tone admitting of no gainsay or appeal. He was always ready for either a fight or a frolic; but had more mischief than ill-will in his composition; and, with all his overbearing roughness, there was strong dash of waggish good humor at bottom. He had three or four boon companions, who regarded him as their model, and at the head of whom he scoured the country, attending every scene of feud or merriment for miles round. In cold weather he was distinguished by a fur cap, surmounted with a flaunting fox's tail; and when the folks at a country gathering descried this well-known crest at a distance, whisking about among a squad of hard riders, they always stood by for a squall. Sometimes his crew would be heard dashing along past the farmhouses at midnight, with whoop and halloo, like a troop of Don Cossacks; and the old dames, startled out of their sleep, would listen for a moment till the hurry-scurry had clattered by, and then exclaim, "Ay, there goes Brom Bones and his gang!" The neighbors looked upon him with a mixture of awe, admiration, and good will; and when any madcap prank, or rustic brawl occurred in the vicinity, always shook their heads, and warranted Brom Bones was at the bottom of it.

This rantipole hero had for some time singled out the blooming Katrina for the object of his uncouth gallantries, and though his amorous toyings were something like the gentle caresses and endearments of a bear, yet it was whispered that she did not altogether discourage his hopes. Certain it is, his advances were signals for rival candidates to retire, who felt no inclination to cross a lion in his amours; insomuch, that when his horse was seen tied to Van Tassel's paling, on a Sunday night, a sure sign that his master was courting, or, as it is termed, "sparking," within, all other suitors passed by in despair, and carried the war into other quarters.

Such was the formidable rival with whom Ichabod Crane had to contend, and, considering all things, a stouter man than he would have shrunk from the competition, and a wiser man would have despaired. He had, however, a happy mixture of pliability and perseverance in his nature; he was in form and spirit like a supple-jack—yielding, but tough; though he bent, he never broke; and though he bowed beneath the slightest pressure, yet, the moment it was away—jerk! he was as erect, and carried his head as high as ever.

To have taken the field openly against his rival would have been madness; for he was not a man to be thwarted in his amours, any more than that stormy lover, Achilles. Ichabod, therefore, made his advances in a quiet and gently-insinuating manner. Under cover of his character of singing-master, he made frequent visits at the farmhouse; not that he had any thing to apprehend from the meddlesome interference of parents, which is so often a stumbling-block in the path of lovers. Balt Van Tassel was an easy indulgent soul; he loved his daughter better even than his pipe, and, like a reasonable man and an excellent father, let her have her way in every thing. His notable little wife, too, had enough to do to attend to her housekeeping and manage her poultry;

for, as she sagely observed, ducks and geese are foolish things, and must be looked after, but girls can take care of themselves. Thus while the busy dame bustled about the house, or plied her spinning-wheel at one end of the piazza, honest Balt would sit smoking his evening pipe at the other, watching the achievements of a little wooden warrior, who, armed with a sword in each hand, was most valiantly fighting the wind on the pinnacle of the barn. In the mean time, Ichabod would carry on his suit with the daughter by the side of the spring under the great elm, or sauntering along in the twilight, that hour so favorable to the lover's eloquence.

I profess not to know how women's hearts are wooed and won. To me they have always been matters of riddle and admiration. Some seem to have but one vulnerable point, or door of access; while others have a thousand avenues, and may be captured in a thousand different ways. It is a great triumph of skill to gain the former, but a still greater proof of generalship to maintain possession of the latter, for the man must battle for his fortress at every door and window. He who wins a thousand common hearts is therefore entitled to some renown; but he who keeps undisputed sway over the heart of a coquette, is indeed a hero. Certain it is, this was not the case with the redoubtable Brom Bones; and from the moment Ichabod Crane made his advances, the interests of the former evidently declined; his horse was no longer seen tied at the palings of Sunday nights, and a deadly feud gradually arose between him and the preceptor of Sleepy Hollow.

Brom, who had a degree of rough chivalry in his nature, would fain have carried matters to open warfare, and have settled their pretensions to the lady, according to the mode of those most concise and simple reasoners, the knights-errant of yore—by single combat; but Ichabod was too conscious of the superior might of his adversary to enter the lists against him: he had overheard a boast of Bones, that he would "double the schoolmaster up, and lay him on a shelf of his own school-house;" and he was too wary to give him an opportunity. There was something extremely provoking in this obstinately pacific system; it left Brom no alternative but to draw upon the funds of rustic waggery in his disposition, and to play off boorish practical jokes upon his rival. Ichabod became the object of whimsical persecution to Bones, and his gang of rough riders. They harried his hitherto peaceful domains; smoked out his singing school, by stopping up the chimney;

broke into the school-house at night, in spite of its formidable fastenings of withe and window stakes, and turned every thing topsy-turvy: so that the poor schoolmaster began to think all the witches in the country held their meetings there. But what was still more annoying, Brom took all opportunities of turning him into ridicule in presence of his mistress, and had a scoundrel dog whom he taught to whine in the most ludicrous manner, and introduced as a rival of Ichabod's to instruct her in psalmody.

In this way matters went on for some time, without producing any material effect on the relative situation of the contending powers. On a fine autumnal afternoon, Ichabod, in pensive mood, sat enthroned on the lofty stool whence he usually watched all the concerns of his little literary realm. In his hand he swayed a ferule, that sceptre of despotic power; the birch of justice reposed on three nails, behind the throne, a constant terror to evil doers; while on the desk before him might be seen sundry contraband articles and prohibited weapons, detected upon the persons of idle urchins; such as half-munched apples, popguns, whirligigs, fly-cages, and whole legions of rampant little paper game-cocks. Apparently there had been some appalling act of justice recently inflicted, for his scholars were all busily intent upon their books, or slyly whispering behind them with one eye kept upon the master; and a kind of buzzing stillness reigned throughout the school-room. It was suddenly interrupted by the appearance of a negro, in tow-cloth jacket and trowsers, a round-crowned fragment of hat, like the cap of Mercury, and mounted on the back of a ragged, wild, half-broken colt, which he managed with a rope by way of halter. He came clattering up to the school door with an invitation to Ichabod to attend a merry-making or "quilting frolic," to be held that evening at Mynheer Van Tassel's; and having delivered his message with that air of importance, and effort at fine language, which a negro is apt to display on petty embassies of the kind, he dashed over the brook, and was seen scampering away up the hollow, full of the importance and hurry of his mission.

All was now bustle and hubbub in the late quiet school-room. The scholars were hurried through their lessons, without stopping at trifles; those who were nimble skipped over half with impunity, and those who were tardy, had a smart application now and then in the rear, to quicken their speed, or help them over a tall word. Books were flung aside without being put away on the shelves, inkstands were overturned, benches thrown down, and the whole school was turned loose an hour before the usual time, bursting forth like a legion of young imps, yelping and racketing about the green in joy at their early emancipation. The gallant Ichabod now spent at least an extra half hour at his toilet, brushing and furbishing up his best, and indeed only, suit of rusty black, and arranging his looks by a bit of broken looking-glass, that hung up in the school-house. That he might make his appearance before his mistress in the true style of a cavalier, he borrowed a horse from the farmer with whom he was domiciliated, a choleric old Dutchman, of the name of Hans Van Ripper, and, thus gallantly mounted, issued forth, like a knight-errant in quest of adventures. But it is meet I should, in the true spirit of romantic story, give some account of the looks and equipments of my hero and his steed. The animal he bestrode was a broken-down plough-horse, that had outlived almost every thing but his viciousness. He was gaunt and shagged, with a ewe neck and a head like a hammer; his rusty mane and tail were tangled and knotted with burrs; one eye had lost its pupil, and was glaring and spectral; but the other had the gleam of a genuine devil in it. Still he must have had fire and mettle in his day, if we may judge from the name he bore of Gunpowder. He had, in fact, been a favorite steed of his master's, the choleric Van Ripper, who was a furious rider, and had infused, very probably, some of his own spirit into the animal; for, old and broken-down as he looked, there was more of the lurking devil in him than in any young filly in the country.

Ichabod was a suitable figure for such a steed. He rode with short stirrups, which brought his knees nearly up to the pommel of the saddle; his sharp elbows stuck out like grasshoppers'; he carried his whip perpendicularly in his hand, like a sceptre, and, as his horse jogged on, the motion of his arms was not unlike the flapping of a pair of wings. A small wool hat rested on the top of his nose, for so his scanty strip of forehead might be called; and the skirts of his black coat fluttered out almost to the horse's tail. Such was the appearance of Ichabod and his steed, as they shambled out of the gate of Hans Van Ripper, and it was altogether such an apparition as is seldom to be met with in broad daylight.

It was, as I have said, a fine autumnal day, the sky was clear and serene, and nature wore that rich and golden livery which we always associate with the idea of abundance. The forests had put on their sober brown and yellow, while some trees of the tenderer kind had been nipped by the frosts into brilliant dyes of orange, purple, and scarlet. Streaming files of wild ducks began to make their appearance high in the air; the bark of the squirrel might be heard from the groves of beech and hickory nuts, and the pensive whistle of the quail at intervals from the neighboring stubble-field.

The small birds were taking their farewell banquets. In the fulness of their revelry, they fluttered, chirping and frolicking, from bush to bush, and tree to tree, capricious from the very profusion and variety around them. There was the honest cock-robin, the favorite game of stripling sportsmen, with its loud querulous note; and the twittering blackbirds flying in sable clouds; and the golden-winged woodpecker, with his crimson crest, his broad black gorget, and splendid plumage; and the cedar bird, with its red-tipt wings and yellow-tipt tail, and its little monteiro cap of feathers; and the blue-jay, that noisy coxcomb, in his gay light-blue coat and white under-clothes; screaming and chattering, nodding and bobbing and bowing, and pretending to be on good terms with every songster of the grove.

As Ichabod jogged slowly on his way, his eye, ever open to every symptom of culinary abundance, ranged with delight over the treasures of jolly autumn. On all sides he beheld vast store of apples; some hanging in oppressive opulence on the trees; some gathered into baskets and barrels for the market; others heaped up in rich piles for the cider-press. Farther on he beheld great fields of Indian corn, with its golden ears peeping from their leafy coverts, and holding out the promise of cakes and hasty pudding; and the yellow pumpkins lying beneath them, turning up their fair round bellies to the sun, and giving ample prospects of the most luxurious of pies; and anon he passed the fragrant buckwheat fields, breathing the odor of the bee-hive, and as he beheld them, soft anticipations stole over his mind of dainty slapjacks, well buttered, and garnished with honey or treacle, by the delicate little dimpled hand of Katrina Van Tassel.

Thus feeding his mind with many sweet thoughts and "sugared suppositions," he journeyed along the sides of a range of hills which look out upon some of the goodliest scenes of the mighty Hudson. The sun gradually wheeled his broad disk down into the west. The wide bosom of the Tappan Zee lay motionless and glassy, excepting that here and there a gentle undulation waved and prolonged the blue shadow of the distant mountain. A few amber clouds floated in the sky, without a breath of air to move them. The horizon was of a fine golden tint, changing gradually into a pure apple green, and from that into the deep blue of the mid-heaven. A slanting ray lingered on the woody crests of the precipices that overhung some parts of the river, giving greater depth to the dark-gray and purple of their rocky sides. A sloop was loitering in the distance, dropping slowly down with the tide, her sail hanging uselessly against the mast; and as the reflection of the sky gleamed along the still water, it seemed as if the vessel was suspended in the air.

It was toward evening that Ichabod arrived at the castle of the Heer Van Tassel, which he found thronged with the pride and flower of the adjacent country. Old farmers, a spare leathern-faced race, in homespun coats and breeches, blue stockings, huge shoes, and magnificent pewter buckles. Their brisk withered little dames, in close crimped caps, long-waisted shortgowns, homespun petticoats, with scissors and pincushions, and gay calico pockets hanging on the outside. Buxom lasses, almost as antiquated as their mothers, excepting where a straw hat, a fine ribbon, or perhaps a white frock, gave symptoms of city innovation. The sons, in short square-skirted coats with rows of stupendous brass buttons, and their hair generally queued in the fashion of the times, especially if they could procure an eel-skin for the purpose, it being esteemed, throughout the country, as a potent nourisher and strenghener of the hair.

Brom Bones, however, was the hero of the scene, having come to the gathering on his favorite steed Daredevil, a creature, like himself, full of mettle and mischief, and which no one but himself could manage. He was, in fact, noted for preferring vicious animals, given to all kinds of tricks, which kept the rider in constant risk of his neck, for he held a tractable well-broken horse as unworthy of a lad of spirit.

Fain would I pause to dwell upon the world of charms that burst upon the enraptured gaze of my hero, as he entered the state parlor of Van Tassel's mansion. Not those of the bevy of buxom lasses, with their luxurious display of red and white; but the ample charms of a genuine Dutch country tea-table, in the sumptuous time of autumn. Such heaped-up platters of cakes of various and almost indescribable kinds, known only to experienced Dutch housewives! There was the doughty dough-nut, the tenderer oly koek, and the crisp and crumbling cruller; sweet cakes and short cakes, ginger cakes and honey cakes, and the whole family of cakes. And then there were apple pies and peach pies and pumpkin pies; besides slices of ham and smoked beef; and moreover delectable dishes of preserved plums, and peaches, and pears, and quinces; not to mention broiled shad and roasted chickens; together with bowls of milk and cream, all mingled higgledy-piggledy, pretty much as I have enumerated them, with the motherly teapot sending up its clouds of vapor from the midst—Heaven bless the mark! I want breath and time to discuss this banquet as it deserves, and am too eager to get on with my story. Happily, Ichabod Crane was not in so great a hurry as his historian, but did ample justice to every dainty.

He was a kind and thankful creature, whose heart dilated in proportion as his skin was filled with good cheer; and whose spirits rose with eating as some men's do with drink. He could not help, too, rolling his large eyes round him as he ate, and chuckling with the possibility that he might one day be lord of all this scene of almost unimaginable luxury and splendor. Then, he thought, how soon he'd turn his back upon the old school-house; snap his fingers in the face of Hans Van Ripper, and every other niggardly patron, and kick any itinerant pedagogue out of doors that should dare to call him comrade!

Old Baltus Van Tassel moved about among his guests with a face dilated with content and good humor, round and jolly as the harvest moon. His hospitable attentions were brief, but expressive, being confined to a shake of the hand, a slap on the shoulder, a loud laugh, and a pressing invitation to "fall to, and help themselves."

And now the sound of the music from the common room, or hall, summoned to the dance. The musician was an old grayheaded negro, who had been the itinerant orchestra of the neighborhood for more than half a century. His instrument was as old and battered as himself. The greater part of the time he scraped on two or three strings, accompanying every movement of the bow with a motion of the head; bowing almost to the ground, and stamping with his foot whenever a fresh couple were to start.

Ichabod prided himself upon his dancing as much as upon his vocal powers. Not a limb, not a fibre about him was idle; and to have seen his loosely hung frame in full motion, and clattering about the room, you would have thought Saint Vitus himself, that blessed patron of the dance, was figuring before you in person. He was the admiration of all the negroes; who, having gathered, of all ages and sizes, from the farm and the neighborhood, stood forming a pyramid of shining black faces at every door and window, gazing with delight at the scene, rolling their white eye-balls, and showing grinning rows of ivory from ear to ear. How could the flogger of urchins be otherwise than animated and joyous? the lady of his heart was his partner in the dance, and smiling graciously in reply to all his amorous oglings; while Brom Bones, sorely smitten with love and jealousy, sat brooding by himself in one corner.

When the dance was at an end, Ichabod was attracted to a knot of the sager folks, who, with old Van Tassel, sat smoking at one end of the piazza, gossiping over former times, and drawing out long stories about the war.

This neighborhood, at the time of which I am speaking, was one of those highly-favored places which abound with chronicle and great men. The British and American line had run near it during the war; it had, therefore, been the scene of marauding, and infested with refugees, cow-boys, and all kinds of border chivalry. Just sufficient time had elapsed to enable each story-teller to dress up his tale with a little becoming fiction, and, in the indistinctness of his recollection, to make himself the hero of every exploit.

There was the story of Doffue Martling, a large blue-bearded Dutchman, who had nearly taken a British frigate with an old iron nine-pounder from a mud breastwork, only that his gun burst at the sixth discharge. And there was an old gentleman who shall be nameless, being too rich a mynheer to be lightly mentioned, who, in the battle of White-plains, being an excellent master of defence, parried a musket ball with a small sword, insomuch that he absolutely felt it whiz round the blade, and glance off at the hilt: in proof of which, he was ready at any time to show the sword, with the hilt a little bent. There were several more that had been equally great in the field, not one of whom but was persuaded that he had a considerable hand in bringing the war to a happy termination.

But all these were nothing to the tales of ghosts and apparitions that succeeded. The neighborhood is rich in legendary treasures of the kind. Local tales and superstitions thrive best in these sheltered long-settled retreats; but are trampled under foot by the shifting throng that forms the population of most of our country places. Besides, there is no encouragement for ghosts in most of our villages, for they have scarecely had time to finish their first nap, and turn themselves in their graves, before their surviving friends have travelled away from the neighborhood; so that when they turn out at night to walk their rounds, they have no acquaintance left to call upon. This is perhaps the reason why we so seldom hear of ghosts except in our long-established Dutch communities.

The immediate cause, however, of the prevalence of supernatural stories in these parts, was doubtless owing to the vicinity of Sleepy Hollow. There was a contagion in the very air that blew from that haunted region; it breathed forth an atmosphere of dreams and fancies infecting all the land. Several of the Sleepy Hollow people were present at Van Tassel's, and, as usual, were doling out their wild and wonderful legends. Many dismal tales were told about funeral trains, and mourning cries and wailings heard and seen about the great tree where the unfortunate Major André was taken, and which stood in the neighborhood. Some mention was made also of the woman in white, that haunted the dark glen at Raven Rock, and was often heard to shriek on winter nights before a storm, having perished there in the snow. The chief part of the stories, however, turned upon the favorite spectre of Sleepy Hollow, the headheadless horseman, who had been heard several times of late, patrolling the country; and, it was said, tethered his horse nightly among the graves in the church-yard.

The sequestered situation of this church seems always to have made it a favorite haunt of troubled spirits. It stands on a knoll, surrounded by locust-trees and lofty elms, from along which its decent whitewashed walls shine modestly forth, like Christian purity beaming through the shades of retirement. A gentle slope descends from it to a silver sheet of water, bordered by high trees, between which, peeps may be caught at the blue hills of the Hudson. To look upon its grass-grown yard, where the sunbeams seem to sleep so quietly, one would think that there at least the dead might rest in peace. On one side of the church extends a wide woody dell, along which raves a large brook among broken rocks and trunks of fallen trees. Over a deep black part of the stream, not far from the church, was formerly thrown a wooden bridge;

the road that led to it, and the bridge itself, were thickly shaded by overhanging trees, which cast a gloom about it, even in the daytime; but occasioned a fearful darkness at night. This was one of the favorite haunts of the headless horseman; and the place where he was most frequently encountered. The tale was told of old Brouwer, a most heretical disbeliever in ghosts, how he met the horseman returning from his foray into Sleepy Hollow, and was obliged to get up behind him; how they galloped over bush and brake, over hill and swamp, until they reached the bridge; when the horseman suddenly turned into a skeleton, threw old Brouwer into the brook, and sprang away over the tree-tops with a clap of thunder.

This story was immediately matched by a thrice marvellous adventure of Brom Bones, who made light of the galloping Hessian as an arrant jockey. He affirmed that, on returning one night from the neighboring village of Sing Sing, he had been overtaken by this midnight trooper; that he had offered to race with him for a bowl of punch, and should have won it too, for Daredevil beat the goblin horse all hollow, but, just as they came to the church bridge, the Hessian bolted, and vanished in a flash of fire.

All these tales, told in that drowsy undertone with which men talk in the dark, the countenances of the listeners only now and then receiving a casual gleam from the glare of a pipe, sank deep in the mind of Ichabod. He repaid them in kind with large extracts from his invaluable author, Cotton Mather, and added many marvellous events that had taken place in his native State of Connecticut, and fearful sights which he had seen in his nightly walks about Sleepy Hollow.

The revel now gradually broke up. The old farmers gathered together their families in their wagons, and were heard for some time rattling along the hollow roads, and over the distant hills. Some of the damsels mounted on pillions behind their favorite swains, and their light-hearted laughter, mingling with the clatter of hoofs, echoed along the silent woodlands, sounding fainter and fainter until they gradually died away—and the late scene of noise and frolic was all silent and deserted. Ichabod only lingered behind, according to the custom of country lovers, to have a tête-à-tête with the heiress, fully convinced that he was now on the high road to success. What passed at this interview I will not pretend to say, for in fact I do not know. Something, however, I fear me, must have gone wrong, for he certainly sallied forth, after no very great interval, with an air quite desolate and chap-fallen.—Oh these women! these women! Could that girl have been playing off any of her coquettish tricks?—Was her encouragement of the poor pedagogue all a mere sham to secure her conquest of his rival?—Heaven only knows, not I!—Let it suffice to say, Ichabod stole forth with the air of one who had been sacking a hen-roost, rather than a fair lady's heart. Without looking to the right or left to notice the scene of rural wealth, on which he had so often gloated, he went straight to the stable, and with several hearty cuffs and kicks, roused his steed most uncourteously from the comfortable quarters in which he was soundly sleeping, dreaming of mountains of corn and oats, and whole valleys of timothy and clover.

It was the very witching time of night that Ichabod, heavy-hearted and crest-fallen, pursued his travel homewards, along the sides of the lofty hills which rise above Tarry Town, and which he had traversed so cheerily in the afternoon. The hour was as dismal as himself. Far below him, the Tappan Zee spread its dusky and indistinct waste of waters, with here and there the tall mast of a sloop, riding quietly at anchor under the land. In the dead hush of midnight, he could even hear the barking of the watch dog from the opposite shore of the Hudson; but it was so vague and faint as only to give an idea of his distance from this faithful companion of man. Now and then, too, the long-drawn crowing of a cock, accidentally awakened, would sound far, far off, from some farmhouse away among the hills—but it was like a dreaming sound in his ear. No signs of life occurred near him, but occasionally the melancholy chirp of a cricket, or perhaps the guttural twang of a bull-frog, from a neighboring marsh, as if sleeping uncomfortably, and turning suddenly in his bed.

All the stories of ghosts and goblins that he had heard in the afternoon, now came crowding upon his recollection. The night grew darker and darker; the stars seemed to sink deeper in the sky, and driving clouds occasionally hid them from his sight. He had never felt so lonely and dismal. He was, moreover, approaching the very place where many of the scenes of the ghost stories had been laid. In the centre of the road stood an enormous tulip-tree, which towered like a giant above all the other trees of the neighborhood, and formed a kind of landmark. Its limbs were gnarled, and fantastic, large enough to form trunks for ordinary trees, twisting down almost to the earth, and rising again into the air. It was connected with the tragical story of the unfortunate André, who had been taken prisoner hard by; and was universally known by the name of Major André's tree. The common people regarded it with a mixture of respect and superstition, partly out of sympathy for the fate of its ill-starred namesake, and partly from the tales of strange sights and doleful lamentations told concerning it.

As Ichabod approached this fearful tree, he began to whistle: he thought his whistle was answered—it was but a blast sweeping sharply through the dry branches. As he approached a little nearer, he thought he saw something white, hanging in the midst of the tree—he paused and ceased whistling; but on looking more narrowly, perceived that it was a place where the tree had been scathed by lightning, and the white wood laid bare. Suddenly he heard a groan—his teeth chattered and his knees smote against the saddle: it was but the rubbing of one huge bough upon another, as they were swayed about by the breeze. He passed the tree in safety, but new perils lay before him.

About two hundred yards from the tree a small brook crossed the road, and ran into a marshy and thickly-wooded glen, known by the name of Wiley's swamp. A few rough logs, laid side by side, served for a bridge over this stream. On that side of the road where the brook entered the wood, a group of oaks and chestnuts, matted thick with wild grapevines, threw a cavernous gloom over it. To pass this bridge was the severest trial. It was at this identical spot that the unfortunate André was captured, and under the covert of those chestnuts and vines were the sturdy yeomen concealed who surprised him. This has ever since been considered a haunted stream, and fearful are the feelings of the schoolboy who has to pass it alone after dark.

As he approached the stream, his heart began to thump; he summoned up, however, all his resolution, gave his horse half a score of kicks in the ribs, and attempted to dash briskly across the bridge; but instead of starting forward, the perverse old animal made a lateral movement, and ran broadside against the fence. Ichabod, whose fears increased with the delay, jerked the reins on the other side, and kicked lustily with the contrary foot: it was all in vain; his steed started, it is true, but it was only to plunge to the opposite side of the road into a thicket of brambles and alder bushes. The schoolmaster now bestowed both whip and heel upon the starveling ribs of old Gunpowder, who dashed forward, snuffling and snorting, but came to a stand just by the bridge, with a suddenness that had nearly sent his rider sprawling over his head. Just at this moment a plashy tramp by the side of the bridge caught the sensitive ear of Ichabod. In the dark shadow of the grove, on the margin of the brook, he beheld something huge, misshapen, black and towering. It stirred not, but seemed gathered up in the gloom, like some gigantic monster ready to spring upon the traveller.

The hair of the affrighted pedagogue rose upon his head with terror. What was to be done? To turn and fly was now too late; and besides, what chance was there of escaping ghost or goblin, if such it was, which could ride upon the wings of the wind? Summoning up, therefore, a show of courage, he demanded in stammering accents— "Who are you?" He received no reply. He repeated his demand in a still more agitated voice. Still there was no answer. Once more he cudgelled the sides of the inflexible Gunpowder, and, shutting his eyes, broke forth with involuntary fervor into a psalm tune. Just then the shadowy object of alarm put itself in motion, and, with a scramble and a bound, stood at once in the middle of the road. Though the night was dark and dismal, yet the form of the unknown might now in some degree be ascertained. He appeared to be a horseman of large dimensions, and mounted on a black horse of powerful frame. He made no offer of molestation or sociability, but kept aloof on one side of the road, jogging along on the blind side of old Gunpowder, who had now got over his fright and waywardness.

Ichabod, who had no relish for this strange midnight companion, and bethought himself of the adventure of Brom Bones with the Galloping Hessian, now quickened his steed, in hopes of leaving him behind. The stranger, however, quickened his horse to an equal pace. Ichabod pulled up, and fell into a walk, thinking to lag behind—the other did the same. His heart began to sink within him; he endeavored to resume his psalm tune, but his parched tongue clove to the roof of his mouth, and he could not utter a stave. There was something in the moody and dogged silence of this pertinacious companion that was mysterious and appalling. It was soon fearfully accounted for. On mounting a rising ground, which brought the figure of his fellow-traveller in relief against the sky, gigantic in height, and muffled in a cloak, Ichabod was horror-struck, on perceiving that he was headless!—but his horror was still more increased, on observing that the head, which should have rested on his shoulders, was carried before him on the pommel of the saddle: his terror rose to desperation; he rained a shower of kicks and blows upon Gunpowder, hoping, by a sudden movement, to give his companion the slip—but the spectre started full jump with him. Away then they dashed, through thick and thin; stones flying, and sparks flashing at every bound. Ichabod's flimsy garments fluttered in the air, as he stretched his long lank body away over his horse's head, in the eagerness of his flight.

They had now reached the road which turns off to Sleepy Hollow; but Gunpowder, who seemed possessed with a demon, instead of keeping up it, made an opposite turn, and plunged headlong down hill to the left. This road leads through a sandy hollow, shaded by trees for about a quarter of a mile, where it crosses the bridge famous in goblin story, and just beyond swells the green knoll on which stands the whitewashed church.

As yet the panic of the steed had given his unskillful rider an apparent advantage in the chase; but just as he had got half way through the hollow, the girths of the saddle gave way, and he felt it slipping from under him. He seized it by the pommel, and endeavored to hold it firm, but in vain; and had just time to save himself by clasping old Gunpowder round the neck, when the saddle fell to the earth, and he heard it trampled under foot by his pursuer. For a moment the terror of Hans Van Ripper's wrath passed across his mind—for it was his Sunday saddle; but this was no time for petty fears; the goblin was hard on his haunches; and (unskilful rider that he was!) he had much ado to maintain his seat; sometimes slipping on one side, sometimes on another, and sometimes jolted on the high ridge of his horse's back-bone, with a violence that he verily feared would cleave him asunder.

An opening in the trees now cheered him with the hopes that the church bridge was at hand. The wavering reflection of a silver star in the bosom of the brook told him that he was not mistaken. He saw the walls of the church dimly glaring under the trees beyond. He recollected the place where Brom Bones's ghostly competitor had disappeared. "If I can but reach that bridge," thought Ichabod, "I am safe." Just then he heard the black steed panting and blowing close behind him; he even fancied that he felt his hot breath. Another convulsive kick in the ribs, and old Gunpowder sprang upon the bridge; he thundered over the resounding planks; he gained the opposite side; and now Ichabod cast a look behind to see if his pursuer should vanish, according to rule, in a flash of fire and brimstone. Just then he saw the goblin rising in his stirrups, and in the very act of hurling his head at him. Ichabod endeavored to dodge the horrible missile, but too late. It encountered his cranium with a tremendous crash—he was tumbled headlong into the dust, and Gunpowder, the black steed, and the goblin rider, passed by like a whirlwind.

The next morning the old horse was found without his saddle, and with the bridle under his feet, soberly cropping the grass at his master's gate. Ichabod did not make his appearance at breakfast—dinner hour came, but no Ichabod. The boys assembled at the school-house, and strolled idly about the banks of the brook; but no schoolmaster. Hans Van Ripper now began to feel some uneasiness about the fate of poor Ichabod, and his saddle. An inquiry was set on foot, and after diligent investigation they came upon his traces. In one part of the road leading to the church was found the saddle trampled in the dirt; the tracks of horses' hoofs deeply dented in the road, and evidently at furious speed, were traced to the bridge, beyond which, on the bank of a broad part of the brook, where the water ran deep and black, was found the hat of the unfortunate Ichabod, and close behind it a shattered pumpkin.

The brook was searched, but the body of the schoolmaster was not to be discovered. Hans Van Ripper, as executor of his estate, examined the bundle which contained all his worldly effects. They consisted of two shirts and a half; two stocks for the neck; a pair or two of worsted stockings; an old pair of corduroy small-clothes; a rusty razor; a book of psalm tunes, full of dogs' ears; and a broken pitchpipe. As to the books and furniture of the school-house, they belonged to the community, excepting Cotton Mather's History of Witchcraft, a New England Almanac, and a book of dreams and fortune-telling; in which last was a sheet of foolscap much scribbled and blotted in several fruitless attempts to make a copy of verses in honor of the heiress of Van Tassel. These magic books and the poetic scrawl were forthwith consigned to the flames by Hans Van Ripper; who from that time forward determined to send his children no more to school; observing, that he never knew any good come of this reading and writing. Whatever money the schoolmaster possessed, and he had received his quarter's pay but a day or two before, he must have had about his person at the time of his disappearance.

The mysterious event caused much speculation at the church on the following Sunday. Knots of gazers and gossips were collected in the churchyard, at the bridge, and at the spot where the hat and the pumpkin had been found. The stories of Brouwer, of Bones, and a whole budget of others, were called to mind; and when they had diligently considered them all, and compared them with the symptoms of the present case, they shook their heads, and came to the conclusion that Ichabod had been carried off by the galloping Hessian. As he was a bachelor, and in nobody's debt, nobody troubled his head any more about him. The school was removed to a different quarter of the hollow, and another pedagogue reigned in his stead.

It is true, an old farmer, who had been down to New York on a visit several years after, and from whom this account of the ghostly adventure was received, brought home the intelligence that Ichabod Crane was still alive; that he had left the neighborhood, partly through fear of the goblin and Hans Van Ripper, and partly in mortification at having been suddenly dismissed by the heiress; that he had changed his quarters to a distant part of the country; had kept school and studied law at the same time, had been admitted to the bar, turned politician, electioneered, written for the newspapers, and finally had been made a justice of the Ten Pound Court. Brom Bones too, who shortly after his rival's disappearance conducted the blooming Katrina in triumph to the altar, was observed to look exceedingly knowing whenever the story of Ichabod was related, and always burst into a hearty laugh at the mention of the pumpkin; which led some to suspect that he knew more about the matter than he chose to tell.

The old country wives, however, who are the best judges of these matters, maintain to this day that Ichabod was spirited away by supernatural means; and it is a favorite story often told about the neighborhood round the winter evening fire. The bridge became more than ever an object of superstitious awe, and that may be the reason why the road has been altered of late years, so as to approach the church by the border of the mill-pond. The school-house being deserted, soon fell to decay, and was reported to be haunted by the ghost of the unfortunate pedagogue; and the ploughboy, loitering homeward of a still summer evening, has often fancied his voice at a distance, chanting a melancholy psalm tune among the tranquil solitudes of Sleepy Hollow.

## POSTSCRIPT
## FOUND IN THE HANDWRITING
## OF MR. KNICKERBOCKER

The preceding Tale is given, almost in the precise words in which I heard it related at a Corporation meeting of the ancient city of Manhattoes, at which were present many of its sages and most illustrious burghers. The narrator was a pleasant, shabby, gentlemanly old fellow, in pepper-and-salt clothes, with a sadly humorous face; and one whom I strongly suspected of being poor,—he made such efforts to be entertaining. When his story was concluded, there was much laughter and approbation, particularly from two or three deputy aldermen, who had been asleep the greater part of the time. There was, however, one tall, dry-looking old gentleman, with beetling eyebrows, who maintained a grave and rather severe face throughout: now and then folding his arms, inclining his head, and looking down upon the floor, as if turning a doubt over in his mind. He was one of your wary men, who never laugh, but upon good grounds—when they have reason and the law on their side. When the mirth of the rest of the company had subsided, and silence was restored, he leaned one arm on the elbow of his chair, and, sticking the other akimbo, demanded, with a slight but exceedingly sage motion of the head, and contraction of the brow, what was the moral of the story, and what it went to prove?

The story-teller, who was just putting a glass of wine to his lips, as a refreshment after his toils, paused for a moment, looked at his inquirer with an air of infinite deference, and, lowering the glass slowly to the table, observed, that the story was intended most logically to prove:—

"That there is no situation in life but has its advantages and pleasures—provided we will but take a joke as we find it:

"That, therefore, he that runs races with goblin troopers is likely to have rough riding of it.

"Ergo, for a country schoolmaster to be refused the hand of a Dutch heiress is a certain step to high preferment in the state."

The cautious old gentleman knit his brows tenfold closer after this explanation, being sorely puzzled by the ratiocination of the syllogism; while, methought, the one in pepper-and-salt eyed him with something of a triumphant leer. At length, he observed, that all this was very well, but still he thought the story a little on the extravagant—there were one or two points on which he had his doubts.

"Faith, sir," replied the story-teller, "as to that matter, I don't believe one-half of it myself."

D. K.

*From* BRACEBRIDGE HALL

# STORY-TELLING

A favorite evening pastime at the Hall, and one which the worthy Squire is fond of promoting, is story-telling, "a good old-fashioned fireside amusement," as he terms it. Indeed, I believe he promotes it chiefly because it was one of the choice recreations in those days of yore, when ladies and gentlemen were not much in the habit of reading. Be this as it may, he will often, at supper table, when conversation flags, call on some one or other of the company for a story, as it was formerly the custom to call for a song; and it is edifying to see the exemplary patience, and even satisfaction, with which the good old gentleman will sit and listen to some hackneyed tale that he has heard for at least a hundred times.

In this way one evening the current of anecdotes and stories ran upon mysterious personages that have figured at different times, and filled the world with doubts and conjecture; such as the Wandering Jew, the Man with the Iron Mask, who tormented the curiosity of all Europe; the Invisible Girl, and last, though not least, the Pigfaced Lady.

At length one of the company was called upon who had the most unpromising physiognomy for a story-teller that ever I had seen. He was a thin, pale, weazen-faced man, extremely nervous, who had sat at one corner of the table, shrunk up, as it were, into himself, and almost swallowed up in the cape of his coat, as a turtle in its shell.

---

EDITOR'S NOTE: *Story-telling* introduces *The Stout Gentleman*; the second pair from *Bracebridge Hall* are similarly related.

The very demand seemed to throw him into a nervous agitation, yet he did not refuse. He emerged his head out of his shell, made a few odd grimaces and gesticulations, before he could get his muscles into order, or his voice under command, and then offered to give some account of a mysterious personage whom he had recently encountered in the course of his travels, and one whom he thought fully entitled of being classed with the Man with the Iron Mask.

I was so much struck with his extraordinary narrative, that I have written it out to the best of my recollection, for the amusement of the reader. I think it has in it all the elements of that mysterious and romantic narrative, so greedily sought after at the present day.

# THE STOUT GENTLEMAN

## A Stage-Coach Romance

I'll cross it, though it blast me!
HAMLET

It was a rainy Sunday in the gloomy month of November. I had been detained, in the course of a journey, by a slight indisposition, from which I was recovering; but was still feverish, and obliged to keep within doors all day, in an inn of the small town of Derby. A wet Sunday in a country inn!—whoever has had the luck to experience one can alone judge of my situation. The rain pattered against the casements; the bells tolled for church with a melancholy sound. I went to the windows in quest of something to amuse the eye; but it seemed as if I had been placed completely out of the reach of all amusement. The windows of my bedroom looked out among tiled roofs and stacks of chimneys, while those of my sitting-room commanded a full view of the stable-yard. I know of nothing more calculated to make a man sick of this world than a stable-yard on a rainy day. The place was littered with wet straw that had been kicked about by travellers and stable-boys. In one corner was a stagnant pool of water, surrounding an island of muck; there were several half-drowned fowls crowded together under a cart, among which was a miserable, crest-fallen cock, drenched out of all life and spirit; his drooping tail matted, as it were, into a single feather, along which the water trickled from his back; near the cart was a half-dozing cow, chewing the cud, and standing patiently to be rained on, with wreaths of vapor rising from her reeking hide; a wall-eyed horse, tired of the loneliness of the stable, was poking his spectral head out of a window, with the rain dripping on it from the eaves; an unhappy cur, chained to a doghouse hard by, uttered something every now and then, between a bark and a yelp; a drab of a kitchen-wench tramped backwards and forwards through the yard in pattens, looking as sulky as the weather itself; every thing, in short, was comfortless and forlorn, excepting a crew of hardened ducks, assembled like boon companions round a puddle, and making a riotous noise over their liquor.

I was lonely and listless, and wanted amusement. My room soon became insupportable. I abandoned it, and sought what is technically called the travellers'-room. This is a public room set apart at most inns for the accommodation of a class of wayfarers, called travellers, or riders; a kind of commercial knights-errant, who are incessantly scouring the kingdom in gigs, on horseback, or by coach. They are the only successors that I know of at the present day to the knights-errant of yore. They lead the same kind of roving, adventurous life, only changing the lance for a driving- whip, the buckler for a pattern-card, and the coat of mail for an upper Benjamin. Instead of vindicating the charms of peerless beauty, they rove about, spreading the fame and standing of some substantial tradesman, or manufacturer, and are ready at any time to bargain in his name; it being the fashion nowadays to trade, instead of fight, with one another. As the room of the hostel, in good old fighting times, would be hung round at night with the armor of way-worn warriors, such as coats of mail, falchions, and yawning helmets; so the travellers'-room is garnished with the harnessing of their successors, with box-coats, whips of all kinds, spurs, gaiters, and oil-cloth covered hats.

I was in hopes of finding some of these worthies to talk with, but was disappointed. There were, indeed, two or three in the room; but I could make nothing of them. One was just finishing his breakfast, quarreling with his bread and butter, and huffing the waiter; another buttoned on a pair of gaiters, with many execrations at Boots for not having cleaned his shoes well; a third sat drumming on the table with his fingers and looking at the rain as it streamed down the window-glass; they all appeared infected by the weather, and disappeared, one after the other, without exchanging a word.

I sauntered to the window, and stood gazing at the people, picking their way to church, with petticoats hoisted midleg high, and dripping umbrellas. The bell ceased to toll, and the streets became silent. I then amused myself with watching the daughters of a tradesman opposite;

who, being confined to the house for fear of wetting their Sunday finery, played off their charms at the front windows, to fascinate the chance tenants of the inn. They at length were summoned away by a vigilant vinegar-faced mother, and I had nothing further from without to amuse me.

What was I to do to pass away the long-lived day? I was sadly nervous and lonely; and everything about an inn seems calculated to make a dull day ten times duller. Old newspapers, smelling of beer and tobacco-smoke, and which I had already read half a dozen times. Good-for-nothing books, that were worse than rainy weather. I bored myself to death with an old volume of the Lady's Magazine. I read all the commonplace names of ambitious travellers scrawled on the panes of glass; the eternal families of the Smiths, and the Browns, and the Jacksons, and the Johnsons, and all the other sons; and I deciphered several scraps of fatiguing in-window poetry which I have met with in all parts of the world.

The day continued lowering and gloomy; the slovenly, ragged, spongy clouds drifted heavily along; there was no variety even in the rain: it was one dull, continued, monotonous patter—patter—patter, excepting that now and then I was enlivened by the idea of a brisk shower, from the rattling of the drops upon a passing umbrella.

It was quite *refreshing* (if I may be allowed a hackneyed phrase of the day) when, in the course of the morning, a horn blew, and a stage-coach whirled through the street, with outside passengers stuck all over it, cowering under cotton umbrellas, and seethed together, and reeking with the streams of wet boxcoats and upper Benjamins.

The sound brought out from their lurking-places a crew of vagabond boys, and vagabond dogs, and the carroty-headed hostler, and that nondescript animal ycleped Boots, and all the other vagabond race that infest the purlieus of an inn; but the bustle was transient; the coach again whirled on its way; and boy and dog, and hostler and Boots, all slunk back again to their holes; the street again became silent, and the rain continued to rain on. In fact, there was no hope of its clearing up; the barometer pointed to rainy weather; mine hostess's tortoise-shell cat sat by the fire washing her face, and rubbing her paws over her ears; and, on referring to the Almanac, I found a direful prediction stretching from the top of the page to the bottom through the whole month, "expect—much—rain—about—this—time!"

I was dreadfully hipped. The hours seemed as if they would never creep by. The very ticking of the clock became irksome. At length the stillness of the house was interrupted by the ringing of a bell. Shortly after I heard the voice of a waiter at the bar: "The stout gentleman in No. 13 wants his breakfast. Tea and bread and butter, with ham and eggs; the eggs not to be too much done."

In such a situation as mine, every incident is of importance. Here was a subject of speculation presented to my mind, and ample exercise for my imagination. I am prone to paint pictures to myself, and on this occasion I had some materials to work upon. Had the guest upstairs been mentioned as Mr. Smith, or Mr. Brown, or Mr. Jackson, or Mr. Johnson, or merely as "the gentleman in No. 13," it would have been a perfect blank to me. I should have thought nothing of it; but "The stout gentleman!"—the very name had something in it of the picturesque. It at once gave the size; it embodied the personage to my mind's eye, and my fancy did the rest.

He was stout, or, as some term it, lusty; in all probability, there-fore, he was advanced in life, some people expanding as they grow old. By his breakfasting rather late, and in his own room, he must be a man accustomed to live at his ease, and about the necessity of early rising; no doubt a round, rosy, lusty old gentleman.

There was another violent ringing. The stout gentleman was im-patient for his breakfast. He was evidently a man of importance; "well to do in the world;" accustomed to be promptly waited upon; of a keen appetite, and a little cross when hungry, "perhaps," thought I, "he may be some London Alderman; or who knows but he may be a Member of Parliament?"

The breakfast was sent up, and there was a short interval of silence; he was, doubtless, making the tea. Presently there was a violent ringing; and before it could be answered, another ringing still more violent. "Bless me! what a choleric old gentleman!" The waiter came down in a huff. The butter was rancid, the eggs were over-done, the ham was too salt;—the stout gentleman was evidently nice in his eating; one of those who eat and growl, and keep the waiter on the trot, and live in a state militant with the household.

The hostess got into a fume. I should observe that she was a brisk, coquettish woman; a little of a shrew, and something of a slammerkin, but very pretty withal; with a nincompoop for a husband, as shrews are apt to have. She rated the servants roundly for their negligence in sending up so bad a breakfast, but said not a word against the stout gentleman; by which I clearly perceived that he must be a man of consequence, entitled to make a noise and to give trouble at a country inn. Other eggs, and ham, and bread and butter were sent up. They appeared to be more graciously received; at least there was no further complaint.

I had not made many turns about the travellers'-room, when there was another ringing. Shortly afterwards there was a stir and an inquest about the house. The stout gentleman wanted the Times or the Chronicle newspaper. I set him down, therefore, for a Whig; or rather, from his being so absolute and lordly where he had a chance, I suspected him of being a Radical. Hunt, I had heard, was a large man; "who knows," thought I, "but it is Hunt himself!"

My curiosity began to be awakened. I inquired of the waiter who was this stout gentleman that was making all this stir; but I could get no information; nobody seemed to know his name. The landlords of bustling inns seldom trouble their heads about the names or occupations of their transient guests. The color of a coat, the shape or size of the person, is enough to suggest a travelling name. It is either the tall gentleman, or the short gentleman, or the gentleman in black, or the gentleman in snuff-color; or, as in the present instance, the stout gentleman. A designation of the kind once hit on answers every purpose, and saves all further inquiry.

Rain—rain—rain! pitiless, ceaseless rain! No such thing as putting a foot out of doors, and no occupation nor amusement within. By and by I heard someone walking overhead. It was in the stout gentleman's room. He evidently was a large man by the heaviness of his tread; and an old man from his wearing such creaking soles. "He is doubtless," thought I, "some rich old square-toes of regular habits, and is now taking exercise after breakfast."

I now read all the advertisements of coaches and hotels that were stuck about the mantelpiece. The Lady's Magazine had become an abomination to me; it was as tedious as the day itself. I wandered out, not knowing what to do, and ascended again to my room. I had not been there long, when there was a squall from a neighboring bedroom. A door opened and slammed violently; a chamber-maid, that I had remarked for having a ruddy, good-humored face, went down stairs in a violent flurry. The stout gentleman had been rude to her!

This sent a whole host of my deductions to the deuce in a moment. This unknown personage could not be an old gentleman; for old gentlemen are not apt to be so obstreperous to chamber-maids. He could not be a young gentleman; for young gentlemen are not apt to inspire such indignation. He must be a middle-aged man, and confounded ugly into the bargain, or the girl would not have taken the matter in such terrible dudgeon. I confess I was sorely puzzled.

In a few minutes I heard the voice of my landlady. I caught a glance of her as she came tramping up stairs;—her face glowing, her cap flaring, her tongue wagging the whole way. "She'd have no such doings in her house, she'd warrant. If gentlemen did spend money freely, it was no rule. She'd have no servant-maids of hers treated in that way, when they were about their work, that's what she wouldn't."

As I hate squabbles, particularly with women, and above all with pretty women, I slunk back into my room, and partly closed the door; but my curiosity was too much excited not to listen. The landlady marched intrepidly to the enemy's citadel, and entered it with a storm: the door closed after her. I heard her voice in a high windy clamor for a moment or two. Then it gradually subsided, like a gust of wind in a garret; then there was a laugh; then I heard nothing more.

After a little while my landlady came out with an odd smile on her face, adjusting her cap, which was a little on one side. As she went downstairs, I heard the landlord ask her what was the matter; she said, "Nothing at all, only the girl's a fool."—I was more than ever perplexed what to make of this unaccountable personage, who could put a good-natured chamber-maid in a passion, and send away a termagant landlady in smiles. He could not be so old, nor cross, nor ugly either.

I had to go to work at his picture again, and to paint him entirely different. I now set him down for one of those stout gentlemen that are frequently met with swaggering about the doors of country inns. Moist, merry fellows, in Belcher handkerchiefs, whose bulk is a little assisted by malt-liquors. Men who have seen the world, and been sworn at Highgate; who are used to tavern-life; up to all the tricks of tapsters, and knowing in the ways of sinful publicans. Free-livers on a small scale; who are prodigal within the compass of a guinea; who call all the waiters by name, tousle the maids, gossip with the landlady at the bar, and prose over a pint of port, or a glass of negus, after dinner.

The morning wore away in forming these and similar surmises. As fast as I wove one system of belief, some movement of the unknown would completely overturn it, and throw all my thoughts again into confusion. Such are the solitary operations of a feverish mind. I was, as I have said, extremely nervous; and the continual meditation on the concerns of this invisible personage began to have its effect:—I was getting a fit of the fidgets.

Dinner-time came. I hoped the stout gentleman might dine in the travellers'-room, and that I might at length get a view of his person; but no—he had dinner served in his own room. What could be the meaning of this solitude and mystery? He could not be a radical; there was something too aristocratical in thus keeping himself apart from the rest of the world, and condemning himself to his own dull company throughout a rainy day. And then, too, he lived too well for a discontented politician. He seemed to expatiate on a variety of dishes, and to sit over his wine like a jolly friend of good living. Indeed, my doubts on this head were soon at an end; for he could not have finished his first bottle before I could faintly hear him humming a tune; and on listening, I found it to be, "God Save the King." 'Twas plain, then, he was no radical, but a faithful subject; one who grew loyal over his bottle, and was ready to stand by king and constitution, when he could stand by nothing else. But who could he be? My conjectures began to run wild. Was he not some personage of distinction travelling incog.? "God knows!" said I, at my wit's end; "it may be one of the royal family for aught I know, for they are all stout gentlemen!"

The weather continued rainy. The mysterious unknown kept his room and, as far as I could judge, his chair, for I did not hear him move. In the meantime, as the day advanced, the travellers'-room began to be frequented. Some, who had just arrived, came in buttoned-up in box-coats; others came home who had been dispersed about the town; some took their dinners, and some their tea. Had I been in a different mood, I should have found entertainment in studying this peculiar class of men. There were two especially, who were regular wags of the road, and up to all the standing jokes of travellers. They had a thousand sly things to say to the waiting-maid, whom they called Louisa, and Ethelinda, and a dozen other fine names, changing the name every time, and chuckling amazingly at their own waggery. My mind, however, had been completely engrossed by the stout gentleman. He had kept my fancy in chase during a long day, and it was not now to be diverted from the scent.

The evening gradually wore away. The travellers read the papers two or three times over. Some drew round the fire and told long stories about their horses, about their adventures, their overturns, and breakings-down. They discussed the credit of different merchants and different inns; and the two wags told several choice anecdotes of pretty chamber-maids, and kind land-ladies. All this passed as they were quietly taking what they called their night-caps, that is to say, strong glasses of brandy and water and sugar, or some other mixture of the kind; and walked off to bed in old shoes cut down into marvelously uncomfortable slippers.

There was now only one man left: a short-legged, long-bodied, plethoric fellow, with a very large, sandy head. He sat by himself, with a glass of port-wine negus, and a spoon; sipping and stirring, and meditating and sipping, until nothing was left but the spoon. He gradually fell asleep bolt upright in his chair, with the empty glass standing before him; and the candle seemed to fall asleep too, for the wick grew long, and black, and cabbaged at the end, and dimmed the little light that remained in the chamber. The gloom that now prevailed was contagious. Around hung the shapeless, and almost spectral, box-coats of departed travellers, long since buried in deep sleep. I only heard the ticking of the clock, with the deep-drawn breathings of the sleeping topers, and the drippings of the rain, drop—drop—drop, from the eaves of the house. The church-bells chimed midnight. All at once the stout gentleman began to walk overhead, pacing slowly backwards and forwards. There was something extremely awful in all this, especially to one in my state of nerves. These ghastly great-coats, these gutteral breathings, and the creaking footsteps of this mysterious being. His steps grew fainter and fainter, and at length died away. I could bear it no longer. I was wound up to the desperation of a hero of romance. "Be he who or what he may," said I to myself, "I'll have a sight of him!" I seized a chamber-candle, and hurried up to No. 13. The door stood ajar. I hesitated—I entered: the room was deserted. There stood a large, broad-bottomed elbow chair at a table, on which was an empty tumbler, and a "Times," newspaper, and the room smelt powerfully of Stilton cheese.

The mysterious stranger had evidently but just retired. I turned off, sorely disappointed, to my room, which had been changed to the front of the house. As I went along the corridor, I saw a large pair of boots, with dirty, waxed tops, standing at the door of a bedchamber. They doubtless belonged to the unknown; but it would not do to disturb so redoubtable a personage in his den: he might discharge a pistol, or something worse, at my head. I went to bed, therefore, and lay awake half the night in a terribly nervous state; and even when I fell asleep, I was still haunted in my dreams by the idea of the stout gentleman and his wax-stopped boots.

I slept rather late the next morning, and was awakened by some stir and bustle in the house, which I could not at first comprehend; until getting more awake, I found there was a mail-coach starting from the door. Suddenly there was a cry from below, "The gentleman has forgot his umbrella! look for the gentleman's umbrella in No. 13!" I heard an immediate scampering of a chamber-maid along the passage, and a shrill reply as she ran, "Here it is! here's the gentleman's umbrella!"

The mysterious stranger then was on the point of setting off. This was the only chance I should ever have of knowing him. I sprang out of bed, scrambled to the window, snatched aside the curtains, and just caught a glimpse of the rear of a person getting in at the coach-door. The skirts of a brown coat parted behind, and gave me a full view of the broad disk of a pair of drab breeches. The door closed—"all right!" was the word—the coach whirled off;—and that was all I ever saw of the stout gentleman!

# THE HAUNTED HOUSE

## From the MSS. of the Late Diedrich Knickerbocker

Formerly almost every place had a house of this kind. If a house was seated on some melancholy place, or built in some old romantic manner, or if any particular accident had happened in it, such as murder, sudden death, or the like, to be sure that house had a mark set on it, and was afterwards esteemed the habitation of a ghost.

BOURNE'S ANTIQUITIES.

In the neighborhood of the ancient city of the Manhattoes there stood, not very many years since, an old mansion, which, when I was a boy, went by the name of the Haunted House. It was one of the very few remains of the architecture of the early Dutch settlers, and must have been a house of some consequence at the time when it was built. It consisted of a centre and two wings, the gable ends of which were shaped like stairs. It was built partly of wood, and partly of small Dutch bricks, such as the worthy colonists brought with them from Holland, before they discovered that bricks could be manufactured elsewhere. The house stood remote from the road, in the centre of a large field, with an avenue of old locust* trees leading up to it, several of which had been shivered by lightning, and two or three blown down. A few apple-trees grew straggling about the field; there were traces also of what had been a kitchen garden; but the fences were broken down, the vegetables had disappeared, or had grown wild, and turned to little better than weeds, with here and there a ragged rose-bush, or a tall sunflower shooting up from among the brambles, and

---

*Acacias

hanging its head sorrowfully, as if contemplating the surrounding desolation. Part of the roof of the old house had fallen in, the windows were shattered, the panels of the doors broken, and mended with rough boards, and two rusty weather-cocks at the ends of the house made a great jingling and whistling as they whirled about, but always pointed wrong. The appearance of the whole place was forlorn and desolate at the best of times; but, in unruly weather, the howling of the wind about the crazy old mansion, the screeching of the weather-cocks, and the slamming and banging of a few loose window-shutters, had altogether so wild and dreary an effect, that the neighborhood stood perfectly in awe of the place, and pronounced it the rendezvous of hobgoblins. I recollect the old building well; for many times, when an idle, unlucky urchin, I have prowled round its precinct, with some of my graceless companions, on holiday afternoons, when out on a freebooting cruise among the orchards. There was a tree standing near the house that bore the most beautiful and tempting fruit; but then it was on enchanted ground, for the place was so charmed by frightful stories that we dreaded to approach it. Sometimes we would venture in a body, and get near the Hesperian tree, keeping an eye upon the old mansion, and darting fearful glances into its shattered windows, when, just as we were about to seize upon our prize, an exclamation from some one of the gang, or an accidental noise, would throw us all into a panic, and we would scamper headlong from the place, nor stop until we had got quite into the road. Then there were sure to be a host of fearful anecdotes told of strange cries and groans, or of some hideous face suddenly seen staring out of one of the windows. By degrees we ceased to venture into these lonely grounds, but would stand at a distance, and throw stones at the building; and there was something fearfully pleasing in the sound as they rattled along the roof, or sometimes struck some jingling fragments of glass out of the windows.

The origin of this house was lost in the obscurity that covers the early period of the province, while under the government of their high mightinesses, the states-general. Some reported it to have been a country residence of Wilhelmus Kieft, commonly called the Testy, one of the Dutch governors of New Amsterdam; others said it had been built by a naval commander who served under Van Tromp, and who, on being disappointed of preferment, retired from the service in disgust, became a philosopher through sheer spite, and brought over all his wealth to the province, that he might live according to his humor, and despise the world. The reason of its having fallen to decay was likewise a matter of dispute; some said it was in chancery, and had already cost more than its worth in legal expense; but the most current, and, of course, the most probable account, was that it was haunted, and that nobody could live quietly in it. There can, in fact, be very little doubt that this last was the case, there were so many corroborating stories to prove it,—not an old woman in the neighborhood could but furnish at least a score. A grayheaded curmudgeon of a negro who lived hard by had a whole budget of them to tell, many of which had happened to himself. I recollect many a time stopping with my schoolmates, and getting him to relate some. The old crone lived in a hovel, in the midst of a small patch of potatoes and Indian corn, which his master had given him on setting him free. He would come to us, with his hoe in his hand, and as we sat perched, like a row of swallows, on the rail of the fence, in the mellow twilight of a summer evening, would tell us such fearful stories, accompanied by such awful rollings of his white eyes, that we were almost afraid of our own footsteps as we returned home afterwards in the dark.

Poor old Pompey! many years are past since he died, and went to keep company with the ghosts he was so fond of talking about. He was buried in a corner of his own little potato patch; the plough soon passed over his grave, and levelled it with the rest of the field, and nobody thought any more of the grayheaded negro. By singular chance I was strolling in that neighborhood, several years afterwards, when I had grown up to be a young man, and I found a knot of gossips speculating on a skull which had been turned up by a ploughshare. They of course determined it to be the remains of some one who had been murdered, and they had raked up with it some of the traditionary tales of the haunted house. I knew it at once to be the relic of poor Pompey, but I held my tongue; for I am too considerate of other people's enjoyment even to mar a story of a ghost or a murder. I took care, however, to see the bones of my old friend buried in a place where they were not likely to be disturbed. As I sat on the turf and watched the interment, I fell into a long conversation with an old gentleman of the neighborhood, John Josse Vandermoere, a pleasant gossiping man, whose whole life was spent in hearing and telling the

news of the province. He recollected old Pompey, and his stories about
the Haunted House; but he assured me he could give me one still
more strange than any that Pompey had related; and on my expressing
a great curiosity to hear it, he sat down beside me on the turf, and
told the following tale. I have endeavored to give it as nearly as possible
in his words; but it is now many years since, and I am grown old,
and my memory is not over good. I cannot therefore vouch for the
language, but I am always scrupulous as to facts.

D. K.

# DOLPH HEYLIGER

"I take the town of concord, where I dwell,
All Kilborn be my witness, if I were not
Begot in bashfulness, brought up in shamefacedness:
Let 'un bring a dog but to my vace that can
Zay I have beat 'un, and without a vault;
Or but a cat will swear upon a book,
I have as much as zet a vire her tail,
And I'll give him or her a crown for 'mends."

TALE OF A TUB

In the early time of the province of New York, while it groaned under the tyranny of the English governor, Lord Cornbury, who carried his cruelties towards the Dutch inhabitants so far as to allow no Dominie, or schoolmaster, to officiate in their language, without his special license; about this time, there lived in the jolly little old city of the Manhattoes, a kind motherly dame, known by the name of Dame Heyliger. She was the widow of a Dutch sea-captain, who died suddenly of a fever, in consequence of working too hard, and eating too heartily, at the time when all the inhabitants turned out in a panic, to fortify the place against the invasion of a small French privateer.* He left her with very little money, and one infant son, the only survivor of several children. The good woman had need of much management to make both ends meet, and keep up a decent appearance. However, as her husband had fallen victim to his zeal for the public safety, it was universally agreed that "something ought to be done for the widow;"

---

*1705

and on the hopes of this "something," she lived tolerably for some years; in the mean time every body pitied and spoke well of her, and that helped along.

She lived in a small house, in a small street, called Garden-street, very probably from a garden which may have flourished there some time or other. As her necessities every year grew greater, and the talk of the public about doing "something for her" grew less, she had to cast about for some mode of doing something for herself, by way of helping out her slender means, and maintaining her independence, of which she was somewhat tenacious.

Living in a mercantile town, she had caught something of the spirit, and determined to venture a little in the great lottery of commerce. On a sudden, therefore, to the great surprise of the street, there appeared at her window a grand array of gingerbread kings and queens, with their arms stuck a-kimbo, after the invariable royal sugar-plums, some with marbles; there were, moreover, cakes of various kinds, and barley-sugar, and Holland dolls, and wooden horses, with here and there gilt-covered picture-books, and now and then a skein of thread, or a dangling pound of candles. At the door of the house sat the good old dame's cat, a decent demure-looking personage, who seemed to scan every body that passed, to criticise their dress, and now and then to stretch her neck, and to look out with sudden curiosity, to see what was going on at the other end of the street; but if by chance any idle vagabond dog came by, and offered to be uncivil—hoity-toity!—how she would bristle up, and growl, and spit, and strike out her paws! She was as indignant as ever was an ancient spinster on the approach of some graceless profligate.

But though the good woman had to come down to those humble means of subsistence, yet she still kept up a feeling of family pride, being descended from the Vanderspiegels, of Amsterdam; and she had the family arms painted and framed, and hung over her mantel-piece. She was, in truth, much respected by all the poorer people of the place; her house was quite a resort of the old wives of the neighborhood; they would drop in there of a winter's afternoon, as she sat knitting on one side of her fireplace, her cat purring on the other, and the tea-kettle singing before it; and they would gossip with her until late in the evening. There was always an arm-chair for Peter de Groodt, sometimes called Long Peter, and sometimes Peter Longlegs, the clerk and sexton of the little Lutheran church, who was her great crony, and indeed the oracle of her fireside. Nay, the Dominie himself did not disdain, now and then, to step in, converse about the state of her mind, and take a glass of her special good cherry brandy. Indeed, he never failed to call on new-year's day, and wish her a happy new year; and the good dame, who was a little vain on some points, always piqued herself on giving him as large a cake as any one in town.

I have said that she had one son. He was the child of her old age; but could hardly have been called the comfort, for, of all unlucky urchins, Dolph Heyliger was the most mischievous. Not that the whisper was really vicious; he was only full of fun and frolic, and had that daring, gamesome spirit, which is extolled in a rich man's child, but execrated in a poor man's. He was continually getting into scrapes: his mother was incessantly harassed with complaints of some waggish pranks which he had played off; bills were sent in for windows that he had broken; in a word, he had not reached his fourteenth year before he was pronounced, by all the neighborhood, to be a "wicked dog, the wickedest dog in the street!" Nay, one old gentleman, in a claret-colored coat, with a thin red face, and ferret eyes, went so far as to assure Dame Heyliger, that her son would, one day or other, come to the gallows!

Yet, notwithstanding all this, the poor old soul loved her boy. It seems as though she loved him the better the worse he behaved; and that he grew more in her favor, the more he grew out of favor with the world. Mothers are foolish, fond-hearted beings; there's no reasoning them out of their dotage; and, indeed, this poor woman's child was all that was left to love her in this world;—so we must not think it hard that she turned a deaf ear to her good friends, who sought to prove to her that Dolph would come to a halter.

To do the varlet justice, too, he was strongly attached to his parent. He would not willingly have given her pain on any account; and when he had been doing wrong, it was but for him to catch his poor mother's eye fixed wistfully and sorrowfully upon him, to fill his heart with bitterness and contrition. But he was a heedless youngster, and could not, for the life of him, resist any new temptation to fun and mischief. Though quick at his learning, whenever he could be brought to apply himself, he was always prone to be led away by idle company, and would play truant to hunt after birds' nests, to rob orchards, or to swim in the Hudson.

In this way he grew up, a tall, lubberly boy; and his mother began to be greatly perplexed what to do with him, or how to put him in a way to do for himself; for he had acquired such an unlucky reputation, that no one seemed willing to employ him.

Many were the consultations that she held with Peter de Groodt, the clerk and sexton, who was her prime counsellor. Peter was as much perplexed as herself, for he had no great opinion of the boy, and thought he would never come to good. He at one time advised her to send him to sea: a piece of advice only given in the most desperate cases; but Dame Heyliger would not listen to such an idea; she could not think of letting Dolph go out of her sight. She was sitting one day knitting by her fireside, in great perplexity, when the sexton entered with an air of unusual vivacity and briskness. He had just come from a funeral. It had been that of a boy of Dolph's years, who had been apprentice to a famous German doctor, and had died of a consumption. It is true, there had been a whisper that the deceased had been brought to his end by being made the subject of the doctor's experiments, on which he was apt to try the effects of a new compound, or a quieting draught. This, however, it is likely, was a mere scandal; at any rate, Peter de Groodt did not think it worth mentioning; though, had we time to philosophize, it would be a curious matter for speculation, why a doctor's family is apt to be so lean and cadaverous, and a butcher's so jolly and rubicund.

Peter de Groodt, as I said before, entered the house of Dame Heyliger with unusual alacrity. A bright idea had popped into his head at the funeral, over which he had chuckled as he shoveled the earth into the grave of the doctor's disciple. It had occurred to him, that, as the situation of the deceased was vacant at the doctor's, it would be the very place for Dolph. The boy had parts, and could pound a pestle, and run an errand with any boy in the town, and what more was wanted in a student?

The suggestion of the sage Peter was a vision of glory to the mother. She already saw Dolph, in her mind's eye, with a cane at his nose, a knocker at his door, and an M.D. at the end of his name—one of the established dignitaries of the town.

The matter, once undertaken, was soon effected: the sexton had some influence with the doctor, they having had much dealing together in the way of their separate professions; and the very next morning he called and conducted the urchin, clad in his Sunday clothes, to undergo the inspection of Dr. Karl Lodovick Knipperhausen.

They found the doctor seated in an elbow-chair, in one corner of his study, or laboratory, with a large volume, in German print, before him. He was a short fat man, with a dark square face, rendered more dark by a black velvet cap. He had a little nobbed nose, not unlike the ace of spades, with a pair of spectacles gleaming on each side of his dusky countenance, like a couple of bow windows.

Dolph felt struck with awe on entering into the presence of this learned man; and gazed about him with boyish wonder at the furniture of this chamber of knowledge; which appeared to him almost as the den of a magician. In the centre stood a claw-footed table, with pestle and mortar, phials and gallipots, and a pair of small burnished scales. At one end was a heavy clothes-press, turned into a receptacle for drugs and compounds; against which hung the doctor's hat and cloak, and gold-headed cane, and on the top grinned a human skull. Along the mantel-piece were glass vessels, in which were snakes and lizards, and a human foetus preserved in spirits. A closet, the doors of which were taken off, contained three whole shelves of books, and some, too, of mighty folio dimensions; a collection, the like of which Dolph had never before beheld. As, however, the library did not take up the whole of the closet, the doctor's thrifty housekeeper had occupied the rest with pots of pickles and preserves; and had hung about the room, among awful implements of the healing art, strings of red pepper and corpulent cucumbers, carefully preserved for seed.

Peter de Groodt and his protégé were received with great gravity and stateliness by the doctor, who was a very wise, dignified little man, and never smiled. He surveyed Dolph from head to foot, above, and under, and through his spectacles, and the poor lad's heart quailed as these great glasses glared on him like two full moons. The doctor heard all that Peter de Groodt had to say in favor of the youthful candidate; and then wetting his thumb with the end of his tongue, he began deliberately to turn over page after page of the great black volume before him. At length, after many hums and haws, and strokings of the chin, and all that hesitation and deliberation with which a wise man proceeds to do what he intended to do from the very first, the doctor agreed to take the lad as a disciple; to give him bed, board, and clothing, and to instruct him in the healing art; in return for which he was to have his services until his twenty-first year.

Behold, then, our hero, all at once transformed from an unlucky urchin, running wild about the streets, to a student of medicine, diligently pounding a pestle, under the auspices of the learned Doctor Karl Lodovick Knipperhausen. It was a happy transition for his fond old mother. She was delighted with the idea of her boy's being brought up worthy of his ancestors; and anticipated the day when he would be able to hold up his head with the lawyer, that lived in the large house opposite; or, peradventure, with the Dominie himself.

Doctor Knipperhausen was a native of the Palatinate in Germany; whence, in company with many of his countrymen, he had taken refuge in England, on account of religious persecution. He was one of nearly three thousand Palatines, who came over from England in 1710, under the protection of Governor Hunter. Where the doctor had studied, how he had acquired his medical knowledge, and where he had received his diploma, it is hard at present to say, for nobody knew at the time; yet it is certain that his profound skill and abstruse knowledge were the talk and wonder of the common people, far and near.

His practice was totally different from that of any other physician—consisting in mysterious compounds, known only to himself, in the preparing and administering of which, it was said, he always consulted the stars. So high an opinion was entertained of his skill, particularly by the German and Dutch inhabitants, that they always resorted to him in desperate cases. He was one of those infallible doctors, that are always effecting sudden and surprising cures, when the patient has been given up by all the regular physicians; unless, as it is shrewdly observed, the case has been left too long before it was put into their hands. The doctor's library was the talk and marvel of the neighborhood, I might almost say of the entire burgh. The good people looked with reverence at a man who had read three whole shelves full of books, and some of them, too, as large as a family Bible. There were many disputes among the members of the little Lutheran church, as to which was the wisest man, the doctor or the Dominie. Some of his admirers even went so far as to say, that he knew more than the governor himself—in a word, it was thought that there was no end to his knowledge!

No sooner was Dolph received into the doctor's family, than he was put in possession of the lodging of his predecessor. It was a garrett-room of a steep-roofed Dutch house, where the rain had pattered on the shingles, and the lightning gleamed, and the wind piped through the crannies in stormy weather; and where whole troops of hungry rats, like Don Cossacks, galloped about, in defiance of traps and ratsbane.

He was soon up to his ears in medical studies, being employed, morning, noon, and night, in rolling pills, filtering tinctures, or pounding the pestle and mortar in one corner of the laboratory; while the doctor would take his seat in another corner, when he had nothing else to do, or expected visitors, and arrayed in his morning-gown and and velvet cap, would pore over the contents of some folio volume. It is true, that the regular thumping of Dolph's pestle, or, perhaps, the drowsy buzzing of the summer flies, would now and then lull the little man into a slumber; but then his spectacles were always wide awake, and studiously regarding the book.

There was another personage in the house, however, to whom Dolph was obliged to pay allegiance. Though a bachelor, and a man of such great dignity and importance, the doctor was, like many other wise men, subject to petticoat government. He was completely under the sway of his housekeeper—a spare, busy, fretting housewife, in a little, round, quilted German cap, with a huge bunch of keys jingling at the girdle of an exceedingly long waist. Frau Ilsé (or Frow Ilsy, as it was pronounced) had accompanied him in his various migrations from Germany to England, and from England to the province; managing his establishment and himself too: ruling him, it is true, with a gentle hand, but carrying a high hand with all the world beside. How she had acquired such ascendency I do not pretend to say. People, it is true, did talk—but have not people been prone to talk ever since the world began? Who can tell how women generally contrive to get the upper hand? A husband, it is true, may now and then be master in his own house; but who ever knew a bachelor that was not managed by his own housekeeper?

Indeed, Frau Ilsy's power was not confined to the doctor's household. She was one of those prying gossips who knew everyone's business better than they do themselves; and whose all-seeing eyes, and all-telling tongues, are terrors throughout a neighborhood.

Nothing of any moment transpired in the world of scandal in this little burgh, but it was known to Frau Ilsy. She had her crew of cronies, that were perpetually hurrying to her little parlor with some precious bit of news; nay, she would sometimes discuss a whole volume of secret history, as she held the street door ajar, and gossiped with one of these garrulous cronies in the very teeth of a December blast.

Between the doctor and the housekeeper it may easily be supposed that Dolph had a busy life of it. As Frau Ilsy kept the keys, and literally ruled the roost, it was starvation to offend her, though he found the study of her temper more perplexing even than that of medicine. When not busy in the laboratory, she kept him running hither and thither on her errands; and on Sundays he was obliged to accompany her to and from church, and carry her Bible. Many a time has the poor varlet stood shivering and blowing his fingers, or holding his frost-bitten nose, in the church-yard, while Isly and her cronies were huddled together, wagging their heads, and tearing some unlucky character to pieces.

With all his advantages, however, Dolph made very slow progress in his art. This was no fault of the doctor's, certainly, for he took unwearied pains with the lad, keeping him close to the pestle and mortar, or on the trot about town with phials and pill-boxes; and if he ever flagged in his industry, which he was rather apt to do, the doctor would fly into a passion, and ask him if he ever expected to learn his profession, unless he applied himself closer to the study. The fact is, he still retained the fondness for sport and mischief that had marked his childhood; the habit, indeed, had strengthened with his years, and gained force from being thwarted and constrained. He daily grew more and more untractable and lost favor in the eyes, both of the doctor and the housekeeper.

In the mean time the doctor went on, waxing wealthy and renowned. He was famous for his skill in managing cases not laid down in the books. He had cured several old women and young girls of witchcraft—a terrible complaint, and nearly as prevalent in the province in those days as hydrophobia is at present. He had even restored one strapping country girl to perfect health, who had gone so far as to vomit crooked pins and needles; which is considered a desperate stage of the malady. It was whispered, also, that he was possessed of the art of preparing love-powders; and many applications had he in consequence from love-sick patients of both sexes. But all these cases formed the mysterious part of his practice, in which, according to the cant phrase, "secrecy and honor might be depended on." Dolph, therefore, was obliged to turn out of the study whenever such consultations occurred, though it is said he learnt more of the secrets of the art at the key-hole, than by all the rest of his studies put together.

As the doctor increased in wealth, he began to extend his possessions, and to look forward, like other great men, to the time when he should retire to the repose of a country seat. For this purpose he had purchased a farm, or, as the Dutch settlers called it, a *bowerie,* a few miles from town. It had been the residence of a wealthy family, that had returned some time since to Holland. A large mansion-house stood in the centre of it, very much out of repair, and which, in consequence of certain reports, had received the appellation of the Haunted House. Either from these reports, or from its actual dreariness, the doctor found it impossible to get a tenant; and that the place might not fall to ruin before he could reside in it himself, he placed a country boor, with his family, in one wing, with the privilege of cultivating the farm on shares.

The doctor now felt all the dignity of a landholder rising within him. He had a little of the German pride of territory in his composition, and almost looked upon himself as owner of a principality. He began to complain of the fatigue of business; and was fond of riding out "to look at his estate." His little expeditions to his lands were attended with a bustle and parade that created a sensation throughout the neighborhood. His wall-eyed horse stood, stamping and whisking off the flies, for a full hour before the house. Then the doctor's saddle-bags would be brought out and adjusted; then,after a little while, his cloak would be rolled up and strapped to the saddle; then his umbrella would be buckled to the cloak; while, in the mean time, a group of ragged boys, that observant class of beings, would gather before the door. At length the doctor would issue forth, in a pair of jack-boots that reached above his knees, and a cocked hat flapped down in front. As he was a short, fat man, he took some time to mount into the saddle; and when there, he took some time to have the saddle and stirrups properly adjusted, enjoying the wonder and admiration of the urchin crowd.

Even after he had set off, he would pause in the middle of the street, or trot back two or three times to give some parting orders; which were answered by the housekeeper from the door, or Dolph from the study, or the black cook from the cellar, or the chambermaid from the garret window; and there were generally some last words bawled after him, just as he was turning the corner.

The whole neighborhood would be aroused by this pomp and circumstance. The cobbler would leave his last; the barber would thrust out his frizzled head, with a comb sticking in it; a knot would collect at the grocer's door, and the word would be buzzed from one end of the street to the other, "The doctor's riding out to his country seat!"

These were golden moments for Dolph. No sooner was the doctor out of sight, than pestle and mortar were abandoned; the laboratory was left to take care of itself, and the student was off on some madcap frolic.

Indeed, it must be confessed, the youngster, as he grew up, seemed in a fair way to fulfill the prediction of the old claret-colored gentleman. He was the ringleader of all holiday sports, and midnight gambols; ready for all kinds of mischievous pranks, and hare-brained adventures.

There is nothing so troublesome as a hero on a small scale, or, rather, a hero in a small town. Dolph soon became the abhorrence of all drowsy, housekeeping old citizens, who hated noise, and had no relish for waggery. The good dames, too, considered him as little better than a reprobate, gathered their daughters under their wings whenever he approached, and pointed him out as a warning to their sons. No one seemed to hold him in much regard, except wild striplings of the place, who were captivated by his open-hearted, daring manners, and the negroes, who always looked upon every idle, do-nothing youngster as a kind of gentleman. Even the good Peter de Groodt, who considered himself a kind of patron of the lad, began to despair of him; and would shake his head dubiously, as he listened to a long complaint from the housekeeper, and sipped a glass of her raspberry brandy.

Still his mother was not to be wearied out of her affection by all the waywardness of her boy; nor disheartened by the stories of his misdeeds, with which her good friends were continually regaling her. She had, it is true, very little of the pleasure which rich people enjoy, in always hearing their children praised; but she considered all this ill-will as a kind of persecution which he suffered, and she liked him the better on that account. She saw him growing up a fine, tall, good-looking youngster, and she looked at him with the secret pride of a mother's heart. It was her great desire that Dolph should appear like a gentleman, and all the money she could save went towards helping out his pocket and his wardrobe. She would look out of the window after him, as he sallied forth in his best array, and her heart would yearn with delight; and once, when Peter de Groodt, struck with the youngster's gallant appearance on a bright Sunday morning, observed, "Well, after all, Dolph does grow a comely fellow!" the tear of pride started in the mother's eye; "Ah, neighbor! neighbor!" exclaimed she, "they may say what they please; poor Dolph will yet hold up his head with the best of them!"

Dolph Heyliger had now nearly attained his one-and-twentieth year, and the term of his medical studies was just expiring; yet it must be confessed, that he knew little more of the profession than when he first entered the doctor's doors. This, however, could not be from any want of quickness of parts, for he showed amazing aptness in mastering other branches of knowledge, which he could only have studied at intervals. He was, for instance, a sure marksman, and won all the geese and turkeys at Christmas-holidays. He was a bold rider; he was famous for leaping and wrestling; he played tolerably on the fiddle; could swim like a fish; and was the best hand in the whole place at fives or ninepins.

All these accomplishments, however, procured him no favor in the eyes of the doctor, who grew more and more crabbed and intolerant the nearer the term of apprenticeship approached. Frau Ilsy, too, was forever finding some occasion to raise a windy tempest about his ears; and seldom encountered him about the house, without a clatter of the tongue; so that at length the jingling of her keys as she approached, was to Dolph like the ringing of the prompter's bell, that gives notice of a theatrical thunder-storm. Nothing but the infinite good-humor of the heedless youngster enabled him to bear all this domestic tyranny without open rebellion. It was evident that the doctor and his house-keeper were preparing to beat the poor youth out of the nest, the moment his term should have expired; a shorthand mode which the doctor had of providing for useless disciples.

Indeed the little man had been rendered more than usually irritable lately, in conseqeunce of various cares and vexations which his country estate had brought upon him. The doctor had been repeatedly annoyed by the rumors and tales which prevailed concerning the old mansion; and found it difficult to prevail even upon the countryman and his family to remain there rent-free. Every time he rode out to the farm he was teased by some fresh complaint of strange noises and fearful sights, with which the tenants were disturbed at night; and the doctor would come home fretting and fuming, and vent his spleen upon the whole household. It was indeed a sore grievance that affected him both in pride and purse. He was threatened with an absolute loss of the profits of his property; and then, what a blow to his territorial consequence, to be the landlord of a haunted house!

It was observed, however, that with all his vexation, the doctor never proposed to sleep in the house himself; nay, he could never be prevailed upon to remain on the premises after dark, but made the best of his way for town as soon as the bats began to flit about in the twilight. The fact was, the doctor had a secret belief in ghosts, having passed the early part of his life in a country where they particularly abound; and indeed the story went, that, when a boy, he had once seen the devil upon the Hartz mountains in Germany.

At length the doctor's vexations on this head were brought to a crisis. One morning as he sat dozing over a volume in his study, he was suddenly startled from his slumbers by the bustling in of the housekeeper.

"Here's a fine to do!" cried she, as she entered the room. "Here's Claus Hopper come in, bag and baggage, from the farm, and swears he'll have nothing more to do with it. The whole family have been frightened out of their wits; for there's such racketing and rummaging about the old house, that they can't sleep quiet in their beds!"

"Donner and blitzen!" cried the doctor impatiently; "will they never have done chattering about that house? What a pack of fools, to let a few rats and mice frighten them out of good quarters!"

"Nay, nay," said the housekeeper, wagging her head knowingly, and piqued at having a good ghost-story doubted, "there's more in it than rats and mice. All the neighborhood talks about the house; and then such sights as have been seen in it! Peter de Groodt tells me, that the family that sold you the house, and went to Holland, dropped several strange hints about it, and said, 'they wished you joy of your bargain;' and you know yourself there's no getting any family to live in it."

"Peter de Groodt's a ninny—an old woman," said the doctor, peevishly; "I'll warrant he's been filling these people's heads full of stories. It's just like his nonsense about the ghost that haunted the church belfry, as an excuse for not ringing the bell that cold night when Harmanus Brinkerhoff's house was on fire. Send Claus to me."

Claus Hopper now made his appearance: a simple country lout, full of awe at finding himself in the very study of Dr. Knipperhausen, and too much embarrassed to enter in much detail of the matters that had caused his alarm. He stood twirling his hat in one hand, resting sometimes on one leg, sometimes on the other, looking occasionally at the doctor, and now and then stealing a fearful glance at the death's head that seemed ogling him from the top of the clothes-press.

The doctor tried every means to persuade him to return to the farm, but all in vain; he maintained a dogged determination on the subject; and at the close of every argument or solicitation would make the same brief, inflexible reply, "Ich kan nicht, mynheer." The doctor was a "little pot, and soon hot;" his patience was exhausted by these continual vexations about his estate. The stubborn refusal of Claus Hopper seemed to him like flat rebellion; his temper suddenly boiled over, and Claus was glad to make a rapid retreat to escape scalding.

When the bumpkin got to the housekeeper's room, he found Peter de Groodt, and several other true believers, ready to receive him. Here he indemnified himself for the restraint he had suffered in the study, and opened a budget of stories about the haunted house that astonished all his hearers. The housekeeper believed them all, as if it was only to spite the doctor for having received her intelligence so uncourteously. Peter de Groodt matched them with many a wonderful legend of the times of the Dutch dynasty, and of the Devil's Stepping-stones; and of the pirate hanged at Gibbet Island, that continued to swing there at night long after the gallows was taken down; and of the ghost of the unfortunate Governor Leisler, hanged for treason, which haunted the old fort and the government-house. The gossiping knot dispersed, each charged with direful intelligence. The sexton disburdened himself at a vestry meeting that was held that very day, and the black cook forsook her kitchen, and spent half the day at the street pump, that gossiping-place for servants, dealing forth the news to all that came for water. In a little time the whole town was in a buzz with tales about the haunted house. Some said that Claus Hopper had seen the devil, while others hinted that the house was haunted by the ghosts of some of the patients whom the doctor had physicked out of the world, and that was the reason why he did not venture to live in it himself.

All this put the little doctor in a terrible fume. He threatened vengeance on any one who should affect the value of his property by exciting popular prejudices. He complained loudly of thus being in a manner dispossessed of his territories by mere bugbears; but he secretly determined to have the house exorcised by the Dominie. Great was his relief, therefore, when in the midst of his perplexities, Dolph stepped forward and undertook to garrison the haunted house. The youngster had been listening to all the stories of Claus Hopper and Peter de Groodt: he was fond of adventure, he loved the marvellous, and his imagination had become quite excited by these tales of wonder. Besides, he had led such an uncomfortable life at the doctor's, being subjected to the intolerable thraldom of early hours, that he was de-lighted at the prospect of having a house to himself, even though it should be a haunted one. His offer was eagerly accepted, and it was determined he should mount guard that very night. His only stipulation was, that the enterprise should be kept secret from his mother; for he knew the poor soul would not sleep a wink if she knew her son was waging war with the powers of darkness.

When night came on he set out on this perilous expedition. The old black cook, his only friend in the household, had provided him with a little mess for supper, and a rush-light; and she tied round his neck an amulet, given her by an African conjurer, as a charm against evil spirits. Dolph was escorted on his way by the doctor and Peter de Groodt, who had agreed to accompany him to the house, and to see him safe lodged. The night was overcast, and it was very dark when they arrived at the grounds which surrounded the mansion. The sexton led the way with a lantern. As they walked along the avenue of acacias, the fitful light, catching from bush to bush, and tree to tree, often startled the doughty Peter, and made him fall back upon his followers; and the doctor grappled still closer hold of Dolph's arm, observing that the ground was very slippery and uneven. At one time they were nearly put to a total rout by a bat, which came flitting about the lantern; and the notes of the insects from the trees, and the frogs from a neighboring pond, formed a most drowsy and doleful concert. The front door of the mansion opened with a grating sound, that made the doctor turn pale. They entered a tolerably large hall, such as is common in American country-houses, and which serves for a sitting-room in warm weather. From this they went up a wide staircase, that groaned and creaked as they trod, every step making its particular note, like the key of a harpsichord. This led to another hall on the second story, whence they entered the room where Dolph was to sleep. It was large, and scantily furnished; the shutters were closed; but as they were much broken, there was no want of a circulation of air. It appeared to have been that sacred chamber, known among Dutch housewives by the name of "the best bed-room;" which is the best furnished room in the house, but in which scarce any body is ever permitted to sleep. Its splendor, however, was all at an end. There were a few broken articles of furniture about the room, and in the centre stood a heavy deal-table and a large arm-chair, both of which had the look of being coeval with the mansion. The fireplace was wide, and had been faced with Dutch tiles, representing Scripture stories; but some of them had fallen out of their places, and lay scattered about the hearth. The sexton lit the rush-light; and the doctor, looking fearfully about the room, was just exhorting Dolph to be of good cheer, and to pluck up a stout heart, when a noise in the chimney, like voices and struggling, struck a sudden panic into the sexton. He took to his heels with the lantern; the doctor followed hard after him; the stairs groaned and creaked as they hurried down, increasing their agitation and speed by its noises. The front door slammed after them; and Dolph heard them scrabbling down the avenue, till the sound of their feet was lost in the distance. That he did not join in this precipitate retreat might have been owing to his possessing a little more courage than his companions, or perhaps that he had caught a glimpse of the cause of their dismay, in a nest of chimney swallows, that came tumbling down into the fireplace.

Being now left to himself, he secured the front door by a strong bolt and bar; and having seen that the other entrances were fastened, returned to his desolate chamber. Having made his supper from the basket which the good old cook had provided, he locked the chamber door, and retired to rest on a mattress in one corner. The night was calm and still; and nothing broke upon the profound quiet, but the lonely chirping of a cricket from the chimney of a distant chamber. The rush-light, which stood in the centre of the deal-table, shed a feeble yellow ray, dimly illumining the chamber, and making uncouth shapes and shadows on the walls, from the clothes which Dolph had thrown over a chair.

With all his boldness of heart, there was something subduing in this desolate scene; and he felt his spirits flag within him, as he lay on his hard bed and gazed about the room. He was turning over in his mind his idle habits, his doubtful prospects, and now and then heaving a heavy sigh, as he thought on his poor old mother; for there is nothing like the silence and loneliness of night to bring dark shadows over the brightest mind. By-and-by he thought he heard a sound as of someone walking below stairs. He listened, and distinctly heard a step on the great staircase. It approached solemnly and slowly, tramp—tramp—tramp! It was evidently the tread of some heavy personage; and yet how could he have got into the house without making a noise? He had examined all the fastenings, and was certain that every entrance was secure. Still the steps advanced, tramp—tramp—tramp! It was evident that the person approaching could not be a robber, the step was too loud and deliberate; a robber would either be stealthy or precipitate. And now the footsteps had ascended the staircase; they were slowly advancing along the passage, resounding through the silent and empty apartments. The very cricket had ceased its melancholy note, and nothing interrupted their awful distinctness. The door, which had been locked on the inside, slowly swung open, as if self-moved. The footsteps entered the room; but no one was to be seen. They passed slowly and audibly across it, tramp—tramp—tramp! but whatever made the sound was invisible. Dolph rubbed his eyes, and stared about him; he could see to every part of the dimly-lighted chamber; all was vacant; yet still he heard those mysterious footsteps, solemnly walking about the chamber. They ceased, and all was dead silence. There was something more appalling in this invisible visitation, than there would have been in any thing that addressed itself to the eyesight. It was awfully vague and indefinite. He felt his heart beat against his ribs; a cold sweat broke out upon his forehead; he lay for some time in a state of violent agitation; nothing, however, occurred to increase his alarm. His light gradually burnt down into the socket, and he fell asleep. When he awoke it was broad daylight; the sun was peering through the cracks of the window shutters, and the birds were merrily singing about the house. The bright cheery day soon put to flight all the terrors of the preceding night. Dolph laughed, or rather tried to laugh, at all that had passed, and endeavored to persuade himself that it was a mere freak of the imagination, conjured up by the stories he had heard; but he was a little puzzled to find the door of his room locked on the inside, notwithstanding that he had positively seen it swing open as the footsteps had entered. He returned to town in a state of considerable perplexity; but he determined to say nothing on the subject, until his doubts were either confirmed or removed by another night's watching. His silence was a grievous disappointment to the gossips who had gathered at the doctor's mansion. They had prepared their minds to hear direful tales, and were almost in a rage at being assured he had nothing to relate.

The next night, then, Dolph repeated his vigil. He now entered the house with some trepidation. He was particular in examining the fastenings of all the doors, and securing them well. He locked the door of his chamber, and placed a chair against it; then having dispatched his supper, he threw himself on his mattress and endeavored to sleep. It was all in vain; a thousand crowding fancies kept him waking. The time slowly dragged on, as if minutes were spinning themselves out into hours. As the night advanced, he grew more and more nervous; and he almost started from his couch when he heard the mysterious footstep again on the staircase. Up it came, as before, solemnly and slowly, tramp—tramp—tramp! It approached along the passage; the door again swung open, as if there had been neither lock nor impediment, and a strange-looking figure stalked into the room. It was an elderly man, large and robust, clothed in the old Flemish fashion. He had on a kind of short cloak, with a garment under it, belted round the waist; trunk hose, with great bunches or bows at the knees; and a pair of russet boots, very large at top, and standing widely from his legs. His hat was broad and slouched, with a feather trailing over one side. His iron-gray hair hung in thick masses on his neck; and he had a short grizzled beard. He walked slowly round the room, as if examining that all was safe; then, hanging his hat on a peg beside the door, he sat down in the elbow-chair, and, leaning his elbow on the table, fixed his eyes on Dolph with an unmoving and deadening stare.

Dolph was not naturally a coward; but he had been brought up in an implicit belief in ghosts and goblins. A thousand stories came swarming to his mind that he had heard about this building; and as he looked at this strange personage, with his uncouth garb, his pale visage, his grizzly beard, and his fixed, staring, fish-like eye, his teeth began to chatter, his hair to rise on his head, and a cold sweat to break out all over his body. How long he remained in this situation he could not tell, for he was like one fascinated. He could not take his gaze off from the spectre; but lay staring at him, with his whole intellect absorbed in the contemplation. The old man remained seated behind the table, without stirring, or turning an eye, always keeping a dead steady glare upon Dolph. At length the household cock, from a neighboring farm, clapped his wings, and gave a loud cheerful crow that rung over the fields. At the sound the old man slowly rose, and took down his hat from the peg; the door opened, and closed after him; he was heard to go slowly down the staircase, tramp—tramp—tramp— and when he had got to the bottom, all was again silent. Dolph lay and listened earnestly; counted every footfall; listened, and listened, if the steps should return, until, exhausted by watching and agitation, he fell into a troubled sleep.

Daylight again brought fresh courage and assurance. He would fain have considered all that had passed as a mere dream; yet there stood the chair in which the unknown had seated himself; there was the table on which he had leaned; there was the peg on which he had hung his hat; and there was the door, locked precisely as he himself had locked it, with the chair placed against it. He hastened down stairs, and examined the doors and windows; all were exactly in the same state in which he had left them, and there was no apparent way by which any being could have entered and left the house, without leaving some trace behind. "Pooh!" said Dolph to himself, "it was all a dream:"— but it would not do; the more he endeavored to shake the scene off from his mind, the more it haunted him.

Though he persisted in a strict silence as to all that he had seen or heard, yet his looks betrayed the uncomfortable night that he had passed. It was evident that there was something wonderful hidden under this mysterious reserve. The doctor took him into the study, locked the door, and sought to have a full and confidential communication; but he could get nothing out of him. Frau Ilsy took him aside into the pantry, but to as little purpose; and Peter de Groodt held him by the button for a full hour, in the church-yard, the very place to get at the bottom of a ghost story, but came off not a whit wiser than the rest. It is always the case, however, that one truth concealed makes a dozen current lies. It is like a guinea locked up in a bank, that has a dozen paper representatives. Before the day was over, the neighborhood was full of reports. Some said that Dolph Heyliger watched in the haunted house, with pistols loaded with silver bullets; others, that he had a long talk with a spectre without a head; others, that Dr. Knipperhausen and the sexton had been hunted down the Bowery lane, and quite into town, by a legion of ghosts of their customers. Some shook their heads, and thought it a shame the doctor should put Dolph to pass the night alone in that dismal house, where he might be spirited away, no one knew whither; while others observed, with a shrug, that if the devil did carry off the youngster, it would be but taking his own.

These rumors at length reached the ears of the good Dame Heyliger, and, as may be supposed, threw her into a terrible alarm. For her son to have opposed himself to danger from living foes, would have been nothing so dreadful in her eyes, as to dare alone the terrors of the haunted house. She hastened to the doctor's, and passed a great part of the day in attempting to dissuade Dolph from repeating his vigil; she told him a score of tales, which her gossiping friends had just related to her, of persons who had been carried off, when watching alone in old ruinous houses. It was all to no effect. Dolph's pride, as well as curiosity, was piqued. He endeavored to calm the apprehensions of his mother. and to assure her that there was no truth in all the rumors she had heard; she looked at him dubiously and shook her head; but finding his determination was not to be shaken, she brought him a little thick Dutch Bible, with brass clasps, to take with him, as a sword wherewith to fight the powers of darkness; and, lest that might not be sufficient, the housekeeper gave him the Heidelberg catechism by way of dagger.

The next night, therefore, Dolph took up his quarters for the third time in the old mansion. Whether dream or not, the same thing was repeated. Towards midnight, when every thing was still, the same

sound echoed through the empty halls—tramp—tramp—tramp! The
stairs were again ascended; the door again swung open; the old man
entered; walked round the room; hung up his hat, and seated himself
by the table. The same fear and trembling came over poor Dolph,
though not in so violent a degree. He lay in the same way, motionless
and fascinated, staring at the figure, which regarded him as before
with a dead, fixed, chilling gaze. In this way they remained for a long
time, till, by degrees, Dolph's courage began gradually to revive.
Whether alive or dead, this being had certainly some object in his
visitation; and he recollected to have heard it said, spirits have no
power to speak until spoken to. Summoning up resolution, therefore,
and making two or three attempts, before he could get his parched
tongue in motion, he addressed the unknown in the most solemn form
of adjuration, and demanded to know what was the motive of his visit.

No sooner had he finished, than the old man rose, took down his
hat, the door opened, and he went out, looking back upon Dolph just
as he crossed the threshold, as if expecting him to follow. The youngster
did not hesitate an instant. He took the candle in his hand, and the
Bible under his arm, and obeyed the tacit invitation. The candle emitted
a feeble, uncertain ray; but still he could see the figure before him,
slowly descend the stairs. He followed trembling. When it had reached
the bottom of the stairs, it turned through the hall towards the back
door of the mansion. Dolph held the light over the balustrades; but,
in his eagerness to catch a sight of the unknown, he flared his feeble
taper so suddenly, that it went out. Still there was sufficient light from
the pale moonbeams, that fell through a narrow window, to give him
an indistinct view of the figure, near the door. He followed, therefore,
down stairs, and turned towards the place; but when he arrived there,
the unknown had disappeared. The door remained fast barred and
bolted; there was no other mode of exit; yet the being, whatever he
might be, was gone. He unfastened the door, and looked out into the
fields. It was a hazy, moonlight night, so that the eye could distinguish
objects at some distance. He thought he saw the unknown in a footpath
which led from the door. He was not mistaken; but how had he got
out of the house? He did not pause to think, but followed on. The old
man proceeded at a measured pace, without looking about him, his
footsteps sounding on the hard ground. He passed through the orchard
of apple-trees, always keeping the footpath. It led to a well, situated

in a little hollow, which had supplied the farm with water. Just at this well Dolph lost sight of him. He rubbed his eyes and looked again; but nothing was to be seen of the unknown. He reached the well, but nobody was there. All the surrounding ground was open and clear; there was no bush nor hiding-place. He looked down the well, and saw, at a great depth, the reflection of the sky in the still water. After remaining here for some time, without seeing or hearing any thing more of his mysterious conductor, he returned to the house, full of awe and wonder. He bolted the door, groped his way back to bed, and it was long before he could compose himself to sleep.

His dreams were strange and troubled. He thought he was following the old man along the side of a great river, until they came to a vessel on the point of sailing; and that his conductor led him on board and then vanished. He remembered the commander of the vessel, a short swarthy man, with crisped black hair, blind of one eye, and lame of one leg; but the rest of his dream was very confused. Sometimes he was sailing; sometimes on shore; now amidst storms and tempests, and now wandering quietly in unknown streets. The figure of the old man was strangely mingled up with the incidents of the dream, and the whole distinctly wound up by his finding himself on board of the vessel again, returning home, with a great bag of money!

When he woke, the gray cool light of dawn was streaking the horizon, and the cocks passing the reveille from farm to farm throughout the country. He arose more harassed and perplexed than ever. He was singularly confounded by all that he had seen and dreamt, and began to doubt whether his mind was not affected, and whether all that was passing in his thoughts might not be mere feverish fantasy. In his present state of mind, he did not feel disposed to return immediately to the doctor's, and undergo the cross-questioning of the household. He made a scanty breakfast, therefore, on the remains of the last night's provisions, and then wandered out into the fields to meditate on all that had befallen him. Lost in thought, he rambled about, gradually approaching the town, until the morning was far advanced, when he was roused by a hurry and a bustle around him. He found himself near the water's edge, in a throng of people, hurrying to a pier, where was a vessel ready to make sail. He was unconsciously carried along by the impulse of the crowd, and found that it was a sloop, on the point of sailing up the Hudson to Albany. There was much leave-taking, and kissing of old women and children, and great activity in carrying on board baskets of bread and cakes, and provisions of all kinds, notwithstanding the mighty joints of meat that dangled over the stern; for a voyage to Albany was an expedition of great moment in those days. The commander of the sloop was hurrying about, and giving a world of orders, which were not very strictly attended to; one man being busy in lighting his pipe, and another in sharpening his snicker-snee.

The appearance of the commander suddenly caught Dolph's attention. He was short and swarthy, with crisped black hair; blind of one eye and lame of one leg—the very commander that he had seen in his dream! Surprised and aroused, he considered the scene more attentively, and recalled stiff further traces of his dream: the appearance of the vessel, of the river, and of a variety of other objects, accorded with the imperfect images vaguely rising to recollection.

As he stood musing on these circumstances, the captain suddenly called out to him in Dutch, "Step on board, young man, or you'll be left behind!" He was startled by the summons; he saw that the sloop was cast loose, and was actually moving from the pier; it seemed as if he was actuated by some irresistible impulse; he sprang upon the deck, and the next moment the sloop was hurried off by the wind and tide. Dolph's thoughts and feelings were all in tumult and confusion. He had been strongly worked upon by the events which had recently befallen him, and could not but think there was some connection between his present situation and his last night's dream. He felt as if under supernatural influence; and tried to assure himself with an old and favorite maxim of his, that "one way or other, all would turn out for the best." For a moment, the indignation of the doctor at his departure, without leave, passed across his mind, but that was matter of little moment; then he thought of the distress of his mother at his strange disappearance, and the idea gave him a sudden pang; he would have entreated to be put on shore; but he knew with such wind and tide the entreaty would have been in vain. Then the inspiring love of novelty and adventure came rushing in full tide through his bosom; he felt himself launched strangely and suddenly on the world, and under full way to explore the regions of wonder that lay up this mighty river, and beyond those blue mountains which had bounded his horizon since childhood. While he was lost in this whirl of thought, the sails strained to the breeze; the shores seemed to hurry away behind him; and before he perfectly recovered his self-possession, the sloop was ploughing her way past Spiking-devil and Yonkers, and the tallest chimneys of the Manhattoes had faded from his sight.

I have said that a voyage up the Hudson in those days was an undertaking of some moment; indeed, it was as much thought of as a voyage to Europe is at present. The sloops were often many days on the way; the cautious navigators taking in sail when it blew fresh, and coming to anchor at night; and stopping to send the boat ashore for milk for tea; without which it was impossible for the worthy old lady passengers to subsist. And there were the much-talked-of perils of the Tappan Zee, and the highlands. In short, a prudent Dutch burgher would talk of such a voyage for months, and even years, beforehand; and never undertook it without putting his affairs in order, making his will, and having prayers said for him in the low Dutch churches.

In the course of such a voyage, therefore, Dolph was satisfied he would have time enough to reflect, and to make up his mind as to what he should do when he arrived at Albany. The captain, with his blind eye, and lame leg, would, it is true, bring his strange dream to mind, and perplex him sadly for a few moments; but of late his life had been made up so much of dreams and realities, his nights and days had been so jumbled together, that he seemed to be moving continually in a delusion. There is always, however, a kind of vagabond consolation in a man's having nothing in this world to lose; with this Dolph comforted his heart, and determined to make the most of the present enjoyment.

In the second day of the voyage they came to the highlands. It was the latter part of a calm, sultry day, that they floated gently with the tide between these stern mountains. There was that perfect quiet which prevails over nature in the languor of summer heat; the turning of a plank, or the accidental falling of an oar on deck, was echoed from the mountain side, and reverberated along the shores; and if by chance the captain gave a shout of command, there were airy tongues which mocked it from every cliff.

Dolph gazed about him in mute delight and wonder at these scenes of nature's magnificence. To the left the Dunderberg reared its woody precipices, height over height, forest over forest, away into the deep summer sky. To the right strutted forth the bold promontory of Antony's Nose, with a solitary eagle wheeling about it; while beyond, mountain succeeded to mountain, until they seemed to lock their arms together, and confine this mighty river in their embraces. There was a feeling of quiet luxury in gazing at the broad, green bosoms here and there scooped out among the precipices; or at woodlands high in air, nodding over the edge of some beetling bluff, and their foliage all transparent in the yellow sunshine.

In the midst of his admiration, Dolph remarked a pile of bright, snowy clouds, peering above the western heights. It was succeeded by another, and another, each seemingly pushing onwards its predecessor, and towering, with dazzling brilliancy, in the deep blue atmosphere: and now muttering peals of thunder were faintly heard rolling behind the mountains. The river, hitherto still and glassy, reflecting pictures of the sky and land, now showed a dark ripple at a distance, as the breeze came creeping up it. The fish-hawks wheeled and screamed, and sought their nests on the high dry trees; the crows flew clamorously to the crevices of the rocks, and all nature seemed conscious of the approaching thunder-gust.

The clouds now rolled in volumes over the mountain-tops; their summits still bright and snowy, but the lower parts of an inky blackness. The rain began to patter down in broad and scattered drops; the wind freshened, and curled up the waves; at length it seemed as if the bellying clouds were torn open by the mountain-tops, and complete torrents of rain came rattling down. The lightning leaped from cloud to cloud, and streamed quivering against the rocks, splitting and rending the stoutest forest-trees. The thunder burst in tremendous explosions; the peals were echoed from mountain to mountain; they crashed upon Dunderberg, and rolled up the long defile of the highlands, each headland making a new echo, until old Bull Hill seemed to bellow back the storm.

For a time the scudding rack and mist, and the sheeted rain, almost hid the landscape from the sight. There was a fearful gloom, illumined still more fearfully by the streams of lightning which glittered among the rain-drops. Never had Dolph beheld such an absolute warring of the elements; it seemed as if the storm was tearing and rending its way through this mountain defile, and had brought all the artillery of heaven into action.

The vessel was hurried on by the increasing wind, until she came to where the river makes a sudden bend, the only one in the whole course of its majestic career.* Just as they turned the point, a violent flaw of wind came sweeping down a mountain gully, bending the forest before it, and, in a moment, lashing up the river into white froth and foam. The captain saw the danger, and cried out to lower the sail. Before the order could be obeyed, the flaw struck the sloop, and threw her on her beam-ends. Everything now was fright and confusion: the flapping of the sails, the whistling and rushing of the wind, the bawling of the captain and crew, the shrieking of the passengers, all mingled with the rolling and bellowing of the thunder. In the midst of the uproar the sloop righted; at the same time the mainsail shifted, the boom came sweeping the quarter-deck, and Dolph, who was gazing unguardedly at the clouds, found himself, in a moment, floundering in the river.

For once in his life one of his idle accomplishments was of use to him. The many truant hours he had devoted to sporting in the Hudson had made him an expert swimmer; yet with all his strength and skill he found great difficulty in reaching the shore. His disappearance from the deck had not been noticed by the crew, who were all occupied by their own danger. The sloop was driven along with inconceivable rapidity. She had hard work to weather a long promontory on the eastern shore, round which the river turned, and which completely shut her from Dolph's view.

It was on a point of the western shore that he landed, and, scrambling up the rocks, threw himself, faint and exhausted, at the foot of a tree. By degrees the thunder-gust passed over. The clouds rolled away to the east, where they lay piled in feathery masses, tinted with the last rosy rays of the sun. The distant play of the lightning might be seen about the dark bases, and now and then might be heard the faint muttering of the thunder. Dolph rose, and sought about to see if any path led from the shore, but all was savage and trackless. The rocks were piled upon each other; great trunks of trees lay shattered about, as they had been blown down by the strong winds which draw through these mountains, or had fallen through age. The rocks, too,

---

*This must have been the bend at West Point.

were overhung with wild vines and briers, which completely matted themselves together, and opposed a barrier to all ingress; every movement that he made shook down a shower from the dripping foliage. He attempted to scale one of these almost perpendicular heights; but, though strong and agile, he found it an Herculean undertaking. Often he was supported merely by crumbling projections of the rock, and sometimes he clung to roots and branches of trees, and hung almost suspended in the air. The wood-pigeon came cleaving his whistling flight by him, and the eagle screamed from the brow of the impending cliff. As he was thus clambering, he was on the point of seizing hold of a shrub to aid his ascent, when something rustled among the leaves, and he saw a snake quivering along like lightning, almost from under his hand. It coiled itself up immediately, in an attitude of defiance, with flattened head, distended jaws, and quickly vibrating tongue, that played like a little flame about its mouth. Dolph's heart turned faint within him, and he had well nigh let go his hold, and tumbled down the precipice. The serpent stood on the defensive but for an instant; and finding there was no attack, glided away into a cleft of the rock. Dolph's eye followed it with fearful intensity, and he saw a nest of adders, knotted, and writhing, and hissing in the chasm. He hastened with all speed from so frightful a neighborhood. His imagination, full of this new horror, saw an adder in every curling vine, and heard the tale of a rattlesnake in every dry leaf that rustled.

At length he succeeded in scrambling to the summit of a precipice; but it was covered by a dense forest. Wherever he could gain a lookout between the trees, he beheld heights and cliffs, one rising beyond another, until huge mountains overtopped the whole. There were no signs of cultivation; no smoke curling among the trees to indicate a human residence. Every thing was wild and solitary. As he was standing on the edge of a precipice overlooking a deep ravine fringed with trees, his feet detached a great fragment of rock; it fell, crashing its way through the treetops, down into the chasm. A loud whoop, or rather yell, issued from the bottom of the glen; the moment after there was the report of a gun; and a ball came whistling over his head, cutting the twigs and leaves, and burying itself deep in the bark of a chestnut-tree.

Dolph did not wait for a second shot, but made a precipitate retreat; fearing every moment to hear the enemy in pursuit. He succeeded however, in returning unmolested to the shore, and determined to penetrate no farther into a country so beset with savage perils. He sat himself down, dripping, disconsolately, on a stone. What was to be done? where was he to shelter himself? The hour of repose was approaching; the birds were seeking their nests, the bat began to flit about in the twilight, and the nighthawk, soaring high in the heaven, seemed to be calling out the stars. Night gradually closed in, and wrapped every thing in gloom; and though it was the latter part of summer, the breeze stealing along the river, and among these dripping forests, was chilly and penetrating, especially to a half-drowned man.

As he sat drooping and despondent in this comfortless condition, he perceived a light gleaming through the trees near the shore, where the winding of the river made a deep bay. It cheered him with the hope of a human habitation, where he might get something to appease the clamorous cravings of his stomach, and what was equally necessary in his shipwrecked condition, a comfortable shelter for the night. With extreme difficulty he made his way toward the light, along ledges of rocks, down which he was in danger of sliding into the river, and over great trunks of fallen trees; some of which had been blown down in the late storm, and lay so thickly together, that he had to struggle through their branches. At length he came to the brow of a rock overhanging a small dell, whence the light proceeded. It was from a fire at the foot of a great tree in the midst of a grassy interval or plat among the rocks. The fire cast up a red glare among the gray crags, and impending trees; leaving chasms of deep gloom, that resembled entrances to caverns. A small brook rippled close by, betrayed by the quivering reflection of the flame. There were two figures moving about the fire, and others squatted before it. As they were between him and the light, they were in complete shadow: but one of them happening to move round to the opposite side, Dolph was startled at perceiving, by the glare falling on painted features, and glittering on silver ornaments, that he was an Indian. He now looked more narrowly, and saw guns leaning against a tree, and a dead body lying on the ground. Here was the very foe that had fired at him from the glen. He endeavored to retreat quietly, not caring to intrust himself to these half-human beings in so savage and lonely a place. It was too late: the Indian, with that eagle quickness of the eye so remarkable in his race, perceived something stirring among the bushes on the rock: he seized one of the guns that leaned against the tree; one moment more, and Dolph might have had his passion for adventure cured by a bullet. He halloed loudly, with the Indian salutation of friendship: the whole party sprang upon their feet; the salutation was returned, and the straggler was invited to join them at the fire.

On approaching, he found, to his consolation, the party was composed of white men, as well as Indians. One, evidently the principal personage, or commander, was seated on a trunk of a tree before the fire. He was a large, stout man, somewhat advanced in life, but hale and hearty. His face was bronzed almost to the color of an Indian's; he had strong but rather jovial features, an aquiline nose, and a mouth shaped like a mastiff's. His face was half thrown in shade by a broad hat, with a buck's tail in it. His gray hair hung short in his neck. He wore a hunting-frock, with Indian leggins, and moccasins, and a tomahawk in the broad wampum-belt round his waist. As Dolph caught a distinct view of his person and features, something reminded him of the old man of the haunted house. The man before him, however, was different in dress and age; he was more cheery too in aspect, and it was hard to find where the vague resemblance lay; but a resemblance there certainly was. Dolph felt some degree of awe in approaching him; but was assured by a frank, hearty welcome. He was still further encouraged by perceiving that the dead body, which had caused him some alarm, was that of a deer; and his satisfaction was complete in discerning, by savory steams from a kettle, suspended by a hooked stick over the fire, that there was a part cooking for the evening's repast.

He had, in fact, fallen in with a rambling hunting party such as often took place in those days among the settlers along the river. The hunter is always hospitable; and nothing makes men more social and unceremonious than meeting in the wilderness. The commander of the party poured out a dram of cheering liquor, which he gave him with a merry leer, to warm his heart; and ordered one of his followers to fetch some garments from a pinnace, moored in a cove close by, while those in which our hero was dripping might be dried before the fire.

Dolph found, as he had suspected, that the shot from the glen, which had come so near giving him his quietus, when on the precipice, was from the party before him. He had nearly crushed one of them by the fragments of rock which he had detached; and the jovial old hunter, in the broad hat and buck-tail, had fired at the place where he saw the bushes move, supposing it to be the sound of some wild animal. He laughed heartily at the blunder; it being what is considered an exceeding good joke among hunters; "but faith, my lad," said he, "if I had but caught a glimpse of you to take sight at, you would have followed the rock. Antony Vander Heyden is seldom known to miss his aim." These last words were at once a clue to Dolph's curiosity; and a few questions let him completely into the character of the man before him, and of his band of woodland rangers. The commander in the broad hat and hunting-frock was no less a personage than the Heer Antony Vander Heyden, of Albany, of whom Dolph had many a time heard. He was, in fact, the hero of many a story; his singular humors and whimsical habits, being matters of wonder to his quiet Dutch neighbors. As he was a man of property, having had a father before him, from whom he inherited large tracts of wild land, and whole barrels full of wampum, he could indulge his humors without control. Instead of staying quietly at home, eating and drinking at regular meal times, amusing himself by smoking his pipe on the bench before the door, and then turning into a comfortable bed at night, he delighted in all kinds of rough, wild expeditions. Never so happy as when on a hunting party in the wilderness, sleeping under trees or bark sheds, or cruising down the river, or on some woodland lake, fishing and fowling, and living the Lord knows how.

He was a great friend to Indians, and to an Indian mode of life; which he considered true natural liberty and manly enjoyment. When at home he had always several Indian hangers-on, who loitered about his house, sleeping like hounds in the sunshine; or preparing hunting and fishing-tackle for some new expedition; or shooting at marks with bows and arrows.

Over these vagrant beings Heer Antony had as perfect command as a huntsman over his pack; though they were great nuisances to the regular people of his neighborhood. As he was a rich man, no one ventured to thwart his humors; indeed, his hearty, joyous manner made him universally popular. He would troll a Dutch song as he tramped along the street; hail every one a mile off, and when he entered a house, would slap the good man familiarly on the back, shake him by the hand till he roared, and kiss his wife and daughter before his face—in short, there was no pride nor ill humor about Heer Antony.

Besides his Indian hangers-on, he had three or four humble friends among the white men, who looked up to him as a patron, and had the run of his kitchen, and the favor of being taken with him occasionally on his expeditions. With a medley of such retainers he was at present on a cruise along the shores of the Hudson, in a pinnace kept for his own recreation. There were two white men with him, dressed partly in the Indian style, with moccasons and hunting-shirts; the rest of his crew consisted of four favorite Indians. They had been prowling about the river, without any definite object, until they found themselves in the highlands; where they had passed two or three days, hunting the deer which still lingered among these mountains.

"It is lucky for you, young man," said Antony Vander Heyden, "that you happened to be knocked overboard to-day; as tomorrow morning we start early on our return homewards; and you might then have looked in vain for a meal among the mountains—but come, lads, stir about! stir about! Let's see what prog we have for supper; the kettle has boiled long enough; my stomach cries cupboard; and I'll warrant our guest is in no mood to dally with his trencher."

There was a bustle now in the little encampment; one took off the kettle and turned a part of the contents into a huge wooden bowl. Another prepared a flat rock for a table; while a third brought various utensils from the pinnace; Heer Antony himself brought a flask or two of precious liquor from his own private locker; knowing his boon companions too well to trust any of them with the key.

A rude but hearty repast was soon spread; consisting of venison smoking from the kettle, with cold bacon, boiled Indian corn, and mighty loaves of good brown household bread. Never had Dolph made a more delicious repast; and when he had washed it down with two or three draughts from the Heer Antony's flask, and felt the jolly liquor sending its warmth through his veins, and glowing round his very heart, he would not have changed his situation, no, not with the governor of the province.

The Heer Antony, too, grew chirping and joyous; told half a dozen fat stories, at which his white followers laughed immoderately, though the Indians, as usual, maintained an invincible gravity.

"This is your true life, my boy!" said he, slapping Dolph on the shoulder; "a man is never a man till he can defy wind and weather, range woods and wilds, sleep under a tree, and live on bass-wood leaves!"

And then would he sing a stave or two of a Dutch drinking song, swaying a short squab Dutch bottle in his hand, while his myrmidons would join in the chorus, until the woods echoed again;—as the good old song has it,

> "They all with a shout made the elements ring
> So soon as the office was o'er;
> To feasting they went, with true merriment,
> And tippled strong liquor gillore."

In the midst of his joviality, however, Heer Antony did not lose sight of discretion. Though he pushed the bottle without reserve to Dolph, he always took care to help his followers himself, knowing the beings he had to deal with; and was particular in granting but a moderate allowance to the Indians. The repast being ended, the Indians having drunk their liquor, and smoked their pipes, now wrapped themselves in their blankets, stretched themselves on the ground, with their feet to the fire, and soon fell asleep, like so many tired hounds. The rest of the party remained chatting before the fire, which the gloom of the forest, and the dampness of the air from the late storm, rendered extremely grateful and comforting. The conversation gradually moderated from the hilarity of supper-time, and turned upon hunting adventures, and exploits and perils in the wilderness, many of which were so strange and improbable, that I will not venture to repeat them, lest the veracity of Antony Vander Heyden and his comrades should be brought into question. There were many legendary tales told, also, about the river, and the settlements on its borders; in which valuable kind of lore the Heer Antony seemed deeply versed. As the sturdy bush-beater sat in a twisted root of a tree, that served him for an arm-chair, dealing forth these wild stories, with the fire gleaming on his strongly-marked visage, Dolph was again repeatedly perplexed by something that reminded him of the phantom of the haunted house; some vague resemblance not to be fixed upon any precise feature or lineament, but pervading the general air of his countenance and figure.

The circumstances of Dolph's falling overboard led to the relation of divers disasters and singular mishaps that had befallen voyagers on this great river, particularly in the earlier periods of colonial history; most of which the Heer deliberately attributed to supernatural causes. Dolph stared at this suggestion; but the old gentleman assured him it was very currently believed by the settlers along the river; that these highlands were under the dominion of supernatural and mischievous beings, which seemed to have taken some pique against the Dutch colonists in the early time of the settlement. In consequence of this, they have ever taken particular delight in venting their spleen, and indulging their humors, upon the Dutch skippers; bothering them with flaws, head-winds, counter-currents, and all kinds of impediments; insomuch, that a Dutch navigator was always obliged to be exceedingly wary and deliberate in his proceedings; to come to anchor at dusk; to drop his peak, or take in sail, whenever he saw a swag-bellied cloud rolling over the mountains; in short, to take so many precautions, that he was often apt to be an incredible time in toiling up the river.

Some, he said, believed these mischievous powers of the air to be evil spirits conjured up by the Indian wizards, in the early times of the province, to revenge themselves on the strangers who had dispossessed them of their country. They even attributed to their incantations the misadventure which befell the renowned Hendrick Hudson, when he sailed so gallantly up this river in quest of a northwest passage, and, as he thought, ran his ship aground; which they affirm was nothing more nor less than a spell of these same wizards, to prevent his getting to China in this direction.

The greater part, however, Heer Antony observed, accounted for all the extraordinary circumstances attending this river, and the perplexities of the skippers who navigated it, by the old legend of the Storm-ship which haunted Point-no-point. On finding Dolph to be utterly ignorant of this tradition, the Heer stared at him for a moment with surprise, and wondered where he had passed his life, to be uninformed on so important a point in history. To pass away the remainder of the evening, therefore, he undertook the tale, as far as his memory would serve, in the very words in which it had been written out by Mynheer Selyne, an early poet of the New Nederlandts. Giving, then, a stir to the fire, that sent up its sparks among the trees like a little volcano, he adjusted himself comfortably in his root of a tree; and throwing back his head, and closing his eyes for a few moments, to summon up his recollection, he related the following legend.

## THE STORM-SHIP

In the golden age of the province of the New Netherlands, when under the sway of Wouter Van Twiller, otherwise called the Doubter, the people of the Manhattoes were alarmed one sultry afternoon, just about the time of the summer solstice, by a tremendous storm of thunder and lightning. The rain fell in such torrents as absolutely to spatter up and smoke along the ground. It seemed as if the thunder rattled and rolled over the very roofs, of the houses; the lightning was seen to play about the church of St. Nicholas, and to strive three times, in vain, to strike its weather-cock. Garret Van Horne's new chimney was split almost from top to bottom; and Doffue Mildeberger was struck speechless from his bald-faced mare, just as he was riding into town. In a word, it was one of those unparalleled storms, which only happen once within the memory of the venerable personage, known in all towns by the appellation of "the oldest inhabitant."

Great was the terror of the good old women of the Manhattoes. They gathered their children together, and took refuge in the cellars; after having hung a shoe on the iron point of every bed-post, lest it should attract the lightning. At length the storm abated; the thunder sank into a growl, and the setting sun, breaking from under the fringed borders of the clouds, made the broad bosom of the bay to gleam like a sea of molten gold.

The word was given from the fort that a ship was standing up the bay. It passed from mouth to mouth, and street to street, and soon put the little capital in a bustle. The arrival of a ship, in those early times of the settlement, was an event of vast importance to the inhabitants. It brought them news from the old world, from the land of their birth, from which they were so completely severed: to the yearly ship, too, they looked for their supply of luxuries, of finery, of comforts, and almost of necessities. The good vrouw could not have her new cap nor new gown until the arrival of the ship; the artist waited for it for his tools, the burgomaster for his pipe and his supply of Hollands, the schoolboy for his top and marbles, and the lordly landholder for the bricks with which he was to build his new mansion. Thus every one, rich and poor, great and small, looked out for the arrival of the ship. It was the great yearly event of the town of New Amsterdam; and from one end of the year to the other, the ship—the ship—the ship— was the continual topic of conversation.

The news from the fort, therefore, brought all the populace down to the Battery, to behold the wished-for sight. It was not exactly the time when she had been expected to arrive, and the circumstance was a matter of some speculation. Many were the groups collected about the Battery. Here and there might be seen a burgomaster, of slow and pompous gravity, giving his opinion with great confidence to a crowd of old women and idle boys. At another place was a knot of old weather-beaten fellows, who had been seamen or fishermen in their times, and were great authorities on such occasions; these gave different opinions, and caused great disputes among their several adherents: but the man most looked up to, and followed and watched by the crowd, was Hans Van Pelt, an old Dutch sea-captain retired from service, the nautical oracle of the place. He reconnoitred the ship through an ancient telescope, covered with tarry canvas, hummed a Dutch tune to himself, and said nothing. A hum, however, from Hans Van Pelt, had always more weight with the public than a speech from another man.

In the mean time the ship became more distinct to the naked eye: she was a stout, round, Dutch-built vessel, with high bow and poop, and bearing Dutch colors. The evening sun gilded her bellying canvas, as she came riding over the long waving billows. The sentinel who had given notice of her approach, declared, that he first got sight of her when she was in the centre of the bay; and that she broke suddenly on his sight, just as if she had come out of the bosom of the black thunder-cloud. The bystanders looked at Hans Van Pelt, to see what he would say to this report: Hans Van Pelt screwed his mouth closer together, and said nothing; upon which some shook their heads, and others shrugged their shoulders.

The ship was now repeatedly hailed, but made no reply, and passing by the fort, stood up on the Hudson. A gun was brought to bear on her, and, with some difficulty, loaded and fired by Hans Van Pelt, the garrison not being expert in artillery. The shot seemed absolutely to pass through the ship, and to skip along the water on the other side, but no notice was taken of it! What was strange, she had all her sails set, and sailed right against wind and tide, which were both down the river. Upon this Hans Van Pelt, who was likewise harbor-master, ordered his boat, and set off to board her; but after rowing two or three hours, he returned without success. Sometimes he would get within one or two hundred yards of her, and then, in a twinkling, she would be a half a mile off. Some said it was because his oarsmen, who were rather pursy and short-winded, stopped every now and then to take breath, and spit on their hands; but this it is probable was a mere scandal. He got near enough, however, to see the crew; who were all dressed in the Dutch style, the officers in doublets and high hats and feathers; not a word was spoken by any one on board; they stood as motionless as so many statues, and the ship seemed as if left to her own government. Thus she kept on, away up the river, lessening and lessening in the evening sunshine, until she faded from sight, like a little cloud melting away in the summer sky.

The appearance of this ship threw the governor into one of the deepest doubts that ever beset him in the whole course of his administration. Fears were entertained for the security of the infant settlements on the river, lest this might be an enemy's ship in disguise, sent to take possession. The governor called together his council repeatedly to assist him with their conjectures. He sat in his chair of state, built of timber from the sacred forest of the Hague, smoking his long jasmin pipe, and listening to all that his counsellors had to say on a subject about which the knew nothing; but in spite of all the conjecturing of the sagest and oldest heads, the governor still continued to doubt.

Messengers were dispatched to different places on the river; but they returned without any tidings—the ship had made no port. Day after day, and week after week, elapsed, but she never returned down the Hudson. As, however, the council seemed solicitous for intelligence, they had it in abundance. The captains of the sloops seldom arrived without bringing some report of having seen the strange ship at different parts of the river; sometimes near the Pallisadoes, sometimes off Croton Point, and sometimes in the highlands; but she never was reported as having been seen above the highlands. The crews of the sloops, it is true, generally differed among themselves in their

accounts of these apparitions; but that may have arisen from the uncertain situations in which they saw her. Sometimes it was by the flashes
of the thunder-storm lighting up a pitchy night, and giving glimpses
of her careering across Tappaan Zee, or the wide waste of Haverstraw
Bay. At one moment she would appear close upon them, as if likely
to run them down, and would throw them into great bustle and alarm;
but the next flash would show her far off, always sailing against the
wind. Sometimes, in quiet moonlight nights, she would be seen under
some high bluff of the highlands, all in deep shadow, excepting her
topsail glittering in the moonbeams; by the time, however, that the
voyagers reached the place, no ship was to be seen; and when they had
passed on for some distance, and looked back, behold! there she was
again, with her topsails in the moonshine! Her appearance was always
just after, or just before, or just in the midst of unruly weather; and
she was known among the skippers and voyagers of the Hudson by
the name of "the storm-ship."

These reports perplexed the governor and his council more than
ever; and it would be endless to repeat the conjectures and opinions
uttered on the subject. Some quoted cases in point, of ships seen off
the coast of New England, navigated by witches and goblins. Old
Hans Van Pelt, who had been more than once to the Dutch colony at
the Cape of Good Hope, insisted that this must be the flying Dutchman,
which had so long haunted Table Bay; but being unable to make port,
had now sought another harbor. Others suggested, that, if it really
was a supernatural apparition, as there was every natural reason to
believe, it might be Hendrick Hudson, and his crew of the Halfmoon;
who, it was well known, had once run aground in the upper part of
the river in seeking a northwest passage to China. This opinion had
very little weight with the governor, but it passed current out of doors;
for indeed it had already been reported, that Hendrick Hudson and
his crew haunted the Kaatskill Mountain; and it appeared very reasonable to suppose, that his ship might infest the river where the
enterprise was baffled, or that it might bear the shadowy crew to their
periodical revels in the mountain.

Other events occurred to occupy the thoughts and doubts of the
sage Wouter and his council, and the storm-ship ceased to be a subject
of deliberation at the board. It continued, however, a matter of popular
belief and marvellous anecdote through the whole time of the Dutch

government, and particularly just before the capture of New Amsterdam, and the subjugation of the province by the English squadron. About that time the storm-ship was repeatedly seen in the Tappaan Zee, and about Weehawk, and even down as far as Hoboken; and her appearance was supposed to be ominous of the approaching squall in public affairs, and the downfall of Dutch domination.

Since that time we have no authentic accounts of her; though it is said she still haunts the highlands, and cruises about Point-no-point. People who live along the river insist that they sometimes see her in summer moonlight; and that in a deep still midnight they have heard the chant of her crew, as if heaving the lead; but sights and sounds are so deceptive along the mountainous shores, and about the wide bays and long reaches of this great river, that I confess I have very strong doubts upon the subject.

It is certain, nevertheless, that strange things have been seen in these highlands in storms, which are considered as connected with the old story of the ship. The captains of the river craft talk of a little bulbous-bottomed Dutch goblin, in trunk hose and sugar-loafed hat, with a speaking trumpet in his hand, which they say keeps about the Dunderberg.* They declare that they have heard him, in stormy weather, in the midst of the turmoil, giving orders in Low Dutch for the piping up of a fresh gust of wind, or the rattling off of another thunder-clap. That sometimes he has been seen surrounded by a crew of little imps in broad breeches and short doublets; tumbling head over heels in the rack and mist, and playing a thousand gambols in the air; or buzzing like a swarm of flies about Antony's Nose; and that, at such times, the hurry-scurry of the storm was always greatest. One time a sloop, in passing by the Dunderberg, was overtaken by a thunder-gust, that came scouring round the mountain, and seemed to burst just over the vessel. Though tight and well ballasted, she labored dreadfully, and the water came over the gunwale. All the crew were amazed, when it was discovered that there was a little white sugar-loaf hat on the mast-head, known at once to be the hat of the Heer of the Dunderberg. Nobody, however, dared to climb to the mast-head, and get rid of this terrible hat. The sloop continued laboring and rocking, as if

---

*i. e. The "Thunder-Mountain," so called from its echoes.

she would have rolled her mast overboard, and seemed in continual danger either of upsetting or of running on shore. In this way she drove quite through the highlands, until she had passed Pollopol's Island, where, it is said, the jurisdiction of the Dunderberg potentate ceases. No sooner had she passed this bourne, than the little hat spun up into the air like a top, whirled up all the clouds into a vortex, and hurried them back to the summit of the Dunderberg; while the sloop righted herself, and sailed on as quietly as if in mill-pond. Nothing saved her from utter wreck but the fortunate circumstance of having a horse-shoe nailed against the mast; a wise precaution against evil spirits, since adopted by all the Dutch captains that navigate this haunted river.

There is another story told of this foul-weather urchin, by Skipper Daniel Ouselsticker, of Fishkill, who was never known to tell a lie. He declared, that, in a severe squall, he saw him seated astride of his bowsprit, riding the sloop ashore, full butt against Antony's Nose, and that he was exorcised by Dominie Van Gieson, of Esopus, who happened to be on board, and who sang the hymn of St. Nicholas; whereupon the goblin threw himself up in the air like a ball, and went off in a whirlwind, carrying away with him the nightcap of the Dominie's wife; which was discovered the next Sunday morning hanging on the weather cock of Esopus church steeple, at least forty miles off! Several events of this kind having taken place, the regular skippers of the river, for a long time, did not venture to pass the Dunderberg, without lowering their peaks, out of homage to the Heer of the mountain; and it was observed that all such as paid this tribute of respect were suffered to pass unmolested.*

---

*Among the superstitions which prevailed in the colonies, during the early times of the settlements, there seems to have been a singular one about phantom ships. The superstitious fancies of men are always apt to turn upon those objects which concern their daily occupations. The solitary ship, which, from year to year, came like a raven in the wilderness, bringing to the inhabitants of a settlement the comforts of life from the world from which they were cut off, was apt to be present to their dreams, whether sleeping or waking. The accidental sight from shore of a sail gliding along the horizon, in those as yet lonely seas, was apt to be a matter of much talk and speculation. There is mention made in one of the early New England writers of a ship navigated

"Such," said Antony Vander Heyden, "are a few of the stories written down by Selyne the poet, concerning this storm-ship; which he affirms to have brought a crew of mischievous imps into the province, from some old ghost-ridden country of Europe. I could give you a host more, if necessary; for all the accidents that so often befall the river craft in the highlands are said to be tricks played off by these imps of the Dunderberg; but I see that you are nodding; so let us turn in for the night."—

The moon had just raised her silver horns above the round back of Old Bull Hill, and lit up the gray rocks and shagged forests, and glittered on the waving bosom of the river. The night dew was falling, and the late gloomy mountains began to soften and put on a gray aerial tint in the dewy light. The hungers stirred the fire, and threw on fresh fuel to qualify the damp of the night air. They then prepared a bed of branches and dry leaves under a ledge of rocks for Dolph; while Antony Vander Heyden, wrapping himself in a huge coat of skins, stretched himself before the fire. It was some time, however, before Dolph could close his eyes. He lay contemplating the strange scene before him: the wild woods and rocks around; the fire throwing fitful gleams on the faces of the sleeping savages; and the Heer Antony, too, who so singularly, yet vaguely, reminded him of the nightly visitant to the haunted house. Now and then he heard the cry of some animal from the forest; or the hooting of the owl; or the notes of the whip-poor-will, which seemed to abound among these solitudes; or the splash

---

by witches, with a great horse that stood by the mainmast. I have met with another story, somewhere, of a ship that drove on shore, in fair, sunny, tranquil weather, with sails all set and a table spread in the cabin, as if to regale a number of guests, yet not a living being on board. These phantom ships always sailed in the eye of the wind; or ploughed their way with great velocity, making the smooth sea foam before their bows, when not a breath of air was stirring.

Moore has finely wrought up one of these legends of the sea into a little tale, which, within a small compass, contains the very essence of this species of supernatural fiction. I allude to his Spectre Ship, bound to Deadman's Isle.

of a sturgeon, leaping out of the river, and falling back full length on its placid surface. He contrasted all this with his accustomed nest in the garret room of the doctor's mansion; where the only sounds at night were the church clock telling the hour; the drowsy voice of the watchman, drawling out all was well; the deep snoring of the doctor's clubbed nose from below stairs; or the cautious labors of some carpenter rat gnawing in the wainscot. His thoughts then wandered to his poor old mother: what would she think of his mysterious disappearance—what anxiety and distress would she not suffer? This thought would continually intrude itself to mar his present enjoyment. It brought with it a feeling of pain, and compunction, and he fell asleep with the tears yet standing in his eyes.

Were all this a mere tale of fancy, here would be a fine opportunity for weaving in strange adventures among these wild mountains, and roving hunters; and, after involving my hero in a variety of perils and difficulties, rescuing him from them all by some miraculous contrivance; but as this is absolutely a true story, I must content myself with simple facts, and keep to probabilities.

At an early hour of the next day, therefore, after a hearty morning's meal, the encampment broke up, and our adventurers embarked in the pinnace of Antony Vander Heyden. There being no wind for the sails, the Indians rowed her gently along, keeping time to a kind of chant of one of the white men. The day was serene and beautiful; the river without a wave; and as the vessel cleft the glassy water, it left a long, undulating track behind. The crows, who had scented the hunters' banquet, were already gathering and hovering in the air, just where a column of thin, blue smoke, rising from among the trees, showed the place of their last night's quarters. As they coasted along the bases of the mountains, the Heer Antony pointed out to Dolph a bald eagle, the sovereign of these regions, who sat perched on a dry tree that projected over the river and, with eye turned upwards, seemed to be drinking in the splendor of the morning sun. Their approach disturbed the monarch's meditations. He first spread one wing, and then the other; balanced himself for a moment; and then, quitting his perch with dignified composure, wheeled slowly over their heads. Dolph snatched up a gun, and sent a whistling ball after him, that cut some of the feathers from his wing; the report of the gun leaped sharply from rock to rock, and awakened a thousand echoes; but the monarch of the air sailed calmly on, ascending higher and higher, and wheeling widely as he ascended, soaring up the green bosom of the woody mountain, until he disappeared over the brow of a beetling precipice. Dolph felt in a manner rebuked by this proud tranquility, and almost reproached himself for having so wantonly insulted this majestic bird. Heer Antony told him, laughing, to remember that he was not yet out of the territories of the lord of the Dunderberg; and an old Indian shook his head, and observed, that there was bad luck in killing an eagle; the hunter, on the contrary, should always leave him a portion of his spoils.

Nothing, however, occurred to molest them on their voyage. They passed pleasantly through magnificent and lonely scenes, until they came to where Pollopol's Island lay, like a floating bower, at the extremity of the highlands. Here they landed, until the heat of the day should abate, or a breeze spring up, that might supersede the labor of the oar. Some prepared the midday meal, while others reposed under the shade of the trees, in luxurious summer indolence, looking drowsily forth upon the beauty of the scene. On the one side were the highlands, vast and cragged, feathered to the top with forests, and throwing their shadows on the glassy water that dimpled at their feet. On the other side was a wide expanse of the river, like a broad lake, with long sunny reaches, and green headlands; and the distant line of Shawangunk mountains waving along a clear horizon, or checkered by a fleecy cloud.

But I forbear to dwell on the particulars of their cruise along the river; this vagrant, amphibious life, careering across silver sheets of water; coasting wild woodland shores; banqueting on shady promontories, with the spreading tree over head, the river curling its light foam to one's feet, and distant mountain, and rock, and tree, and snowy cloud, and deep blue sky, all mingling in summer beauty before one; all this, though never cloying in the enjoyment would be but tedious in narration.

When encamped by the water-side, some of the party would go into the woods and hunt; others would fish: sometimes they would amuse themselves by shooting at a mark, by leaping, by running, by wrestling; and Dolph gained great favor in the eyes of Antony Vander Heyden, by his skill and adroitness in all these exercises; which the Heer considered as the highest of manly accomplishments.

Thus did they coast jollily on, choosing only the pleasant hours for voyaging; sometimes in the cool morning dawn, sometimes in the sober evening twilight, and sometimes when the moonshine spangled the crisp curling waves that whispered along the sides of their little bark. Never had Dolph felt so completely in his element; never had he met with any thing so completely to his taste as this wild, haphazard life. He was the very man to second Antony Vander Heyden in his rambling humors, and gained continually on his affections. The heart of the old bush-whacker yearned toward the young man, who seemed thus growing up in his own likeness; and as they approached to the end of their voyage, he could not help inquiring a little into his history. Dolph frankly told him his course of life, his severe medical studies, his little proficiency, and his very dubious prospects. The Heer was shocked to find that such amazing talents and accomplishments were to be cramped and buried under a doctor's wig. He had a sovereign contempt for the healing art, having never had any other physician than the butcher. He bore a mortal grudge to all kinds of study also, ever since he had been flogged about an unintelligible book when he was a boy. But to think that a young fellow like Dolph, of such wonderful abilities, who could shoot, fish, run, jump, ride, and wrestle, should be obliged to roll pills, and administer juleps for a living—'twas monstrous! He told Dolph never to despair, but to "throw physic to the dogs;" for a young fellow of his prodigious talents could never fail to make his way. "As you seem to have no acquaintance in Albany," said Heer Antony, "you shall go home with me, and remain under my roof until you can look about you; and in the mean time we can take an occasional bout at shooting and fishing, for it is a pity that such talents should lie idle."

Dolph, who was at the mercy of chance, was not hard to be persuaded. Indeed, on turning over matters in his mind, which he did very sagely and deliberately, he could not but think that Antony Vander Heyden was, "somehow or other," connected with the story of the Haunted House; that the misadventure in the highlands, which had thrown them so strangely together, was, "somehow or other," to work out something good: in short, there is nothing so convenient as this "somehow or other" way of accommodating one's self to circumstances; it is the main stay of a heedless actor, and tardy reasoner, like Dolph

Heyliger; and he who can, in this loose, easy way, link foregone evil to anticipated good.

On their arrival at Albany, the sight of Dolph's companion seemed to cause universal satisfaction. Many were the greetings at the river-side, and the salutations in the streets; the dogs bounded before him; the boys whooped as he passed; every body seemed to know Antony Vander Heyden. Dolph followed on in silence, admiring the neatness of this worthy burgh; for in those days Albany was in all its glory, and inhabited almost exclusively by the descendants of the original Dutch settlers, not having as yet been discovered and colonized by the restless people of New England. Every thing was quiet and orderly; every thing was conducted calmly and leisurely; no hurry, no bustle, no struggling and scrambling for existence. The grass grew about the unpaved streets, and relieved the eye by its refreshing verdure. Tall sycamores or pendant willows shaded the houses, with caterpillars swinging, in long silken strings, from their branches; or moths, flut-tering about like coxcombs, in joy at their gay transformation. The houses were built in the old Dutch style, with the gable ends towards the street. The thrifty housewife was seated on a bench before her door, in close-crimped cap, bright flowered gown, and white apron, busily employed in knitting. The husband smoked his pipe on the opposite bench, and the little pet negro girl, seated on the step at her mistress's feet, was industriously plying her needle. The swallows sported about the eaves, or skimmed along the streets, and brought back some rich booty for their clamorous young; and the little house-keeping wren flew in and out of a Lilliputian house, or an old hat nailed against the wall. The cows were coming home, lowing through the streets, to be milked at their owner's door; and if, perchance, there were any loiterers, some negro urchin, with a long goad, was gently urging them homewards.

As Dolph's companion passed on, he received a tranquil nod from the burghers, and a friendly word from their wives; all calling him familiarly by the name of Antony; for it was the custom in this strong-hold of the patriarchs, where they had all grown up together from childhood, to call each other by the christian name. The Heer did not pause to have his usual jokes with them, for he was impatient to reach his home. At length they arrived at his mansion. It was of some magnitude, in the Dutch style, with large iron figures on the gables, that gave the date of its erection, and showed that it had been built in the earliest times of the settlement.

The news of Heer Antony's arrival had preceded him, and the whole household was on the look-out. A crew of negroes, large and small, had collected in front of the house to receive him. The old, white-headed ones, who had grown gray in his service, grinned for joy, and made many awkward bows and grimaces, and the little ones capered about his knees. But the most happy being in the household was a little, plump, blooming lass, his only child, and the darling of his heart. She came bounding out of the house; but the sight of a strange young man with her father called up, for a moment, all the bashfulness of a homebred damsel. Dolph gazed at her with wonder and delight; never had he seen, as he thought, any thing so comely in the shape of a woman. She was dressed in the good old Dutch taste, with long stays, and full, short petticoats, so admirably adapted to show and set off the female form. Her hair, turned up under a small round cap, displayed the fairness of her forehead; she had fine, blue, laughing eyes; a trim, slender waist, and soft swell—but, in a word, she was a little Dutch divinity; and Dolph, who never stopped half-way in a new impulse, fell desperately in love with her.

Dolph was now ushered into the house with a hearty welcome. In the interior was a mingled display of Heer Antony's taste and habits, and of the opulence of his predecessors. The chambers were furnished with good old mahogany; the beaufets and cupboards glittered with embossed silver, and painted china. Over the parlor fireplace was, as usual, the family coat of arms, painted and framed; above which was a long duck fowling-piece, flanked by an Indian pouch, and a powder-horn. The room was decorated with many Indian articles, such as pipes of peace, tomahawks, scalping-knives, hunting-pouches, and belts of wampum; and there were various kins of fishing-tackle, and two or three fowling-pieces in the corners. The household affairs seemed to be conducted, in some measure, after the master's humors; corrected perhaps, by a little quiet management of the daughter's. There was a great degree of patriarchal simplicity, and good-humored indulgence. The negroes came into the room without being called, merely to look at their master, and hear of his adventures; they would stand listening at the door until he had finished a story, and then go off on a broad grin, to repeat it in the kitchen. A couple of pet negro children were playing about the floor with the dogs, and sharing with them their bread and butter. All the domestics looked hearty and happy; and when the table was set for the evening repast, the variety and abundance of good household luxuries bore testimony to the open-handed liberality of the Heer, and the notable housewifery of his daughter.

In the evening there dropped in several of the worthies of the place, the Van Renssellaers, and the Gansevoorts, and the Rosebooms, and others of Antony Vander Heyden's intimates, to hear an account of his expedition; for he was the Sinbad of Albany, and his exploits and adventures were favorite topics of conversation among the inhabitants. While these sat gossiping together about the door of the hall, and telling long twilight stories, Dolph was cozily seated, entertaining the daughter on a window-bench. He had already got on intimate terms; for those were not times of false reserve and idle ceremony; and, besides, there is something wonderfully propitious to a lover's suit, in the delightful dusk of a long summer evening; it gives courage to the most timid tongue, and hides the blushes of the bashful. The stars alone twinkled brightly; and now and then a firefly streamed his transient light before the window, or, wandering into the room, flew gleaming about the ceiling.

What Dolph whispered in her ear that long summer evening, it is impossible to say; his words were so low and indistinct, that they never reached the ear of the historian. It is probable, however, that they were to the purpose for he had a natural talent at pleasing the sex, and was never long in company with a petticoat, without paying proper court to it. In the mean time the visitors, one by one, departed; Antony Vander Heyden, who had fairly talked himself silent, sat nodding alone in his chair by the door, when he was suddenly aroused by a hearty salute with which Dolph Heyliger had unguardedly rounded off one of his periods, and which echoed through the still chamber like the report of a pistol. The Heer started up, rubbed his eyes, called for lights, and observed, that it was high time to go to bed; though, on parting for the night, he squeezed Dolph heartily by the hand, looked kindly in his face, and shook his head knowingly; for the Heer well remembered what he himself had been at the youngster's age.

The chamber in which our hero was lodged was spacious, and panelled with oak. It was furnished with clothes-presses, and mighty chests of drawers, well waxed, and glittering with brass ornaments.

These contained ample stock of family linen; for the Dutch housewives had always a laudable pride in showing off their household treasures to strangers.

Dolph's mind, however, was too full to take particular note of the objects around him: yet he could not help continually comparing the free, open-hearted cheeriness of this establishment, with the starveling, sordid, joyless housekeeping, at Doctor Knipperhausen's. Still something marred the enjoyment; the idea that he must take leave of his hearty host, and pretty hostess, and cast himself once more adrift upon the world. To linger here would be folly: he should only get deeper in love: and for a poor varlet, like himself, to aspire to the daughter of the great Heer Vander Heyden—it was madness to think of such a thing! The very kindness that the girl had shown towards him prompted him, on reflection, to hasten his departure; it would be a poor return for the frank hospitality of his host, to entangle his daughter's heart in an injudicious attachment. In a word, Dolph was like many other young reasoners, of exceeding good hearts, and giddy heads; who think after they act, and act differently from what they think; who make excellent determinations over night, and forget to keep them next morning.

"This is a fine conclusion, truly, of my voyage," said he, as he almost buried himself in a sumptuous feather-bed, and drew the fresh white sheets up to his chin. "Here am I, instead of finding a bag of money to carry home, launched in a strange place, with scarcely a stiver in my pocket; and, what is worse, have jumped ashore up to my very ears in love with the bargain. However," added he, after some pause, stretching himself, and turning himself in bed, "I'm in good quarters for the present, at least; so I'll e'en enjoy the present moment, and let the next take care of itself; I dare say all will work out, 'somehow or other,' for the best."

As he said these words he reached out his hand to extinguish the candle, when he was suddenly struck with astonishment and dismay, for he thought he beheld the phantom of the haunted house, staring on him from a dusky part of the chamber. A second look reassured him, as he perceived that what he had taken for the spectre was, in fact, nothing but a Flemish portrait, hanging in a shadowy corner, just behind a clothes-press. It was, however, the precise representation of his nightly visitor. The same cloak and belted jerkin, the same grizzled beard and fixed eye, the same broad slouched hat, with a feather hanging over one side. Dolph now called to mind the resemblance he had frequently remarked between his host and the old man of the haunted house; and was fully convinced they were in some way connected, and that some especial destiny had governed his voyage. He lay gazing on the portrait with almost as much awe as he had gazed on the ghostly original, until the shrill house-clock warned him of the lateness of the hour. He put out the light; but remained for a long time turning over these curious circumstances and coincidences in his mind, until he fell asleep. His dreams partook of the nature of his waking thoughts. He fancied that he still lay gazing on the picture, until, by degrees, it became animated; that the figure descended from the wall, and walked out of the room; that he followed it, and found himself by the well, to which the old man pointed, smiled on him, and disappeared.

In the morning, when he waked, he found his host standing by his bedside, who gave him a hearty morning's salutation, and asked him how he had slept. Dolph answered cheerily; but took occasion to inquire about the portrait that hung against the wall. "Ah," said Heer Antony, "that's a portrait of old Killian Vander Spiegel, once a burgomaster of Amsterdam, who, on some popular troubles, abandoned Holland, and came over to the province during the government of Peter Stuyvesant. He was my ancestor by the mother's side, and an old miserly curmudgeon he was. When the English took possession of New Amsterdam, in 1664, he retired into the country. He fell into a melancholy, apprehending that his wealth would be taken from him, and that he would come to beggary. He turned all his property into cash, and used to hide it away. He was for a year or two concealed in various places, fancying himself sought after by the English, to strip him of his wealth; and finally he was found dead in his bed one morning, without any one being able to discover where he had concealed the greater part of his money."

When his host had left the room, Dolph remained for some time lost in thought. His whole mind was occupied by what he had heard. Vander Spiegel was his mother's family name; and he recollected to have heard her speak of this very Killian Vander Spiegel as one of her ancestors. He had heard her say, too, that her father was Killian's rightful heir, only that the old man died without leaving any thing to be inherited. It now appeared that Heer Antony was likewise a descendant, and perhaps an heir also, of this poor rich man; and that thus the Heyligers and the Vander Heydens were remotely connected. "What," thought he, "if after all, this is the interpretation of my dream, that this is the way I am to make my fortune by this voyage to Albany, and that I am to find the old man's hidden wealth in the bottom of that well? But what an odd roundabout mode of communicating the matter! Why the plague could not the old goblin have told me about the well at once, without sending me all the way to Albany, to hear a story that was to send me all the way back again?"

These thoughts passed through his mind while he was dressing. He descended the stairs, full of perplexity, when the bright face of Marie Vander Heyden suddenly beamed in smiles upon him, and seemed to give him a clue to the whole mystery. "After all," thought he, "the old goblin is in the right. If I am to get his wealth, he means that I shall marry his pretty descendant; thus both branches of the family will again be united, and the property go on in the proper channel."

No sooner did this idea enter his head, than it carried conviction with it. He was now all impatience to hurry back and secure the treasure, which, he did not doubt, lay at the bottom of the well, and which he feared every moment might be discovered by some other person. "Who knows," thought he, "but this night-walking old fellow of the haunted house may give a hint to some shrewder fellow than myself, who will take a shorter cut to the well than by the way of Albany?" He wished a thousand times that the babbling old ghost was laid in the Red Sea, and his rambling portrait with him. He was in a perfect fever to depart. Two or three days elapsed before any opportunity presented for returning down the river. They were ages to Dolph, notwithstanding that he was basking in the smiles of the pretty Marie, and daily getting more and more enamored.

At length the very sloop from which he had been knocked overboard, prepared to make sail. Dolph made an awkward apology to his host for his sudden departure. Antony Vander Heyden was sorely astonished. He had concerted half a dozen excursions into the wilderness; and his Indians were actually preparing for a grand expedition to one of the lakes. He took Dolph aside, and exerted his eloquence to get him to abandon all thoughts of business and to remain with him, but in vain; and he at length gave up the attempt, observing, "that it was a thousand pities so fine a young man should throw himself away." Heer Antony, however, gave him a hearty shake by the hand at parting, with a favorite fowling-piece, and an invitation to come to his house whenever he revisited Albany. The pretty little Marie said nothing; but as he gave her a farewell kiss, her dimpled cheek turned pale, and a tear stood in her eye.

Dolph sprang lightly on board of the vessel. They hoisted sail; the wind was fair; they soon lost sight of Albany, its green hills, and embowered islands. They were wafted gayly past the Kaatskill mountains, whose fairy heights were bright and cloudless. They passed prosperously through the highlands, without any molestation from the Dunderberg goblin and his crew; they swept on across Haverstraw Bay, and by Croton Point, and through the Tappaan Zee, and under the Pallisadoes, until, in the afternoon of the third day, they saw the promontory of Hoboken hanging like a cloud in the air; and, shortly after, the roofs of the Manhattoes rising out of the water.

Dolph's first care was to repair to his mother's house; for he was continually goaded by the idea of the uneasiness she must experience on his account. He was puzzling his brains, as he went along, to think how he should account for his absence without betraying the secrets of the haunted house. In the midst of these cogitations, he entered the street in which his mother's house was situated, when he was thunderstruck at beholding it a heap of ruins.

There had evidently been a great fire, which had destroyed several large houses, and the humble dwelling of poor Dame Heyliger had been involved in the conflagration. The walls were not so completely destroyed, but that Dolph could distinguish some traces of the scene of his childhood. The fireplace, about which he had often played, still remained, ornamented with Dutch tiles, illustrating passages in Bible history, on which he had many a time gazed with admiration. Among the rubbish lay the wreck of the good dame's elbow-chair, from which she had given him so many a wholesome precept; and hard by it was the family Bible, with brass clasps; now alas! reduced to a cinder.

For a moment Dolph was overcome by this dismal sight, for he was seized with the fear that his mother had perished in the flames. He was relieved, however, from this horrible apprehension, by one of the neighbors, who happened to come by and informed him that his mother was yet alive.

The good woman had, indeed, lost every thing by this unlooked-for calamity; for the populace had been so intent upon saving the fine furniture of her rich neighbors, that the little tenement, and the little all of poor Dame Heyliger, had been suffered to consume without interruption; nay, had it not been for the gallant assistance of her old crony, Peter de Groodt, the worthy dame and her cat might have shared the fate of their habitation.

As it was, she had been overcome with fright and affliction, and lay ill in body and sick at heart. The public, however, had showed her its wonted kindness. The furniture of her rich neighbors being, as far as possible, rescued from the flames; themselves duly and ceremoniously visited and condoled with on the injury of their property, and their ladies commiserated on the agitation of their nerves; the public, at length, began to recollect something about poor dame Heyliger. She forthwith became again a subject of universal sympathy; every body pitied her more than ever; and if pity could but have been coined into cash—good Lord! how rich she would have been!

It was now determined, in good earnest, that something ought to be done for her without delay. The dominie, therefore, put up prayers for her on Sunday, in which all the congregation joined most heartily. Even Cobus Groesbeek, the alderman, and Mynheer Milledollar, the great Dutch merchant, stood up in their pews, and did not spare their voices on the occasion; and it was thought the prayers of such great men could not but have their due weight. Doctor Knipperhausen, too, visited her professionally, and gave her abundance of advice gratis, and was universally lauded for his charity. As to her old friend, Peter de Groodt, he was a poor man, whose pity, and prayers, and advice, could be of but little avail, so he gave her all that was in his power— he gave her shelter.

To the humble dwelling of Peter de Groodt, then, did Dolph turn his steps. On his way thither, he recalled all the tenderness and kindness of his simple-hearted parent, her indulgence of his errors, her blindness to his faults; and then he bethought himself of his own idle, harum-scarum life. "I've been a complete sink-pocket, that's the truth of it. —But," added he briskly, and clasping his hands, "only let her live— only let her live—and I'll show myself indeed a son!"

As Dolph approached the house he met Peter de Groodt coming out of it. The old man started back aghast, doubting whether it was not a ghost that stood before him. It being bright daylight, however, Peter soon plucked up heart, satisfied that no ghost dare show his face in such clear sunshine. Dolph now learned from the worthy sexton the consternation and rumor to which his mysterious disappearance had given rise. It had been universally believed that he had been spirited away by those hobgoblin gentry that infested the haunted house; and old Abraham Vandozer, who lived by the great buttonwood trees, near the three-mile stone, affirmed, that he had heard a terrible noise in the air, as he was going home late at night, which seemed just as if a flock of wild-geese were overhead, passing off towards the northward. The haunted house was, in consequence, looked upon with ten times more awe than ever; nobody would venture to pass a night in it for the world, and even the doctor had ceased to make his expeditions to it in the daytime.

It required some preparation before Dolph's return could be made known to his mother, the poor soul having bewailed him as lost; and her spirits having been sorely broken down by a number of comforters, who daily cheered her with stories of ghosts, and of people carried away by the devil. He found her confined to her bed, with the other member of the Heyliger family, the good dame's cat, purring beside her, but sadly singed, and utterly despoiled of those whiskers which were the glory of her physiognomy. The poor woman threw her arms about Dolph's neck: "My boy! my boy! art thou still alive?" For a time she seemed to have forgotten all her losses and troubles in her joy at his return. Even the sage grimalkin showed indubitable signs of joy at the return of the youngster. She saw, perhaps, that they were a forlorn and undone family, and felt a touch of that kindliness which fellow-suffers only know. But, in truth, cats are a slandered people; they have more affection in them than the world commonly gives them credit for.

The good dame's eyes glistened as she saw one being, at least, beside herself, rejoiced at her son's return. "Tib knows thee! poor dumb beast!" said she, smoothing down the mottled coat of her favorite; then recollecting herself, with a melancholy shake of the head, "Ah, my poor Dolph!" exclaimed she, "thy mother can help thee no longer!

She can no longer help herself! What will become of thee, my poor boy!"

"Mother," said Dolph, "don't talk in that strain; I've been too long a charge upon you; it's now my part to take care of you in your old days. Come! be of good cheer! you and I, and Tib will all see better days. I'm here, you see, young, and sound, and hearty; and don't let us despair; I dare say things will all, somehow or other, turn out for the best."

While this scene was going on with the Heyliger family, the news was carried to Doctor Knipperhausen, of the safe return of his disciple. The little doctor scarce knew whether to rejoice or be sorry at the tidings. He was happy at having the foul reports which had prevailed concerning his country mansion thus disproved; but he grieved at having his disciple, of whom he had supposed himself farily disencumbered, thus drifting back, a heavy charge upon his hands. While balancing between these two feelings, he was determined by the counsels of Frau Ilsy, who advised him to take advantage of the truant absence of the youngster, and shut the door upon him for ever.

At the hour of bed-time, therefore, when it was supposed the recreant disciple would seek his old quarters, every thing was prepared for his reception. Dolph, having talked his mother into a state of tranquillity, sought the mansion of his quondam master, and raised the knocker with a faltering hand. Scarcely, however, had it given a dubious rap, when the doctor's head, in a red night-cap, popped out of one window, and the housekeeper's, in a white night-cap, out of another. He was now greeted with a tremendous volley of hard names and hard language, mingled with invaluable pieces of advice, such as are seldom ventured to be given excepting to a friend in distress, or a culprit at the bar. In a few moments not a window in the street but had its particular night-cap, to the shrill treble of Frau Ilsy, and the guttural croaking of Dr. Knipperhausen; and the word went from window to window, "Ah! here's Dolph Heyliger come back, and at his old pranks again." In short, poor Dolph found he was likely to get nothing from the doctor but good advice; a commodity so abundant as even to be thrown out of the window; so he was fain to beat a retreat, and take up his quarters for the night under the lowly roof of honest Peter de Groodt.

The next morning, bright and early, Dolph was out at the haunted house. Every thing looked just as he had left it. The fields were grass-grown and matted, and appeared as if nobody had traversed them since his departure. With palpitating heart he hastened to the well. He looked down into it and saw that it was of great depth, with water at the bottom. He had provided himself with a strong line, such as the fisherman use on the banks of Newfoundland. At the end was a heavy plummet and a large fish-hook. With this he began to sound the bottom of the well, and to angle about in the water. The water was of some depth; there was also much rubbish, stones from the top having fallen in. Several times his hook got entangled, and he came near breaking his line. Now and then, too, he haled up mere trash, such as the skull of a horse, an iron hoop, and a shattered iron-bound bucket. He had now been several hours employed without finding any thing to repay his trouble, or to encourage him to proceed. He began to think himself a great fool, to be thus decoyed into a wild-goose-chase by mere dreams, and was on the point of throwing line and all into the well, and giving up all further angling.

"One more cast of the line," said he, "and that shall be the last." As he sounded, he felt the plummet slip, as it were, through the interstices and loose stones; and as he drew back the line, he felt that the hook had taken hold of something heavy. He had to manage his line with great caution, lest it should be broken by the strain upon it. By degrees the rubbish which lay upon the article he had hooked gave way; he drew it to the surface of the water, and what was his rapture at seeing something like silver glittering at the end of his line! Almost breathless with anxiety, he drew it up to the mouth of the well, surprised at its great weight, and fearing every instant that his hook would slip from its hold, and his prize tumble again to the bottom. At length he landed it safe beside the well. It was a great silver porringer, of an ancient form, richly embossed, and with armorial bearings engraved on its side, similar to those over his mother's mantelpiece. The lid was fastened down by several twists of wire; Dolph loosened them with a trembling hand, and, on lifting the lid, behold! the vessel was filled with broad golden pieces, of a coinage which he had never seen before! It was evident he had lit on the place where Killian Vander Spiegel had concealed his treasure.

Fearful of being seen by some straggler, he cautiously retired, and buried his pot of money in a secret place. He now spread terrible stories about the haunted house, and deterred every one from aproaching it, while he made frequent visits to it in stormy days, when no one was stirring in the neighboring fields; though, to tell the truth, he did not care to venture there in the dark. For once in his life he was diligent and industrious, and followed up his new trade of angling with such perseverance and success, that in a little while he had hooked up wealth enough to make him, in those moderate days, a rich burgher for life.

It would be tedious to detail minutely the rest of this story. To tell how he gradually managed to bring his property into use without exciting surprise and inquiry—how he satisfied all scruples with regard to retaining the property, and at the same time gratified his own feelings, by marrying the pretty Marie Vander Heyden—and how he and Heer Antony had many a merry and roving expedition together.

I must not omit to say, however, that Dolph took his mother home to live with him, and cherished her in her old days. The good dame, too, had the satisfaction of no longer hearing her son made the theme of censure; on the contrary, he grew daily in public esteem; every body spoke well of him and his wines; and the lordliest burgomaster was never known to decline his invitation to dinner. Dolph often related, at his own table, the wicked pranks which had once been the abhorrence of the town; but they were now considered excellent jokes, and the gravest dignitary was fain to hold his sides when listening to them. No one was more struck with Dolph's increasing merit than his old master the doctor; and so forgiving was Dolph, that he absolutely employed the doctor as his family physician, only taking care that his prescriptions should be always thrown out of the window. His mother had often her junto of old cronies to take a snug cup of tea with her in her comfortable little parlor; and Peter de Groodt, as he sat by the fireside, with one of her grandchildren on his knee, would many a time congratulate her upon her son turning out so great a man; upon which the good old soul would wag her head with exultation, and exclaim, "Ah, neighbor, neighbor! did I not say that Dolph would one day or other hold up his head with the best of them?"

Thus did Dolph Heyliger go on, cheerily and prosperousiy, growing merrier as he grew older and wiser, and completely falsifying the old proverb about money got over the devil's back; for he made good use of the community. He was a great promoter of public institutions, such as beef-steak societies and catch-clubs. He presided at all public dinners, and was the first that introduced turtle from the West Indies. He improved the breed of race-horses and game-cocks, and was so great a patron of modest merit, that any one who could sing a good song, or tell a good story, was sure to find a place at his table.

He was a member, too, of the corporation, made several laws for the protection of game and oysters, and bequeathed to the board a large silver punch-bowl, made out of the identical porringer before mentioned, and which is in the possession of the corporation to this very day.

Finally, he died, in a florid old age, of an apoplexy at a corporation feast, and was buried with great honors in the yard of the little Dutch church in Garden-street, where his tombstone may still be seen, with a modest epitaph in Dutch, by his friend Mynheer Justus Benson, an ancient and excellent poet of the province.

The foregoing tale rests on better authority than most tales of the kind, as I have it at second hand from the lips of Dolph Heyliger himself. He never related it till towards the latter part of his life, and then in great confidence, (for he was very discreet,) to a few of his particular cronies at his own table, over a supernumerary bowl of punch; and, strange as the hobgoblin parts of the story may seem, there never was a single doubt expressed on the subject by any of his guests. It may not be amiss, before concluding, to observe that, in addition to his other accomplishments, Dolph Heyliger was noted for being the ablest drawer of the long-bow in the whole province.

By a Nervous Gentleman

# ADVENTURE OF
# THE GERMAN STUDENT

On a stormy night, in the tempestuous times of the French revolution, a young German was returning to his lodgings, at a late hour, across the old part of Paris. The lightning gleamed, and the loud claps of thunder rattled through the lofty narrow streets—but I should first tell you something about this young German.

Gottfried Wolfgang was a young man of good family. He had studied for some time at Göttingen, but being of a visionary and enthusiastic character, he had wandered into those wild and speculative doctrines which have so often bewildered German students. His secluded life, his intense application, and the singular nature of his studies, had an effect on both mind and body. His health was impaired; his imagination diseased. He had been indulging in fanciful speculations on spiritual essences, until, like Swedenborg, he had an ideal world of his own around him. He took up a notion, I do not know from what cause, that there was an evil influence hanging over him; an evil genius or spirit seeking to ensnare him and ensure his perdition. Such an idea working on his melancholy temperament, produced the most gloomy effects. He became haggard and desponding. His friends discovered the mental malady preying upon him, and determined that the best cure was a change of scene; he was sent, therefore, to finish his studies amidst the splendors and gayeties of Paris.

Wolfgang arrived at Paris at the breaking out of the revolution. The popular delirium at first caught his enthusiastic mind, and he was

captivated by the political and philosophical theories of the day: but
the scenes of blood which followed shocked his sensitive nature, dis-
gusted him with society and the world, and made him more than ever
a recluse. He shut himself up in a solitary apartment in the *Pays
Latin*, the quarter of students. There, in a gloomy street not far from
the monastic walls of the Sorbonne, he pursued his favorite speculations. Sometimes he spent hours together in the great libraries of Paris,
those catacombs of departed authors, rummaging among their hoards
of dusty and obsolete works in quest of food for his unhealthy appetite.
He was, in a manner, a literary ghoul, feeding in the charnel-house
of decayed literature.

Wolfgang, though solitary and recluse, was of an ardent temperament, but for a time it operated merely upon his imagination. He
was too shy and ignorant of the world to make any advances to the
fair, but he was a passionate admirer of female beauty, and in his
lonely chamber would often lose himself in reveries on forms and faces
which he had seen, and his fancy would deck out images of loveliness
far surpassing the reality.

While his mind was in this excited and sublimated state, a dream
produced an extraordinary effect upon him. It was of a female face of
transcendent beauty. So strong was the impression made, that he dreamt
of it again and again. It haunted his thoughts by day, his slumbers by
night; in fine, he became passionately enamoured of this shadow of a
dream. This lasted so long that it became one of those fixed ideas which
haunt the minds of melancholy men, and are at times mistaken for
madness.

Such was Gottfried Wolfgang, and such his situation at the time
I mentioned. He was returning home late one stormy night, through
some of the old gloomy streets of the *Marais*, the ancient part of Paris.
The loud claps of thunder rattled among the high houses of the narrow
streets. He came to the Place de Grève, the square where public
executions are performed. The lightning quivered about the pinnacles
of the ancient Hôtel de Ville, and shed flickering gleams over the open
space in front. As Wolfgang was crossing the square, he shrank back
with horror at finding himself close by the guillotine. It was the height
of the reign of terror, when this dreadful instrument of death stood
ever ready, and its scaffold was continually running with the blood of
the virtuous and the brave. It had that very day been actively employed

in the work of carnage, and there it stood in grim array, amidst a silent and sleeping city, waiting for fresh victims.

Wolfgang's heart sickened within him, and he was turning shuddering from the horrible engine, when he beheld a shadowy form cowering as it were at the foot of the steps which led up to the scaffold. A succession of vivid flashes of lightning revealed it more distinctly. It was a female figure, dressed in black. She was seated on one of the lower steps of the scaffold, leaning forward, her face hid in her lap; and her long dishevelled tresses hanging to the ground, streaming with the rain which fell in torrents. Wolfgang paused. There was something awful in this solitary monument of woe. The female had the appearance of being above the common order. He knew the times to be full of vicissitude, and that many a fair head, which had once been pillowed on down, now wandered houseless. Perhaps this was some poor mourner whom the dreadful axe had rendered desolate, and who sat here heart-broken on the strand of existence, from which all that was dear to her had been launched into eternity.

He approached, and addressed her in the accents of sympathy. She raised her head and gazed wildly at him. What was his astonishment at beholding, by the bright glare of the lightning, the very face which had haunted him in his dreams. It was pale and disconsolate, but ravishingly beautiful.

Trembling with violent and conflicting emotions, Wolfgang again accosted her. He spoke something of her being exposed at such an hour of the night, and to the fury of such a storm, and offered to conduct her to her friends. She pointed to the guillotine with a gesture of dreadful signification.

"I have no friend on earth!" said she.

"But you have a home," said Wolfgang.

"Yes—in the grave!"

The heart of the student melted at the words.

"If a stranger dare make an offer," said he, "without danger of being misunderstood, I would offer my humble dwelling as a shelter; myself as a devoted friend. I am friendless myself in Paris, and a stranger in the land; but if my life could be of service, it is at your disposal, and should be sacrificed before harm or indignity should come to you."

There was an honest earnestness in the young man's manner that had its effect. His foreign accent, too, was in his favor; it showed him not to be a hackneyed inhabitant of Paris. Indeed, there is an eloquence in true enthusiasm that is not to be doubted. The homeless stranger confided herself implicitly to the protection of the student.

He supported her faltering steps across the Pont Neuf, and by the place where the statue of Henry the Fourth had been overthrown by the populace. The storm had abated, and the thunder rumbled at a distance. All Paris was quiet; that great volcano of human passion slumbered for a while, to gather fresh strength for the next day's eruption. The student conducted his charge through the ancient streets of the *Pays Latin,* and by the dusky walls of the Sorbonne, to the great dingy hotel which he inhabited. The old portress who admitted them stared with surprise at the unusual sight of the melancholy Wolfgang with a female companion.

On entering his apartment, the student, for the first time, blushed at the scantiness and indifference of his dwelling. He had but one chamber—an old-fashioned saloon—heavily carved, and fantastically furnished with the remains of former magnificence, for it was one of those hotels in the quarter of the Luxembourg palace which had once belonged to nobility. It was lumbered with books and papers, and all the usual apparatus of a student, and his bed stood in a recess at one end.

When lights were brought, and Wolfgang had a better opportunity of contemplating the stranger, he was more than ever intoxicated by her beauty. Her face was pale, but of a dazzling fairness, set off by a profusion of raven hair that hung clustering about it. Her eyes were large and brilliant, with a singular expression approaching almost to wildness. As far as her black dress permitted her shape to be seen, it was of perfect symmetry. Her whole appearance was highly striking, though she was dressed in the simplest style. The only thing approaching to an ornament which she wore, was a broad black band round her neck, clasped by diamonds.

The perplexity now commenced with the student how to dispose of the helpless being thus thrown upon his protection. He thought of abandoning his chamber to her, and seeking shelter for himself elsewhere. Still he was so fascinated by her charms, there seemed to be such a spell upon his thoughts and senses, that he could not tear himself from her presence. Her manner, too, was singular and unaccountable. She spoke no more of the guillotine. Her grief had abated. The attentions of the student had first won her confidence, and then, apparently, her heart. She was evidently an enthusiast like himself, and enthusiasts soon understand each other.

In the infatuation of the moment, Wolfgang avowed his passion for her. He told her the story of his mysterious dream, and how she had possessed his heart before he had even seen her. She was strangely affected by his recital, and acknowledged to have felt an impulse towards him equally unaccountable. It was the time for wild theory and wild actions. Old prejudices and superstitions were done away; every thing was under the sway of the "Goddess of Reason." Among other rubbish of the old times, the forms and ceremonies of marriage began to be considered superfluous bonds for honorable minds. Social compacts were the vogue. Wolfgang was too much of a theorist not to be tainted by the liberal doctrines of the day.

"Why should we separate?" said he: "our hearts are united; in the eyes of reason and honor we are as one. What need is there of sordid forms to bind high souls together?"

The stranger listened with emotion: she had evidently received illumination at the same school.

"You have no home nor family," continued he; "let me be every thing to you, or rather let us be every thing to one another. If form is necessary, form shall be observed—there is my hand. I pledge myself to you for ever."

"For ever?" said the stranger, solemnly.

"For ever!" repeated Wolfgang.

The stranger clasped the hand extended to her: "Then I am yours," murmured she, and sank upon his bosom.

The next morning the student left his bride sleeping, and sallied forth at an early hour to seek more spacious apartments, suitable to the change in his situation. When he returned, he found the stranger lying with her head hanging over the bed, and one arm thrown over it. He spoke to her, but received no reply. He advanced to awaken her from her uneasy posture. On taking her hand, it was cold—there was no pulsation—her face was pallid and ghastly. —In a word, she was a corpse.

Horrified and frantic, he alarmed the house. A scene of confusion ensued. The police was summoned. As the officer of police entered the room, he started back on beholding the corpse.

"Great heaven!" cried he, "how did this woman come here?"

"Do you know any thing about her?" said Wolfgang eagerly.

"Do I?" exclaimed the officer: "she was guillotined yesterday."

He stepped forward; undid the black collar round the neck of the corpse, and the head rolled on the floor!

The student burst into a frenzy. "The fiend! the fiend has gained possession of me!" shrieked he: "I am lost for ever."

They tried to soothe him, but in vain. He was possessed with the frightful belief that an evil spirit had reanimated the dead body to ensnare him. He went distracted, and died in a mad-house.

Here the old gentleman with the haunted head finished his narrative.

"And is this really a fact?" said the inquisitive gentleman.

"A fact not to be doubted," replied the other. "I had it from the best authority. The student told it me himself. I saw him in a mad-house in Paris."

# THE MONEY-DIGGERS

## Found Among the Papers
## of the Late Diedrich Knickerbocker

> "Now I remember those old women's words,
> Who in my youth would tell me winter's tales:
> And speak of sprites and ghosts that glide ny night
> About the place where treasure hath been hid."
>
> MARLOW'S *Jew of Malta*

## HELL-GATE

About six miles from the renowned city of the Manhattoes, in that Sound or arm of the sea which passes between the main-land and Nassau, or Long Island, there is a narrow strait, where the current is violently compressed between shouldering promontories, and horribly perplexed by rocks and shoals. Being, at the best of times, a very violent, impetuous current, it takes these impediments in mighty dudgeon; boiling in whirlpools; brawling and fretting in ripples; raging and roaring in rapids and breakers; and, in short, indulging in all kinds of wrong-headed paroxysms. At such times, woe to any unlucky vessel that ventures within its clutches.

This termagant humor, however, prevails only at certain times of tide. At low water, for instance, it is as pacific a stream as you would wish to see; but as the tide rises, it begins to fret; at half-tide it roars with might and main, like a bull bellowing for more drink; but when the tide is full, it relapses into quiet, and, for a time, sleeps as soundly as an alderman after dinner. In fact, it may be compared to a quar-

---

EDITOR'S NOTE: *The Money-Diggers* is reprinted here in its entirety.

relsome toper, who is a peaceable fellow enough when he has no liquor at all, or when he has a skinfull; but who, when half-seas over, plays the very devil.

This mighty, blustering, bullying, hard-drinking little strait was a place of great danger and perplexity to the Dutch navigators of ancient days; hectoring their tub-built barks in a most unruly style; whirling them about in a manner to make any but a Dutchman giddy, and not unfrequently stranding them upon rocks and reefs, as it did the famous squadron of Oloffe the Dreamer, when seeking a place to found the city of the Manhattoes. Whereupon, out of sheer spleen, they denominated it *Helle-gat*, and solemnly gave it over to the devil. This appellation has since been aptly rendered into English by the name of Hell-gate, and into nonsense by the name of *Hurl-gate*, according to certain foreign intruders, who neither understood Dutch nor English— may St. Nicholas confound them!

This strait of Hell-gate was a place of great awe and perilous enterprise to me in my boyhood; having been much of a navigator on those small seas, and having more than once run the risk of shipwreck and drowning in the course of certain holiday voyages, to which, in common name, and partly from various strange circumstances connected with it, this place had far more terrors in the eyes of my truant companions and myself than had Scylla and Charybdis for the navigators of yore.

In the midst of this strait, and hard by a group of rocks called the Hen and Chickens, there lay the wreck of a vessel which had been entangled in the whirlpools and stranded during a storm. There was a wild story told to us of this being the wreck of a pirate, and some tale of bloody murder which I cannot now recollect, but which made us regard with great awe, and keep far from it in our cruisings, Indeed, the desolate look of the forlorn hulk, and the fearful place where it lay rotting, were enough to awaken strange notions. A row of timber-heads, blackened by time, just peered above the surface at high water; but at timbers, partly stripped of their planks, and dripping with sea-weeds, looked like the huge skeleton of some sea-monster. There was also the stump of a mast, with a few ropes and blocks swinging about and whistling in the wind, while the sea-gull wheeled and screamed around the melancholy carcass. I have a faint recollection of some hobgoblin tale of sailors' ghosts being seen about this wreck at night, with bare skulls, and blue lights in their sockets instead of eyes, but I have forgotten all the particulars.

In fact, the whole of this neighborhood was like the straits of Pelorus of yore, a region of fable and romance to me. From the strait to the Manhattoes, the borders of the Sound are greatly diversified, being broken and indented by rocky nooks overhung with trees, which give them a wild and romantic look. In the time of my boyhood, they abounded with traditions about pirates, ghosts, smugglers, and buried money; which had a wonderful effect upon the young minds of my companions and myself.

As I grew to more mature years, I made diligent research after the truth of these strange traditions; for I have always been a curious investigator of the valuable but obscure branches of the history of my native province. I found infinite difficulty, however, in arriving at any precise information. In seeking to dig up one fact, it is incredible the number of fables that I unearthed. I will say nothing of the devil's stepping-stones, by which the arch-fiend made his retreat from Connecticut to Long Island, across the Sound; seeing the subject is likely to be learnedly treated by a worthy friend and contemporary historian, whom I have furnished with particulars thereof.* Neither will I say any thing of the black man in a three-cornered hat, seated in the stern of a jolly-boat, who used to be seen about Hell-gate in stormy weather, and who went by the name of the pirate's *spuke*, (i.e., pirate's ghost,) and whom, it is said, old Governor Stuyvesant once shot with a silver bullet; because I never could meet with any person of stanch credibility who professed to have seen this spectrum, unless it were the widow of Manus Conklen, the blacksmith, of Frogsneck; but then, poor woman, she was a little purblind, and might have been mistaken; though they say she saw farther than other folks in the dark.

All this, however, was but little satisfactory in regard to the tales of pirates and their buried money, about which I was most curious; and the following is all that I could, for a long time, collect, that had any thing like an air of authenticity.

---

*For a very interesting and authentic account of the devil and his stepping-stones, see the valuable Memoir read before the New-York Historical Society, since the death of Mr. Knickerbocker, by his friend, an eminent jurist of the place.

# KIDD THE PIRATE

In old times, just after the territory of the New-Netherlands had been wrested from the hands of their High Mightinesses, the Lords States-General of Holland, by King Charles the Second, and while it was as yet in an unquiet state, the province was a great resort of random adventurers, loose livers, and all that class of hap-hazard fellows who live by their wits, and dislike the old-fashioned restraint of law and gospel. Among these, the foremost were the buccaneers. These were rovers of the deep, who, perhaps, in time of war had been educated in those schools of piracy, the privateers; but having once tasted the sweets of plunder, had ever retained a hankering after it. There is but a slight step from the privateersman to the pirate; both fight for the love of plunder; only that the latter is the bravest, as he dares both the enemy and the gallows.

But in whatever school they had been taught, the buccaneers that kept about the English colonies were daring fellows, and made sad work in times of peace among the Spanish settlements and Spanish merchantmen. The easy access to the harbor of the Manhattoes, the number of hiding-places about its waters, and the laxity of its scarcely-organized government, made it a great rendezvous of the pirates; where they might dispose of their booty, and concert new depredations. As they brought home with them wealthy lading of all kinds, the luxuries of the tropics, and the sumptuous spoils of the Spanish provinces, and disposed of them with the proverbial carelessness of freebooters, they were welcome visitors to the thrifty traders of the Manhattoes. Crews of these desperadoes, therefore, the runagates of every country and every clime, might be seen swaggering in open day about the streets of the little burgh, elbowing its quiet mynheers; trafficking away their rich outlandish plunder at half or quarter price to the wary merchant; and then squandering their prize-money in taverns, drinking, gambling, singing, swearing, shouting, and astounding the neighborhood with midnight brawl and ruffian revelry.

At length these excesses rose to such a height as to become a scandal to the provinces, and to call loudly for the interposition of government. Measures were accordingly taken to put a stop to the widely-extended evil, and to ferret this vermin brood out of the colonies.

Among the agents employed to execute this purpose was the no-torious Captain Kidd. He had long been an equivocal character; one of those nondescript animals of the ocean that are neither fish, flesh, nor fowl. He was somewhat of a trader, something more of a smuggler, with a considerable dash of the picaroon. He had traded for many years among the pirates, in a little rakish, mosquito-built vessel, that could run into all kinds of waters. He knew all their haunts and lurking-places; was always hooking about on mysterious voyages, and was as busy as a Mother Cary's chicken in a storm.

This nondescript personage was pitched upon by government as the very man to hunt the pirates by sea, upon the good old maxim of "setting a rogue to catch a rogue;" or as otters are sometimes used to catch their cousins-german, the fish.

Kidd accordingly sailed for New-York, in 1695, in a gallant vessel called the Adventure Galley, well armed and duly commissioned. On arriving at his old haunts, however, he shipped his crew on new terms; enlisted a number of his old comrades, lads of the knife and the pistol; and then set sail for the East. Instead of cruising against pirates, he turned pirate himself; steered to the Madeiras, to Bonavista, and Mad-agascar, and cruised about the entrance of the Red Sea. Here, among other maritime robberies, he captured a rich Quedah merchantman, manned by Moors, though commanded by an Englishman. Kidd would fain have passed this off for a worthy exploit, as being a kind of crusade against the infidels; but government had long since lost all relish for such Christian triumphs.

After roaming the seas, trafficking his prizes, and changing from ship to ship, Kidd had the hardihood to return to Boston, laden with booty, with a crew of swaggering companions at his heels.

Times, however, were changed. The buccaneers could no longer show a whisker in the colonies with impunity. The new governor, Lord Bellamont, had signalized himself by his zeal in extirpating these offenders; and was doubly exasperated against Kidd, having been in-strumental in appointing him to the trust which he had betrayed. No sooner, therefore, did he show himself in Boston, than the alarm was given of his reappearance, and measures were taken to arrest this cutpurse of the ocean. The daring character which Kidd had acquired, however, and the desperate fellows who followed like bull-dogs at his heels, caused a little delay in his arrest. He took advantage of this, it is said, to bury the greater part of his treasures, and then carried a high head about the streets of Boston. He even attempted to defend himself when arrested, but was secured and thrown into prison, with his followers. Such was the formidable character of this pirate, and his crew, that it was thought advisable to despatch a frigate to bring them to England. Great exertions were made to screen him from justice, but in vain; he and his comrades were tried, condemned, and hanged at Execution Dock in London. Kidd died hard, for the rope with which he was first tied up broke with his weight, and he tumbled to the ground. He was tied up a second time, and more effectually; hence came, doubtless, the story of Kidd's having a charmed life, and that he had to be twice hanged.

Such is the main outline of Kidd's history; but it has given birth to an innumerable progeny of traditions. The report of his having buried great treasures of gold and jewels before his arrest, set the brains of all the good people along the coast in a ferment. There were rumors on rumors of great sums of money found here and there, sometimes in one part of the country, sometimes in another; of coins with Moorish inscriptions, doubtless the spoils of his eastern prizes, but which the common people looked upon with superstitious awe, regarding the Moorish letters as diabolical or magical characters.

Some reported the treasure to have been buried in solitary, unsettled places, about Plymouth and Cape Cod; but by degrees various other parts, not only on the eastern coast, but along the shores of the Sound, and even of Manhattan and Long Island, were gilded by these rumors. In fact, the rigorous measures of Lord Bellamont spread sudden consternation among the buccaneers in every part of the provinces: they secreted their money and jewels in lonely out-of-the-way places, about the wild shores of the rivers and sea-coast, and dispersed themselves over the face of the country. The hand of justice prevented many of them from ever returning to regain their buried treasures, which remained, and remain probably to this day, objects of enterprise for the money-digger.

This is the cause of those frequent reports of trees and rocks bearing mysterious marks, supposed to indicate the spots where treasures lay hidden; and many have been the ransackings after the pirate's booty. In all the stories which once abounded of these enterprises, the devil played a conspicuous part. Either he was conciliated by ceremonies and invocations, or some solemn compact was made with him. Still he was ever prone to play the money-diggers some slippery trick. Some would dig so far as to come to an iron chest, when some baffling circumstance was sure to take place. Either the earth would fall in and fill up the pit, or some direful noise or apparition would frighten the party from the place: sometimes the devil himself would appear, and bear off the prize when within their very grasp; and if they revisited the place the next day, not a trace would be found of their labors of the preceding night.

All these rumors, however, were extremely vague, and for a long time tantalized, without gratifying, my curiosity. There is nothing in this world so hard to get at as truth, and there is nothing in this world but truth that I care for. I sought among all my favorite sources of authentic information, the oldest inhabitants, and particularly the old Dutch wives of the province;—but though I flatter myself that I am better versed than most men in the curious history of my native province, yet for a long time my inquiries were unattended with any substantial result.

At length it happened that, one calm day in the latter part of summer, I was relaxing myself from the toils of severe study, by a day's amusement in fishing in those waters which had been the favorite resort of my boyhood. I was in company with several worthy burghers of my native city, among whom were more than one illustrious member of the corporation, whose names, did I dare to mention them, would do honor to my humble page. Our sport was indifferent. The fish did not bite freely, and we frequently changed our fishing-ground without bettering our luck. We were at length anchored close under a ledge of rocky coast on the eastern side of the island of Manhatta. It was a still, warm day. The stream whirled and dimpled by us, without a wave or even a ripple; and every thing was so calm and quiet, that it was almost startling when the kingfisher would pitch himself from the branch of some high tree, and after suspending himself for a moment in the air to take his aim, would souse into the smooth water after his prey. While we were lolling in our boat, half drowsy with the warm stillness of the day, and the dulness of our sport, one of our party, a worthy alderman, was overtaken by a slumber, and, as he dozed, suffered the sinker of his drop-line to lie upon the bottom of the river. On waking, he found he had caught something of importance from the weight. On drawing it to the surface, we were much surprised to find it a long pistol of very curious and outlandish fashion, which, from its rusted condition, and its stock being wormeaten and covered with barnacles, appeared to have lain a long time under water. The unexpected appearance of this document of warfare, occasioned much speculation among my pacific companions. One supposed it to have fallen there during the revolutionary war; another, from the peculiarity of its fashion, attributed it to the voyagers in the earliest days of the settlement; perchance to the renowned Adrian Block, who explored the Sound, and discovered Block Island, since so noted for its cheese. But a third, after regarding it for some time, pronounced it to be of veritable Spanish workmanship.

"I'll warrant," said he, "if this pistol could talk, it would tell strange stories of hard fights among the Spanish Dons. I've no doubt but it is a relic of the buccaneers of old times—who knows but it belonged to Kidd himself?"

"Ah! that Kidd was a resolute fellow," cried an old ironfaced Cape Cod whaler.—"There's a fine old song about him all to the tune of—

> My name is Captain Kidd,
> As I sailed, as I sailed.—

And then it tells about how he gained the devil's good graces by burying the Bible:

> I had the Bible in my hand,
> As I sailed, as I sailed,
> And I buried it in the sand,
> As I sailed.—

"Odsfish, if I thought this pistol had belonged to Kidd, I should set great store by it, for curiosity's sake. By the way, I recollect a story about a fellow who once dug up Kidd's buried money, which was written by a neighbor of mine, and which I learnt by heart. As the fish don't bite just now, I'll tell it to you, by way of passing away the time."—And so saying, he gave us the following narration.

# THE DEVIL & TOM WALKER

A few miles from Boston in Massachusetts, there is a deep inlet, winding several miles into the interior of the country from Charles Bay, and terminating in a thickly-wooded swamp or morass. On one side of this inlet is a beautiful dark grove; on the opposite side the land rises abruptly from the water's edge into a high ridge, on which grow a few scattered oaks of great age and immense size. Under one of these gigantic trees, according to old stories, there was a great amount of treasure buried by Kidd the pirate. The inlet allowed a facility to bring the money in a boat secretly and at night to the very foot of the hill; the elevation of the place permitted a good look-out to be kept that no one was at hand; while the remarkable trees formed good landmarks by which the place might easily be found again. The old stories add, moreover, that the devil presided at the hiding of the money, and took it under his guardianship; but this, it is well known, he always does with buried treasure, particularly when it has been ill-gotten. Be that as it may, Kidd never returned to recover his wealth; being shortly after seized at Boston, sent out to England, and then hanged for a pirate.

About the year 1727, just at the time that earthquakes were pre-valent in New-England, and shook many tall sinners down upon their knees, there lived near this place a meagre, miserly fellow, of the name of Tom Walker. He had a wife as miserly as himself: they were so miserly that they even conspired to cheat each other. Whatever the woman could lay hands on, she hid away; a hen could not cackle but she was on the alert to secure the new-laid egg. Her husband was continually prying about to detect her secret hoards, and many and fierce were the conflicts that took place about what ought to have been common property. They lived in a forlorn-looking house that stood alone, and had an air of starvation. A few straggling savin-trees, emblems of sterility, grew near it; no smoke ever curled from its chimney; no traveller stopped at its door. A miserable horse, whose ribs were as articulate as the bars of a gridiron, stalked about a field, where a thin carpet of moss, scarcely covering the ragged beds of puddingstone, tantalized and balked his hunger; and sometimes he would lean his head over the fence, look piteously at the passer-by, and seem to petition deliverance from this land of famine.

The house and its inmates had altogether a bad name. Tom's wife was a tall termagant, fierce of temper, loud of tongue, and strong of arm. Her voice was often heard in wordy warfare with her husband; and his face sometimes showed signs that their conflicts were not confined to words. No one ventured, however, to interfere between them. The lonely wayfarer shrunk within himself at the horrid clamor and clapper-clawing; eyed the den of discord askance; and hurried on his way, rejoicing, if a bachelor, in his celibacy.

One day that Tom Walker had been to a distant part of the neighborhood, he took what he considered a short cut homeward, through the swamp. Like most short cuts, it was an ill-chosen route. The swamp was thickly grown with great gloomy pines and hemlocks, some of them ninety feet high, which made it dark at noonday, and a retreat for all the owls of the neighborhood. It was full of pits and quagmires, partly covered with weeds and mosses, where the green surface often betrayed the traveller into a gulf of black, smothering mud: there were also dark and stagnant pools, the abodes of the tadpole, the bull-frog, and the water-snake; where the trunks of pines and hemlocks lay half-drowned, half-rotting, looking like alligators sleeping in the mire.

Tom had long been picking his way cautiously through this treacherous forest; stepping from tuft to tuft of rushes and roots, which afforded precarious footholds among deep sloughs; or pacing carefully, like a cat, along the prostrate trunks of trees; startled now and then by the sudden screaming of the bittern, or the quacking of a wild duck rising on the wing from some solitary pool. At length he arrived at a piece of firm ground, which ran out like a peninsula into the deep bosom of the swamp. It had been one of the strong-holds of the Indians during their wars with the first colonists. Here they had thrown up a kind of fort, which they had looked upon as almost impregnable, and had used as a place of refuge for their squaws and children. Nothing remained of the old Indian fort but a few embankments, gradually sinking to the level of the surrounding earth, and already overgrown in part by oaks and other forest trees, the foliage of which formed a contrast to the dark pines and hemlocks of the swamp.

It was late in the dusk of evening when Tom Walker reached the old fort, and he paused there awhile to rest himself. Any one but he would have felt unwilling to linger in this lonely, melancholy place, for the common people had a bad opinion of it, from the stories handed down from the time of the Indian wars; when it was asserted that the savages held incantations here, and made sacrifices to the evil spirit. Tom Walker, however, was not a man to be troubled with any fears of the kind. He reposed himself for some time on the trunk of a fallen hemlock, listening to the boding cry of the tree-toad, and delving with his walking-staff into a mound of black mould at his feet. As he turned up the soil unconsciously, his staff struck against something hard. He raked it out of the vegetable mould, and lo! a cloven skull, with an Indian tomahawk buried deep in it, lay before him. The rust on the weapon showed the time that had elapsed since this death-blow had been given. It was a dreary memento of the fierce struggle that had taken place in this last foothold of the Indian warriors.

"Humph!" said Tom Walker, as he gave it a kick to shake the dirt from it.

"Let that skull alone!" said a gruff voice. Tom lifted up his eyes, and beheld a great black man seated directly opposite him on the stump of a tree. He was exceedingly surprised, having neither heard nor seen any one approach; and he was still more perplexed on observing, as well as the gathering gloom would permit, that the stranger was neither negro nor Indian. It is true he was dressed in a rude half Indian garb, and had a red belt or sash swathed round his body; but his face was neither black nor copper-color, but swarthy and dingy, and begrimed with soot, as if he had been accustomed to toil among fires and forges. He had a shock of coarse black hair, that stood out from his head in all directions, and bore an axe on his shoulder.

He scowled for a moment at Tom with a pair of great red eyes.

"What are you doing on my grounds?" said the black man, with a hoarse growling voice.

"Your grounds!" said Tom with a sneer, "no more your grounds than mine; they belong to Deacon Peabody."

"Deacon Peabody be d—d," said the stranger, "as I flatter myself he will be, if he does not look more to his own sins and less to those of his neighbors. Look yonder, and see how Deacon Peabody is faring."

Tom looked in the direction that the stranger pointed, and beheld one of the great trees, fair and flourishing without, but rotten at the core, and saw that it had been nearly hewn through, so that the first high wind was likely to blow it down. On the bark of the tree was scored the name of Deacon Peabody, an eminent man, who had waxed wealthy by driving shrewd bargains with the Indians. He now looked round, and found most of the tall trees marked with the name of some great man of the colony, and all more or less scored by the axe. The one on which he had been seated, and which had evidently just been hewn down, bore the name of Crowninshield; and he recollected a mighty rich man of that name, who made a vulgar display of wealth, which it was whispered he had acquired by buccaneering.

"He's just ready for burning!" said the black man, with a growl of triumph. You see I am likely to have a good stock of firewood for winter."

But what right have you," said Tom, "to cut down Deacon Peabody's timber?"

"The right of a prior claim," said the other. "This woodland belonged to me long before one of your white-faced race put foot upon the soil."

"And pray, who are you, if I may be so bold?" said Tom.

"Oh, I go by various names. I am the wild huntsman in some countries; the black miner in others. In this neighborhood I am known by the name of the black woodsman. I am he to whom the red men consecrated this spot, and in honor of whom they now and then roasted a white man, by way of sweet-smelling sacrifice. Since the red men have been exterminated by you white savages, I amuse myself by presiding at the persecutions of Quakers and Anabaptists; I am the great patron and prompter of slave-dealers, and the grand-master of the Salem witches."

"The upshot of all which is, that, if I mistake not," said Tom, sturdily, "you are he commonly called Old Scratch."

"The same, at your service!" replied the black man, with a half civil nod.

Such was the opening of this interview, according to the old story; though it has almost too familiar an air to be credited. One would think that to meet with such a singular personage, in this wild, lonely place, would have shaken any man's nerves; but Tom was a hard-minded fellow, not easily daunted, and he had lived so long with a termagant wife, that he did not even fear the devil.

It is said that after this commencement they had a long and earnest conversation together, as Tom returned homeward. The black man told him of great sums of money buried by Kidd the pirate, under the oak-trees on the high ridge, not far from the morass. All these were under his command, and protected by his power, so that none could find them but such as propitiated his favor. These he offered to place within Tom Walker's reach, having conceived an especial kindness for him; but they were to be had only on certain conditions. What these conditions were may easily be surmised, though Tom never disclosed them publicly. They must have been very hard, for he required time to think of them, and he was not a man to stick at trifles where money was in view. When they had reached the edge of the swamp, the stranger paused—"What proof have I that all you have been telling me is true?" said Tom. "There's my signature," said the black man, pressing his finger on Tom's forehead. So saying, he turned off among the thickets of the swamp, and seemed, as Tom said, to go down, down, down, into the earth, until nothing but his head and shoulders could be seen, *and so on,* until he totally disappeared.

When Tom reached home, he found the black print of a finger burnt, as it were, into his forehead, which nothing could obliterate.

The first news his wife had to tell him was the sudden death of Absalom Crowninshield, the rich buccaneer. It was announced in the papers with the usual flourish, that "A great man had fallen in Israel."

Tom recollected the tree which his black friend had just hewn down, and which was ready for burning. "Let the freebooter roast," said Tom "who cares!" He now felt convinced that all he had heard and seen was no illusion.

He was not prone to let his wife into his confidence; but as this was an uneasy secret, he willingly shared it with her. All her avarice was awakened at the mention of hidden gold, and she urged her husband to comply with the black man's terms, and secure what would make them wealthy for life. However Tom might have felt disposed to sell himself to the Devil, he was determined not to do so to oblige his wife; so he flatly refused, out of the mere spirit of contradiction. Many and bitter were the quarrels they had on the subject; but the more she talked, the more resolute was Tom not to be damned to please her.

At length she determined to drive the bargain on her own account, and if she succeeded, to keep all the gain to herself. Being of the same

fearless temper as her husband, she set off for the old Indian fort
towards the close of a summer's day. She was many hours absent.
When she came back, she was reserved and sullen in her replies. She
spoke something of a black man, whom she had met about twilight,
hewing at the root of a tall tree. He was sulky, however, and would
not come to terms: she was to go again with a propitiatory offering,
but what it was she forbore to say.

The next evening she set off again for the swamp, with her apron
heavily laden. Tom waited and waited for her, but in vain; midnight
came, but she did not make her appearance: morning, noon, night
returned, but still she did not come. Tom now grew uneasy for her
safety, especially as he found she had carried off in her apron the silver
teapot and spoons, and every portable article of value. Another night
elapsed, and other morning came; but no wife. In a word, she was
never heard of more.

What was her real fate nobody knows, in consequence of so many
pretending to know. It is one of those facts which have become confounded by a variety of historians. Some asserted that she lost her way
among the tangled mazes of the swamp, and sank into some pit or
slough; others, more uncharitable, hinted that she had eloped with the
household booty, and made off to some other province; while others
surmised that the tempter had decoyed her into a dismal quagmire,
on the top of which her hat was found lying. In confirmation of this,
it was said a great black man, with an axe on his shoulder, was seen
late that very evening coming out of the swamp, carrying a bundle
tied in a check apron, with an air of surly triumph.

The most current and probable story, however, observes, that Tom
Walker grew so anxious about the fate of his wife and his property,
that he set out at length to seek them both at the Indian fort. During
a long summer's afternoon he searched about the gloomy place, but
no wife was to be seen. He called her name repeatedly, but she was
nowhere to be heard. The bittern alone responded to his voice, as he
flew screaming by; or the bull-frog croaked dolefully from a neighboring pool. At length, it is said, just in the brown hour of twilight,
when the owls began to hoot, and the bats to flit about, his attention
was attracted by the clamor of carrion crows hovering about a cypress-
tree. He looked up, and beheld a bundle tied in a check apron, and
hanging in the branches of the tree, with a great vulture perched hard

by, as if keeping watch upon it. He leaped with joy; for he recognized his wife's apron, and supposed it to contain the household valuables.

"Let us get hold of the property," said he, consolingly to himself, "and we will endeavor to do without the woman."

As he scrambled up the tree, the vulture spread its wide wings, and sailed off screaming into the deep shadows of the forest. Tom seized the checked apron, but woeful sight! found nothing but a heart and liver tied up in it!

Such, according to this most authentic old story, was all that was to be found of Tom's wife. She had probably attempted to deal with the black man as she had been accustomed to deal with her husband; but though a female scold is generally considered a match for the devil, yet in this instance she appears to have had the worst of it. She must have died game, however; for it is said Tom noticed many prints of cloven feet deeply stamped about the tree, and found handfuls of hair, that looked as if they had been plucked from the coarse black shock of the woodman. Tom knew his wife's prowess by experience. He shrugged his shoulders, as he looked at the signs of a fierce clapper-clawing. "Egad," said he to himself, "Old Scratch must have had a tough time of it!"

Tom consoled himself for the loss of his property, with the loss of his wife, for he was a man of fortitude. He even felt something like gratitude towards the black woodman, who, he considered, had done him a kindness. He sought, therefore, to cultivate a further acquaintance with him, but for some time without success; the old black-legs played shy, for whatever people may think, he is not always to be had for calling for: he knows how to play his cards when pretty sure of his game.

At length, it is said, when delay had whetted Tom's eagerness to the quick, and prepared him to agree to any thing rather than not gain the promised treasure, he met the black man one evening in his usual woodman's dress, with his axe on his shoulder, sauntering along the swamp, and humming a tune. He affected to receive Tom's advances with great indifference, made brief replies, and went on humming his tune.

By degrees, however, Tom brought him to business, and they began to haggle about the terms on which the former was to have the pirate's treasure. There was one condition which need not be mentioned, being generally understood in all cases where the devil grants favors; but there were others about which, though of less importance, he was inflexibly obstinate. He insisted that the money found through his means should be employed in his service. He proposed, therefore, that Tom should employ it in the black traffick; that is to say, that he should fit out a slave-ship. This, however, Tom resolutely refused: he was bad enough in all conscience; but the devil himself could not tempt him to turn slave-trader.

Finding Tom so squeamish on this point, he did not insist upon it, but proposed, instead, that he should turn usurer; the devil being extremely anxious for the increase of usurers, looking upon them as his peculiar people.

To this no objections were made, for it was just to Tom's taste.

"You shall open a broker's shop in Boston next month," said the black man.

"I'll do it to-morrow, if you wish," said Tom Walker.

"You shall lend money at two per cent. a month."

"Egad, I'll charge four!" replied Tom Walker.

"You shall extort bonds, foreclose mortgages, drive the merchants to bankruptcy——"

"I'll drive them to the d——l," cried Tom Walker.

"You are the usurer for my money!" said the black-legs with delight. "When will you want the rhino?"

"This very night."

"Done!" said the devil.

"Done!" said Tom Walker.—So they shook hands and struck a bargain.

A few days' time saw Tom Walker seated behind his desk in a counting-house in Boston.

His reputation for a ready-moneyed man, who would lend money out for a good consideration, soon spread abroad. Everybody remembers the time of Governor Belcher, when money was particularly scarce. It was a time of paper credit. The country had been deluged with government bills; the famous Land Bank had been established; there had been a rage for speculating; the people had run mad with schemes for new settlements; for building cities in the wilderness; land jobbers went about with maps of grants, and townships, and Eldorados, lying nobody knew where, but which everybody was ready to purchase.

In a word, the great speculating fever which breaks out every now and then in the country, had raged to an alarming degree, and every body was dreaming of making sudden fortunes from nothing. As usual the fever had subsided; the dream had gone off, and the imaginary fortunes with it; the patients were left in doleful plight, and the whole country resounded with the consequent cry of "hard times."

At this propitious time of public distress did Tom Walker set up as usurer in Boston. His door was soon thronged by customers. The needy and adventurous; the gambling speculator; the dreaming land-jobber; the thriftless tradesman; the merchant with cracked credit; in short, every one driven to raise money by desperate means and desperate sacrifices, hurried to Tom Walker.

Thus Tom was the universal friend of the needy, and acted like a "friend in need;" that is to say, he always exacted good pay and good security. In proportion to the distress of the applicant was the hardness of his terms. He accumulated bonds and mortgages; gradually squeezed his customers closer and closer: and sent them at length, dry as a sponge, from his door.

In this way he made money hand over hand; became a rich and mighty man, and exalted his cocked hat upon 'Change. He built himself, as usual, a vast house, out of ostentation; but left the greater part of it unfinished and unfurnished, out of parsimony. He even set up a carriage in the fulness of his vainglory though he nearly starved the horses which drew it; and as the ungreased wheels groaned and screeched on the axle-trees, you would have thought you heard the souls of the poor debtors he was squeezing.

As Tom waxed old, however, he grew thoughtful. Having secured the good things of this world, he began to feel anxious about those of the next. He thought with regret on the bargain he had made with his black friend, and set his wits to work to cheat him out of the conditions. He became, therefore, all of a sudden, a violent church-goer. He prayed loudly and strenuously, as if heaven were to be taken by force of lungs. Indeed, one might always tell when he had sinned most during the week, by the clamor of his Sunday devotion. The quiet Christians who had been modestly and steadfastly travelling Zion-ward, were struck with self-reproach at seeing themselves so suddenly outstripped in their career by this new-made convert. Tom was as rigid in religious as in money matters; he was a stern supervisor and

censurer of his neighbors, and seemed to think every sin entered up to their account became a credit on his own side of the page. He even talked of the expediency of reviving the persecution of Quakers and Anabaptists. In a word, Tom's zeal became as notorious as his riches.

Still, in spite of all this strenuous attention to forms, Tom had a lurking dread that the devil, after all, would have his due. That he might not be taken unawares, therefore, it is said he always carried a small Bible in his coat-pocket. He had also a great folio Bible on his counting-house desk, and would frequently be found reading it when people called on business; on such occasions he would lay his green spectacles in the book, to mark the place, while he turned round to drive some usurious bargain.

Some say that Tom grew a little crack-brained in his old days, and that fancying his end approaching, he had his horse new shod, saddled and bridled, and buried with his feet uppermost; because he supposed that at the last day the world would be turned upside down; in which case he should find his horse standing ready for mounting, and he was determined at the worst to give his old friend a run for it. This, however, is probably a mere old wives' fable. If he really did take such a precaution, it was totally superfluous; at least so says the authentic old legend which closes his story in the following manner.

One hot summer afternoon in the dog-days, just as a terrible black thundergust was coming up, Tom sat in his counting-house in his white linen cap and India silk morning-gown. He was on the point of foreclosing a mortgage, by which he would complete the ruin of an unlucky land speculator for whom he had professed the greatest friendship. The poor land-jobber begged him to grant a few months' indulgence. Tom had grown testy and irritated, and refused another day.

"My family will be ruined and brought upon the parish," said the land-jobber. "Charity begins at home," replied Tom; "I must take care of myself in these hard times."

"You have made so much money out of me," said the speculator.

Tom lost his patience and his piety—"The devil take me," said he, "if I have made a farthing!"

Just then there were three loud knocks at the street door. He stepped out to see who was there. A black man was holding a black horse, which neighed and stamped with impatience.

"Tom, you're come for," said the black fellow, gruffly. Tom shrank back but too late. He had left his little Bible at the bottom of his coat-pocket, and his big Bible on the desk buried under the mortgage he was about to foreclose: never was sinner taken more unawares. The black man whisked him like a child into the saddle, gave the horse the lash, and away he galloped, with Tom on his back, in the midst of the thunderstorm. The clerks stuck their pens behind their ears, and stared after him from the windows. Away went Tom Walker, dashing down the streets; his white cap bobbing up and down, his morning-gown fluttering in the wind, and his steed striking fire out of the pavement at every bound. When the clerks turned to look for the black man he had disappeared.

Tom Walker never returned to foreclose the mortgage. A countryman who lived on the border of the swamp, reported that in the height of the thundergust he had heard a great clattering of hoofs and a howling along the road, and running to the window caught sight of a figure, such as I have described, on a horse that galloped like mad across the fields, over the hills, and down into the black hemlock swamp towards the old Indian fort; and that shortly after a thunderbolt falling in that direction seemed to set the whole forest in a blaze.

The good people of Boston shook their heads and shrugged their shoulders, but had been so much accustomed to witches and goblins, and tricks of the devil, in all kinds of shapes, from the first settlement of the colony, that they were not so much horror-struck as might have been expected. Trustees were appointed to take charge of Tom's effects. There was nothing, however, to administer upon. On searching his coffers all his bonds and mortgages were found reduced to cinders. In place of gold and silver his iron chest was filled with chips and shavings; two skeletons lay in his stable instead of his half-starved horses, and the very next day his great house took fire and was burnt to the ground.

Such was the end of Tom Walker and his ill-gotten wealth. Let all griping money-brokers lay this story to heart. The truth of it is not to be doubted. The very hole under the oak-trees, whence he dug Kidd's money, is to be seen to this day; and the neighboring swamp and old Indian fort are often haunted in stormy nights by a figure on horseback, in morning-gown and white cap, which is doubtless the troubled spirit of the usurer. In fact, the story has resolved itself into a proverb, and is the origin of that popular saying, so prevalent throughout New England, of "The Devil and Tom Walker."

---

Such, as nearly as I can recollect, was the purport of the tale told by the Cape Cod whaler. There were divers trivial particulars which I have omitted, and which whiled away the morning very pleasantly, until the time of tide favorable to fishing being passed, it was proposed to land, and refresh ourselves under the trees, till the noontide heat should have abated.

We accordingly landed on a delectable part of the island of Mannahata, in that shady and embowered tract formerly under the dominion of the ancient family of the Hardenbrooks. It was a spot well known to me in the course of the aquatic expeditions of my boyhood. Not far from where we landed there was an old Dutch family vault, constructed in the side of a bank, which had been an object of great awe and fable among my schoolboy associates. We had peeped into it during one of our coasting voyages, and been startled by the sight of mouldering coffins and musty bones within; but what had given it the most fearful interest in our eyes, was its being in some way connected with the pirate wreck which lay rotting among the rocks of Hell-gate. There were stories also of smuggling connected with it, particularly relating to a time when this retired spot was owned by a noted burgher, called Ready Money Provost; a man of whom it was whispered that he had many mysterious dealings with parts beyond the seas. All these things, however, had been jumbled together in our minds in that vague way in which such themes are mingled up in the tales of boyhood.

While I was pondering upon these matters, my companions had spread a repast, from the contents of our well-stored pannier, under a broad chestnut, on the greensward which swept down to the water's edge. Here we solaced ourselves on the cool grassy carpet during the warm sunny hours of mid-day. While lolling on the grass, indulging in that kind of musing reverie of which I am fond, I summoned up the dusky recollections of my boyhood respecting this place, and repeated them like the imperfectly remembered traces of a dream, for the amusement of my companions. When I had finished, a worthy old burgher, John Josse Vandermoere, the same who once related to me the adventures of Dolph Heyliger, broke silence, and observed, that he recollected a story of money-digging, which occurred in this very neighborhood, and might account for some of the traditions which I had heard in my boyhood. As we knew him to be one of the most authentic narrators in the province, we begged him to let us have the particulars, and accordingly, while we solaced ourselves with a clean long pipe of Blasc Moore's best tobacco, the authentic John Josse Vandermoere related the following tale.

# WOLFERT WEBBER, OR GOLDEN DREAMS

In the year of grace one thousand seven hundred and—blank—for I do not remember the precise date; however, it was somewhere in the early part of the last century, there lived in the ancient city of the Manhattoes a worthy burgher, Wolfert Webber by name. He was descended from Old Cobus Webber of the Brille in Holland, one of the original settlers, famous for introducing the cultivation of cabbages, and who came over to the province during the protectorship of Oloffe Van Kortlandt, otherwise called the Dreamer.

The field in which Cobus Webber first planted himself and his cabbages had remained ever since in the family, who continued in the same line of husbandry with that praiseworthy perseverance for which our Dutch burghers are noted. The whole family genius, during several generations, was devoted to the study and development of this one noble vegetable; and to this concentration of intellect may doubtless be ascribed the prodigious renown to which the Webber cabbages attained.

The Webber dynasty continued in uninterrupted succession; and never did a line give more unquestionable proofs of legitimacy. The eldest son succeeded to the looks, as well as the territory of his sire; and had the portraits of this line of tranquil potentates been taken, they would have presented a row of heads marvellously resembling in shape and magnitude the vegetables over which they reigned.

The seat of government continued unchanged in the family mansion:—a Dutch-built house, with a front, or rather gable-end of yellow brick, tapering to a point, with the customary iron weathercock at the top. Every thing about the building bore the air of long-settled ease and security. Flights of martins peopled the little coops nailed against its walls, and swallows built their nests under the eaves; and every one knows that these house-loving birds bring good luck to the dwelling where they take up their abode. In a bright summer morning in early summer, it was delectable to hear their cheerful notes, as they sported about in the pure sweet air, chirping forth, as it were, the greatness and prosperity of the Webbers.

Thus quietly and comfortably did this excellent family vegetate under the shade of a mighty button-wood tree, which by little and little grew so great as entirely to overshadow their palace. The city gradually spread its suburbs round their domain. Houses sprang up to interrupt their prospects. The rural lanes in the vicinity began to grow into the bustle and populousness of streets; in short, with all the habits of rustic life they began to find themselves the inhabitants of a city. Still, however, they maintained their hereditary character, and hereditary possessions, with all the tenacity of petty German princes in the midst of the empire. Wolfert was the last of the line, and succeeded to the patriarchal bench at the door, under the family tree, and swayed the sceptre of his fathers, a kind of rural potentate in the midst of the metropolis.

To share the cares and sweets of sovereignty, he had taken unto himself a helpmate, one of that excellent kind, called stirring women; that is to say, she was one of those notable little housewives who are always busy where there is nothing to do. Her activity, however, took one particular direction; her whole life seemed devoted to intense knitting; whether at home or abroad, walking or sitting, her needles were continually in motion, and it is even affirmed that by her un-wearied industry she very nearly supplied her household with stockings throughout the year. This worthy couple were blessed with one daughter, who was brought up with great tenderness and care; uncommon pains had been taken with her education, so that she could stitch in every variety of way; make all kinds of pickles and preserves, and mark her own name on a sampler. The influence of her taste was seen also in the family garden, where the ornamental began to mingle with the useful; whole rows of fiery marigolds and splendid hollyhocks bordered the cabbage-beds; and gigantic sunflowers lolled their broad jolly faces over the fences, seeming to ogle most affectionately the passers-by.

Thus reigned and vegetated Wolfert Webber over his paternal acres, peacefully and contentedly. Not but that, like all other sovereigns, he had his occasional cares and vexations. The growth of his native city sometimes caused him annoyance. His little territory gradually became hemmed in by streets and houses, which intercepted air and sunshine. He was now and then subjected to the irruptions of the border population that infest the streets of a metropolis; who would make midnight forays into his dominions, and carry off captive whole platoons of his noblest subjects. Vagrant swine would make a descent, too, now and then, when the gate was left open, and lay all waste before them; and mischievous urchins would decapitate the illustrious sunflowers, the glory of the garden, as they lolled their heads so fondly over the walls. Still all these were petty grievances, which might now and then ruffle the surface of his mind, as a summer breeze will ruffle the surface of a mill-pond; but·they could not disturb the deep-seated quiet of his soul. He would but seize a trusty staff, that stood behind the door, issue suddenly out, and anoint the back of the aggressor, whether pig or urchin, and then return within doors, marvellously refreshed and tranquillized.

The chief cause of anxiety to honest Wolfert, however, was the growing prosperity of the city. The expenses of living doubled and trebled; but he could not double and treble the magnitude of his cabbages; and the number of competitors prevented the increase of price; thus, therefore, while every one around him grew·richer, Wolfert grew poorer, and he could not, for the life of him, perceive how the evil was to be remedied.

This growing care, which increased from day to day, had its gradual effect upon our worthy burgher; insomuch, that it at length implanted two or three wrinkles in his brow; things unknown before in the family of the Webbers; and it seemed to pinch up the corners of his cocked hat into an expression of anxiety, totally opposite to the tranquil, broad-brimmed, low-crowned beavers of his illustrious progenitors.

Perhaps even this would not have materially disturbed the serenity of his mind, had he had only himself and his wife to care for; but there was his daughter gradually growing to maturity; and all the world knows that when daughters begin to ripen, no fruit nor flower requires so much looking after. I have no talent at describing female charms else fain would I depict the progress of this little Dutch beauty. How her blue eyes grew deeper and deeper, and her cherry lips redder and redder; and how she ripened and ripened, and rounded and rounded in the opening breath of sixteen summers, until, in her seventeenth spring, she seemed ready to burst out of her bodice, like a half blown rose-bud.

Ah, well-a-day would I could but show her as she was then, tricked out on a Sunday morning, in the hereditary finery of the old Dutch clothes-press, of which her mother had confided to her the key. The wedding-dress of her grandmother, modernized for use, with sundry ornaments, handed down as heirlooms in the family. Her pale brown hair smoothed with buttermilk in flat waving lines on each side of her fair forehead. The chain of yellow virgin gold, that encircled her neck; the little cross, that just rested at the entrance of a soft valley of happiness, as if it would sanctify the place. The—but, pooh!—it is not for an old man like me to be prosing about female beauty; suffice it to say, Amy had attained her seventeenth year. Long since had her sampler exhibited hearts in couples desperately transfixed with arrows, and true lovers' knots worked in deep blue silk; and it was evident she began to languish for some more interesting occupation than the rearing of sunflowers or pickling of cucumbers.

At this critical period of female existence, when the heart within a damsel's bosom, like its emblem, the miniature which hangs without, is apt to be engrossed by a single image, a new visitor began to make his appearance under the roof of Wolfert Webber. This was Dirk Waldron, the only son of a poor widow, but who could boast of more fathers than any lad in the province; for his mother had had four husbands, and this only child; so that though born in her last wedlock, he might fairly claim to be the tardy fruit of a long course of cultivation. This son of four fathers, united the merits and the vigor of all his sires. If he had not had a great family before him, he seemed likely to have a great one after him; for you had only to look at the fresh bucksome youth, to see that he was formed to be the founder of a mighty race.

This youngster gradually became an intimate visitor of the family. He talked little, but he sat long. He filled the father' pipe when it was empty, gathered up the mother's knitting-needle, or ball of worsted when it fell to the ground; stroked the sleek coat of the tortoise-shell cat, and replenished the teapot for the daughter from the bright copper kettle that sang before the fire. All these quiet little offices may seem of trifling import; but when true love is translated into Low Dutch, it is in this way that it eloquently expresses itself. They were not lost upon the Webber family. The winning youngster found marvellous favor in the eyes of the mother; the tortoise-shell cat, albeit the most staid and demure of her kind, gave indubitable signs of approbation of his visits, the teakettle seemed to sing out a cheering note of welcome at his approach, and if the sly glances of the daughter might be rightly read, as she sat bridling and dimpling, and sewing by her mother's side, she was not a whit behind Dame Webber, or grimalkin, or the teakettle, in good will.

Wolfert alone saw nothing of what was going on. Profoundly wrapt up in meditation on the growth of the city and his cabbages, he sat looking in the fire, and puffing his pipe in silence. One night, however, as the gentle Amy, according to custom, lighted her lover to the outer door, and he, according to custom, took his parting salute, the smack resounded so vigorously through the long, silent entry, as to startle even the dull ear of Wolfert. He was slowly roused to a new source of anxiety. It had never entered into his head that this mere child, who, as it seemed, but the other day had been climbing about his knees, and playing with dolls and baby-houses, could all at once be thinking of lovers and matrimony. He rubbed his eyes, examined into the fact, and really found that while he had been dreaming of other matters, she had actually grown to be a woman, and what was worse, had fallen in love. Here arose new cares for Wolfert. He was a kind father, but he was a prudent man. The young man was a lively, stirring lad; but then he had neither money nor land. Wolfert's ideas all ran in one channel; and he saw no alternative in case of a marriage, but to portion off the young couple with a corner of his cabbage garden, the whole of which was barely sufficient for the support of his family.

Like a prudent father, therefore, he determined to nip this passion in the bud, and forbade the youngster the house; though sorely did it go against his fatherly heart, and many a silent tear did it cause in the bright eye of his daughter. She showed herself, however, a pattern of filial piety and obedience. She never pouted and sulked; she never flew in the face of parental authority; she never flew into a passion, nor fell into hysterics, as many romatic novel-read young ladies would do. Not she, indeed! She was none such heroical rebellious trumpery, I'll warrant ye. On the contrary, she acquiesced like an obedient daughter, shut the street door in her lover's face, and if ever she did grant him an interview, it was either out of the kitchen window, or over the garden fence.

Wolfert was deeply cogitating these matters in his mind, and his brow wrinkled with unusual care, as he wended his way one Saturday afternoon to a rural inn, about two miles from the city. It was a favorite resort of the Dutch part of the community, from being always held by a Dutch line of landlords, and retaining an air and relish of the good old times. It was a Dutch-built house, that had probably been a country seat of some opulent burgher in the early time of the settlement. It stood near a point of land, called Corlear's Hook, which stretches out into the Sound, and against which the tide, at its flux and reflux, sets with extraordinary rapidity. The venerable and somewhat crazy mansion was distinguished from afar, by a grove of elms and sycamores that seemed to wave a hospitable invitation, while a few weeping-willows, with their dank, drooping foliage, resembling fallen waters, gave an idea of coolness, that rendered it an attractive spot during the heats of summer.

Here, therefore, as I said, resorted many of the old inhabitants of the Manhattoes, where, while some played at shuffleboard and quoits and ninepins, others smoked a deliberate pipe, and talked over public affairs.

It was on a blustering autumnal afternoon that Wolfert made his visit to the inn. The grove of elms and willows was stripped of its leaves, which whirled in rustling eddies about the fields. The nine-pin alley was deserted, for the premature chilliness of the day had driven the company within doors. As it was Saturday afternoon, the habitual club was in session, composed principally of regular Dutch burghers, though mingled occasionally with persons of various character and country, as is natural in a place of such motley population.

Beside the fireplace, in a huge leather-bottomed arm-chair, sat the dictator of this little world, the venerable Rem, or as it was pronounced, Ramm Rapelye. He was a man of Walloon race, and illustrious for the antiquity of his line; his great-grandmother having been the first white child born in the province. But he was still more illustrious for his wealth and dignity: he had long filled the noble office of alderman, and was a man to whom the governor himself took off his hat. He had maintained possession of the leather-bottomed chair from time immemorial; and had gradually waxed in bulk as he sat in his seat of government, until in the course of years he filled its whole magnitude. His word was decisive with his subjects; for he was so rich a man, that he was never expected to support any opinion by argument. The landlord waited on him with peculiar officiousness; not that he paid better than his neighbors, but then the coin of a rich man seems always to be so much more acceptable. The landlord had ever a pleasant word and a joke, to insinuate in the ear of the august Ramm. It is true, Ramm never laughed, and, indeed, ever maintained a mastiff-like gravity, and even surliness of aspect; yet he now and then rewarded mine host with a token of approbation; which though nothing more nor less than a kind of grunt, still delighted the landlord more than a broad laugh from a poorer man.

"This will be a rough night for-the money-diggers," said mine host, as a gust of wind howled round the house, and rattled at the windows.

"What! are they at their works again?" said an English half-pay captain, with one eye, who was a very frequent attendant at the inn.

"Aye, are they," said the landlord, "and well may they be. They've had luck of late. They say a great pot of money has been dug up in the fields, just behind Stuyvesant's orchard. Folks think it must have been buried there in old times, by Peter Stuyvesant, the Dutch governor."

"Fudge!" said the one-eyed man of war, as he added a small portion of water to a bottom of brandy.

"Well, you may believe it or not as you please," said mine host, somewhat nettled; "but every body knows that the old governor buried a great deal of his money at the time of the Dutch troubles, when the English red coats seized on the province. They say, too, the old gentleman walks; aye, and in the very same dress that he wears in the picture that hangs up in the family house."

"Fudge!" said the half-pay officer.

"Fudge, if you please!—But didn't Corney Van Zandt see him at midnight, stalking about in the meadow with his wooden leg, and a drawn sword in his hand, that flashed like fire? And what can he be walking for, but because people have been troubling the place where he buried his money in old times?"

Here the landlord was interrupted by several guttural sounds from Ramm Rapelye, betokening that he was laboring with the unusual production of an idea. As he was too great a man to be slighted by a prudent publican, mine host respectfully paused until he should deliver himself. The corpulent frame of this mighty burgher now gave all the symptoms of a volcanic mountain on the point of an eruption. First, there was a certain heaving of the abdomen, not unlike an earthquake; then was emitted a cloud of tobacco-smoke from that crater, his mouth; then there was a kind of rattle in the throat, as if the idea were working its way up through a region of phlegm; then there were several disjointed members of a sentence thrown out, ending in a cough; at length his voice forced its way into a slow, but absolute tone of a man who feels the weight of his purse, if not of his ideas; every portion of his speech being marked by a testy puff of tobacco-smoke.

"Who talks of old Peter Stuyvesant's walking?—puff—Have people no respect for persons?—puff—puff—Peter Stuyvesant knew better what to do with his money than to bury it—puff—I know the Stuyvesant family—puff—every one of them—puff—not a more respectable family in the province—puff—old standards—puff—warm householders—puff—none of your upstarts—puff—puff—puff.—Don't talk to me of Peter Stuyvesant's walking—puff—puff—puff—puff."

Here the redoubtable Ramm contracted his brow, clasped up his mouth, till it wrinkled at each corner, and redoubled his smoking with such vehemence, that the cloudy volumes soon wreathed round his head, as the smoke envelopes the awful summit of Mount Etna.

A general silence followed the sudden rebuke of this very rich man. The subject, however, was too interesting to be readily abandoned. The conversation soon broke forth again from the lips of Peechy Prauw Van Hook, the chronicler of the club, one of those prosing, narrative old men who seem to be troubled with an incontinence of words, as they grow old.

Peechy could, at any time, tell as many stories in an evening as his hearers could digest in a month. He now resumed the conversation, by affirming that, to his knowledge, money had, at different times, been digged up in various parts of the island. The lucky persons who had discovered them had always dreamt of them three times beforehand, and what was worthy of remark, those treasures had never been found but by some descendant of the good old Dutch families, which clearly proved that they had been buried by Dutchmen in the olden time.

"Fiddlestick with your Dutchmen!" cried the half-pay officer. "The Dutch had nothing to do with them. They were all buried by Kidd the pirate, and his crew."

Here a key-note was touched that roused the whole company. The name of Captain Kidd was like a talisman in those times, and was associated with a thousand marvellous stories.

The half-pay officer took the lead and in his narrations fathered upon Kidd all the plunderings and exploits of Morgan, Blackbeard, and the whole list of bloody buccaneers.

The officer was a man of great weight among the peaceable members of the club, by reason of his warlike character and gunpowder tales. All his golden stories of Kidd, however, and of the booty he had buried, were obstinately rivalled by the tales of Peechy Prauw, who, rather than suffer his Dutch progenitors to be eclipsed by a foreign freebooter, enriched every field and shore in the neighborhood with the hidden wealth of Peter Stuyvesant and his contemporaries.

Not a word of this conversation was lost upon Wolfert Webber. He returned pensively home, full of magnificent ideas. The soil of his native island seemed to be turned into gold dust; and every field to teem with treasure. His head almost reeled at the thought how often he must have heedlessly rambled over places where countless sums lay, scarcely covered by the turf beneath his feet. His mind was in an uproar with this whirl of new ideas. As he came in sight of the venerable mansion of his forefathers, and the little realm where the Webbers had so long, and so contentedly flourished, his gorge rose at the narrowness of his destiny.

"Unlucky Wolfert!" exclaimed he; "others can go to bed and dream themselves into whole mines of wealth; they have but to seize a spade in the morning, and turn up doubloons like potatoes; but thou must dream of hardships, and rise to poverty—must dig thy field from year's end to year's end, and yet raise nothing but cabbages!"

Wolfert Webber went to bed with a heavy heart; and it was long before the golden visions that disturbed his brain permitted him to sink into repose. The same visions, however, extended into his sleeping thoughts, and assumed a more definite form. He dreamt that he had discovered an immense treasure in the centre of his garden. At every stroke of the spade he laid bare a golden ingot; diamond crosses sparkled out of the dust; bags of money turned up their bellies, corpulent with pieces-of-eight, or venerable doubloons; and chests, wedged close with moidores, ducats, and pistareens, yawned before his ravished eyes, and vomited forth their glittering contents.

Wolfert awoke a poorer man than ever. He had no heart to go about his daily concerns, which appeared so paltry and profitless; but sat all day long in the chimney corner, picturing to himself ingots and heaps of gold in the fire. The next night his dream was repeated. He was again in his garden, digging, and laying open stores of hidden wealth. There was something very singular in this repetition. He passed another day of reverie, and though it was cleaning day, and the house, as usual in Dutch households, completely topsy-turvy, yet he sat unmoved amidst the general uproar.

The third night he went to bed with a palpitating heart. He put on his red night-cap wrong side outwards, for good luck. It was deep midnight before his anxious mind could settle itself into sleep. Again the golden dream was repeated, and again he saw his garden teeming with ingots and money-bags.

Wolfert rose the next morning in complete bewilderment. A dream, three times repeated, was never known to lie; and if so, his fortune was made.

In his agitation he put on his waistcoat with the hind part before, and this was a corroboration of good luck. He no longer doubted that a huge store of money lay buried somewhere in his cabbage field, coyly waiting to be sought for; and he repined at having so long been scratching about the surface of the soil instead of digging to the centre.

He took his seat at the breakfast table full of these speculations; asked his daughter to put a lump of gold into his tea, and on handing his wife a plate of slap-jacks, begged her to help herself to a doubloon.

His grand care now was how to secure this immense treasure without its being known. Instead of his working regularly in his grounds in the daytime, he now stole from his bed at night, and with spade and pickaxe, went to work to rip up and dig about his paternal acres from one end to the other. In a little time the whole garden, which had presented such a goodly and regular appearance, with its phalanx of cabbages, like a vegetable army in battle array, was reduced to a scene of devastation; while the relentless Wolfert, with night-cap on head, and lantern and spade in hand, stalked through the slaughtered ranks, the destroying angel of his own vegetable world. Every morning bore testimony to the ravages of the preceding night in cabbages of all ages and conditions, from the tender sprout to the full-grown head, piteously rooted from their quiet beds like worthless weeds, and left to wither in the sunshine. In vain Wolfert's wife remonstrated; in vain his darling daughter wept over the destruction of some favorite marigold. "Thou shalt have gold of another guess sort," he would cry, chucking her under the chin; "thou shalt have a string of crooked ducats for thy wedding necklace, my child." His family began really to fear that the poor man's wits were diseased. He muttered in his sleep at night about mines of wealth, about pearls and diamonds, and bars of gold. In the daytime he was moody and abstracted, and walked about as if in a trance. Dame Webber held frequent councils with all the old women of the neighborhood; scarce an hour in the day but a knot of them might be seen wagging their white caps together round her door, while the poor woman made some piteous recital. The daughter, too, was fain to seek for more frequent consolation from the stolen interviews of her favored swain, Dirk Waldron. The delectable little Dutch songs, with which she used to dulcify the house, grew less and less frequent, and she would forget her sewing, and look wistfully in her father's face as he sat pondering by the fireside. Wolfert caught her eye one day fixed on him thus anxiously, and for a moment was roused from his golden reveries.— "Cheer up, my girl," said he, exultingly, "why dost thou droop?— thou shalt hold up thy head one day with the Brinckerhoffs, and the Schermerhorns, the Van Hornes, and the Van Dams.—By Saint Nicholas, but the patroon himself shall be glad to get thee for his son!"

Amy shook her head at his vainglorious boast, and was more than ever in doubt of the soundness of the good man's intellect.

In the mean time Wolfert went on digging and digging; but the field was extensive, and as his dream had indicated no precise spot, he had to dig at random. The winter set in before one-tenth of the scene of promise had been explored.

The ground became frozen hard, and the nights too cold for the labors of the spade.

No sooner, however, did the returning warmth of spring loosen the soil, and the small frogs begin to pipe in the meadows, but Wolfert resumed his labors with renovated zeal. Still, however, the hours of industry were reversed.

Instead of working cheerily all day, planting and setting out his vegetables, he remained thoughtfully idle, until the shades of night summoned him to his secret labors. In this way he continued to dig from night to night, and week to week, and month to month, but not a stiver did he find. On the contrary, the more he digged, the poorer he grew. The rich soil of his garden was digged away, and the sand and gravel from beneath was thrown to the surface, until the whole field presented an aspect of sandy barrenness.

In the mean time, the seasons gradually rolled on. The little frogs which had piped in the meadows in early spring, croaked as bull-frogs during the summer heats, and then sank into silence. The peach-tree budded, blossomed, and bore its fruit. The swallows and martins came, twittered about the roof, built their nests, reared their young, held their congress along the eaves, and then winged their flight in search of another spring. The caterpillar spun its winding-sheet, dangled in it from the great button-wood tree before the house; turned into a moth, fluttered with the last sunshine of summer, and disappeared; and finally the leaves of the button-wood tree turned yellow, then brown, then rustled one by one to the ground, and whirling about in little eddies of wind and dust, whispered that winter was at hand.

Wolfert gradually woke from his dream of wealth as the year declined. He had reared no crop for the supply of his household during the sterility of winter. The season was long and severe, and for the first time the family was really straitened in its comforts. By degrees a revulsion of thought took place in Wolfert's mind, common to those whose golden dreams have been disturbed by pinching realities. The idea gradually stole upon him that he should come to want. He already considered himself one of the most unfortunate men in the province, having lost such an incalculable amount of undiscovered treasure, and now, when thousands of pounds had eluded his search, to be perplexed for shillings and pence was cruel in the extreme.

Haggard care gathered about his brow; he went about with a money-seeking air, his eyes bent downwards into the dust, and carrying his hands in his pockets, as men are apt to do when they have nothing else to put into them. He could not even pass the city almshouse without giving it a rueful glance, as if destined to be his future abode.

The strangeness of his conduct and of his looks occasioned much speculation and remark. For a long time he was suspected of being crazy, and then every body pitied him; and at length it began to be suspected that he was poor, and then every body avoided him.

The rich old burghers of his acquaintance met him outside of the door when he called, entertained him hospitably on the threshold, pressed him warmly by the hand at parting, shook their heads as he walked away, with the kind-hearted expression of "poor Wolfert," and turned a corner nimbly if by chance they saw him approaching as they walked the streets. Even the barber and the cobbler of the neighborhood, and a tattered tailor in an alley hard by, three of the poorest and merriest rogues in the world, eyed him with that abundant sympathy which usually attends a lack of means; and there is not a doubt but their pockets would have been at his command, only that they happened to be empty.

Thus every body deserted the Webber mansion, as if poverty were contagious, like the plague; every body but honest Dirk Waldron, who still kept up his stolen visits to the daughter, and indeed seemed to wax more affectionate as the fortunes of his mistress were in the wane.

Many months had elapsed since Wolfert had frequented his old resort, the rural inn. He was taking a long lonely walk one Saturday afternoon, musing over his wants and disappointments, when his feet took instinctively their wonted direction, and on awaking out of a reverie, he found himself before the door of the inn. For some moments he hesitated whether to enter, but his heart yearned for companionship; and where can a ruined man find better companionship than at a tavern, where there is neither sober example nor sober advice to put him out of countenance?

Wolfert found several of the old frequenters of the inn at their usual places; but one was missing, the great Ramm Rapelye, who for many years had filled the leather-bottomed chair of state. His place was supplied by a stranger, who seemed, however, completely at home in the chair and the tavern. He was rather under size, but deep chested, square, and muscular. His broad shoulders, double joints, and bow knees, gave tokens of prodigious strength. His face was dark and weather beaten; a deep scar, as if from the slash of a cutlass, had almost divided his nose, and made a gash in his upper lip, through which his teeth shone like a bull-dog's. A mop of iron gray hair gave a grisly finish to this hard favored visage. His dress was of an amphibious character. He wore an old hat edged with tarnished lace, and cocked in martial style, on one side of his head; a rusty blue military coat with brass buttons, and a wide pair of short petticoat trowsers, or rather breeches, for they were gathered up at the knees. He ordered every body about him with an authoritative air; talking in a brattling voice, that sounded like the crackling of thorns under a pot; d——d the landlord and servants with perfect impunity, and was waited upon with greater obsequiousness than had ever been shown to the mighty Ramm himself.

Wolfert's curiosity was awakened to know who and what was this stranger, who had thus usurped absolute sway in this ancient domain. Peechy Prauw took him aside, into a remote corner of the hall, and there, in an under voice, and with a great caution, imparted to him all that he knew on the subject. The inn had been aroused several months before, on a dark stormy night, by repeated long shouts, that seemed like the howlings of a wolf. They came from the water-side; and at length were distinguished to be hailing the house in the sea-faring manner, "House-a-hoy!" The landlord turned out with his head waiter, tapster, hostler, and errand-boy—that is to say, with his old negro Cuff. On approaching the place whence the voice proceeded, they found this amphibious-looking personage at the water's edge, quite alone, and seated on a great oaken sea-chest How he came there, whether he had been set on shore from some boat, or had floated to land on his chest, nobody could tell, for he did not seem disposed to answer questions; and there was something in his looks and manners that put a stop to all questioning. Suffice it to say, he took possession of a corner room of the inn, to which his chest was removed with great difficulty. Here he had remained ever since, keeping about the inn and its vicinity. Sometimes, it is true, he disappeared for one, two, or three days at a time, going and returning without giving any notice or account of his movements. He always appeared to have plenty of money, though often of very strange outlandish coinage; and he regularly paid his bill every evening before turning in.

He had fitted up his room to his own fancy, having slung a hammock from the ceiling instead of a bed, and decorated the walls with rusty pistols and cutlasses of foreign workmanship. A greater part of his time was passed in this room, seated by the window, which commanded a wide view of the Sound, a short old-fashioned pipe in his mouth, a glass of rum-toddy at his elbow, and a pocket telescope in his hand, with which he reconnoitred every boat that moved upon the water. Large square-rigged vessels seemed to excite but little attention; but the moment he descried any thing with a shoulder-of-mutton sail, or that a barge, or yawl, or jolly-boat hove in sight, up went the telescope, and he examined it with the most scrupulous attention.

All this might have passed without much notice, for in those times the province was so much the resort of adventurers of all characters and climes, that any oddity in dress or behavior attracted but small attention. In a little while, however, this strange sea-monster, thus strangely cast upon dry land, began to encroach upon the long-established customs and customers of the place, and to interfere in a dictatorial manner in the affairs of the nine-pin alley and the barroom, until in the end he usurped an absolute command over the whole inn. It was all in vain to attempt to withstand his authority. He was not exactly quarrelsome, but boisterous and peremptory, like one accustomed to tyrannize on a quarter-deck; and there was a dare-devil air about every thing he said and did, that inspired wariness in all bystanders. Even the half-pay officer, so long the hero of the club, was soon silenced by him; and the quiet burghers stared with wonder at seeing their inflammable man of war so readily and quietly extinguished.

And then the tales that he would tell were enough to make a peaceable man's hair stand on end. There was not a sea-fight, nor marauding nor freebooting adventure that had happend within the last twenty years, but he seemed perfectly versed in it. He delighted to talk of the exploits of the buccaneers in the West Indies, and on the Spanish Main. How his eyes would glisten as he described the way-laying of treasure-ships, the desperate flights, yard-arm and yard-arm—broadside and broadside—the boarding and capturing of huge

Spanish galleons! With what chuckling relish would he describe the descent upon some rich Spanish colony; the rifling of a church; the sacking of a convent! You would have thought you heard some gormandizer dilating upon the roasting of a savory goose at Michaelmas as he described the roasting of some Spanish Don to make him discover his treasure—a detail given with a minuteness that made every rich old burgher present turn uncomfortably in his chair. All this would be told with infinite glee, as if he considered it an excellent joke; and then he would give such a tyrannical leer in the face of his next neighbor, that the poor man would be fain to laugh out of sheer faintheartedness. If any one, however, pretended to contradict him in any of his stories he was on fire in an instant. His very cocked hat assumed a momentary fierceness, and seemed to resent the contradiction. "How the devil should you know as well as I?—I tell you it was as I say;" and he would at the same time let slip a broadside of thundering oaths and tremendous sea-phrases, such as had never been heard before within these peaceful walls.

Indeed, the worthy burghers began to surmise that he knew more of those stories than mere hearsay. Day after day their conjectures concerning him grew more and more wild and fearful. The strangeness of his arrival, the strangeness of his manners, the mystery that surrounded him, all made him something incomprehensible in their eyes. He was a kind of monster of the deep to them—he was a merman— he was a behemoth—he was a leviathan—in short, they knew not what he was.

The domineering spirit of this boisterous sea-urchin at length grew quite intolerable. He was no respecter of persons; he contradicted the richest burghers without hesitation; he took possession of the sacred elbow-chair, which time out of mind, had been the seat of sovereignty of the illustrious Ramm Rapelye. Nay, he even went so far in one of his rough jocular moods, as to slap that mighty burgher on the back, drink his toddy, and wink in his face, a thing scarcely to be believed. From this time Ramm Rapelye appeared no more at the inn; his example was followed by several of the most eminent customers, who were too rich to tolerate being bullied out of their opinions, or being obliged to laugh at another man's jokes. The landlord was almost in despair; but he knew not how to get rid of this sea-monster and his sea-chest, who seemed both to have grown like fixtures, or excrescences, on his establishment.

Such was the account whispered cautiously in Wolfert's ear, by the narrator, Peechy Prauw, as he held him by the button in a corner of the hall, casting a wary glance now and then towards the door of the bar-room, lest he should be overheard by the terrible hero of his tale.

Wolfert took his seat in a remote part of the room in silence; impressed with profound awe of this unknown, so versed in freebooting history. It was to him a wonderful instance of the revolutions of mighty empires, to find the venerable Ramm Rapelye thus ousted from the throne, and a rugged tarpawling dictating from his elbow chair, hectoring the patriarchs, and filling this tranquil little realm with brawl and bravado.

The stranger was on this evening in a more than usually communicative mood, and was narrating a number of astounding stories of plunderings and burnings on the high seas. He dwelt upon them with peculiar relish, heightening the frightful particulars in proportion to their effect on his peaceful auditors. He gave a swaggering detail of the capture of a Spanish merchantman. She was lying becalmed during a long summer's day, just off from the island which was one of the lurking-places of the pirates. They had reconnoitred her with their spy-glasses from the shore, and ascertained her character and force. At night a picked crew of daring fellows set off for her in a whale boat. They approached with muffled oars, as she lay rocking idly with the undulations of the sea, and her sails flapping against the masts. They were close under the stern before the guard on deck was aware of their approach. The alarm was given; the pirates threw hand-grenades on deck, and sprang up the main chains sword in hand.

The crew flew to arms, but in great confusion; some were shot down, others took refuge in the tops; others were driven overboard and drowned, while others fought hand to hand from the main-deck to the quarter-deck, disputing gallantly every inch of ground. There were three Spanish gentlemen on board with their ladies, who made the most desperate resistance. They defended the companion-way, cut down several of their assailants, and fought like very devils, for they were maddened by the shrieks of the ladies from the cabin. One of the Dons was old, and soon dispatched. The other two kept their ground vigorously, even though the captain of the pirates was among their assailants. Just then there was shout of victory from the main-deck. "The ship is ours!" cried the pirates.

One of the Dons immediately dropped his sword and surrendered; the other, who was a hot-headed youngster, and just married, gave the captain a slash in the face that laid all open. The captain just made out to articulate the words "no quarter."

"And what did they do with their prisoners?" said Peechy Prauw, eagerly.

"Threw them all overboard," was the answer. A dead pause followed the reply. Peechy Prauw sunk quietly back, like a man who had unwarily stolen upon the lair of a sleeping lion. The honest burghers cast fearful glances at the deep scar slashed across the visage of the stranger, and moved their chairs a little farther off. The seaman, however, smoked on without moving a muscle, as though he either did not perceive or did not regard the unfavorable effect he had produced upon his hearers.

The half-pay officer was the first to break the silence; for he was continually tempted to make ineffectual head against this tyrant of the seas, and to regain his lost consequence in the eyes of his ancient companions. He now tried to match the gunpowder tales of the stranger by others equally tremendous. Kidd, as usual, was his hero, concerning whom he seemed to have picked up many of the floating traditions of the province. The seaman had always evinced a settled pique against the one-eyed warrior. On this occasion he listened with peculiar impatience. He sat with one arm akimbo, the other elbow on the table, the hand holding on to the small pipe he was pettishly puffing; his legs crossed; drumming with one foot on the ground, and casting every now and then the side-glance of a basilisk at the prosing captain. At length the latter spoke of Kidd's having ascended the Hudson with some of his crew, to land his plunder in secrecy.

"Kidd up the Hudson!" burst forth the seaman, with a tremendous oath—"Kidd never was up the Hudson!"

"I tell you he was," said the other. "Aye, and they say he buried a quantity of treasure on the little flat that runs out into the river, called the Devil's Dans Kammer."

"The Devil's Dans Kammer in your teeth!" cried the seaman. "I tell you Kidd never was up the Hudson. What a plague do you know of Kidd and his haunts?"

"What do I know?" echoed the half-pay officer. "Why, I was in London at the time of his trial; aye, and I had the pleasure of seeing him hanged at Execution Dock."

"Then, sir, let me tell you that you saw as pretty a fellow hanged as ever trod shoe-leather. Aye!" putting his face nearer to that of the officer, "and there was many a land-lubber looked on that might much better have swung in his stead!"

The half-pay officer was silenced; but the indignation thus pent up in his bosom glowed with intense vehemence in his single eye, which kindled like a coal.

Peechy Prauw, who never could remain silent, observed that the gentleman certainly was in the right. Kidd never did bury money up the Hudson, nor indeed in any of those parts, though many affirmed such to be the fact. It was Bradish and others of the buccaneers who had buried money; some said in Turtle Bay, others on Long Island, others in the neighborhood of Hellgate. Indeed, added he, I recollect an adventure of Sam, the negro fisherman, many years ago, which some think had something to do with the buccaneers. As we are all friends here, and as it will go no further, I'll tell it to you.

"Upon a dark night many years ago, as Black Sam was returning from fishing in Hell-gate——"

Here the story was nipped in the bud by a sudden movement from the unknown, who laying his iron fist on the table, knuckles downward, with a quiet force that indented the very boards, and looking grimly over his shoulder, with the grin of an angry bear—"Heark'ee, neighbor," said he, with significant nodding of the head, "you'd better let the buccaneers and their money alone—they're not for old men and old women to meddle with. They fought hard for their money; they gave body and soul for it; and wherever it lies buried, depend upon it he must have a tug with the devil who gets it!"

This sudden explosion was succeeded by a bland silence throughout the room. Peechy Prauw shrunk within himself, and even the one-eyed officer turned pale. Wolfert, who from a dark corner of the room had listened with intense eagerness to all this talk about buried treasure, looked with mingled awe and reverence at this bold buccaneer; for such he really suspected him to be. There was a chinking of gold and a sparkling of jewels in all his stories about the Spanish Main that gave a value to every period; and Wolfert would have given any thing for the rummaging of the ponderous sea-chest, which his imagination crammed full of golden chalices, crucifixes, and jolly round bags of doubloons.

The dead stillness that had fallen upon the company was at length interrupted by the stranger, who pulled out a prodigious watch of curious and ancient workmanship, and which in Wolfert's eyes had a decidedly Spanish look. On touching a spring it struck ten o'clock; upon which the sailor called for his reckoning, and having paid it out of a handful of outlandish coin, he drank off the remainder of his beverage, and without taking leave of any one, rolled out of the room, muttering to himself, as he stamped up stairs to his chamber.

It was some time before the company could recover from the silence into which they had been thrown. The very footsteps of the stranger, which were heard now and then as he traversed his chamber, inspired awe.

Still the conversation in which they had been engaged was too interesting not to be resumed. A heavy thundergust had gathered up unnoticed while they were lost in talk, and the torrents of rain that fell forbade all thoughts of setting off for home until the storm should subside. They drew nearer together, therefore, and entreated the worthy Peechy Prauw to continue the tale which had been so discourteously interrupted. He readily complied, whispering, however, in a tone scarcely above his breath, and drowned occasionally by the rolling of the thunder; and he would pause every now and then, and listen with evident awe, and as he heard the heavy footsteps of the stranger pacing over head.

The following is the purport of his story.


ADVENTURE OF THE BLACK FISHERMAN


Every body knows Black Sam, the old negro fisherman, or, as he is commonly called, Mud Sam, who has fished about the Sound for the last half century. It is now many years since Sam, who was then as active a young negro as any in the province, and worked on the farm of Killian Suydam on Long Island, having finished his day's work at an early hour, was fishing, one still summer evening, just about the neighborhood of Hell-gate.

He was in a light skiff, and being well acquainted with the currents and eddies, had shifted his station according to the shifting of the tide, from the Hen and Chickens to the Hog's Back, from the Hog's Back to the Pot, and from the Pot to the Frying-Pan; but in the eagerness of his sport he did not see that the tide was rapidly ebbing, until the roaring of the whirlpools and eddies warned him of his danger; and he had some difficulty in shooting his skiff from among the rocks and breakers, and getting to the point of Blackwell's Island. Here he cast anchor for some time, waiting the turn of the tide to enable him to return homewards. As the night set in, it grew blustering and gusty. Dark clouds came bundling up in the west; and now and then a growl of thunder or a flash of lightning told that a summer storm was at hand. Sam pulled over, therefore, under the lee of Manhattan Island, and coasting along, came to a snug nook, just under a steep beetling rock, where he fastened his skiff to the root of a tree that shot out from a cleft, and spread its broad branches like a canopy over the water. The gust came scouring along; the wind threw up the river in white surges; the rain rattled among the leaves; the thunder bellowed worse than that which is now bellowing; the lightning seemed to lick up the surges of the stream; but Sam, snugly sheltered under rock and tree, lay crouching in his skiff, rocking upon the billows until he fell asleep. When he woke all was quiet. The gust had passed away, and only now and then a faint gleam of lightning in the east showed which way it had gone. The night was dark and moonless; and from the state of the tide Sam concluded it was near midnight. He was on the point of making loose his skiff to return homewards, when he saw a light gleaming along the water from a distance, which seemed rapidly approaching. As it drew near he perceived it came from a lantern in the bow of a boat gliding along under shadow of the land. It pulled up in a small cove, close to where he was. A man jumped on shore, and searching about with the lantern, exclaimed, "This is the place—here's the iron ring." The boat was then made fast, and the man returning on board, assisted his comrades in conveying something heavy on shore. As the light gleamed among them, Sam saw that they were five stout desperate-looking fellows, in red woollen caps, with a leader in a three-cornered hat, and that some of them were armed with dirks, or long knives, and pistols. They talked low to one another, and occasionally in some outlandish tongue which he could not understand.

On landing they made their way among the bushes, taking turns to relieve each other in lugging their burden up the rocky bank. Sam's curiosity was now fully aroused; so leaving his skiff he clambered silently up a ridge that overlooked their path. They had stopped to rest for a moment, and the leader was looking about among the bushes with his lantern. "Have you brought the spades?" said one. "They are here," replied another, who had them on his shoulder. "We must dig deep, where there will be no risk of discovery," said a third.

A cold chill ran through Sam's veins. He fancied he saw before him a gang of murderers, about to bury their victim. His knees smote together. In his agitation he shook the branch of a tree with which he was supporting himself as he looked over the edge of the cliff.

"What's that?" cried one of the gang. "Some one stirs among the bushes!"

The lantern was held up in the direction of the noise. One of the red-caps cocked a pistol, and pointed it towards the very place where Sam was standing. He stood motionless—breathless; expecting the next moment to be his last. Fortunately his dingy complexion was in his favor, and made no glare among the leaves.

"'Tis no one," said the man with the lantern. "What a plague! you would not fire off your pistol and alarm the country!"

The pistol was uncocked; the burden was resumed, and the party slowly toiled along the bank. Sam watched them as they went, the light sending back fitful gleams through the dripping bushes, and it was not till they were fairly out of sight that he ventured to draw breath freely. He now thought of getting back to his boat, and making his escape out of the reach of such dangerous neighbors; but curiosity was all-powerful. He hesitated and lingered and listened. By and by he heard the strokes of spades. "They are digging the grave!" said he to himself; and the cold sweat started upon his forehead. Every stroke of a spade, as it sounded through the silent groves, went to his heart; it was evident there was as little noise made as possible; every thing had an air of terrible mystery and secrecy. Sam had a great relish for the horrible,—a tale of murder was a treat for him; and he was a constant attendant at executions. He could not resist an impulse, in spite of every danger, to steal nearer to the scene of mystery, and overlook the midnight fellows at their work. He crawled along cautiously, therefore, inch by inch; stepping with the utmost care along the dry leaves, lest their rustling should betray him. He came at length to where a steep rock intervened between him and the gang; for he saw the light of their lantern shining up against the branches of the trees on the other side. Sam slowly and silently clambered up the surface of the rock, and raising his head above its naked edge, beheld the villains immediately below him, and so near, that though he dreaded discovery, he dared not withdraw lest the least movement should be heard. In this way he remained, with his round black face peering above the edge of the rock, like the sun just emerging above the edge of the horizon, or the round-cheeked moon on the dial of a clock.

The red-caps had nearly finished their work; the grave was filled up, and they were carefully replacing the turf. This done, they scattered dry leaves over the place. "And now," said the leader, "I defy the devil himself to find it out."

"The murderers!" exclaimed Sam, involuntarily.

The whole gang started, and looking up, beheld the round black head of Sam just above them. His white eyes strained half out of their orbits; his white teeth chattering, and his whole visage shining with cold perspiration.

"We're discovered!" cried one.

"Down with him!" cried another.

Sam heard the cocking of a pistol, but did not pause for the report. He scrambled over rock and stone, through brush and brier; rolled down banks like a hedge-hog; scrambled up others like a catamount. In every direction he heard some one or other of the gang hemming him in. At length he reached the rocky ridge along the river; one of the red-caps was hard behind him. A steep rock like a wall rose directly in his way; it seemed to cut off all retreat, when fortunately he spied the strong cord-like branch of a grape-vine reaching half way down it. He sprang at it with the force of a desperate man, seized it with both hands, and being young and agile, succeeded in swinging himself to the summit of the cliff. Here he stood in full relief against the sky, when the red-cap cocked his pistol and fired. The ball whistled by Sam's head. With the lucky thought of a man in an emergency, he uttered a yell, fell to the ground, and detached at the same time a fragment of the rock, which tumbled with a loud splash into the river.

"I've done his business," said the red-cap to one or two of his comrades as they arrived panting. "He'll tell no tales, except to the fishes in the river."

His pursuers now turned to meet their companions. Sam sliding silently down the surface of the rock, let himself quietly into his skiff, cast loose the fastening, and abandoned himself to the rapid current, which in that place runs like a mill-stream, and soon swept him off from the neighborhood. It was not, however, until he had drifted a great distance that he ventured to ply his oars; when he made his skiff dart like an arrow through the strait of Hell-gate, never heeding the danger of Pot, Frying Pan, nor Hog's Back itself: nor did he feel himself thoroughly secure until safely nestled in bed in the cockloft of the ancient farm-house of the Suydams.

Here the worthy Peechy Prauw paused to take breath, and to take a sip of the gossip tankard that stood at his elbow. His auditors remained with open mouths and outstretched necks, gaping like a nest of swallows for an additional mouthful.

"And is that all?" exclaimed the half-pay officer.

"That's all that belongs to the story," said Peechy Prauw.

"And did Sam never find out what was buried by the red-caps?" said Wolfert, eagerly, whose mind was haunted by nothing but ingots and doubloons.

"Not that I know of" said Peechy; "he had not time to spare from his work, and, to tell the truth, he did not like to run the risk of another race among the rocks. Besides, how should he recollect the spot where the grave had been digged? every thing would look so different by daylight. And then, where was the use of looking for a dead body, when there was no chance of hanging the murderers?"

"Aye, but are you sure it was a dead body they buried?" said Wolfert.

"To be sure," cried Peechy Prauw, exultingly. "Does it not haunt in the neighborhood to this very day?"

"Haunts!" exclaimed several of the party, opening their eyes still wider, and edging their chairs still closer.

"Aye, haunts," repeated Peechy; "have none of you heard of father Red-cap, who haunts the old burnt farm-house in the woods, on the border of the Sound, near Hell-gate?"

"Oh, to be sure, I've heard tell of something of the kind, but then I took it for some old wives' fable."

"Old wives' fable or not," said Peechy Prauw, "that farmhouse stands hard by the very spot. It's been unoccupied time out of mind, and stands in a lonely part of the coast; but those who fish in the neighborhood have often heard strange noises there; and lights have been seen about the wood at night; and an old fellow in a red cap has been seen at the windows more than once, which people take to be the ghost of the body buried there. Once upon a time three soldiers took shelter in the building for the night, and rummaged it from top to bottom, when they found old father Red-cap astride of a cider-barrel in the cellar, with a jug in one hand and a goblet in the other. He offered them a drink out of his goblet, but just as one of the soldiers was putting it to his mouth—whew!—a flash of fire blazed through the cellar, blinded every mother's son of them for several minutes, and when they recovered their eye-sight, jug, goblet, and Red-cap had vanished, and nothing but the empty cider-barrel remained."

Here the half-pay officer, who was growing very muzzy and sleepy, and nodding over his liquor, with half-extinguished eye, suddenly gleamed up like an expiring rushlight.

"That's all fudge!" said he, as Peechy finished his last story.

"Well, I don't vouch for the truth of it myself," said Peechy Prauw, "though all the world knows that there's something strange about that house and grounds; but as to the story of Mud Sam, I believe it just as well as if it had happened to myself."

---

The deep interest taken in this conversation by the company had made them unconscious of the uproar abroad among the elements, when suddenly they were electrified by a tremendous clap of thunder. A lumbering crash followed instantaneously, shaking the building to its very foundation. All started from their seats, imagining it the shock of an earthquake, or that old father Red-cap was coming among them in all his terrors. They listened for a moment, but only heard the rain pelting against the windows, and the wind howling among the trees. The explosion was soon explained by the apparition of an old negro's bald head thrust in at the door, his white goggle eyes contrasting with his jetty poll, which was wet with rain, and shone like a bottle. In a jargon but half intelligible, he announced that the kitchen chimney had been struck with lightning.

A sullen pause of the storm, which now rose and sunk in gusts, produced a momentary stillness. In this interval the report of a musket was heard, and a long shout, almost like a yell resounded from the shores. Every one crowded to the window; another musket-shot was heard, and another long shout, mingled wildly with a rising blast of wind. It seemed as if the cry came up from the bosom of the waters; for though incessant flashes of lightning spread a light about the shore, no one was to be seen.

Suddenly the window of the room overhead was opened, and a loud halloo uttered by the mysterious stranger. Several hailings passed from one party to the other, but in a language which none of the company in the bar-room could understand; and presently they heard the window closed, and a great noise overhead, as if all the furniture were pulled and hauled about the room. The negro servant was summoned, and shortly afterwards was seen assisting the veteran to lug the ponderous sea-chest down stairs.

The landlord was in amazement. "What, you are not going on the water in such a storm?"

"Storm!" said the other, scornfully, "do you call such a sputter of weather a storm?"

"You'll get drenched to the skin—You'll catch your death!" said Peechy Prauw, affectionately.

"Thunder and lightning!" exclaimed the veteran, "don't preach about weather to a man that has cruised in whirlwinds and tornadoes."

The obsequious Peechy was again struck dumb. The voice from the water was heard once more in a tone of impatience; the bystanders stared with redoubled awe at this man of storms, who seemed to have come up out of the deep, and to be summoned back to it again. As, with the assistance of the negro, he slowly bore his ponderous sea-chest towards the shore, they eyed it with a superstitious feeling; half doubting whether he were not really about to embark upon it and launch forth upon the wild waves. They followed him at a distance with a lantern.

"Dowse the light!" roared the hoarse voice from the water. "No one wants light here!"

"Thunder and lightning!" exclaimed the veteran, turning short upon them; "back to the house with you!"

Wolfert and his companions shrunk back in dismay. Still their curiosity would not allow them entirely to withdraw. A long sheet of lightning now flickered across the waves, and discovered a boat, filled with men, just under a rocky point, rising and sinking with the heaving surges, and swashing the waters at every heave. It was with difficulty held to the rocks by a boat-hook, for the current rushed furiously round the point. The veteran hoisted one end of the lumbering sea-chest on the gunwale of the boat, and seized the handle at the other end to lift it in, when the motion propelled the boat from the shore; the chest slipped off from the gunwale, and, sinking into the waves, pulled the veteran headlong after it. A loud shriek was uttered by all on shore, and a volley of execrations by those on board; but boat and man were hurried away by the rushing swiftness of the tide. A pitchy darkness succeeded; Wolfert Webber indeed fancied that he distinguished a cry for help, and that he beheld the drowning man beckoning for assistance; but when the lightning again gleamed along the water, all was void; neither man nor boat was to be seen; nothing but the dashing and weltering of the waves as they hurried past.

The company returned to the tavern to await the subsiding of the storm. They resumed their seats, and gazed on each other with dismay. The whole transaction had not occupied five minutes, and not a dozen words had been spoken. When they looked at the oaken chair, they could scarcely realize the fact that the strange being who had so lately tenanted it, full of life and Herculean vigor, should already be a corpse. There was the very glass he had just drunk from; there lay the ashes from the pipe which he had smoked, as it were, with his last breath. As the worthy burghers pondered on these things, they felt a terrible conviction of the uncertainty of existence, and each felt as if the ground on which he stood was rendered less stable by his awful example.

As, however, the most of the company were possessed of that valuable philosophy which enables a man to bear up with fortitude against the misfortunes of his neighbors, they soon managed to console themselves for the tragic end of the veteran. The landlord was particularly happy that the poor dear man had paid his reckoning before he went; and made a kind of farewell speech on the occasion.

"He came," said he, "in a storm, and he went in a storm; he came in the night, and he went in the night; he came nobody knows whence, and he has gone nobody knows where. For aught I know he has gone to sea once more on his chest, and may land to bother some people on the other side of the world! Though it's a thousand pities," added he, "if he has gone to Davy Jones' locker, that he had not left his own locker behind him."

"His locker! St. Nicholas preserve us!" cried Peechy Prauw. "I'd not have had that sea-chest in the house for any money; I'll warrant he'd come racketing after it at nights, and making a haunted house of the inn. And, as to his going to sea in his chest, I recollect what happened to Skipper Onderdonk's ship on his voyage from Amsterdam."

"The boatswain died during a storm, so they wrapped him up in a sheet, and put him in his own sea-chest, and threw him overboard; but they neglected in their hurry-skurry to say prayers over him—and the storm raged and roared louder than ever, and they saw the dead man seated in his chest, with his shroud for a sail, coming hard after the ship; and the sea breaking before him in great sprays like fire; and there they kept scudding day after day, and night after night, expecting every moment to go to wreck; and every night they saw the dead boatswain in his sea-chest trying to get up with them, and they heard his whistle above the blasts of wind, and he seemed to send great seas mountain high after them, that would have swamped the ship if they had not put up the dead-lights. And so it went on till they lost sight of him in the fogs off Newfoundland and supposed he had veered ship and stood for Dead Man's Isle. So much for burying a man at sea without saying prayers over him."

The thundergust which had hitherto detained the company was now at an end. The cuckoo clock in the hall told midnight; every one pressed to depart, for seldom was such a late hour of the night trespassed on by these quiet burghers. As they sallied forth, they found the heavens once more serene. The storm which had lately obscured them had rolled away, and lay piled up in fleecy masses on the horizon, lighted up by the bright crescent of the moon, which looked like a little silver lamp hung up in a palace of clouds.

The dismal occurrence of the night, and the dismal narrations they had made, had left a superstitious feeling in every mind. They cast a fearful glance at the spot where the buccaneer had disappeared, almost expecting to see him sailing on his chest in the cool moonshine. The trembling rays glittered along the waters, but all was placid; and the current dimpled over the spot where he had gone down. The party huddled together in a little crowd as they repaired homewards; particularly when they passed a lonely field where a man had been murdered; and even the sexton, who had to complete his journey alone, though accustomed, one would think, to ghosts and goblins, went a long way round, rather than pass by his own church-yard.

Wolfert Webber had now carried home a fresh stock of stories and notions to ruminate upon. These accounts of pots of money and Spanish treasures, buried here and there and every where, about the rocks and bays of these wild shores, made him almost dizzy. "Blessed St. Nicholas!" ejaculated he half aloud, "is it not possible to come upon one of these golden hoards, and to make one's self rich in a twinkling? How hard that I must go on, delving and delving, day in and day out, merely to make a morsel of bread, when one lucky stroke of a spade might enable me to ride in my carriage for the rest of my life!"

As he turned over in his thoughts all that had been told of the singular adventure of the negro fisherman, his imagination gave a totally different complexion to the tale. He saw in the gang of redcaps nothing but a crew of pirates burying their spoils, and his cupidity was once more awakened by the possibility of at length getting on the traces of some of this lurking wealth. Indeed, his infected fancy tinged every thing with gold. He felt like the greedy inhabitant of Bagdad, when his eyes had been greased with the magic ointment of the dervise, that gave him to see all the treasures of the earth. Caskets of buried jewels, chests of ingots, and barrels of outlandish coins, seemed to court him from their concealments, and supplicate him to relieve them from their untimely graves.

On making private inquiries about the grounds said to be haunted by father Red-cap, he was more and more confirmed in his surmise. He learned that the place had several times been visited by experienced money-diggers, who had heard black Sam's story, though none of them had met with success. On the contrary, they had always been dogged with ill-luck of some kind or other, in consequence, as Wolfert concluded, of not going to work at the proper time, and with the proper ceremonials. The last attempt had been made by Cobus Quackenbos, who dug for a whole night, and met with incredible difficulty, for as fast as he threw one shovel full of earth out of the hole, two were thrown in by invisible hands. He succeeded so far, however, as to uncover an iron chest, when there was a terrible roaring, ramping, and raging of uncouth figures about the hole, and at length a shower of blows, dealt by invisible cudgels, fairly belabored him off of the forbidden ground. This Cobus Quackenbos had declared on his death-bed, so that there could not be any doubt of it. He was a man that had devoted many years of his life to money-digging, and it was thought would have ultimately succeeded, had he not died recently of a brain-fever in the alms-house.

Wolfert Webber was now in a worry of trepidation and impatience; fearful lest some rival adventurer should get a scent of the buried gold. He determined privately to seek out the black fisherman, and get him to serve as guide to the place where he had witnessed the mysterious scene of interment. Sam was easily found; for he was one of those old habitual beings that live about a neighborhood until they wear them-selves a place in the public mind, and become, in a manner, public characters. There was not an unlucky urchin about town that did not know Sam the fisherman, and think that he had a right to play his tricks upon the old negro. Sam had led an amphibious life for more than half a century, about the shores of the bay, and the fishing-grounds of the Sound. He passed the greater part of his time on and in the water, particularly about Hell-gate; and might have been taken, in bad weather, for one of the hobgoblins that used to haunt that strait. There would he be seen, at all times, and in all weathers; sometimes in his skiff, anchored among the eddies, or prowling, like a shark about some wreck, where the fish are supposed to be most abundant. Sometimes seated on a rock from hour to hour, looking in the mist and drizzle, like a solitary heron watching for its prey. He was well acquainted with every hole and corner of the Sound; from the Wall-about to Hell-gate, and from Hell-gate even unto the Devil's Stepping-Stones; and it was even affirmed that he knew all the fish in the river by their Christian names.

Wolfert found him at his cabin, which was not much larger than a tolerable dog-house. It was rudely constructed of fragments of wrecks and drift-wood, and built on the rocky shore, at the foot of the old fort, just about what at present forms the point of the Battery. A "most ancient and fish-like smell" pervaded the place. Oars, paddles, and fishing rods were leaning against the wall of the fort; a net was spread on the sands to dry; a skiff was drawn up on the beach, and at the door of his cabin was Mud Sam himself, indulging in the true negro luxury of sleeping in the sunshine.

Many years had passed away since the time of Sam's youthful adventure, and the snows of many a winter had grizzled the knotty wool upon his head. He perfectly recollected the circumstances, however, for he had often been called upon to relate them, though in his version of the story he differed in many points from Peechy Prauw; as is not unfrequently the case with authentic historians. As to the subsequent researches of money-diggers, Sam knew nothing about them; they were matters quite out of his line; neither did the cautious Wolfert care to disturb his thoughts on that point. His only wish was to secure the old fisherman as a pilot to the spot, and this was readily effected. The long time that had intervened since his nocturnal adventure had effaced all Sam's awe of the place, and the promise of a trifling reward roused him at once from his sleep and his sunshine.

The tide was adverse to making the expedition by water, and Wolfert was too impatient to get to the land of promise, to wait for its turning; they set off, therefore, by land. A walk of four or five miles brought them to the edge of a wood, which at that time covered the greater part of the eastern side of the island. It was just beyond the pleasant region of Bloomen-dael. Here they struck into a long lane, straggling among trees and bushes, very much overgrown with weeds and mullen-stalks, as if but seldom used, and so completely overshadowed as to enjoy but a kind of twilight. Wild vines entangled the trees and flaunted in their faces; brambles and briers caught their clothes as they passed; the garter-snake glided across their path; the spotted toad hopped and waddled before them, and the restless cat-bird mewed at them from every thicket. Had Wolfert Webber been deeply read in romantic legend, he might have fancied himself entering upon forbidden, enchanted ground; or that these were some of the guardians set to keep watch upon buried treasure. As it was, the loneliness of the place, and the wild stories connected with it, had their effect upon his mind.

On reaching the lower end of the lane, they found themselves near the shore of the Sound in a kind of amphitheatre, surrounded by forest trees. The area had once been a grassplot, but was now shagged with briers and rank weeds. At one end, and just on the river bank, was a ruined building, little better than a heap of rubbish, with a stack of chimneys rising like a solitary tower out of the centre. The current of the Sound rushed along just below it; with wildly grown trees drooping their branches into its waves.

Wolfert had not a doubt that this was the haunted house of Father Red-cap, and called to mind the story of Peechy Prauw. The evening was approaching, and the light falling dubiously among the woody places, gave a melancholy tone to the scene, well calculated to foster any lurking feeling of awe or superstition. The night-hawk, wheeling about in the highest regions of the air, emitted his peevish, boding cry. The woodpecker gave a lonely tap now and then on some hollow tree, and the fire-bird* streamed by them with his deep-red plumage.

They now came to an inclosure that had once been a garden. It extended along the foot of a rocky ridge, but was little better than a wilderness of weeds, with here and there a matted rose bush, or a peach or plum tree grown wild and ragged, and covered with moss. At the lower end of the garden they passed a kind of vault in the side of a bank, facing the water. It had the look of a root-house. The door, though decayed, was still strong, and appeared to have been recently patched up. Wolfert pushed it open. It gave a harsh grating upon its hinges, and striking against something like a box, a rattling sound ensued, and a skull rolled on the floor. Wolfert drew back shuddering, but was reassured on being informed by the negro that this was a family vault, belonging to one of the old Dutch families that owned this estate; an assertion corroborated by the sight of coffins of various sizes piled within. Sam had been familiar with all these scenes when a boy, and now knew that he could not be far from the place of which they were in quest.

They now made their way to the water's edge, scrambling along ledges of rocks that overhung the waves, and obliged often to hold by shrubs and grape-vines to avoid slipping into the deep and hurried stream. At length they came to a small cove, or rather indent of the shore. It was protected by steep rocks, and overshadowed by a thick copse of oaks and chestnuts, so as to be sheltered and almost concealed. The beach shelved gradually within the cove, but the current swept deep, and black, and rapid, along its jutting points. The negro paused;

---

*Orchard Oriole.

raised his remnant of a hat, and scratched his grizzled poll for a moment, as he regarded this nook; then suddenly clapping his hands, he stepped exultingly forward, and pointed to a large iron ring, stapled firmly in the rock, just where a broad shelf of stone furnished a commodious landing-place. It was the very spot where the red-caps had landed. Years had changed the more perishable features of the scene; but rock and iron yield slowly to the influence of time. On looking more closely, Wolfert remarked three crosses cut in the rock just above the ring, which had no doubt some mysterious signification. Old Sam now readily recognized the overhanging rock under which his skiff had been sheltered during the thundergust. To follow up the course which the midnight gang had taken, however, was a harder task. His mind had been so much taken up on that eventful occasion by the persons of the drama, as to pay but little attention to the scenes; and these places look so different by night and day. After wandering about for some time, however, they came to an opening among the trees which Sam thought resembled the place. There was a ledge of rock of moderate height like a wall on one side, which he thought might be the very ridge whence he had overlooked the diggers. Wolfert examined it narrowly, and at length discovered three crosses similar to those on the above ring, cut deeply into the face of the rock, but nearly obliterated by moss that had grown over them. His heart leaped with joy, for he doubted not they were the private marks of the buccaneers. All now that remained was to ascertain the precise spot were the treasure lay buried; for otherwise he might dig at random in the neighborhood of the crosses, without coming upon the spoils, and he had already had enough of such profitless labor. Here, however, the old negro was perfectly at a loss, and indeed perplexed him by a variety of opinions; for his recollections were all confused. Sometimes he declared it must have been at the foot of a mulberry-tree hard by; then beside a great white stone; then under a small green knoll, a short distance from the ledge of rocks; until at length Wolfert became as bewildered as himself.

The shadows of evening were now spreading themselves over the woods, and rock and tree began to mingle together. It was evidently too late to attempt any thing farther at present; and, indeed, Wolfert had come unprovided with implements to prosecute his researches, Satisfied, therefore, with having ascertained the place, he took note of all its landmarks, that he might recognize it again, and set out on his return homewards, resolved to prosecute this golden enterprise without delay.

The leading anxiety which had hitherto absorbed every feeling, being now in some measure appeased, fancy began to wander, and to conjure up a thousand shapes and chimeras as he returned through this haunted region. Pirates hanging in chains seemed to swing from every tree, and he almost expected to see some Spanish Don, with his throat cut from ear to ear, rising slowly out of the ground, and shaking the ghost of a money-bag.

Their way back lay through the desolate garden, and Wolfert's nerves had arrived at so sensitive a state that the flitting of a bird, the rustling of a leaf, or the falling of a nut, was enough to startle him. As they entered the confines of the garden, they caught sight of a figure at a distance advancing slowly up one of the walks, and bending under the weight of a burden. They paused and regarded him attentively. He wore what appeared to be a woolen cap, and still more alarming, of a most sanguinary red.

The figure moved slowly on, ascended the bank, and stopped at the very door of the sepulchral vault. Just before entering it he looked around. What was the affright of Wolfert, when he recognized the grisly visage of the drowned buccaneer! He uttered an ejaculation of horror. The figure slowly raised his iron fist, and shook it with a terrible menace. Wolfert did not pause to see any more, but hurried off as fast as his legs could carry him, nor was Sam slow in following at his heels, having all his ancient terrors revived. Away, then, did they scramble through bush and brake, horribly frightened at every bramble that tugged at their skirts, nor did they pause to breathe, until they had blundered their way through this perilous wood, and fairly reached the high road to the city.

Several days elapsed before Wolfert could summon courage enough to prosecute the enterprise, so much had he been dismayed by the apparition, whether living or dead, of the grisly buccaneer. In the mean time, what a conflict of mind did he suffer! He neglected all his concerns, was moody and restless all day, lost his appetite, wandered in his thoughts and words, and committed a thousand blunders. His rest was broken; and when he feel asleep, the nightmare, in shape of a huge money-bag, sat squatted upon his breast. He babbled about incalculable sums; fancied himself engaged in money-digging; threw the bedclothes right and left, in the idea that he was shovelling away the dirt; groped under the bed in quest of the treasure, and lugged forth, as he supposed, and inestimable pot of gold.

Dame Webber and her daughter were in despair at what they conceived a returning touch of insanity. There are two family oracles, one or other of which Dutch housewives consult in all cases of great doubt and perplexity—the dominie and the doctor. In the present instance they repaired to the doctor. There was at that time a little dark mouldy man of medicine, famous among the old wives of the Manhattoes for his skill, not only in the healing art, but in all matters of strange and mysterious nature. His name was Dr. Knipperhausen, but he was more commonly known by the appellation of the High German Doctor.* To him did the poor women repair for council and assistance touching the mental vagaries of Wolfert Webber.

They found the doctor seated in his little study, clad in his dark camlet robe of knowledge, with his black velvet cap; after the manner of Boorhaave, Van Helmont, and other medical sages; a pair of green spectacles set in black horn upon his clubbed nose, and poring over a German folio that reflected back the darkness of his physiognomy. The doctor listened to their statement of the symptoms of Wolfert's malady with profound attention; but when they came to mention his raving about buried money, the little man pricked up his ears. Alas, poor women! they little knew the aid they had called in.

Dr. Knipperhausen had been half his life engaged in seeking the short cuts to fortune, in quest of which so many a long lifetime is wasted. He had passed some years of his youth among the Harz mountains of Germany, and had derived much valuable instruction from the miners, touching the mode of seeking treasure buried in the earth. He had prosecuted his studies also under a travelling sage who united the mysteries of medicine with magic and legerdemain. His mind therefore had become stored with all kinds of mystic lore; he had dabbled a little in astrology, alchemy, divination; knew how to detect stolen money, and to tell where springs of water lay hidden; in

---

*The same, no doubt, of whom mention is made in the history of Dolph Heyliger.

a word, by the dark nature of his knowledge he had acquired the name of the High German Doctor, which is pretty nearly equivalent to that of necromancer. The doctor had often heard rumors of treasure being buried in various parts of the island, and had long been anxious to get on the traces of it. No sooner were Wolfert's waking and sleeping vagaries confided to him, than he beheld in them the confirmed symptoms of a case of money-digging, and lost no time in probing it to the bottom. Wolfert had long been sorely oppressed in mind by the golden secret, and as a family physician is a kind of father confessor, he was glad of any opportunity of unburdening himself. So far from curing, the doctor caught the malady from his patient. The circumstances unfolded to him awakened all his cupidity; he had not a doubt of money being buried somewhere in the neighborhood of the mysterious crosses, and offered to join Wolfert in the search. He informed him that much secrecy and caution must be observed in enterprises of the kind; that money is only to be digged for at night; with certain forms and ceremonies; and burning of drugs; the repeating of mystic words, and above all, that the seekers must first be provided with a divining rod, which had the wonderful property of pointing to the very spot on the surface of the earth under which treasure lay hidden. As the doctor had given much of his mind to these matters, he charged himself with all the necessary preparations, and, as the quarter of the moon was propitious, he undertook to have the divining rod ready by a certain night.*

---

*The following note was found appended to this passage in the hand-writing of Mr. Knickerbocker. "There has been much written against the divining rod by those light minds who are ever ready to scoff at the mysteries of nature; but I fully join with Dr. Knipperhausen in giving it my faith. I shall not insist upon its efficacy in discovering the concealment of stolen goods, the boundary stones of fields, the traces of robbers and murderers, or even the existence of subterraneous springs and streams of water: albeit, I think these properties not to be readily discredited; but of its potency in discovering veins of precious metal, and hidden sums of money and jewels, I have not the least doubt. Some said that the rod turned only in the hands of persons who had been born in particular months of the year; hence astrologers had recourse to planetary influence when they would procure a talisman. Others declared that the properties of the rod were either an effect of chance, or the fraud of the holder, or the work of the devil. Thus saith the reverend father

Wolfert's heart leaped with joy at having met with so learned and able a coadjutor. Every thing went on secretly, but swimmingly. The doctor had many consultations with his patient, and the good woman of the household lauded the comforting effect of his visits. In the mean time the wonderful divining rod, that great key to nature's secrets, was duly prepared. The doctor had thumbed over all his books of knowledge for the occasion; and the black fisherman was engaged to take them in his skiff to the scene of enterprise; to work with spade and pickaxe in unearthing the treasure; and to freight his bark with the weighty spoils they were certain of finding.

At length the appointed night arrived for this perilous undertaking. Before Wolfert left his home he counselled his wife and daughter to go to bed, and feel no alarm if he should not return during the night. Like reasonable women, on being told not to feel alarm they fell immediately into a panic. They saw at once by his manner that something unusual was in agitation; all their fears about the unsettled state of his mind were revived with tenfold force: they hung about him, entreating him not to expose himself to the night air, but all in vain. When once Wolfert was mounted on his hobby, it was no easy matter to get him out of the saddle. It was a clear starlight night, when he issued out of the portal of the Webber palace. He wore a large flapped

---

Gaspard Sebett in his Treatise on Magic; 'Propter haec et similia argumenta audacter ego promisero vim conversivam virgulae bifurcatae nequaquam naturalem esse, sed vel casu vel fraude virgulam tractantis vel ope diaboli,'&c.

"Georgius Agricola also was of opinion that it was a mere delusion of the devil to inveigle the avaricious and unwary into his clutches, and in his treatise 'de re Metallica,' lays particular stress on the mysterious words pronounced by those persons who employed the divining rod during his time. But I make not a doubt that the divining rod is one of those secrets of natural magic, the mystery of which is to be explained by the sympathies existing between physical things operated upon by the planets, and rendered efficacious by the strong faith of the individual. Let the divining rod be properly gathered at the proper time of the moon, cut into the proper form, used with the necessary ceremonies, and with a perfect faith in its efficacy, and I can confidently recommend it to my fellow-citizens as an infallible means of discovering the places on the Island of the Manhattoes where treasure hath been buried in the olden time.

D.K."

hat tied under the chin with a handkerchief of his daughter's, to secure him from the night damp, while Dame Webber threw her long red cloak about his shoulders, and fastened it round his neck.

The doctor had been no less carefully armed and accoutred by his housekeeper, the vigilant Frau Ilsy; and sallied forth in his camlet robe by way of surcoat; his black velvet cap under his cocked hat, a thick clasped book under his arm, a basket of drugs and dried herbs in one hand, and in the other the miraculous rod of divination.

The great church clock struck ten as Wolfert and the doctor passed by the church yard, and the watchman bawled in hoarse voice a long and doleful "all's well!" A deep sleep had already fallen upon this primitive little burgh: nothing disturbed this awful silence, excepting now and then the bark of some profligate night-walking dog, or the serenade of some romantic cat. It is true, Wolfert fancied more than once that he heard the sound of a stealthy footfall at a distance behind them; but it might have been merely the echo of their own steps along the quiet streets. He thought also at one time that he saw a tall figure skulking after them—stopping when they stopped, and moving on as they proceeded; but the dim and uncertain lamp-light threw such vague gleams and shadows, that this might all have been mere fancy.

They found the old fisherman waiting for them, smoking his pipe in the stern of the skiff, which was moored just in front of his little cabin. A pickaxe and spade were lying in the bottom of the boat, with a dark lantern, and a stone bottle of good Dutch courage, in which honest Sam no doubt put even more faith than Dr. Knipperhausen in his drugs.

Thus then did these three worthies embark in their cockleshell of a skiff upon the nocturnal expedition, with a wisdom and valor equalled only by the three wise men of Gotham, who adventured to sea in a bowl. The tide was rising and running rapidly up the Sound. The current bore them along, almost without the aid of an oar. The profile of the town lay all in shadow. Here and there a light feebly glimmered from some sick chamber, or from the cabin window of some vessel at anchor in the stream. Not a cloud obscured the deep starry firmament, the lights of which wavered on the surface of the placid river; and a shooting meteor, streaking its pale course in the very direction they were taking, was interpreted by the doctor into a most propitious omen.

In a little while they glided by the point of Corlaer's Hook with the rural inn which had been the scene of such night adventures. The family had retired to rest, and the house was dark and still. Wolfert felt a chill pass over him as they passed the point where the buccaneer had disappeared. He pointed it out to Dr. Knipperhausen. While regarding it, they thought they saw a boat actually lurking at the very place; but the shore cast such a shadow over the border of the water that they could discern nothing distinctly. They had not proceeded far when they heard the low sounds of distant oars, as if cautiously pulled. Sam plied his oars with redoubled vigor, and knowing all the eddies and currents of the stream, soon left their followers, if such they were, far astern. In a little while they stretched across Turtle bay and Kip's bay, then shrouded themselves in the deep shadows of the Manhattan shore, and glided swiftly along, secure from observation. At length the negro shot his skiff into a little cove, darkly embowered by trees, and made it fast to the well-known iron ring. They now landed, and lighting the lantern, gathered their various implements and proceeded slowly through the bushes. Every sound startled them, even that of their own footsteps among the dry leaves; and the hooting of a screech owl, from the shattered chimney of the neighboring ruin, made their blood run cold.

In spite of all Wolfert's caution in taking note of the landmarks, it was some time before they could find the open place among the trees, where the treasure was supposed to be buried. At length they came to the ledge of rock; and on examining its surface by the aid of the lantern, Wolfert recognized the three mystic crosses. Their hearts beat quick, for the momentous trial was at hand that was to determine their hopes.

The lantern was now held by Wolfert Webber, while the doctor produced the divining rod. It was a forked twig, one end of which was grasped firmly in each hand, while the centre, forming the stem, pointed perpendicularly upwards. The doctor moved this wand about, with a certain distance of the earth, from place to place, but for some time without any effect, while Wolfert kept the light of the lantern turned full upon it, and watched it with the most breathless interest. At length the rod began slowly to turn. The doctor grasped it with greater earnestness, his hands trembling with the agitation of his mind. The wand continued to turn gradually, until at length the stem had

reversed its position, and pointed perpendicularly downward, and remained pointing to one spot as fixedly as the needle to the pole.

"This is the spot!" said the doctor, in an almost inaudible tone.
Wolfert's heart was in his throat.

"Shall I dig?" said the negro, grasping the spade.

"*Pots tausends*, no!" replied the little doctor, hastily. He now
ordered his companions to keep close by him, and to maintain the most
inflexible silence. That certain precautions must be taken and ceremonies used to prevent the evil spirits which kept about buried treasure
from doing them any harm. He then drew a circle about the place,
enough to include the whole party. He next gathered dry twigs and
leaves and made a fire, upon which he threw certain drugs and dried
herbs which he had brought in his basket. A thick smoke rose, diffusing
a potent odor, savoring marvellously of brimstone and assafoetida,
which, however grateful it might be to the olfactory nerves of spirits,
nearly strangled poor Wolfert, and produced a fit of coughing and
wheezing that made the whole grove resound. Dr. Knipperhausen then
unclasped the volume which he had brought under his arm, which
was printed in red and black characters in German text. While Wolfert
held the lantern, the doctor, by the aid of his spectacles, read off several
forms of conjuration in Latin and German. He then ordered Sam to
seize the pickaxe and proceed to work. The close-bound soil gave
obstinate signs of not having been disturbed for many a year. After
having picked his way through the surface, Sam came to a bed of sand
and gravel, which he threw briskly to right and left with the spade.

"Hark!" said Wolfert, who fancied he heard a trampling among
the dry leaves, and a rustling through the bushes. Sam paused for a
moment, and they listened. No footstep was near. The bat flitted by
them in silence; a bird, roused from its roost by the light which glared
up among the trees, flew circling about the flame. In the profound
stillness of the woodland, they distinguish the current rippling along
the rocky shore, and the distant murmuring and roaring of Hell-gate.

The negro continued his labors, and had already digged a considerable hole. The doctor stood on the edge, reading formulae every
now and then from his black-letter volume, or throwing more drugs
and herbs upon the fire; while Wolfert bent anxiously over the pit,
watching every stroke of the spade. Any one witnessing the scene thus
lighted up by fire, lantern, and the reflection of Wolfert's red mantle,

might have mistaken the little doctor for some foul magician, busied in his incantations, and the grizzly-headed negro for some swart goblin, obedient to his commands.

At length the spade of the fisherman struck upon something that sounded hollow. The sound vibrated to Wolfert's heart. He struck his spade again.—

"'Tis a chest," said Sam.

"Full of gold, I'll warrant it!" cried Wolfert, clasping his hands with rapture.

Scarcely had he uttered the words when a sound from above caught his ear. He cast up his eyes, and lo! by the expiring light of the fire he beheld, just over the disk of the rock, what appeared to be the grim visage of the drowned buccaneer, grinning hideously down upon him.

Wolfert gave a loud cry, and let fall the lantern. His panic communicated itself to his companions. The negro leaped out of the hole; the doctor dropped his book and basket, and began to pray in German. All was horror and confusion. The fire was scattered about, the lantern extinguished. In their hurry-scurry they ran against and confounded one another. They fancied a legion of hobgoblins let loose upon them, and that they saw, by the fitful gleams of the scattered embers, strange figures, in red caps, gibbering and ramping around them. The doctor ran one way, the negro another, and Wolfert made for the water side. As he plunged struggling onwards through brush and brake, he heard the tread of some one in pursuit. He scrambled frantically forward. The footsteps gained upon him. He felt himself grasped by his cloak, when suddenly his pursuer was attacked in turn: a fierce fight and struggle ensued—a pistol was discharged that lit up rock and bush for a second, and showed two figures grappling together—all was then darker than ever. The contest continued—the combatants clinched each other, and panted, and groaned, and rolled among the rocks. There was snarling and growling as of a cur, mingled with curses, in which Wolfert fancied he could recognize the voice of the buccaneer. He would fain have fled, but he was on the brink of a precipice, and could go no further.

Again the parties were on their feet; again there was a tugging and struggling, as if strength alone could decide the combat, until one was precipitated from the brow of the cliff, and sent headlong into the deep stream that whirled below. Wolfert heard the plunge, and a kind of strangling, bubbling murmur, but the darkness of the night hid every thing from him, and the swiftness of the current swept every thing instantly out of hearing. One of the combatants was disposed of, but whether friend of foe, Wolfert could not tell, nor whether they might not both be foes. He heard the survivor approach, and his terror revived. He saw, where the profile of the rocks rose against the horizon, a human form advancing. He could not be mistaken: it must be the buccaneer. Whither should he fly!—a precipice was on one side—a murderer on the other. The enemy approached—he was close at hand. Wolfert attempted to let himself down the face of the cliff. His cloak caught in a thorn that grew on the edge. He was jerked from off his feet, and held dangling in the air, half-choked by the string with which his careful wife had fastened the garment around his neck. Wolfert thought his last moment was arrived; already had committed his soul to St. Nicholas, when the string broke, and he tumbled down the bank, bumping from rock to rock, and bush to bush, and leaving the red cloak fluttering like a bloody banner in the air.

It was a long while before Wolfert came to himself. When he opened his eyes, the ruddy streaks of morning were already shooting up the sky. He found himself grievously battered, and lying in the bottom of a boat. He attempted to sit up, but was too sore and stiff to move. A voice requested him in friendly accents to lie still. He turned his eyes towards the speaker: it was Dirk Waldron. He had dogged the party, at the earnest request of Dame Webber and her daughter, who with the laudable curiosity of their sex, had pried into the secret consultations of Wolfert and the doctor. Dirk had been completely distanced in following the light skiff of the fisherman, and had just come in to rescue the poor money-digger from his pursuer.

Thus ended this perilous enterprise. The doctor and Black Sam severally found their way back to the Manhattoes, each having some dreadful tale of peril to relate. As to poor Wolfert, instead of returning in triumph laden with bags of gold, he was borne home on a shutter, followed by a rabble-rout of curious urchins. His wife and daughter saw the dismal pageant from a distance, and alarmed the neighborhood with their cries: they thought the poor man had suddenly settled the great debt of nature in one of his wayward moods. Finding him, however, still living, they had him speedily to bed, and a jury of old matrons of the neighborhood assembled, to determine how he should be doctored. The whole town was in a buzz with the story of the money-diggers. Many repaired to the scene of the previous night's adventures: but though they found the very place of the digging, they discovered nothing that compensated them for their trouble. Some say they found the fragments of an oaken chest, and an iron pot-lid, which savored strongly of hidden money; and that in the old family vault there were traces of bales and boxes, but this is all very dubious.

In fact, the secret of all this story has never to this day been discovered: whether any treasure were ever actually buried at that place; whether, if so, it were carried off at night by those who had buried it; or whether it still remains there under the guardianship of gnomes and spirits until it shall be properly sought for, is all matter of conjecture. For my part I incline to the latter opinion; and make no doubt that great sums lie buried, both there and in other parts of this island and its neighborhood, ever since the times of the buccaneers and the Dutch colonists; and I would earnestly recommend the search after them to such of my fellow-citizens as are not engaged in any other speculations.

There were many conjectures formed, also, as to who and what was the strange man of the seas who had domineered over the little fraternity of Corlaer's Hook for a time; disappeared so strangely, and reappeared so fearfully. Some supposed him a smuggler stationed at that place to assist his comrades in landing their goods among the rocky coves of the island. Others, that he was one of the ancient comrades of Kidd or Bradish, returned to convey away treasures formerly hidden in the vicinity. The only circumstance that throws any thing like a vague light on this mysterious matter, is a report which prevailed of a strange foreign-built shallop, with much the look of a picaroon, having been seen hovering about the Sound for several days without landing or reporting herself, though boats were seen going to and from her at night: and that she was seen standing out of the mouth of the harbor, in the gray of the dawn after the catastrophe of the money-diggers.

I must not omit to mention another report, also, which I confess is rather apocryphal, of the buccaneer, who was supposed to have been drowned, being seen before daybreak, with a lantern in his hand, seated astride of his great sea-chest, and sailing through Hell-gate, which just then began to roar and bellow with redoubled fury.

While all the gossip world was thus filled with talk and rumor, poor Wolfert lay sick and sorrowful in his bed, bruised in body and sorely beaten down in mind. His wife and daughter did all they could to bind up his wounds, both corporal and spiritual. The good old dame never stirred from his bedside, where she sat knitting from morning till night; while his daughter busied herself about him with the fondest care. Nor did they lack assistance from abroad. Whatever may be said of the desertion of friends in distress, they had no complaint of the kind to make. Not an old wife of the neighborhood but abandoned her work to crowd to the mansion of Wolfert Webber, to inquire after his health, and the particulars of his story. Not one came moreover without her little pipkin of pennyroyal, sage, balm, or other herb tea, delighted at an opportunity of signalizing her kindness and her doctorship. What drenchings did not the poor Wolfert undergo, and all in vain! It was a moving sight to behold him wasting away day by day; growing thinner and thinner, and ghastlier and ghastlier, and staring with rueful visage from under an old patchwork counterpane, upon the jury of matrons kindly assembled to sigh and groan and look unhappy around him.

Dirk Waldron was the only being that seemed to shed a ray of sunshine into this house of mourning. He came in with cheery look and manly spirit, and tried to reanimate the expiring heart of the poor money-digger, but it was all in vain. Wolfert was completely done over. If any thing was wanting to complete his despair, it was a notice served upon him in the midst of his distress, that the corporation were about to run a new street through the very centre of his cabbage garden. He now saw nothing before him but poverty and ruin; his last reliance, the garden of his forefathers, was to be laid waste, and what then was to become of his poor wife and child?

His eyes filled with tears as they followed the dutiful Amy out of the room one morning. Dirk Waldron was seated beside him; Wolfert grasped his hand, pointed after his daughter, and for the first time since his illness, broke the silence he had maintained.

"I am going!" said he, shaking his head feebly, "and when I am gone—my poor daughter——"

"Leave her to me, father!" said Dirk, manfully—"I'll take care of her!"

Wolfert looked up in the face of the cheery, strapping youngster, and saw there was none better able to take care of a woman. "Enough," said he—"she is yours!—and now fetch me a lawyer—let me make my will and die."

The lawyer was brought—a dapper, bustling, round-headed little man, Roorback (or Rollebuck as it was pronounced) by name. At the sight of him the women broke into loud lamentations, for they looked upon the signing of a will as the signing of a death warrant. Wolfert made a feeble motion for them to be silent. Poor Amy buried her face and her grief in the bed curtain. Dame Webber resumed her knitting to hide her distress, which betrayed itself however in a pellucid tear, which trickled silently down, and hung at the end of her peaked nose; while the cat, the only unconcerned member of the family, played with the good dame's ball of worsted, as it rolled about the floor.

Wolfert lay on his back, his night-cap drawn over his forehead; his eyes closed; his whole visage the picture of death. He begged the lawyer to be brief, for he felt his end approaching, and that he had not time to lose. The lawyer nibbed his pen, spread out his paper, and prepared to write.

"I give and bequeath," said Wolfert, faintly, "my small farm—"

"What—all!" exclaimed the lawyer.

Wolfert half opened his eyes and looked upon the lawyer.

"Yes—all," said he.

"What! all that great patch of land with cabbages and sun-flowers, which the corporation is just going to run a main street through?"

"The same," said Wolfert, with a heavy sigh, and sinking back upon his pillow.

"I wish him joy that inherits, it!" said the little lawyer, chuckling, and rubbing his hands involuntarily.

"What do you mean?" said Wolfert, again opening his eyes.

"That he'll be one of the richest men in the place!" cried the little Rollebuck.

The expiring Wolfert seemed to step back from the threshold of existence: his eyes again lighted up; he raised himself in his bed, shoved back his red worsted night cap, and stared broadly at the lawyer.

"You don't say so!" exclaimed he.

"Faith, but I do!; rejoined the other. "Why, when that great field and that huge meadow come to be laid out in streets, and cut up into snug building lots—why, whoever owns it need not pull off his hat to the patroon!"

"Say you so?" cried Wolfert, half thrusting one leg out of bed, "why, then I think I'll not make my will yet!"

To the surprise of every body the dying man actually recovered. The vital spark, which had glimmered faintly in the socket, received fresh fuel from the oil of gladness, which the little lawyer poured into his soul. It once more burnt up into a flame.

Give physic to the heart, ye who would revive the body of a spirit-broken man! In a few days Wolfert left his room; in a few days more his table was covered with deeds, plans of streets, and building lots. Little Rollebuck was constantly with him, his right-hand man and adviser; and instead of making his will, assisted in the more agreeable task of making his fortune. In fact Wolfert Webber was one of those worthy Dutch burghers of the Manhattoes whose fortunes have been made, in a manner, in spite of themselves; who have tenaciously held on to their hereditary acres, raising turnips and cabbages about the skirts of the city, hardly able to make both ends meet, until the corporation has cruelly driven streets through their abodes, and they have suddenly awakened out of their lethargy, and, to their astonishment, found themselves rich men.

Before many months had elapsed, a great bustling street passed through the very center of the Webber garden, just where Wolfert had dreamed of finding a treasure. His golden dream was accomplished; he did indeed find an unlooked-for source of wealth; for, when his paternal lands were distributed into building lots, and rented out to safe tenants, instead of producing a paltry crop of cabbages, they returned him an abundant crop of rent; insomuch that on quarter-day, it was a goodly sight to see his tenants knocking at the door, from morning till night, each with a little round-bellied bag of money, a golden produce of the soil.

The ancient mansion of his forefathers was still kept up; but instead of being a little yellow-fronted Dutch house in a garden, it now stood boldly in the midst of a street, the grand home of the neighborhood; for Wolfert enlarged it with a wing on each side, and a cupola or tea room on top, where he might climb up and smoke his pipe in hot weather; and in the course of time the whole mansion was overrun by the chubby-faced progeny of Amy Webber and Dirk Waldron.

As Wolfert waxed old, and rich, and corpulent, he also set up a great ginger-bread colored carriage, drawn by a pair of black Flanders mares, with tails that swept the ground; and to commemorate the origin of his greatness, he had for his crest, a full blown cabbage painted on the panels, with the pithy motto **ALLES KOPF**, that is to say, ALL HEAD; meaning thereby that he had risen by sheer head-work.

To fill the measure of his greatness, in the fulness of time the renowned Ramm Rapelye slept with his fathers, and Wolfert Webber succeeded to the leather-bottomed arm-chair, in the inn parlor at Corlaer's Hook; where he long reigned greatly honored and respected, insomuch that he was never known to tell a story without its being believed, nor to utter a joke without its being laughed at.

# Appendix

*As Irving indicated in his note to "Rip Van Winkle," he was relying on German folk materials to supply the Romantic wonder his native land lacked. Precisely which of the German folktale collections he read is difficult to establish with certainty because several contain the same stories, but a curious confusion in the note is circumstantial evidence that points directly at Otmar's* Volks-Sagen. *The "superstition about the Emperor Frederick der Rothbart, and the Kypphäuser mountain [surely a misprint for* Kyffhäuser*]" that he cites was doubtless one source, but the greater indebtedness was to the story of Peter Klaus. In Otmar, these are adjacent tales. (Two scholarly studies explore these influences on Irving. Henry A. Pochmann's "Irving's German Sources in The Sketch Book" appeared in* Studies in Philology, *XXVII (1930), 477-507. A more extensive survey of the mythic antecedents is Philip Young's superb essay, "Fallen from Time: The Mythic Rip Van Winkle," first published in* Kenyon Review, *XXII (1960), 547-73, and reprinted in his book,* Three Bags Full.*)*

*Oddly, despite Irving's acknowledgment, the fact that "Rip Van Winkle" had a German root has been treated as its author's dirty secret. Charges of plagiarism were leveled in the decade following its publication, and long after Irving's death, a peculiar Dutch scholar stridently accused him of fraud. Comparison of "Rip Van Winkle" with the two tales (reprinted below in English translation) should clearly demonstrate that the genius of the story-telling was emphatically Irving's own.*

*"The Legend of Sleepy Hollow" also reveals a debt to the German Romanticism that, at the start of the nineteenth century, produced numerous gatherings of tales revolving around the supernatural. In this case, the source was the fifth legend of Rübezahl in* Volksmärchen der Deutschen *by Musaeus, but the loan is almost entirely confined to the figure of the headless horseman. Although it seems virtually certain that Irving worked with a copy of Musaeus close by, he invented a wholly new base for his story.*

## The Enchanted Emperor

Once upon a time, on the third day of Easter, a miner who lived alone, peacefully and piously, went to the Kyffhäuser. There he found, sitting on a high watchtower, a monk with a long white beard that reached down to his knees. When the monk saw the miner, he closed the great book he was reading and, in a friendly manner, said to him, "Come with me to Emperor Frederick, who has been waiting for us for an hour. The dwarf has already brought me the springroot."

Like ice, a chill went through the miner's body, but the monk spoke so soothingly that he followed quite happily, promising, come what may, not to utter a sound. At last they arrived at a clearing, which was surrounded by a wall. There the monk drew a large circle and wrote strange signs in the sand with his crook. Then he read, long and aloud, prayers from the great book, which, however, the miner did not understand. Finally, he struck the earth three times with his staff and cried out, "Open."

A dull rumbling, like a distant thunderstorm, swells from beneath their feet and the earth trembles. Now the miner sinks, along with the monk who has grabbed his hand. The circled ground sinks very softly into the deep, and they along with it. As they step from it, the ground slowly rises up again. Now they are in a great vault.

The monk proceeds with a firm step; the miner follows with shaking knees. Thus they walk through several passages until it begins to grow quite dark all around them. But soon they find an eternal lamp, which reveals that they are in a spacious crossroads. Here the monk lights two torches, for himself and his companion. They go on, and all of a sudden they are standing before a large iron church door.

The monk prays, then, holding the springroot, which springs all enchanted bolts, against the lock, he commands, "Open, door." With thundercracks, all the iron bolts and locks burst loose of themselves, and they see in front of them a round chapel.

The floor was mirror smooth, like ice. Here (so the monk afterwards told the miner) anyone who had not lived a chaste and pure life would break both legs and could never return from the place. The shine from the torches set the round vault's ceiling and walls ablaze. Great crystal and diamond spikes hung down, and between them, even larger spikes of purest gold. In one corner stood a golden altar; in the other, a golden baptismal font on silver feet.

The monk now signaled to his companion to remain standing in the middle and placed a torch in each of his hands. He himself approached a door, made wholly of silver, and knocked three times with his crook, whereupon the door sprang open.

Directly across from the door, seated on a golden throne, was the Emperor Frederick—no, not a statue carved in stone, but his living, breathing image. The gold crown on his head bobbed repeatedly as he knitted his great eyebrows. His long red beard (the same beard which, according to the centuries-old fable, is supposed to have given rise to the old proverb: "They are fighting over the Emperor's beard which no one has yet seen") had grown through the stone table in front of him; it stretched all the way to his feet. At the sight, the miner's eyes and ears failed him.

Finally the monk came back and silently drew his companion away. The silver door closed by itself. The iron door slammed behind them with a frightening clap. As they passed through the crossroads into the vault's entrance, the circumscribed ground slowly sank to meet them. They both stepped onto it and were softly lifted to the high ground.

After their ascent, the monk gave the miner two small ingots, of an unknown ore, that he had brought from the chapel. His descendants still retain the ingots as a memento.

## Peter Klaus the Goatherd

In the village of Littendorf at the foot of a mountain lived Peter Klaus, a goatherd, who was in the habit of pasturing his flock upon the Kyffhäuser. Towards evening he generally let them browse upon a nearby green, surrounded with an old ruined wall, where he could take a muster of his whole flock.

One day, he noticed that one of his prettiest goats usually disappeared soon after arriving at this spot, and did not reenter the fold until late evening. By watching repeatedly, he discovered that she slipped through a gap in the old wall, whither he followed her. It led him into a passage which widened as it opened onto a cavern, where he saw the goat feeding on oats that were falling through crevices above. He looked up and turned his ear to this odd shower of grain, but he could discover nothing. Where the devil could it be coming from? At length he heard the neighing and stamping of horses overhead; listening, he concluded that the oats must have fallen through the manger when they were fed. Why these horses were in this uninhabited part of the mountain was a mystery to the poor goatherd, but so it was. Soon their groom appeared, and without saying a word, beckoned him to follow. Peter obeyed and followed him up some steps that led him into an open court-yard encircled by old walls. On one side was a still more spacious cavern, surrounded by rocky heights that only admitted a kind of twilight through the overhanging trees and shrubs. Proceeding, he came to a smooth-shaven green, where he saw twelve ancient knights, none of whom spoke a word, engaged in a game of nine pins. His guide now beckoned to Peter, in silence, to pick up the nine pins; then he went his way. Trembling in every joint, Peter did not dare disobey. As he performed his task, he cast an occasional stolen glance at the players, whose long beards and slashed doublets had long been out of fashion. By degrees his looks grew bolder. Taking particular notice of everything around him, he observed, among other things, a tankard near him filled with a wine of excellent aroma. He took a good draught, which seemed to inspire him with life. Whenever he began to feel tired of running, he returned with fresh ardor to the tankard, which never failed to renew his strength. But, finally, it quite overpowered him, and he fell asleep.

When he next opened his eyes, he found himself again on the grassy green, in the same spot where he was in the habit of pasturing his goats. After rubbing his eyes, he looked round, but he could see neither his dog nor his flock. The long rank grass that grew about him, and trees and bushes he had never before seen astonished him. Shaking his head, he walked on a little farther, looking for the old sheep path and the hillocks and roads where he daily drove his flock, but he could find no trace of them. Yet the village, the same Sittendorf, lay just before him. Scratching his head, he hastened downhill at a quick pace to inquire after his flock.

All the people whom he met upon his entrance were strangers to him: they wore different clothes, and even spoke in a style different from that of his old neighbors. When he asked about his goats, they only stared at him, fixing their eyes on his chin. Without thinking, he put his hand to his mouth, and to his great astonishment found he had a beard, at least a foot long. Perhaps, he thought, he and all the world about him were in a dream, and yet he knew well enough that the mountain he had just come down was the Kyffhäuser. And the cottages, with their gardens and lawns, were much as he had left them. Besides, in answer to a passenger's inquiry as to what place this was, the lads who had all collected round him answered, "Sittendorf, Sir."

Still shaking his head, he went farther into the village to look for his own house. He found it, but greatly altered for the worse; a strange goatherd in an old tattered frock lay before the door, and near him, his old dog, which growled and bared its teeth at Peter when he called. He went through the entrance which had once a door, but all within was empty and deserted. Like a drunken man, Peter staggered out of the house and called the names of his wife and children. But no one heard him, and no one gave answer.

Soon, however, a crowd of women and children drew round the inquisitive stranger with the long hoary beard and asked him what he wanted. To evade their inquiries, because it would seem passing strange to be asking after his own wife and children, as well as about himself, while standing in front of his own house, he pronounced the first name to come into his head: "Kurt Steffen, the blacksmith." Most of the spectators were silent, and only looked at him wistfully; then, at last, an old woman said: "Why, for these twelve years he has been at Sachsenburg, whence I suppose you are not come today." "Where is Valentine Meier, the tailor?" "The Lord rest his soul," cried another old woman leaning on her crutch, "for more than fifteen years he has been lying in a house he will never leave."

Peter recognized two of the speakers as his young neighbors, suddenly grown very old, but he had no desire to ask more questions. At this moment, with a year-old baby in her arms and a girl about four taking holding her hand, a sprightly young woman made her way through the crowd of spectators. As much as it was possible, these three resembled the wife he was seeking. "What are your names?" he asked in a tone of astonishment. "Mine is Maria." "And your father's?" Peter resumed. "Peter Klaus, God rest his soul! It is now twenty years since we all looked for him day and night upon the Kyffhäuser after his flock came home without him. At that time," the woman added, "I was only seven years old."

The goatherd could no longer bear this: "I am Peter Klaus," he said, "Peter and no other," and he took his daughter's child and kissed it. The spectators appeared dumbstruck, until first one and then another began to say, "Yes, indeed, this is Peter Klaus! Welcome, good neighbor. After twenty years' absence, welcome home."